AUTHOR'S NOTE

If you've read the first two books in this series, you'll see that they're different from a lot of my other books. They're difficult. More painful. More frustrating.

Real.

Because in real life, life isn't easy and smooth. Love sure as shit isn't either.

This series has kind of turned into my version of 'real' love stories. These characters make mistakes. They follow their head to protect their hearts. They run away. They don't do what characters are supposed to do in romance novels.

If you're not ready for something difficult, frustrating, real, you should probably put this down and come back to it later.

Because I'm warning you now, this story isn't easy. You're gonna want to slap Polly and Heath. Shake some sense into them. Tell them to get their shit together.

But I tried to make this real.

When two people are in love, and I mean real, tear your hair out,

miserable, heart-wrenching love, they do not have their shit together.
I hope you fall in love with these beautifully flawed people just like I did.

Anne

xxx

THE PROBLEM WITH PEACE

GREENSTONE SECURITY #3

ANNE MALCOM

DEDICATION

For everyone who doesn't have their shit together.

PROLOGUE

I SMOOTHED my dress for the hundredth time.

It was as smooth as it was ever going to be.

Not that it *needed* to be smooth.

It was kind of the point of this whole wedding.

It was a *Polly* wedding after all.

I had flowers in my hair.

I was barefoot.

My dress was simple white lace, form-fitting. Chosen not because it was my dream wedding dress, but because Craig had mentioned casually how he loved seeing me in tight things. It was pointedly uttered as I was reading a bridal magazine and dog-earring a page with a long flowing princess style dress that wasn't exactly the 'meringue' dress, but it didn't hug my curves either. I'd always dreamed of a whimsical dress, only hinting at the things that my husband would discover later on in the night.

"You've got a beautiful body, sweetheart," he said, circling me from behind. "I just want to see it on our wedding day, know it's

all mine." He kissed the side of my neck, chasing away the small amount of disappointment I had at his words.

I wasn't worried about forgoing my ideal dress for what Craig liked. Because I loved him. And I loved making him happy. It wasn't a hardship. This day was for us, after all, not about the vanity of me wearing a big poofy dress.

Plus, the poofy dress wouldn't go with the 'Polly' wedding everyone imagined. The one on the rooftop of my loft, decorated with fairy lights and low-key music. Ordained by my friend who read everyone's auras before the ceremony. Lucy and Rosie had scowled and muttered under their breath at this. But they did it. Every single one of my family did it. They indulged me.

Because it was *me*.

This was the wedding everyone *expected* from me.

Not the one *I* envisioned.

Not the one I'd dreamed of on and off since I was old enough to read romance novels. And solidified when I was eighteen years old when I was in a crowded and foul-smelling bar.

Where I was wearing that whimsical, flowing dress, lightly beaded, a long flowing train, in a church—the one on the corner across from our house in Amber—despite the fact I wasn't religious. I believed in the power of the universe, and some kind of higher being. But I didn't think that higher being had a book of rules about how to act. Yet I liked churches. I liked the simple peace they offered when one didn't get caught up of the politics of it all.

But Craig had been against that.

He wasn't religious. He didn't believe in a higher being. And he didn't want to have to have meetings with the priest to get permission to be married in the church.

"I'm not asking anyone's permission for marrying the woman I love," he growled.

this is it. The moment in life you've got a chance to go beyond the ordinary. Beyond even the extraordinary."

He mocked me with words from the past.

And they hit their mark.

Too bad they didn't change anything.

He froze, his eyes the only thing moving, they were roving over every inch of me, like he was committing me to memory, like he was taking me in right before he walked out of my life forever.

Which was good.

That needed to happen.

"You're makin' a mistake, Sunshine," he murmured. "And I'm not gonna save you from it. Not gonna fight you when you *chose* to belong to another man. Even though we both know the parts you don't want anyone to see belong to fucking *me*."

He didn't give me the chance to speak, because his mouth crashed down on mine.

He was kissing me.

While I was in my wedding dress.

Minutes away from marrying another man.

A man I loved.

Who was kind.

Simple.

Beautiful.

And none of that mattered.

Because the kiss wasn't kind.

Or simple.

Or beautiful.

How could a kiss like this be beautiful? It was impossible. Because it was full of truth. Full of goodbye.

I shouldn't have kissed him back. Shouldn't have met his ferocity with some of my own, the kind that had lain dormant for years.

No, I shouldn't have done that.

But I was me, and I spent my life doing things I shouldn't do.

So I kissed him back.

Betrayed Craig.

Myself.

And then it was over.

I was no longer in his arms, he had retreated fast across the room, rubbing the back of his hand along his mouth, as if he were rubbing away my kiss. Rubbing away all evidence of me.

There was no tenderness in his eyes.

No kindness.

He wasn't going to wish me well or tell me to be happy.

But he was going to say something. He *had* to say something. In moments like these, the man always said something. One last plea. One last hurl of ugly beautiful promises.

And I would've relented.

Despite everything that I knew would end us, that I knew would make me hate myself in the future, if he'd opened his mouth and said one more thing, outstretched his hand, I would've taken it.

But he didn't.

He glared at me with a mixture of love and hatred, the latter being the prevailing emotion, and then he turned and walked out.

Without a word.

Because this wasn't a movie or a fairy tale.

Woodenly, I turned back to the mirror. My eyes were no longer darkened underneath, my face flush in all the right places and my lips pink and swollen.

My hair was mussed, but artfully so the flowers I'd woven into them didn't look as purposeful as before.

I smoothed my dress again, my hand flat on my stomach to calm the sickness swirling at the base of it.

A single tear trailed down my cheek.

I wiped it away with the back of my hand.

And then I turned to go and marry another man.

I promised myself I'd forget that moment. I'd love Craig with my whole heart. Whatever was left. And this moment with Heath would be buried among the many in the graveyard of our past together.

But promises were broken much easier than they were made.

Especially the ones I made to myself.

Especially when they had anything to do with Heath.

CHAPTER ONE

Six Years Earlier

"I THINK I MIGHT GO!" I yelled at Harry over the music.

It wasn't that I didn't like music so loud that you couldn't talk unless you screamed in your date's ears. Or crowded bars with sticky floors and water stained glasses. Or the patrons of that bar veering toward the unseemly at best and criminals at worst.

No, all of that was completely fine with me. I wasn't one to shy away from such things, and these were the only type of bars that didn't card.

But the music was bad.

The company was only slightly better.

Harry had seemed cool and hip when surrounded by the overwhelmingly normal crowd of our high school. He wore scuffed Doc Martins. Band tee shirts that pretty much no one had ever heard of. His hair was always artfully messed so it draped over his features effortlessly and beautifully. He carried around books of poetry and then also played music so loud from his iPod that you could hear it down the halls.

He seemed such a contrast, complex and soulful. I'd obviously fell in total lust with him and damn near melted when he asked me to come to a 'gig' in L.A. with him and his 'crew.'

My parents knew exactly where I was because I was legally an adult, they couldn't stop me. Lucy had told me to call her if I needed bail money and hooked pepper spray onto my keychain.

It had been fun at first. His friends were all pseudo arty hipsters who took themselves a little seriously but were still fun to be around. But then he started slamming too many tequila shots and got sloppy and handsy and betrayed his true persona as a sleazy teenage boy after one thing.

So I was leaving.

I wasn't quite sure how I was going to leave, since everyone we'd drove here with had dispersed in the bar and even if I found someone who had the keys to the van parked somewhere down the street, no one could drive.

I'd call a cab. Figure it out. My friend Allie dropped out of school and got a job on some sitcom here, I'd crash with her. Things tended to work themselves out.

But first I had to escape Harry's sweaty hands that had tightened around my upper arms when I'd screamed that I was leaving.

"But baby, why?" he yelled, trying to yank me closer to him.

I yanked back. "How about 'cause I'm not your baby?"

He furrowed his brows in a confusion only an arrogant drunk boy can have when presented with a girl that didn't want to worship at their feet.

Or even go to first base with them.

He let me go.

Which I was thankful for.

ego and entitlement with *more violence.* Because I've got a feeling you're better than that."

I swallowed roughly before I spoke again.

"And you're a man to keep his promises, are you not?" I repeated my previous question, my voice as uneven as my heartbeat.

He gave me a long intense look that did not belong between two strangers. Something tugged at the bottom of my stomach with that stare, with my hands pressed into his chest, with the nearness of his body, and the energy around it.

I was in tune with energy. I studied it. And I'd always believed that people gave off certain vibrations when two souls recognized each other, for good or for bad, those vibrations became more intense.

Of course, every single member of my family thought this was "new age bullshit"— it was just Lucy that *said* that, but the sentiment was echoed by everyone else.

But I believed in it. Because it happened with people. People who would become important to me in the future sparked something.

This was different than that.

This was an inferno.

Not entirely unpleasant. But not as nice as any kind of 'love at first sight' was communicated in any movie.

"Yeah, Sunshine," he murmured, somehow getting himself heard above the music. "I'm a man who keeps promises."

Something about that sentence was so final. So ominous.

And I wanted *more.*

"You want to make a promise to buy me a beer?" I asked, deciding that I could not possibly leave this bar now.

I would stay in this place, for as long as this man was going to be in it.

And I was going to be leaving with him, I decided.

He glanced down to my hands, which were still fisting his tee. I probably should've let go, it wasn't exactly socially acceptable to be fondling a man's pecs when you didn't even know his last name. Or first name for that matter.

I *should've* let go.

I did not.

"I shouldn't," he said, moving his gaze upward at the same time my heart sank.

Another intense look.

"But I will," he added.

I exhaled a breath I didn't even know I was holding.

"YOU KNOW, I don't even know your name," I said after taking the beer he handed me.

He had first directed us to a miraculously quiet corner of the bar that did not need yelling or require the dodging of drunk teenagers.

"And what does a name change about this situation?"

"Well, not much," I pondered. "But it does mean I can stop calling you 'that guy who almost punched another guy's teeth out for me.'" I paused, arching my brow. "It's a little long."

His smirk widened, though his eyes hardened at the mention of the circumstances of our meeting. He was *that* guy. The protective, alpha guy. Usually I didn't go for instincts left around from a bygone era where women were encouraged—no, *forced* to be helpless and men were the 'protectors.'

But I was going for him.

In a big way.

"Heath," he said, watching me drink my beer.

I swallowed the liquid self-consciously. Another abnormal thing.

Nerves.

I was not a girl that got nervous, in any situation, but especially in front of guys. Maybe I hadn't cared enough in order to be nervous? Because wasn't that what nerves were? A fear that you're not going to live up to someone's expectations?

I didn't want to live up to anyone's expectations because I didn't believe in them.

Of course until about ten minutes ago.

"Heath," I repeated, tasting the name and mixing it in with the beer. "It suits you."

"Do names really suit people?"

I shrugged. "Well, if it was Chester then I don't think it would."

He smirked and took a long pull of his beer while he watched me. He didn't rush to fill the silence between us.

It was an unusual thing to do with someone you just met. Usually long and comfortable silences were reserved for the most intimate of relationships. Girlfriends you've known forever and who could say everything with a raised brow. In my case, it was my older sister who blew up cars for fun.

And Rosie.

She also blew up cars for fun.

Normally those cars belonged to guys I'd dated.

But I didn't do silence with anyone else. Mostly because everyone I spent time with was loud. And I was loud when I was with them. Always searching for a new adventure, a new experience.

Now I was learning that silence with an attractive stranger staring at you was the best kind of adventure.

"You got a name?" he asked finally. "I can keep callin' you

'that girl that lights up a piece of shit bar and makes me make promises that I shouldn't be makin', and not breaking ones I itch to make'...but it's a little long too."

My breath left me in a whoosh.

He thought I *lit up a bar*?

Not exactly poetry, but I thought poetry was pretentious and I didn't get it anyway.

"Polly," I said on little more than a whisper.

His eyes flared, something passed over his face.

"Does it suit me?" I asked, finding my normal flirty persona from where his stare had made me fumble and drop it on the sticky floor.

"Nah," he said after a long pause. "I don't think anything as simple as a name can suit you, especially not one word. But it does the best it can."

Holy. Shit.

That was poetry.

"I totally wouldn't have flunked English if you were around," I said.

He was taking a pull of his beer when I spoke, and he made a choking sound as he tried to laugh while swallowing.

I smirked.

It was strange to see a man like him, a man who looked like he could conquer anything with his muscles and general air of alpha, be taken down by a smart comment and a badly timed sip of beer.

He made a throat clearing sound that I felt right in between my legs.

How a throat clearing could turn me on I had no idea.

But it did.

"You okay?" I asked innocently.

He glared at me in response. But a friendly glare. One that I definitely felt in between my legs.

CHAPTER TWO

"GOTTA ASK YOU SOMETHING," he said an inordinate amount of time later.

Minutes could have passed. Hours. Lightyears.

Heck, the world could've ended outside, and I wouldn't have known. Or cared. And I was a person kind of concerned with the end of the world, about recycling, about climate change, about the destruction of rainforests and the consumption of fossil fuels. I was passionate about it. Lucy called it "more annoying than slow walkers in airports."

But I hadn't known passion until him.

I hadn't known *life* until him.

Of course that was a ridiculous thing to think about a man who I'd met in a bar and who I'd been making out with against a slightly sticky wall for however long. But that was me. I embraced feelings that other people might call ridiculous, or try to taint with logic.

"Anything," I whispered.

His eyes flared. "How old are you?"

"Eighteen," I said immediately, wishing it wasn't the truth, wishing I was older and more worldly.

"Fuck," he murmured, hands tightening around me. "You're too young."

My stomach dropped.

"A good man would stop this right here," he continued, moving his hand so he could tug lightly on my hair.

My stomach continued to drop.

He moved his gaze up and down my body with deliberate slowness. "I'm takin' you home."

I gaped at him and tried not to show my disappointment. "Home?" I asked, my voice small.

I'd thought this had been good for him too, despite the reaction to my age. I was legal, after all. The hardness against my stomach was evidence that he wasn't turned off by me. The darkness on his face sure made it seem that it was something more than him being turned on. That this was more than physical. But maybe I was misreading. Maybe I was seeing things I wanted to see. It wouldn't be the first time. Everyone in my life knew I had the tendency to block out the darker and harder aspects of life, pretend they weren't there so I could have my sunshine.

But this wasn't sunshine.

Not with him.

It was dark, unyielding and unpredictable.

But maybe I was imagining it. Or pretending that he was having this same visceral reaction. Maybe he kissed like a man so he could totally see that I kissed like a girl.

"Yeah," he rasped, his thumb brushing my swollen bottom lip.

I sucked in a ragged breath at the gesture.

I did not know people did that in real life.

But they did.

And it was awesome.

"I can, you don't have to—I can find my own way home," I whispered.

I was originally trying to make it sound like I wasn't a heartbroken little girl that her passionate liaison was ending without even...ending. I was trying to sound like a strong independent woman who didn't need the man who kissed the heck of out her to drop her off at home.

His body hardened. "Oh, you're not findin' your way anywhere, Little Girl," he growled.

He stepped back, taking me with him, his hand grasping mine in a grip that was just a little too tight—in other words, perfect.

"I'm plannin' on getting lost tonight. In you. And you're getting lost too."

And then he started walking. I went with him mostly as a result of his powerful stride and his firm hold on me. But once the words penetrated, I all but skipped behind him. The bar was loud and crowded, a mess of writhing bodies that it hadn't been before.

I didn't see how he was going to navigate through the number of drunken bodies clogging up the path to the exit. But I needn't have worried. The crowd seemed to fricking melt for him. We were outside before I knew what had happened. The air was shockingly fresh and jolting, goose bumps immediately rose on my arms.

Heath was yanking his leather jacket off and it was situated on my shoulders in a moment.

"Now you're going to be cold," I murmured, inhaling his purely male scent, hoping it imprinted onto my skin. That it would somehow sink into my bones.

"But you'll be warm," he said, his lips coming down on mine for a quick and brutal kiss.

And then he was walking us along the sidewalk.

To get lost.

And I found myself hoping I'd never be found again.

I WAS NERVOUS.

I hadn't given myself time to properly and truly get nervous. To think about what I was doing. Mostly because Heath demanded every ounce of my attention, there was no room for nerves when he was kissing me, when his hands were on me. There was only enough room to remember to breathe.

But now I was nervous.

Because it was *real*.

I was going to give him my virginity.

There was no hesitation in that. I knew instinctively that he was the perfect person for me to give it to. He was the person I didn't know I was waiting for.

I went on intuition.

I might've still been a girl, but he awakened the woman in me, including my woman's intuition.

I knew he'd take care of me. That he *wanted* to. It was evident in everything he did. From putting his jacket on me to opening my car door, to not moving the car until my seatbelt was buckled, to his hand settling on my thigh the entire ride.

And then to him directing me to the bedroom and then leaving to get me a glass of freakin' *water*.

Because that was the kind of guy he was.

"You hungry?" he called from the kitchen.

Not that he even really needed to raise his voice since the kitchen was approximately two doors away from the bedroom.

"No thanks," I called back.

My stomach was far too unstable for such things like food.

I was sitting awkwardly on the end of the bed, not quite sure if I should undress, lay seductively splayed across the dark gray comforter, or get right under the covers.

All of these options seemed awkward, not that sitting ramrod straight at the end of the bed was exactly any better.

To distract myself, I looked around. Not that there was much to look at. He'd told me that this was his 'crash pad' in L.A.

And considering he was away for years at a time, it was a surprise he even had a pad, crash or otherwise.

I'd asked him about this on the drive.

"Why don't you just get a hotel when you come back?"

He glanced at me across the cab. "'Cause after a year livin' hard and rough and not knowin' if I'd be alive to have a shitty sleep in a shitty cot, I like knowin' that I'll be coming back to a bed that's mine, even if it's in a crappy apartment. It's somethin'."

All of this was spoken with a harsh nonchalance that I was getting to understand was Heath's default when talking about things that were heavy or emotional.

It got to me.

A lot.

He didn't have a *home.*

I was a huge believer in a home being people more than a place. A family, adopted or otherwise—I was lucky to have both, plus a physical home of my own with memories that sank into the very foundation—to be a constant, people you could always go to, always count on.

And Heath hadn't mentioned family. Friends.

Granted we barely knew each other, but he already knew I had two sisters, one adopted, one blood related, a mother that texted me to make sure I was still in the country—and being serious—a father that brewed his own beer, and that my friend

Allie wanted to star in her own movie but instead was playing a serial killer's latest victim on some crime show.

He'd listened. Asked questions. Seemed utterly engaged in my long-winded, enthusiastic and totally crazy stories that should've made a guy I met at a bar run a mile.

He didn't run a mile.

He kissed me until I was crazy and then took me home.

To his 'crash pad' that served as the one constant he could come back to after months, years of war.

It wasn't in a terrible area of L.A., not that I was one to care about 'areas.' But the cars parked on the street were nice, the apartment buildings all well-kept, and the streets were well lit.

He lived in one of the highest buildings on the block, top floor but where that didn't mean a penthouse, it just meant the exact same, shoebox apartment without hearing the neighbors practicing tap dancing on the floor above.

You walked in with a small and modern kitchen on the left, an equally small and sparsely furnished living room directly ahead, with doors opening off to a small balcony.

His hall consisted of one door to the bathroom, one to his bedroom.

From what I saw of the place, it was lacking any kind of personality but was meticulously clean.

The bed I was sitting on had army corners and everything. I had yanked at the comforter just to create some disorder because the pure crispness of it all made me uncomfortable.

The room had a large dresser, not a single thing sitting on top of it. Not a photo, not a jumbled array of aftershave and deodorant.

Not one thing.

Ditto with his bedside tables.

There was a lamp on either side and a digital alarm clock.

He said he didn't want a hotel room because he wanted a home. Hotel rooms had more personality than this.

My heart burned with the knowledge that this was his version of a home.

It was only as I was blinking away tears at that thought did I realize that the man I'd been crying for was standing in the door, with one glass of water in his hand and his eyes on me.

I wondered how long he'd been there, staring at me while I had grieved over his version of a home. Or lack thereof.

"Your bed is far too neat," I said.

He blinked.

"Like, I know it's good to make beds when we're not sleeping in them," I continued. "Believe me, I know, since my entire family are *bed makers*."

Heath's jaw ticked. "You say that like they're serial killers."

"They might be," I deadpanned. "Serial killers like order after all." I paused. "Now would be a terrible time to find out you're a serial killer. Now I'm alone and at your mercy."

The jaw tick disappeared. And pure male hunger replaced it.

My inner thighs clenched together as I responded to the look physically.

He moved then, rounding the bed to place the water on the bedside table and then yanking me up off the bed and into his arms.

He toyed with a strand of my hair, his hand biting into my hip. "No, Sunshine," he murmured, not taking his eyes from me. "I'm the one at your fuckin' mercy."

Cue another thigh clench.

A fricking huge one.

And a stutter in my heartbeat.

A fricking huge one.

He didn't move to kiss me, didn't brutally throw me down on the bed like the darkness in his eyes communicated.

"I haven't done this before," I said, trying to sound proud of my virginity instead of slightly ashamed, as I did right now.

Which was completely and utterly unreasonable. Up until tonight, or right this second, I had been proud that I didn't give in to society's pressures of 'losing it' like some sort of race where there were no winners but a small number of losers who would take home an STI or an unplanned pregnancy as their prize.

My whole identity was about being me in spite of what the world told me to be. But now, I had a vague sense of regret that I hadn't gotten the messy, awkward—I had no such romantic notions about the first time being 'magical'—act out of the way so it wouldn't be messy with Heath. It was awkward already because I was being awkward. Which was not something I was familiar with. Because I liked this man. Really liked him. I felt like there was a lot riding on this.

On us.

I wanted to not be an awkward virgin.

So then I would know about sex, and not seem like the little girl in the bar he'd rescued, and she was now offering up her virtue as thanks.

I supposed it was a modern-day fairy tale if I wanted to look at it that way.

Because I had retreated into my head, as I often did, it took me a long moment to realize that Heath hadn't replied to my admission.

I blinked him into focus.

Then I blinked away my response at hot freaking hot he was.

He hadn't moved since I spoke.

Crap.

His eyes locked on mine as if he sensed I was now mentally present and not thinking about fairy tales.

"You're a virgin?"

Though there was an inflection at the end, it was obvious it wasn't a question.

But I answered it anyway, just so I could fill up the silence that was no longer comfortable between us.

I couldn't read anything from his voice or his tight expression. And I was guessing his lack of expression was a bad thing.

"Is that a problem?"

"Yeah, Sunshine, it's a problem," he replied, voice clipped.

I cringed.

Of course it was a problem. He was a *man*. A real one. One who was only here temporarily. He didn't need to be tangled up with a girl still in high school, and a *virgin* at that.

His hands moved so they were on either side of my neck.

His expression was no longer blank.

"It's a problem because it's not a gift you should be giving to a man who you met in a bar," he rasped. "A man like me. It's a problem because a man like me knows that gift isn't meant for him. Maybe if I was a different version of the same man, I might be able to make sure you give it to the right person." His grip tightened, toying with the idea of pain, but stopping short. "But I'm this version. So even though it's yours to give, and not mine to take. I'm going to take it anyway."

I didn't even have time to let his words sink in, let them chase away all feelings of awkwardness with pure need because he was kissing me.

Kissing me.

Brutal. Hard. Soul destroying.

"But we're at the point of no return, *I'm* at the point of no return. So I'm gonna take it," he murmured against my mouth.

"And I'm going to give you fuckin' everything that a *boy* couldn't give you."

And then he kissed me again.

Every time he kissed me it was different than the last. Because it was more than a kiss. We were getting more tangled up in each other with every second spent together. Tangled in a way that my insides—my heart—would stay that way even when he left me, never to be seen again.

He was taking something from me, but it was a connection that I'd never lose. And he'd told me I was going to lose him, this, from the start, I found myself desperate for something to hold onto when he became nothing but a memory.

I blinked when he was no longer kissing me. His body was no longer tangled in mine.

He was almost pressed up against his dresser, the space between us obvious but somehow more erotic than the way he'd been kissing me moments ago. And if you'd asked me moments ago if there could be something more erotic than the way he was kissing me I would've told you, you were straight up crazy.

But his stare turned my body to flames, my knees to jelly.

I was breathing heavily, audibly.

He was a statue.

"Take off your clothes," he demanded, voice hoarse.

"Do you not want to do that?" I asked, my voice once more being back to shy and uneasy.

Virginal.

He shook his head violently once. "No fucking way. This is an image that I'm gonna be searing into my brain. I need to watch. Need to be able to drink in every inch of you, naked before me, right before I touch every single part of you that hasn't been anyone's but yours. Before I take it for myself."

My knees trembled again, threatening to give way

completely. I had never been spoken to like this. With a voice dripping in sex. In desire.

My hand shook as I directed it to the top button of my dress. Not from fear. Despite the way his face had changed, turn almost feral, I wasn't afraid of him. No, I was afraid of myself. Of what the romantic in me would turn this into. Of what I'd torture myself with.

But thoughts of the future didn't have a place in the present. I never thought of the consequences. A character fault, a lot of people, including my guidance counselor, would tell me. I wasn't about to start being a better person right now, especially if it meant I had to do anything but undress in front of the man in front of me.

I had three buttons undone before I even realized what I was doing.

The fabric slipped off my shoulders and down so my already hard nipples were exposed to the air.

Heath let out a sound that was a merge between a hiss and a growl when my breasts were totally exposed to him.

My heart bounced against my now naked chest with a force that threatened to shatter through my entire ribcage.

Boys had seen my boobs before. I wasn't exactly shy. Plus, I had good boobs. Not overly large, but not small either. Round, perky, with average sized nipples.

And of course, my virginity was completely technical, so my boobs had had attention before.

Or I thought they had.

But Heath's gaze was more than any fumbling set of hands could ever have been.

His hands were fisted at his sides and his knuckles were turning white with the force his was obviously exerting to keep them there.

My nipples ached for a touch that I knew would not be fumbling or awkward. But I also ached for more of this, of this distance that was more intimate than anything I'd ever experienced.

"Keep going," he growled.

I'd just been standing there, half-naked, my hands poised on the button above my bellybutton, staring at his fists and imagining them on me.

I did as he asked. Immediately.

My dress pooled around my ankles a moment later.

I was still wearing my shoes. That and a white pair of panties.

Nothing else.

But Heath's stare, of course. And that covered me in a way clothes never would.

His jaw was iron.

My fingers went to the edges of my panties.

"No," he snapped.

I paused immediately.

He was in front of me in a slice of a moment.

He wasn't touching me.

"Lie down," he ordered.

I ached to touch him, to press my naked body to his clothed one, to wrap myself up in him and kiss him since it felt like an eternity since I'd done that.

Instead, I did as he asked.

The comforter felt rough against my skin. But the air itself felt coarse against my skin. Because I'd never been this naked—truly naked—in my life.

I expected Heath to cover his body with mine, or at least start undressing, but instead, he knelt at the side of the bed, never taking his eyes from mine.

His hand circled my ankle and lifted my leg, working the straps of my wedges so they fell to the floor with a resounding thump. He continued upward from my ankles so slowly it was torture, I felt like I was coming apart from my skin but unable to move.

I inhaled roughly as his hands got to the top of my thighs and his thumb brushed against the apex of my legs, right above that magical spot that was all but crying out for his attention, for a release.

My entire body reacted to the barely-there touch.

Violently.

I almost lost it all then. Just from his hand *brushing* me.

I'd had orgasms before. All but one self-induced. The one was only because the boy in question had done extensive research on the female anatomy and obviously learned nothing from that, but was very open to direction.

So I knew what it felt like.

But the soft brush of his thumb against me showed me that I knew nothing. Not a damn thing.

"Heath," I whispered, my voice raspy and thin.

His eyes darkened. "Like that, Sunshine," he murmured, moving his hands up the side of my thighs so they were fastened on the edges of my panties. "You breathing my name when I'm close enough to taste how much you want me. How sweet your pussy's gonna be."

My core spasmed from just those words. Words pushing me closer to the edge.

Heath purposefully moved his eyes from mine to the triangle of lace covering me. Another nudge toward the edge.

My heartbeat was thunder inside my chest. A fricking earthquake inside my bones.

Then he moved his hands down my sides. And since my

panties were clutched in his grip, they came too. Instinctively, I lifted my hips up slightly so he could get them down.

He let out another strangled hiss.

Because he couldn't speak.

Because of what *I* was doing to him. Upon first glance, him being fully clothed and me being naked on the bed would've seemed like an obvious exchange of power. I'd assumed that he held it all, until that moment. It was me. Naked, and at his mercy, I had the power. Power to make his body so tight he was shaking with the force of making his movements so small and tender.

Power to make his gaze turn animalistic with the need for me.

And power to literally take the words from his mouth when I exposed myself to him. His eyes were fastened on my core as he moved my panties down my legs.

It should've been embarrassing, uncomfortable to have a man so close to a place that hadn't been intimately inspected in such a way...well, ever. A place that was hidden and personal, sacred.

But it wasn't.

Because his gaze told me that he considered it just that. Sacred.

He was literally on his knees in front of me.

Like he was fricking worshipping me.

Me.

His hands were up at my hips and he dragged me across the bed until my legs rested on his shoulders and I was inches away from his mouth. The apex of my hips was right in his fricking face.

My body was an inferno.

Heath moved his gaze from in between my legs to my eyes.

My thighs clenched instinctively from that gaze, from this whole fricking situation.

"Gonna bet you taste sweeter than you look," he rasped.

And then he put his mouth there.

Like right fricking *there.*

Again, boys had tried to put it there. But they didn't know where *there* was, or what to do with it. It just turned into an awkward and unsatisfying act.

I cried out the second Heath put his mouth on me.

My hands fisted the comforter to the point I feared I might rip the fabric apart. I'd thought he was worshipping me with his eyes.

I was so fricking wrong.

I didn't know worship until he worked his mouth against me.

My climax came fast and hard. Hard enough for stars to invade my vision, my body, to the point I must've blacked out because as soon as I started to come back to earth, his fingers were inside me, gentle and expertly working me back up, back down, back somewhere beautiful and almost unbearable at the same time.

His eyes were locked against mine the entire time his mouth was working me to release, *that* was something one could only call life-shattering.

Not only did he give me something I'd thought was a myth, but he watched me lose control, completely unravel. There was something intimate about that. More intimate than his mouth on me, his fingers inside me.

Something that added yet another layer to whatever this was.

But something that was pushed away at the same time Heath gently, tenderly pushed my spent body backward, so I was once again splayed on the bed.

He stood.

I blinked him into stark focus.

In another blink, his tee was off, and I was completely and fully lucid. A torso like that would turn Charlie Cheswick lucid.

I'd known he'd have a great body, because, well, I had eyes. But seeing a hint of it covered in clothes was impactful enough. Actually gazing upon his sculpted abs, his defined pecs, the wide shoulders and muscled biceps was something else.

But there was something else.

Because I expected him to be smooth, like his pressed exterior. And the skin I'd seen had been smooth. Like granite. But dotted around his torso were puckered pieces of flesh, where something had violently torn through his flesh, scarring it forever.

He told me about his violent life.

He wore it behind his eyes.

But it was something else entirely to see the evidence of it on his skin.

"You're beautiful," I whispered, because somehow the ugliness of whatever had marked him only made him more so.

If he was one of those men who took offense to being called beautiful because it threatened his masculinity, he didn't show it.

Wearing a pink fricking teddy and matching shoes wouldn't threaten his masculinity.

"*You're* beautiful," he said, his eyes feasting on me lying there, naked, propped up on my elbows.

"Unbutton your pants," I commanded.

His mouth turned up, but he was still in intense alpha male mode, so a full-on grin wasn't possible. "You telling me what to do too, Sunshine?" he asked.

I nodded. "Turnabout's fair play."

The mouth turn disappeared as he kicked off his boots and did as I asked. I itched to be as cool and erotic as him and not take my eyes off his when he did so. But I wasn't. I was greedy. I wanted to imprint every part of his body onto my memory. And he was hotter than any man I'd seen in real life. And he was undressing.

For me.

So yeah, I was looking at the goods when he took his pants off.

And his underwear.

My stomach clenched when he was naked, oh so gloriously naked in front of me.

Naked and *hard.*

I wasn't a stranger to this specific male appendage. I'd seen them up close, and been kind of, underwhelmed with them. Plus, they weren't exactly...nice to look at.

I wasn't underwhelmed right now. Heath standing in front of me, naked after just making me orgasm in a way I never thought possible was beyond purely *nice.* As was his manhood that was easily the most impressive I'd ever seen in my young life.

My core twitched just looking at it, craving him inside me.

Then I swallowed, thinking an utterly cliché virginal thought of 'how the fricking heck is *that* going to fit in *there*?'

But he would fit. Because we fit. And I was ready. Beyond ready for him. He'd made sure of that. My muscles were not tight with nerves as they had been before. My muscles were all but liquid underneath my skin.

I did feel a spark of nerves, but it was physically impossible to manifest the entire nervous reaction that all girls got right before the act itself.

I did find it physically possible to push off the bed and stand on shaky feet in front of Heath.

He immediately gripped my hips to steady me, as if he glimpsed that small shake to my body. But then again, he was responsible for it, and he was very in tune with my body, as he demonstrated earlier.

"For what I've got planned, you're gonna be on the bed," he murmured, yanking my naked body to his.

I let out a gasp as our bare skin touched and a very obvious part of him pressed into me.

"Well, for the first time, at least," he continued, eyes dark. "Once you're ready, I'll educate you on the many places that aren't a bed that I can fuck you on."

My pussy clenched at the promise. At the need for him to make good on it. And he would. He was a man who kept his promises, after all.

"Well, for what I've got planned, I've got to be right about," I trailed my fingers down his chest, dancing over his scars and then moving to kneel at his feet. "Right about here," I breathed against him and his entire body stiffened.

"Fuck," he hissed. "Baby, this is meant to be about you," he protested in a thick voice.

I looked up at him while I fastened my hand around his length.

He let out another curse.

"Oh, but what was it I said before?" I asked sweetly, moving slowly up and down. "Turnabout's fair play."

And then I moved my mouth to fasten right onto that beautiful cock of his.

It was not an act I'd enjoyed in the past. Especially because every teenage boy is desperate for it and it never really felt organic. But with Heath, I *loved* it.

With every swipe of my tongue, with every time I twisted my hand and mouth in opposite directions—*Cosmopolitan* told me to do this—I coaxed his surrender. I was in control, I had the power.

I would've stayed for a lot longer if I could've, despite the fact my knees were protesting, and my jaw was beginning to ache.

But Heath had other ideas.

I was hauled up his body and his hand clutched my neck.

"Fuck, baby," he growled. "Are you real? 'Cause I swear to Christ, I'm worried about the state of reality right now."

I pressed my lips to his and he didn't hesitate to open to me, the act of kissing him after what I was just doing sending shoots of desire down my stomach.

"We don't need to worry about the state of reality," I whispered against his mouth. "We need to worry about the state of my virginity and it's still intact. I'd like for you to rectify that immediately."

His eyes lost their lazy satisfaction and his hand tightened on my neck to the point of pain. "Sunshine, we don't have to do that. You can stay perfectly intact. For someone who isn't gonna leave with no return date, no fuckin' forwarding address. Someone better. I'm happy with this." His hand trailed downwards to gently tweak my nipple.

I let out a little moan.

His hand trailed lower. Way lower.

I let out what could only be described as a cry of pleasure.

His eyes flared. "I'm more than happy with this," he murmured. "We can continue to do this. I'm not gonna push you."

I took his wrist in my grasp, moved his fingers to intertwine with mine and then led him to my entrance. Coaxed him inside me.

He let out a growl and moved his fingers inside me while I somehow managed the feat of walking us backward, so the bed hit the backs of my thighs.

"You don't need to push me," I said, voice broken with the movement of his fingers. "I'm going to push you. I'm going to have to demand you make love to me. Right now."

Another eye flare.

His fingers stopped moving. They left me gently.

He didn't speak. Instead, he pushed me onto the bed.

A drawer opened and closed.

Foil crinkled.

Ah, he was thinking of practical things that hadn't even crossed my mind. Despite the fact I'd preached safe sex to my much more sexually active friends. I didn't used to understand how anyone could get so caught up in something and not remember to protect themselves.

But it was impossible to protect myself emotionally.

Heath was doing what he could physically.

His body covered mine seconds later. And he was kissing me. Again, this was different than every one before. Probably because we were both naked, on a bed and all of his delicious manly parts were rubbing against all the right places.

But also because this kiss was the last kiss we'd have...before. Everything would change after.

He pulled back so his eyes met mine. "I'm not gonna lie to you, baby, this is gonna hurt, though I'm sure you know that. But the next time I'll make it better for you. I'll make you scream so loud that you'll lose your voice the same second you lose everything but my cock inside you."

Wetness rushed between my legs at his words.

"Heath," I whispered, wrapping my leg around his hip and pulling him down.

His lips pressed against mine at the same time he pressed against me.

The sensation of him pressing into me, probing all the sensitive areas he'd worshipped before he yanked me closer to a climax I didn't think I'd have the energy to reach again so soon.

But then he pressed harder, pressed inside.

And at first, the pleasure battled with the pain, my primed body submitting to him.

But there was only so much submitting my body could do before he had to push through without submission. With pain.

"Polly," he murmured. "Look at me. Need your beautiful eyes."

I didn't even realize I'd had them squeezed shut in my discomfort.

When I opened them, Heath's eyes searched mine. His entire body was taut, his jaw tight enough to shatter if he clenched it any more.

"Keep lookin' at me," he demanded. Then he thrust into me with a brutality that I knew was actually gentler than the slow and agonizing movements of before.

I cried out in mostly pain and a leftover of pleasure. I kept my promise, I didn't squeeze my eyes shut through the burning pain of him breaking through that wall, of that unpleasant fullness that almost felt like I was being torn in two.

Heath's mouth pressed onto mine, gently at first, then more insistent. He demanded a response out of me and I gave it to him. And I got so lost in the kiss that I didn't flinch when he started to move, when my sensitive body started to protest.

I kept kissing him.

I dug my nails into the skin of his back.

He growled against my mouth.

And whether it was the kiss, the growl, or Heath himself, the pain started to subside. Slowly. Much slower than his thrusts, but enough for each to yield less pain and more of that beautiful pleasure that seemed like it was from a lifetime ago.

I no longer felt too full with Heath inside me.

I felt perfect.

He stopped moving. "Polly?" he demanded in concern.

I sunk my nails into his back again moving my palm to his ass to yank him closer into me. He let out a hiss.

"Don't stop," I breathed.

"The Devil himself wouldn't stop me," he rasped as he started moving again.

And my hips started to move with him. My body. *Everything* responded to him. The pain was a dull ache, still there, still insistent, but it was drowning in the sea of sensation Heath had thrown me into.

CHAPTER THREE

IT HAD BEEN HOURS.

We hadn't left the bed, apart to meet basic human needs.

I would've forgone food entirely, but Heath was insistent of the fact that I needed to replenish my energy.

And to be fair, he'd used up a great deal of it.

I was quite happy for him to use up all of it.

For him to use up all of me.

Because I wasn't falling for him.

I'd fallen.

Hard.

"You know, I thought this was a modern-day fairy tale," I said, spooning ice cream into my mouth. "But I don't think the princes do the things to princesses like you just did to me."

I was wearing his tee, sitting on his counter, swinging my aching legs as he leaned against his fridge, watching me.

Shirtless.

Wearing sweats low on his hips.

Commando.

And he had just done *things*.

Things I didn't think my body could handle.

Things I didn't know my body craved.

He was silent for a moment after I spoke, then he moved taking the spoon from me just as I'd been about to put it to my mouth. He ate the ice cream on my spoon with a smirk before setting it and the tub aside.

He pushed my legs wider so he could step between them. My core responded immediately, despite the dull ache.

"You want a fairy tale," he murmured, playing with my hair. "See, that's your problem. You want something that someone's already written for you. And that ain't you, babe, I'm fucking pleased to tell you. The person you are, the story you live, it won't fit in a book. It's not ever going to be flattened down to live in some two-dimensional world. You're too big for that. You're too bright. You're sunshine in a life that has always been midnight."

I blinked away the prickling of tears at the back of my eyes. Because his words were unbelievable. They were not something you uttered to a girl that you met at a bar, the girl who gave you her virginity for reasons unknown.

But maybe they weren't unknown. Because no matter how free-spirited I was, I wasn't a girl to give something so precious to just *anyone*.

Not to the boy who rented a hotel room on prom night.

Not to the boy who wrote a love song about me.

Or the one who inscribed our initials on a tree.

No.

I was going to give it to a man who told me I was his freaking sunshine after knowing me for twenty-eight hours.

Yeah, I was counting.

"How do you know me when you've only known me for twenty-eight hours?" I whispered. Then I realized I was vocalizing the fact that I knew the exact number of hours we'd been together for. "You know, approximately," I said quickly.

"Can't tell you how I know," he said. "Just know that I do."

Silence echoed between us with the power of the truth.

"You say you live in a world of make-believe yet somehow you're the realest person I've ever met," he murmured, eyes roving over me.

"Maybe everything was make-believe until I met you," I whispered.

"Fuck," he hissed inches from my mouth. "You can't say shit like that. We can't say anything else. It's too dangerous."

I knew what he meant.

Because I felt it too. Every word we said meant something. We were sharing things. And tangling ourselves in each other in impossible ways. Impossible because we both knew this had an expiry date.

"So let's not say anything else," I said against his mouth.

And then I kissed him.

But that was much more dangerous.

"CAN I ASK YOU SOMETHING?"

I didn't know how long we'd been lying there in the shadow of the full moon.

It wasn't lost on me that it was a full moon. The full moon had power. It poured energy into the world and amplified both good and bad experiences. I was a believer in such things.

But I couldn't believe it was the full moon that gave power to this particular experience. The one that had my body aching and sated and thrumming with the sheer amount of worship set upon it.

No, that was all Heath.

His arms tightened around me. I liked that. A lot. That when I spoke, he had to physically pull me closer to his naked body before he answered.

"You're asking me if you can ask me a question?" he teased. "You're naked in my arms, Sunshine. Know how sweet your pussy tastes, know what it's like to be inside it. Think you can just go straight ahead and ask whatever you want."

I giggled. "Don't be crass."

He pulled me farther up his body so I was all but splayed upon his chest and tilted my chin up to meet his shadowed face. "I seem to recall you enjoying me being crass," he murmured against my mouth.

Even though the area between my legs was tender, it pulsed with the sex in his tone, needing more of him.

I smiled. "I seem to recall the same thing. But it's a little foggy. Maybe you're going to have to refresh my memory."

"Fuck, baby, you're gonna wear me out," he growled, catching my bottom lip in his teeth.

His hands moved up and down my back. "And you're testing all my willpower. 'Cause I know you're hurting, so I'm gonna wait. It might fuckin' kill me, but I'm waiting." His arms tightened around me once more. "So how about you ask that question to distract me."

"You're on short leave, right?" I asked.

He was right, my question did distract him, and it wasn't even the real question. It was the precursor to the question. But nonetheless, his body froze around mine, and I felt the change in his demeanor instantly.

"Yeah, babe," he said. "Wheels up on Monday."

I ignored the dull burn in my throat that came with this knowledge. Not just that he was leaving and I was likely to never see him again, though that sucked, but because he was going somewhere violent. Somewhere he could get hurt.

Die.

Best-case scenario had him coming back a little less than he was before. A little less than he was right now. Because war took from everyone. And I couldn't stand the thought of it taking from him.

"So you're stateside for three days?" I clarified.

"Yeah, not including flight time. Hardly worth the trip, but it's better than the alternative, which was stayin' put."

"And when you got here, from a war zone, you came to a shitty bar in West Hollywood to listen to a crappy band and drink warm beer," I said.

"There a question in there, Sunshine?"

I traced lines with my finger on his pec. "You know there is."

He sighed, long and hard. "My buddy, Duke, he's from bumfuck nowhere in the middle of Dakota. Total travel time to get him home puts him there for just under fourteen hours. But he did it, grin on his face because he's going to see his folks, his sister just had a baby and his girl is there. Most of the men on the bird over here had similar stories. People to go back to. People that care if they come back." He paused. "I'm not most men."

Sadness bloomed in my heart, cold and painful. "You don't have anyone?" I asked.

"I guess I could visit my parents. Might be sober enough to recognize me," he said. "But considering I left at sixteen when I got big enough to fight back and win against my pops, I doubt they would welcome me with open arms. Never been welcomed with open arms since I can remember. Doubt even when I was born."

I struggled to not bawl all over his chest since his voice

betrayed no emotion at the fact his parents beat him and didn't care about him.

Obviously, there was emotion there. But the more hurt there was in some people, the tougher they seemed.

"What about friends?" I asked.

"Hung out in rough crowds before I left home," he said. "Not people I imagine stayed off drugs or outta prison. Bounced around from sixteen to eighteen, didn't stay anywhere long enough to make friends. And then I went straight into the Marines. So my friends are the ones I'll be getting on a plane with come Monday."

I digested this.

Or I tried to.

I could not imagine, I could not *fathom* a life like that. My life was full, bursting with people who I adored. I decorated my life with people I loved. It was what filled me up. I tried to think about not having a mom and dad who loved me for exactly who I was, tried to think of them hurting me.

Bile rose in my throat at the mere thought of it.

I struggled to imagine a life where I didn't have Lucy, Rosie, Ashley—my safety nets and my shields from the world. People who would die for me, commit felonies for me. People made up big chunks of my heart.

"I'm sorry that you didn't have people to treat you in the way you should've been treated," I whispered.

"I'm not," he replied.

I stilled.

"'Cause if I had somewhere to go tonight, maybe that asshole would've got what he wanted," he said not taking his eyes from mine. "And if I went through all that shit just so I could stop the world from marking you with that kind of ugliness, then I'm at peace with that."

I blinked rapidly.

I had no idea what to say to that.

How in the *heck* did someone respond to that? Because he wasn't just saying it. Heath didn't just say things unless he meant them. And he meant it. He meant that he was happy to go through *years* of utter misery to help protect me from a handful of *moments* of it.

"My life was ugly, it is ugly," he murmured. "But you changed that."

Again, my heart stuttered. Bled.

"Everyone is looking for something that will make the world a little less ugly," I whispered finally.

My words gave him pause. Actual visible pause, and then his brows furrowed in that attractive and familiar way, scrunching up his features like a man staring at a puzzle without the right pieces. "That's not something that I'd expect you to say."

I smiled. And it wasn't happy. It felt rather sad and melancholy. Because it was filled with truth. "Of course not. I am the literal Pollyanna, right? I'm not meant to see the ugliness, I'm the carefree, rather flaky yet loveable romantic. But there is no way to exist in this world and be carefree. It's an impossibility. We're all pretending. Just like you're pretending to be all... you."

He raised his brow in the moonlight. "*All me*?" he repeated. His voice now held a hint of teasing, just like his eyes. "And what is 'all me'?"

I grinned shyly. "I don't know. The strong and tough Marine who comes to a woman's aid in a bar when really he needs someone to come to his aid. Show him that life isn't just wars in one country and savage drunks in another. A person who fights ugly for a living and maybe needs a little beauty in his life."

All teasing glint left his eyes. He searched my face for a long time. "Jesus," he muttered. "I think I've found that beauty,

Sunshine." He stroked the side of my face in a way that unnerved me.

It was nice, of course, because whenever he touched me, it was nice. But there was something poignant, final, about it. Like in *The Way We Were* when Katie realizes she still loves Hubbel but there is no way they would ever be together, so they just bask in that last moment flirting with different futures, different pasts, until they go back to their mutual realities which will retreat their relationship into a memory.

But then again, I tended to romanticize moments.

"You know I've fought in battles, some of them I didn't think I'd be comin' back from. Survivin'," he murmured, he grasped the side of my neck with one hand, the other biting into my bare hip. He stroked the side of my jaw with his thumb. "Somehow I did. But I don't think I'll survive you."

And then he kissed me.

And neither of us survived that weekend.

Not really.

I fell in love with him that night, when I was too young, too naïve and too fearless.

When he left, I experienced the broken heart that would've jaded a lot of people. Turned them cold and cynical and closed. But I was determined, even though I was broken, even though I'd given him everything, my most precious of things, I would not give him that.

He could take my virginity and my heart, but he would not take that zest for life that was central to me. The zest for love. For the fairy tale.

He gave me first-hand experience of the fact it wasn't real.

And I spent years after that trying to prove him wrong.

Trying to fall in love with a thousand different guys so I could fall out of love with one.

Because I did still love him.

Even though he treated me horrendously. Callously. Even though his actions were unforgivable.

Actions were unforgivable. But love was not as easily swayed.

Broken hearts sometimes crave the person that broke them. No matter how unhealthy, ugly, and painful that need is, it doesn't go away.

But I tried to cover it up.

Ignore it.

Prove to him that he did not own me.

Give my heart to everyone because I maintained the illusion that it didn't belong to any of them. Not even me.

Four Years Later

"Polly!" Lucy yanked me into an uncharacteristic hug.

Lucy wasn't a hugger.

I was. I was usually the one that had to wrangle her into any kind of affection. It wasn't because she didn't feel it, though it would seem like it on first glance. She was always wearing black, always elegant and in heels, her beautifully sharp features mostly sculpted into a mask of indifference. Even when she was hurting. *Especially* when she was hurting.

Which had been a lot from the moment she'd met Keltan.

Because people are not all smiles and happiness when they fall in love. No, if it's real and true—like what Lucy and Keltan had—the smiles were rare, and misery was common.

A year ago, when this all began, Lucy smiled more than ever.

Which was the obvious sign of her misery, since she usually put more effort into looking happy when she was miserable.

There was nothing I could do, apart from hope that the universe gave my sister peace.

And a year later, a year full of misery and pain disguised by fake grins, her smile was real. Genuine.

It filled my heart.

"Sorry I'm late," I said once she released me, fighting the tears that prickled the backs of my eyes. Tears of utter and complete relief that my sister was getting exactly what she deserved.

She grinned wider. "Oh, you're not late." She turned on her heel and walked farther into Keltan's impressive apartment. I took this as my cue to follow. "I told you to come two hours earlier than I wanted you here," she called over her shoulder, shouting because of the low thump of the music growing as we entered.

Of course, she knew me so well.

I didn't *mean* to be late.

I tried my hardest to be early.

But Rain really needed my feedback on her routine for this comedy show she was doing. She was nervous. Her. The girl that flashed a cop to get herself out of a ticket. So I stayed and listened and laughed and gave her a little of what she needed. Most of it was going to come from her, she just needed someone to help her figure that out.

"Sorry we don't have any kale juice or kombucha or whatever it is you're into these days," Lucy continued as I caught up with her. "But how about a beer?"

I grinned. "Beer sounds great."

I smiled at a few people I kind of knew, but most were strangers. I smiled at them too. Not enough people smiled at strangers.

I hadn't exactly mingled with Lucy's L.A. crowd. I didn't do much mingling with her friends back in Amber either. Apart from Rosie, and Ashley. And the Sons of Templar now and again.

But the three of them did their best to keep me away from the notorious biker club saying I'd "bring trouble even someone like Gage couldn't handle."

But that was okay with me. As much as I respected their free-spirited life outsides the bounds of society, I was kind of against violence. Kind of being utterly and completely.

And they lived violent lives.

My crowd veered to a little more peaceful end of the spectrum. Not that I stuck to one 'crowd.' I wasn't in a group in high school, I was the nomad who was friends with everyone and no one, who had a different boyfriend who took her to different parties where she met different people every week.

I was addicted to that. Knowing different people, how they lived their lives, how I could fit into some version of it. Sometimes I did. For a while at least.

It was only here in my loft in L.A. with the group of misfits that I was thinking *maybe* I might fit. But since I was exploring that, I hadn't hung out with Lucy and Keltan much. To be fair, they'd only just gotten their shit together after over a year of painful separation.

They definitely didn't need Lucy's little sister cramping their style.

I knew Keltan owned a security company. Knew it was kind of famous. I kind of guessed there would be hot guys at this party, because if Keltan was anything to go by, then yeah.

Not my type.

Maybe because they were too conventional alpha male for me.

Or maybe because they reminded me of someone.

When I saw him, I thought I was hallucinating. Thought I'd let my mind stray to him and for that reason, he'd appeared. But if I was hallucinating, then I'd see him exactly how he was imprinted into my memory. Not with almost everything about him different apart from his eyes and the way they stared into me.

"Holy shit," I murmured under my breath as Lucy handed me the bottle.

She frowned, not yet catching on to who I was staring at. "What? Is it not gluten-free? Is it made by corporate America so you can't possibly contribute to the capitalist pigs by drinking it?" she asked dryly.

I barely heard her, though it was the truth.

Something worse than the capitalist ethos taking over the minds of our society was happening right now.

He was coming over.

Oh shit, *he was coming over*.

At a loss of what to do, I lifted the beer to my face and chugged. Yes, faced with the man I'd been fantasizing about for years, instead of looking my best and giving him an intense look like he was giving me, I chugged my beer like a frat boy on rush week.

"Alright, so your latest boyfriend owns a brewery," Lucy teased, still thankfully oblivious.

Then he was there.

In front of us.

And everything came crashing into me. The power of the memories I'd carried and nurtured and pretended that it was something but not the thing.

Because there was more than something, something exciting, something passionate, something a little like love. There was all of that, and then there was *the thing*.

That connection.

The stifling and uncomfortable vibration in the air the second our eyes locked. The tightness in my lungs as invisible hands squeezed at them. The needles pressing farther into my heart with every rapid beat. The pulsating throb in between my legs.

"Ah, Heath, of course you'd lumber over here with less than chivalrous thoughts about the newest beautiful woman to enter the room," Lucy said with a smirk. "I'm afraid this beautiful woman is taken by a man I presume owns a brewery and sleeps in his mom's basement." She gave me a wink.

I was trying to remember how to breathe.

"Also," Lucy continued. "There's the fact that she's my baby sister and I'd just have to castrate you with a dull butter knife if you even got any ideas," she said sweetly.

I recovered quicker than I thought possible, reaching out to the hand Heath had extended after Lucy had finished her threats that worked as her version of an introduction.

"Nice to meet you," I said with a voice that was little more than a squeak.

Lucy introduced us because obviously we were strangers. To her, there was no way this man who worked for Keltan, and me had ever crossed paths before. No way would I—or could I—educate her on the truth.

The handshake was a bad idea.

No, scratch that. The handshake was a terrible idea.

The second his hand engulfed mine, my entire body went flush. I was catapulted roughly and painfully into that beautiful and ugly past.

Everything was stark and blurry at the same time.

I tried to yank my hand back, for continued survival more than anything else. And because there was only so long I could hold it together with Lucy looking on.

But his grip tightened.

Almost to the point of pain.

He frowned at me.

No, he *glared.*

He hadn't spoken yet.

I prayed that he played along with my farce. The lie that felt uncomfortable and itchy the second I decided to roll with it. I didn't lie. Didn't act. But here I was, doing both. Because I had no other choice.

"Polly," he drawled, the word tearing at all those wounds that I'd thought were healed. My inner thighs clenched with the memory of him saying my name.

When he'd taken my virginity.

"Nice to meet you," he murmured, letting go of my hand, but not of my soul.

I exhaled roughly. But the expelling of breath didn't give me relief. My lungs were still starved and flooded with oxygen at the same time.

Lucy saved the day.

As she tended to do with me.

"Wine," she near screamed, thrusting it at me, snatching my empty beer bottle.

I took it like a life raft, more for something to hold onto than anything else. Something to anchor me to the present so I didn't do anything dangerous like try to get lost in the past.

I didn't do that.

I *never* did that.

I never worried about yesterday and I never fretted for tomorrow.

My family thought that the reason for this was the reason for everything else I did...because I was just *Polly.*

But the real reason for this was standing right in front of me, hands clenched at his sides, the pieces of me ground up in those closed fists.

Lucy snatched my hand not holding the wine and started to

drag me toward the sofa, oblivious to the fact I was leaving a huge chunk of myself in the clenched fists of the man she'd 'introduced' me to.

"Now, I need to hear about this cult you're living in. And make sure you don't drink the Gatorade," she demanded, eyes narrowed.

I frowned. "It's not a cult, it's a community of..."

And then I lost myself in the familiar. In reassuring Lucy that my latest situation would not result in my getting on the news as the fifteenth wife of an eighty-year-old man and no, I was not preparing for any sort of apocalypse.

Familiar.

But made utterly freaking alien by the man watching me, yanking at the tapestry I'd knit over the broken pieces of myself.

There was only so long I could handle that.

There was only so long any human being could handle that.

So I left, feigning an event that I had to go to. Which wasn't a lie. There was an indie rock band playing in the Hills. And I *had* been planning on going. Jett, my kind of boyfriend, who I *thought* I'd been kind of obsessed with—until now of course—was a member of the band and I had wanted to see him.

But now I didn't want to see him because Heath had made me see myself, really see me, the me I'd become after four years of denial, and I didn't like it one bit.

Lucy had let me leave easily enough—well, with a raised brow and an insistence to take the taser she'd shoved into my purse.

Heath had been clenching a beer, his eyes on me, gaze heavier than anything physical could've been. His stare was physical. It didn't bow down to the years between us, the years that should've chipped away at the feelings, the memories, until they were nothing but pebbles to be carried around, maybe stumbled upon in the wrong moments of remembering.

But this was not a pebble.

This was a mountain, heavy and all-consuming.

And I needed to run from it.

So I ran.

I wasn't surprised he'd followed me home.

Not that I knew that much about him—two nights, no matter how amazing and life-changing, cannot tell you everything about a person. But it told me *enough*.

As did the way he looked at me the entire night. The way he totally and utterly shredded my insides with that intense and knowing stare.

Like somehow he'd learned everything about me in those two nights all those years ago, and he'd held onto it, carried it with him, and then the stare presented me with the truth of that.

I thought I was prepared when I opened the door he had been banging on moments after I'd closed it.

I was not.

All of my breath left my body in a low exhale seeing him standing in front of me.

I expected him to burst into the living room, that for once, was empty. It was almost a miracle. The common area was never empty, due to the kind of people that were drawn to living arrangements like this. People who didn't live by conventional means, by society's timetable. At the loft, there was no such thing as 'proper' hours. People had breakfast at midnight. Dinner at eight in the morning. Did yoga at three in the morning. Decided to take up the drums in the middle of the day.

It wasn't for everyone.

Or even the majority.

Which was kind of the point.

In the majority, people like us were lonely. But here, loneliness was actively fought against, and almost impossible.

And I'd never felt lonely.

Because I'd never let myself. My life was designed to look like chaos. But it was really carefully planned to avoid my own demons.

Tonight had straightened up my chaos. Lined up everything so I couldn't avoid what I was trying to hide. I'd felt exceptionally lonely when I got back to the empty loft. I'd been lonely walking the bustling streets of L.A., amongst the throngs of people, until I got home to rare silence.

Until the banging on my door.

Until he yanked me outside and then began pacing the hallway, running his fingers through his hair.

He shouldn't be doing that.

Because it made my own fingers itch to do that. I didn't get to that first night. He was still in the Marines then. They had buzz cuts.

He'd grown it.

It suited him.

It didn't soften his face as it would have with other men.

It made him harsher.

Wilder.

Before, that wildness was hidden, only slightly, behind his military issue haircut. Behind his clean-shaven face, his neatly pressed clothes. I saw it of course, felt it, biblically, in the night we do not think of.

When he shed his clothes that night, he shed whatever personality the trials and horrors of war had forced him to wear. I saw it. I imprinted that onto my skin. My soul. My broken heart.

I imagined he put it right back on—that military issue personality that matched the buzzcut—when he left me in bed that

Sunday morning we do not think of. Seeing him in the flesh, he must've. Because he was *here.* And I knew a lot about war. Because I campaigned for peace. And you had to know the enemy and all that.

I knew it was only those people that wore the uniform on their bodies as well as their souls that survived.

Not just physically, but managed to survive enough when they got home not to spiral into a haze of drugs, alcohol, homelessness. I knew this because I volunteered at three different homeless shelters. The number of veterans amongst the residents in such places was staggering.

But Heath had shed that uniform completely and utterly on the outside, maybe because he knew he couldn't shed it from his soul. Or maybe I was reading too much into the fact he'd grown the previous buzz cut into a shaggy, shiny and beautiful mane that brushed his shoulders. That his strong and angled jaw was now hidden by a long and trimmed beard. That his previously large but lean muscles were now bursting from the long-sleeved tee he had pushed the sleeves up to reveal corded arms.

He was wearing all black, down to his scuffed motorcycle boots.

I'd thought he was beautiful before.

But this was something less than beautiful. Something so much *more.*

His eyes darted around the hallway, flickering like the tired light three doors down.

Mine stayed on him.

They couldn't move.

And then he yanked me in. Not with his body, he still kept space between us. No, with his fricking *gaze* centered on me. Familiar and alien at the same time. Comforting and terrifying.

Calm and chaotic.

"*This* is where you live?" he hissed.

I jerked back.

Of all the things I thought he might say, this was not it.

Which was actually a good thing, because I likely wouldn't have been able to react properly—with strength and willpower—to anything else.

The words, the judgment in them—judgment he seemed certain he had the right to possess—had my back straightening.

"This is where I live," I agreed, my tone daring him to say more. I folded my arms and arched my brow.

His eyes flickered to my chest as I did so and I hated I felt that flicker right in between my legs.

"You shouldn't live here," he clipped, folding his own arms and widening his stance as if it were to reinforce the point that he had muscles, a great beard, and a penis and therefore his word was law.

I was sure that was the case with plenty of women.

And I didn't judge them one bit.

Because it was tempting to let the beautiful man with great muscles, a greater beard, and an excellent penis—with equally excellent skills in using it—lay down whatever law he saw fit.

I had certainly fallen victim to a handsome face, pretty words, and a talented tongue.

His being the first.

Hence me not letting him lay anything. Especially me.

I wouldn't survive it.

"You shouldn't be here," I returned.

His eyes hardened at my response. As if he weren't expecting such a show from me. And I guessed he was right. I didn't argue. Not if I could avoid it. The cold and harsh tone of my voice was foreign to me. I had an expression on my face that would likely be foreign too. It *felt* unnatural. Because I didn't frown. I tried to give myself a reason to smile, to be kind, understanding and happy every day.

I truly believed happiness was a decision.

It was the hardest one to make, especially every single morning, but it's how I lived my life.

Until now.

Because if I was going to survive this encounter, it wasn't with the decision to be happy. It was the decision to be miserable. To be ruthless. With Heath. And most of all, myself.

"You treated me like a stranger," he accused, instead of continuing the apartment conversation.

I wished we'd continued that conversation, because this was a lot more dangerous. But the only way through it was, well, *through it.*

Though I did consider running back into the loft, slamming the deadbolt, and hiding in the bathtub for the foreseeable future.

I didn't do that.

Instead, I sank further into the persona that felt so uncomfortable.

"You took my virginity, showed me two nights of...something and then left me in the morning without so much as a goodbye," I hissed back. "You *are* a stranger."

He flinched at my words.

I tried not to let that affect me. So he had a minor physical reaction to my recounting of the event. I *lived* it. And I had critical physical and emotional reactions for *years* after.

He didn't get to act outraged.

I paused.

Breathed.

I remembered what I'd been chasing since that night. Peace.

I'd never get it, of course. But what was the point in yelling at him? Accusing him? Spouting ugliness out into the present when

I carried enough of it with me from the past? Me being angry and bitter would change nothing.

It would be giving him more of me.

He was waiting, bracing, watching me. Probably expecting more shouting. Screeching. There was something about his expression that looked like he wanted it. That he was ready to take it. Because he knew it was wrong, what he'd done.

"It's the past," I said, my voice little more than a whisper. "Whatever that was has happened. It's history. And so are we. It would just be easier for all involved if we pretend it never happened."

Lie.

Lie.

Big fat *lie.*

That was another thing I didn't do. Like ever. Lie. Because I tried to act in a way that I'd want people to act toward me. Sometimes I'd tell a friend that her new hemp shoes were totally cute and that could've been considered a lie. But not when it didn't hurt anyone's peace. Plus, my abhorrence for hemp shoes was only *my* truth, not Marianne's. So on the whole, I didn't lie.

But I did it all fricking evening, with my *sister*, of all people.

And now to *him*.

It all revealed the lies I'd been telling myself all along.

"Bullshit."

The single word echoed through the hallway.

"Excuse me?"

He didn't blink at my tone, didn't change his expression, this new version of him didn't seem to have the same fluid ability as the man I'd met in a bar years before.

For a moment, I got the certainty that he'd taken something with him when he left, but he also left something too. Something I didn't know I possessed until right now.

But of course, that was crazy. Impossible.

Wasn't it?

"You heard me," he said, voice mild and his indifference sweeping that thought away. "I said it's fuckin' bullshit."

There was more bite in his words now.

More emotion.

Namely anger.

At *me*.

As if I wasn't the one who woke up alone and confused, covered in memories of a man who had disappeared from reality.

I was the one that woke up to a note.

You will always be my Sunshine, but my life isn't ready for that yet.
H

That was it.

The entire mother effing note.

And I hadn't seen him for four years, yet this was him shouting at me, throwing anger at me.

"Are you fricking kidding me?" I demanded, my voice a visible snap of the last thread of my temper. "You think after a *weekend four years ago* we can just jump back into what we were? When what we were was forty-eight hours in a *fantasy*. I don't live in a fantasy. Despite what people might tell you, or what you might tell yourself. I've moved on. I'm different." I looked him up and down, hopefully keeping my mask of fury firmly intact. "And you obviously are. And this isn't a fantasy. This is reality." I paused, unable to banish him from my life as I had intended. Not when he was standing right in front of me. The universe put him here for a reason.

I wouldn't survive him if I gave him my heart.

But I wouldn't survive if I made him walk away either.

The pause yawned on as I considered my options.

"So how about we just be friends?" The words were weak and impossible to say, and even more impossible to make a reality.

Heath stepped forward, face granite. "Because I don't have platonic feelings toward you, Sunshine," he said, voice rough, caressing my spine and feeding a hunger between my legs. "I didn't back then and I sure as fuck don't now. I don't want to be your friend. I'm gonna be *your man*."

I folded my arms in frustration. Mostly at him, but also at myself for responding so viscerally to him. "You don't know what kind of feelings you have toward me," I hissed. "You have memories you carried through a war, through the years, just like me. And revisionist history isn't just something that happens in politics or the corrupt education system, it's rampant in emotional history too. So you think you know that weekend, you think you know *me*, but you've changed, tweaked when the details got fuzzy. You don't know me for who I am. You know me from who you made me into."

I threw the words out of desperation more than anything. And if the expression on his face was anything to go by, they hit their mark.

"You think the details of you that night are fucking fuzzy for me?" he asked slowly, voice flat.

I nodded, trying to make the gesture decisive.

"You were wearing a dress that was too short and you didn't have a fuckin' jacket on even though it was January in L.A., not winter like anywhere else, but chilly enough to need a fuckin' jacket. Your dress had sunflowers on it, huge bright yellow ones," he said.

I sucked in a breath of surprise.

But he wasn't done.

He was so far from done.

"You were wearing some sort of corked wedges, like you were going to a fucking garden party in August instead of a shitty gig in a shitty bar in a shitty area in L.A.'s version of winter," he continued, voice harsh. "Your hair was split into two pigtails, and they drove me fuckin' *wild.* They were loose, you had curls escaping out of them."

His hand reached up as if to hold onto one of the curls—much longer now—escaping my messy bun, but then he caught himself halfway, yanking his hand back down into a fist at his side.

"You were glowing, like a fuckin' *sun* in the middle of that bar," he ground out, eyes not leaving mine. "Some sweaty, fat, drunk asshole had his hands on you. You weren't fighting him like most girls were. You weren't even fucking looking around for anyone to help you. You were lost in your head, and you had a soft look on your face that even the hardness of a place like that, a situation like that couldn't take off. You were a lamb in a den of wolves. And it looked like I was saving you, but really I just wanted you for myself."

His voice was raspier now. Full of desire from the past, and plenty being built in the present.

My panties were soaked. My breathing shallow. Heart shattering as it thundered against my ribs.

And. He. Wasn't. Done.

"Your hands on my chest were the lightest and smallest thing that had ever been on there, but somehow they cracked my fuckin' ribcage," he rasped. "You tasted like strawberry when you kissed me because you wanted to see what it felt like. You told me you believed in peace but didn't judge me from making my living fighting a war."

He paused, and his eyes darkened even more as his gaze tore through my clothes, searing my skin. My fricking soul.

"You were wearing white lace panties underneath your dress. No fuckin' bra." He paused, his eyes at my chest He visibly shuddered at the memory of my freaking bare breasts.

I almost leaned in then. Almost swallowed his painful and beautiful words with a kiss.

Almost.

Heath watched me as if he knew what I was battling. "Had I known that you weren't wearin' a fucking bra that night would've ended at my apartment much fuckin' earlier," he continued. "Your pussy was the sweetest, warmest and most beautiful place I've ever been able to make my home in."

My core clenched at his words. It ached for his touch. For him to fill me up bodily like his words were filling me up. But I didn't move. I couldn't.

"And I told you I didn't have a home apart from that shitty apartment and it broke your heart," he said, voice softer now. And the softness was tearing through me like a serrated blade. "Saw it because you don't wear your heart on your sleeve, you wear it in every inch of you," he murmured. "It radiates from the *air* around you. And it broke for me, the man who was a stranger, who knew you more intimately than anyone had before."

He let the words sink into the air. Into the energy between us. Let them chip away at the lies I'd told myself about what that night had been.

"And when I left you in bed, you reached for me, and mumbled 'I love you,' in your fuckin' sleep," he said, going for the final blow. "And I thought, fucking seriously, about snatching you up, putting you in my truck and just...driving. I seriously considered abandoning the family who'd made me into a man, the thing that defined me better than the first eighteen years of my life. I almost risked it all, ruined it all—happily—for you in that moment."

My eyes watered, my vision wavered at his words. At the emotion in them. At the truth in them. My brain ached for that moment to have come into actuality so I could've taken his hand, driving through the years with him at my side and the world on our backs. I yearned for a past I'd never known and never would know.

"And the worst thing was, I knew you, knew your soul and knew that you would've gone if I asked you," he said, voice quieter now. "You would've committed to a life on the road, on the run from Uncle Sam and the world itself. *That's* what made me leave. And that's what made me commit every single fucking detail of you to my memory. No revising. Not embellishment. Because you can't fucking embellish perfection. Don't do this, us, the injustice of saying it was anything less than it was. You're lying to me and you're lying to your fucking self."

The end of his speech was no longer gentle. Not that the words had ever been gentle. Nothing about this, us, was gentle. It wasn't some kind of easy or joyous reunion. It was torture.

He hadn't moved. He was still watching me, waiting for a response.

But what in the actual heck did I say to that? A part of me knew what to say.

Nothing.

It wasn't the time to say anything. It was a time to jump back into his arms. To kiss him and let the years dissolve around us.

But I couldn't.

I was afraid.

And not too proud to admit it.

"Polly!" The voice cracked through the moment.

Both Heath and I moved our gazes to a group of people storming through the hall.

Jett was front and center.

Oblivious, and likely wasted, he bowled forward and snatched me into his arms.

"Babe! You missed the show," he said. "I'd be mad at you, if you weren't so cute." He kissed my forehead. "And because we're doing an encore show in your living room."

People shouted "fuck yeah!" in response to this, as the small crowd pushed past all the emotional demons that had filled up the hall with their instruments, with their half-full beers.

Heath stood in the middle of it all, unmoving, glaring at Jett. Or more accurately, his arms around me. Jett noticed this, belatedly. He moved and slung his arm around my shoulder. "Oh hey, dude."

Jett looked the part of an indie rocker. He had silver on every single finger. Wore a ripped black tee. His skinny arms were covered in mismatched and random tattoos. He was wearing dirty Chuck Taylors.

But he really had a kind heart, which was what drew me to him.

"You a friend of Polly's?" he asked.

Heath glared at me now. "I don't know, am I, Polly?"

The question was much more than that. It was an invitation to step out of Jett's kind and safe embrace into Heath's harsh and dangerous one.

I painted a smile on my face. "Yeah, he's a friend."

Nothing changed outwardly on Heath's expression.

But everything changed.

CHAPTER FOUR

Three Weeks Later

I WASN'T PAYING attention when a knock came at the door. It should've been something to pay attention to, considering no one knocked here. Most people walked right in. We operated on an open-door policy. Obviously I didn't tell my family about that because they would get all *judgy* about it.

No one stole anything.

No one was hurt.

The world didn't tilt on its axis because we didn't believe in locked doors.

It was a little slice of peace, of magic, this loft. People came and went, they gave what they could, took what was offered and it worked.

Not something the outside world would understand because we were conditioned to think it didn't work that way. That money and greed drove everyone. You could never get something for nothing, and people always had an ulterior motive.

Not here.

So the knocking thing was weird.

But weird was a construct. Just like normal. There was nothing constructed or constant about the lifestyle here, and that was the beauty of it. So I didn't think much about the knock. It was outside the norm, but that was all the better.

Plus, I was focused on the pasta I was making. It wasn't exactly working with coconut flour. Bringing white flour into this kitchen was pretty much taken as an act of war. Mainly because of the fact that modified grains were now used to produce said flour, and we did not support that.

"We could turn it into a savory cake," Rain offered, swinging her legs from where she sat on the counter. She was sucking a lollipop, watching me and reading *A Communist Manifesto* at the same time.

We'd moved in within days of each other.

Became fast friends.

Even though she wasn't exactly friendly looking on the outside with jet black hair, wore clothes to match the shade, her eyes always heavily made up with smudged eyeliner, she had piercings on her eyebrow and nose, tattoos crawling up her neck.

She exuded the mood of someone who was perpetually sad. Because people that wore black all the time and dressed like goths were all about violent music and misery, in society's eyes at least.

But that was the opposite of the truth. She was perpetually happy. Never in a bad mood. Always smiling. Always positive. Despite the crappy hand life had dealt her.

I frowned at the mush in front of me. "Do you think it would bake without setting the oven on fire? I don't want to do that twice in one week."

That time I had been trying to make pizza with cauliflower. We ended up ordering in. The firefighters even stayed for a slice.

Rain shrugged. "Let's find out. And if you do, then I'll be able to get the phone number of that firefighter that was *totally* flirting with me. Plus, I've got a friend who works at a restaurant and can likely get us an oven real cheap, read, free." She waggled her brows at me meaningfully. She wasn't exactly averse to breaking the law. I knew she was some kind of hacker and I didn't think anything she did on her computer was anywhere near legal.

I was reasonably sure she was high up in the ranks of the notorious group 'Anonymous' even though their ethos was built around the idea that there were no ranks, which was how they survived despite the FBI imprisoning various members.

I didn't have strict ideas about following rules or the law and I knew Rain well enough to know that whatever she was doing was for the greater good. Or at least her version of the greater good, and it certainly wasn't hurting anyone.

But virtually stealing something from someone with too much money and not enough morals was not the same as stealing an oven from a restaurant. Especially if *I* was the reason for it.

I was about to lecture her about how we couldn't steal ovens, but Lionel's voice floated through the loft. He'd been the one to open the door, it had taken him a couple of long moments to even get to the door, likely because of the bong on the table but also because of the fact he wasn't used to the knocking either.

"You know, you have to tell me if you're a cop, it's the law," he drawled, sounding a lot more alert than he was before. But alert in a way of a high person trying their hardest to sound sober. Which of course wasn't alert. Like at all.

There was a pause.

"Dude! You can't just waltz right in here! You don't have a warrant. Anything you find is inadmissible in court. We have rights!" Lionel yelled, his voice still slow but trying to catch up with him nonetheless.

I would've been laughing at this had I not had my eyes on the man storming across the room. The man who only had eyes for me.

Rain popped her lollipop from her mouth. "Wow," she breathed. "I'd steal a thousand ovens if he could arrest me. But if he's a cop, then I'm a Real Housewife."

I froze with Heath's presence usually. Especially with everything that was going on. Because I hadn't seen him in a handful of weeks. Not since our meeting in the hallway. And I hadn't stopped thinking about him.

I had tried to convince myself in these weeks that Heath had a part of me that didn't exist anymore, the part that was eighteen and nurtured fantasies and had the naivety of youth to rely on.

But seeing him told me I'd been lying.

Heath had *everything*.

And he took it strolling across the room.

I wiped my hands just in time for him to round the counter.

"What are you doing here?" I demanded, my voice shaking slightly.

Not because of his mere presence, but because of something behind his eyes. Something that was more than us.

And it was bad. It had to be bad if it was more than us.

He was on me in two seconds, his hands framing either side of my face. And I knew it was bad. Because he was touching me tenderly, without the anger that had been present in our last discussion. In our last argument.

Heath wasn't a man to forgive such things easily. To forget. So the tenderness was a cushion for something. Something bad.

"Sunshine, before I say what I'm gonna say, I need you to

breathe. Need you to promise you're gonna breathe," he said, his voice a rasp that was cut with something.

Something that terrified me.

Pain.

I couldn't speak so instead I responded with a strangled inhale.

He stroked my cheek with his thumb, tenderly, gently.

And then he fucking destroyed my world.

I PACED.

Because I couldn't sit still at the best of times.

This was not the best of times.

My sister, my savior, my best friend had been *stabbed on the street* and was now in critical condition.

"What does critical condition even *mean*?" I asked the room. The room being Heath. There were a lot of people waiting to hear news. Keltan included. But he wasn't waiting.

No, he was yelling at doctors, fighting with security when they stopped him from pushing through the double doors that led to the place where people were saved, or they weren't.

And my sister was behind those doors.

My sister who had been stabbed.

On the street.

Keltan was covered in blood.

Her blood.

That had given me pause when I'd walked in. When *we'd* walked in.

Heath hadn't let go of my hand the entire time since he gave me the news. He'd held it silently on the ride, let it go only to round the truck and open the door for me and help me out, as if he knew that I couldn't handle such basic things when my sister was in the hospital.

Stabbed.

And that's all I knew.

That's all Heath knew because as soon as he heard, he came looking for me.

It should've been sweet.

It should've filled me with warmth, his dedication to me when I'd done nothing but push him away when I saw him that day at the party.

But it didn't fill me with anything.

Because I felt empty. Hollowed out.

I wasn't empty when we walked through the automatic doors leading to the triage waiting room. I was full. Absolutely bursting with terror so visceral that my stomach lurched dangerously.

Because I saw Keltan.

I saw the utter hopelessness and emptiness on his face.

And the blood covering his white tee. Or what used to be a white tee.

It was crimson now.

There were dark red stains on his hands. Going up his arms. He looked like he'd just murdered someone. Or tried to save someone who had been murdered.

"That's blood," I said, standing woodenly in the spot right in the middle of the door. It was an inconsiderate place to stand, but I couldn't move. No way in goddess's green earth could I move from this spot. I wanted to go backward, like all the way backward to the loft where my biggest problem was a small kitchen fire.

But I couldn't.

There was no way I could go forward, where my biggest problem was facing a man wearing my sister's blood on his tee. I couldn't move forward into the world in front of me. The world that might not contain Lucy.

So I stayed put. In the middle. If I stayed here long enough maybe reality might change into something less ugly and sickening.

But I couldn't take my eyes off Keltan's hands. His tee.

"He is covered in Lucy's blood," I whispered to no one. "That's too much blood for a person to wear on the outside of their body. That's meant to be inside someone's body. That's meant to be inside Lucy."

Suddenly, the limbo I'd been so sure was safe was just as ugly and sickening as that world ahead. There was no escape from the image of Lucy, bleeding, dying, her skin ripped open with violence and pain.

My stomach lurched again.

I yanked my hand from Heath's and sprinted in the direction of a bathroom.

I made it just in time to empty the contents of my stomach.

But not the contents of my heart. They were shedding my insides.

At some point, hands gathered up my hair, held it back. Another hand rubbed my back in slow circles.

It should've touched me somewhere deep, Heath quietly doing what he could in the face of my pain.

But I was empty again.

Heath had not left me since I threw up in the bathroom. He was sitting on a chair in a beige waiting room, elbows on his knees watching me.

He didn't try to tell me to sit down, to calm down, because he was Heath and he didn't do things that he knew were stupid. Telling me to do either of these things would've been stupid. So he was just...there.

"Critical condition," I repeated, still pacing.

I hadn't cried.

I'd thrown up.

I had worn out the soles of my shoes with the pacing. But no tears. Because tears were the first sign of grief. Of loss.

I stopped pacing to face Heath.

"Critical," I whispered. "Critical means that they don't want to tell you something to give you hope. Because there's no hope."

Heath was out of his chair and in front of me in a moment, his hands framing either side of my face. "You stop that shit right fucking now," he growled. "You are the one person in the world that has hope in her fucking bones. In her soul. You give it to the hopeless. You gave it to a tortured man four years ago and you carried him through what came after. And if you can do that for someone else, someone damned, you sure as fuck can do that for your sister. Don't you dare abandon that hope."

He wasn't speaking gently with me. Trying to handle me with care. Trying to mind the broken pieces. Which was good. They were broken anyway, no matter what happened from here on out, they'd stay that way, a reminder of how the world can smash everything apart in a handful of moments.

"What if critical turns to..." I trailed off, my voice literally unable to form the word.

Death.

The thought was poison in my mind.

"If it does. We'll handle it. You'll handle it. You'll get through," he said.

I flinched because he wasn't placating me with false promises that most people made in situations like this. Because he didn't make promises he couldn't keep.

That hadn't changed in the years between us.

Nothing had changed in four years as much as things had in the last four hours.

I searched his eyes for strength, for comfort. He gave me the former. But not the latter, because no matter how I responded to his hands on mine, to his sheer presence, there was no comfort in this moment. Not even Heath could change that. The only person who could change that was behind double doors in 'critical condition.'

"Polly?" The strangled voice jerked me out of Heath's gaze and he dropped his hands.

My mom and dad entered the room, each of them pale, drawn and terrified.

I ran into my father's arms. He kissed my head.

No one said anything.

We couldn't.

We were all too busy hoping.

MY FIRST FULL and clean inhale was marred by cleaning products.

Probably because I was surrounded by them. Because I was currently hiding in some sort of cleaning closet.

Yes, I was hiding in a hospital closet, breathing because I could finally do that now.

Because hope somehow won.

Lucy woke up.

She survived.

And she had it in her to joke about how bad her hair looked and demanded someone go and get her "Egyptian Cotton sheets and a pair of Versace pajamas."

But there was no missing the gray pallor to her face. The

shadow of death still lurking in the room, hiding underneath that sterile lemony scent.

But I'd smiled at her bedside. Overjoyed, just like my parents had been, through their tears. Keltan hadn't left her side.

He'd changed out of his bloodstained clothes.

In fact, he'd changed the next time I saw him after I'd thrown up at the sight of him.

I wondered if Heath had anything to do with it.

Of course Heath had something to do with it.

He hadn't left. He'd left me to sit with my family, with a panicked Rosie who arrived a few hours before Lucy woke up.

She'd immediately yanked me into her arms and I relaxed into her small but strong embrace. I hadn't seen her in a year. Not since she up and disappeared to who knew where doing who knew what.

Whatever it was, was bad. Because even though this place, this situation changed us all, there was something deeper behind her eyes, something darker than the Rosie I'd seen before.

"We're going to kick her ass when she wakes up," Rosie murmured after letting me go but still holding tight onto my hands.

That was her way of saying "she has to wake up because I couldn't handle it if she didn't."

But she did.

So no one would actually have to live the reality of a world without her. But we would always live this memory.

I had slipped out of the room when I got enough reality to chase away the worst of my memories. Of my demons.

And now I was here, hiding in some supplies closet because I didn't know where to go to breathe. To let my tears fall.

Because I couldn't do it in the open, under harsh hospital

lights, where people might see. Where I might catch a glimpse of myself.

The door opened and light flooded in. I was about to prepare some kind of excuse to whatever hospital employee opened the door, but it closed quickly again, and I was in muscled arms and pressed into a warm and muscled body.

"How did you know I'd be in here?" I whispered against Heath's mouth.

The tightness of the space meant we were pressed up against each other out of necessity. But it was not just necessary because of the space.

He didn't answer. A magician never gives away his tricks, after all.

Instead of answering, he kissed me.

Kissed me.

After years.

He kissed me like no time had passed, but somehow like an eternity had gone by in our separation.

I should've pushed him away. Should've grasped onto all the reasons that were so tangible before this day.

But instead, I grasped onto him. And I kissed him back with everything I had. All of my grief, sorrow, anger, frustration. All of the emotions that I never let ripple the smooth and happy façade.

My hands went underneath his tee, raking up that hard and warm skin that I hadn't let myself remember.

He continued to kiss me, clutch my neck with one hand, the other went right to my ass, yanking my body farther against him, grinding me onto his hard length.

I moaned into his mouth.

He wasn't kissing me to give me comfort, tenderness, after one of the hardest moments in my life. After being faced with the ugliest of all realities.

No, he was kissing me in the midst of that ugly reality. Giving me another one.

I moved my hands from underneath his tee to move downward, to work his belt with a desperation that crossed over into insanity.

He didn't stop kissing me as I fumbled with his belt, trying to free him in the small space.

But then I no longer had purchase on his belt because I was being lifted up. My panties pushed to the side, and he surged into me.

I cried out into his mouth, wrapping my legs around him as he fucked me ruthlessly, brooms and cleaning products falling around us with the force of his thrusts.

My orgasm came quick and intense. Life-shattering. Life ending. His mouth left mine and the palm of his hand muffled my cries in a way his kiss couldn't. He didn't stop as I tumbled over the edge, as my orgasm threatened to destroy me. No, he continued with his movements, harsh and beautiful and almost unbearable.

And just as I thought the aftershocks were subsiding, his entire body tightened, his hand left my mouth and he was kissing me again, making a noise at the back of his throat as he found his release inside me.

And that sent me over the edge again, so I tightened around him, milking his release from him.

Stillness eventually took over the chaos that had seemed so permanent. Heath's forehead was resting on mine.

We were both breathing heavily.

He was still inside me.

Slowly, without a word, he lifted me from him and placed me on my feet.

Evidence of his release began to trickle down my leg. He

moved to snatch a rogue cloth and gently cleaned me with a tenderness that had been absent the entire time he'd been fucking me.

And this was *fucking*.

Pure and simple.

No, not at all pure and the farthest from simple anyone could ever get.

But this moment, afterward, the one that should've been filled with chaos as the reality of what had just happened settled in—me fucking the man I was trying to keep away from in a supply closet hours after my sister almost died—it was quiet. Peaceful.

Simple.

Heath pulled my dress down and then buckled his belt.

I stayed silent.

He lifted his hands to frame my face again, brushing my bottom lip with his thumb.

I opened my mouth to say something, something stupid and reckless and dangerous.

But then the door opened, harsh light flooded in and an orderly gaped between us and then grinned wickedly at Heath.

It was the harsh and sterile light and the leer from the young orderly that chased away the words that I was about to say. I took the slackening of Heath's hands as an opportunity and pushed past the orderly to run out the door.

Away from Heath.

He didn't chase me.

It didn't work that way between us.

CHAPTER FIVE

IT DIDN'T FIX US.

Staring death in the face, or more accurately having death stare me in the face with its horrific, sickening and inescapable reality.

I didn't go back on everything with the brutal reminder of how short life was. It was tempting. Oh so tempting when I spent the next two days at my sister's side, Heath's touch chasing away the grip of death.

I wanted him.

With my bones.

With my soul.

But it was my heart that stopped me.

My broken, damaged and cowardly heart.

And it continued to stop me as I watched Lucy marry Keltan from her hospital bed. With Heath staring at me during the whole thing.

I didn't look at him.

I couldn't.

And when it was appropriate, I ran from the room. Much like I'd run from that supply closet.

This time Heath chased me.

"Not so fast, Sunshine."

He had yanked me into an empty exam room before I could escape.

Not that there was any escaping Heath.

"I gave you time," he said, stalking toward me as I backed farther into the room.

I hit a bed and my retreat was hampered. And also the bed was not a good thing to have in the immediate vicinity considering the look in Heath's eyes. Considering *Heath*. The electric connection we shared that had every cell in my body calling out for him.

"I gave you time," he continued eyes dark, hands grasping my hips. The way he pressed against the thin fabric of my dress told me that he'd leave bruises.

And if there was ever a physical embodiment of the reasons why this wouldn't work, it was that. He couldn't touch me without leaving bruises. He couldn't look at me without leaving scars.

"I know you needed it," Heath rasped. "Time. Knew it would do more harm than good to chase you after everything that happened. Know you're a woman that enjoys the loud, but you need the quiet when everything becomes too much." He cupped my face. "These past few days have been too fucking much," he murmured.

My eyes watered.

I couldn't handle it. Him being kind. Gentle.

I couldn't handle him knowing me so fricking well when I was a stranger to myself.

"What happened between us was wrong," I whispered.

His eyes flickered with hardness. With anger. "No, what happened between us was the only right thing in a fucking wrong situation," he growled. "It should've happened the *second* I saw you again. The second for whatever reason, I was given another chance. Should've ripped you out of that hipster fucker's arms. But I was trying to do it right. Trying to give you time. Waiting for you to come to me." His gaze tore through me. "Why didn't you come to me, Polly?"

I could've told him the truth. That I spent hours fighting with myself. Driving through the city, driving past his old apartment, visiting ghosts and wondering if there was such a thing as the resurrection of broken hearts.

I could've told him that I wanted to come to him with every fiber of my being, but I couldn't because no matter how adventurous I seemed outwardly, my heart didn't need adventure. Couldn't survive it. It needed peace. And I knew he couldn't give me that.

But I knew if I said all that, poured out my truth, that it'd be over. That when I laid out all those reasons that seemed so concrete inside my head, they'd dissipate to dust in front of Heath. In front of what he had.

So I didn't tell him the real truth.

"Because back then, we had a weekend. A weekend to see all the beautiful things between us. To focus on them," I said, trying to remember the words I'd rehearsed for this exact moment. And I had rehearsed them. Because I knew this moment would come. After seeing Heath's gaze when I said to Jett that we were friends. He'd walked away after that, but his eyes held a promise. That he'd be coming back.

Which was why he was right, I had dodged him. I'd been careful to never stay in one place too long, my days were never the same, I slept even less than usual. In an ideal world, I was hard to pin down, hard to find.

But this was far from an ideal world. So I was almost impossible to find. Both Lucy and Rosie had commented and complained about it, more worried about my 'cult' than ever.

Obviously they still didn't know the truth.

They couldn't. Because they were the truest, most unflattering emotional mirrors. And they'd call me on my shit.

"Despite what we said to the contrary, that was a fantasy," I said, keeping my eyes and my voice clear with effort. "We're in reality now. And we need to face who we are. Who we really are. I'm a girl who marches for peace, loses her keys daily, is never going to keep to a schedule and wants to travel the world."

I forced myself to keep his eyes, which were hardening with every one of my words.

"You're a man who makes his bed with military corners. You live and ordered and violent life. You're a grown up. A real one. Not me, who's just pretending. That's who we are. Who we were before. And for a weekend, we fit." I sucked in a breath at the impact of those memories. "Because we knew there was an expiration date. But our lives are too different for us to work in reality. We are too different to work in reality. People don't change, Heath," I said. "No matter how long it's been. At our core, we haven't changed. And we won't. I don't want either of us to. No matter how much I wanted us...that's the crux of it."

"You're tellin' me we can't be together because of how I make my fuckin' bed?" he hissed.

"Among other things," I replied, my voice shaking only slightly.

He stared at me for a long time. "That's bullshit, Polly. And you fucking know it."

Did I?

I wasn't sure what I knew anymore.

But I did know that I couldn't survive trying this, jumping into this like I jumped into everything else, like I had that night all those years ago, and have it leave me.

Have Heath leave me.

Again.

I prayed he didn't push me. Didn't press his body any closer to mine. Didn't kiss me.

Because I knew for certain if he did any of those things it'd be done. Over.

My resolve would be shattered. I'd give in. I'd jump.

And then eventually, something would happen. I would happen. And I'd do what I always did. Fuck something up. Do something oh so Polly.

Heath was staring at me, his features morphing, shifting.

He didn't say anything. He didn't press his body closer to mine. Didn't kiss me.

And I should've been relieved when he stepped back, running his hands through his hair in frustration.

But I wasn't.

"I'm not gonna try to convince you what's right when you're trying so hard to convince yourself of what is wrong, Polly," he said. "You're not a girl that lives in a fairy tale, no matter what the world thinks. I know you. And you think you're looking for a knight to save you from yourself. To chase you. To convince you to take a chance. I'm not a knight. Not gonna save you. Mostly 'cause no one can save you from yourself."

And then he turned on his heel and left.

And he didn't save me.

I didn't save me either.

I jumped farther in that false fairy tale, that false reality.

Because I was Polly.

And I was fucking things up.

Irrevocably.

One Month Later

A lot could change in a month.

Especially when you were willing yourself to change in that month.

Especially when you'd convinced you had to change in order to survive. That you were really saving yourself, and more importantly, *him*.

I didn't change by getting my life together, by finding a 'real' job, moving into a 'real' apartment, or truly trying to figure out who the heck I was.

I changed the ultimate Polly way.

With a guy.

"I know this is exceptionally cheesy, but I'm going to say it anyway in the vain hope that you find it endearing enough to give me a chance," a voice said from beside me.

I looked up from my matcha latte.

I was faced with an attractive man.

A very attractive man.

He was tall but not too tall. Tanned enough to show me he went out in the sun, but not too much to tell me he lay in a sunbed. His features were masculine but not sharp. He had muscles peeking out from his simple white tee, but they weren't excessive.

Weren't like...no. I was not allowed to think of him.

His eyes were what got me. They were blue, blindingly so. Kind. Smiling. Clear. Free of demons. Of danger.

I put down my book.

"I'm listening," I said with a smile.

He smiled back. It was easy. Natural. "You are quite easily the most beautiful woman I've ever seen. And I couldn't physically bring myself to go a second longer without talking to you. Without knowing your name."

It was cliché.

And cheesy.

But it was also nice.

Easy.

Natural.

Simple.

So I gave him my name.

And my heart.

The smallest and last undamaged piece that I tried to convince myself didn't belong to someone else.

THREE WEEKS PASSED WITH CRAIG. Three weeks I threw myself into with more force than I had with any other man.

Except...him.

I threw myself in, convinced myself this was it, this was right because there was no other choice.

And it was right.

Craig was easy to be around. He complimented me daily, even if they were rather cheesy, over the top poetic compliments.

They came from his heart.

He gave me his heart.

He was easy to love. I knew that because I was falling in some kind of love with him.

I was *making* myself fall in love.

That's what the fairy tales didn't tell you. About the girl who made decisions with her head instead of her heart, who chose to love the man who was safer, instead of the man she had no choice in loving.

And that's what had me saying yes when Craig went down on one knee after less than a month of dating.

"I know it's been three weeks, but I can't go another three seconds without knowing I'm going to spend eternity with you," he said, holding a large, obviously very expensive diamond. It was beautiful. So very beautiful, I knew that scores of women would actually scream when presented with it.

I hated myself for having the thought in the middle of a romantic and beautiful proposal—but it so wasn't me. I would've liked something smaller, something vintage. Something with a story.

"Polly, I know you want to take adventures, and I promise I'll take you on as many as I can. If you promise to take this adventure with me."

I jerked myself out of my head and scolded myself for having such thoughts, especially when Craig was spinning literal poetry. On one knee. In his bedroom. With rose petals scattered around us.

My heart should've been full.

It wasn't.

Until I forced it to be so.

"Yes," I whispered.

It was then that I realized that he'd slipped the large and cold diamond on my finger before I'd spoken.

L.A. WAS NOT a place you ran into people you knew. It was too large, too sprawling. Everyone was rushing to one place or another. They were stuck in traffic, in line at some juice bar, trying to get into some party, trying to get out of some party that was nowhere near as fabulous everyone said it would be.

So you didn't run into people you knew. Or friends. It was hard enough to purposefully run into friends when you tried to plan it. Especially my friends.

And we were trying to make a plan for all of my friends to be at the loft at the same time for my last night living there.

I was moving in with Craig.

Which made sense. I was marrying him.

"I thought you'd be glad to be leaving that place," he said when I'd shed a little tear while boxing up my stuff. He looked around. "We'll be somewhere with proper plumbing, furniture...privacy," he said, staring at the door where the sounds of Rain's hard rock was vibrating the door.

It was safe to say Craig didn't understand the loft.

But that was okay.

No one understood the loft.

Even the people that loved me the most.

The people who were shocked but supportive about my quickly upcoming nuptials.

After a lot of teasing about Craig's name.

"It's so...normal," Lucy said, nose screwed up.

"I was sure your fiancé would be called Stryker, or Matthias," Rosie said. "You know, something weird. Craig isn't weird. And that's weird."

Once they got over his name was Craig, they were supportive...ish.

Granted, we'd only been engaged for less than twenty-four hours. I was sure they didn't plan on it sticking.

I was Polly, after all.

We were grocery shopping. Such a mundane, normal and peaceful thing for a couple to do.

So obviously my peace was shattered with the man standing in the cereal aisle.

I froze.

Right in the middle of the aisle.

Craig noticed.

"Polly? What are you—"

"Don't say my name," I hissed, preparing to run.

But the man standing the cereal aisle with four women staring at him, almost drooling, had badass super senses and heard my name, so he turned.

And his eyes met mine.

I hadn't seen him in almost months.

Since the day at the hospital.

If I was honest with myself, I'd expected to see him. Expected him to come after me. To shake me out of my idiocy. That's what the hero did, after all.

But Heath promised he wasn't going to save me from my worst enemy.

Myself.

And Heath kept his promises.

So the first time I was seeing him was in the cereal aisle of Whole Foods, with my new fiancé standing next to me.

I expected him to look at me with that hardness in his eyes that had calcified when I'd pushed him away. But at first, for that beautiful moment within a moment, they were soft. They weren't chiseled away from the years, from my stupidity, my cowardice, the violence that had settled in his soul.

And then the moment was over.

Craig's hand slipped into mine.

Heath's eyes went to our intertwined hands.

And they hardened.

I thought he'd walk away.

Of course he didn't.

Heath was not a man to shy away from a battle.

"Heath," I said when he came to stand in front of me.

In front of *us*.

"Polly," he replied. The way he uttered my name was some kind of accusation.

Craig squeezed my hand a little too hard.

"Heath, this is Craig," I stuttered, moving my eyes back and forward between the men.

Heath didn't move his gaze from mine.

Craig held out his hand.

An awkward moment clutched us as Heath ignored the hand, ignored Craig's existence.

Then he took it.

"Craig is my..." I trailed off because I couldn't physically say it. Not in front of Heath. In front of the person I was with him.

"Fiancé," Craig finished for me, letting go of Heath's hand and pulling me into his body, kissing my head. "That's the first time I've gotten to introduce myself as your fiancé," he murmured, loud enough for Heath to hear. "I like it."

I should've too.

Even in the midst of this moment, I should've liked the way it sounded against the air.

But Heath owned the air around me.

So the word I'd convinced myself fit just great, itched, tore at my skin.

I smiled at Craig.

I was a coward and avoided Heath's eyes.

"Sorry, how do you know Polly?" Craig asked, voice still

pleasant but there was an underlying hardness, suspicion and he held me a little tighter as he said it.

"He works for Keltan," I said quickly before Heath could open his mouth. Though he didn't seem too eager to speak. He seemed frozen in front of us.

Craig's face was vacant.

"Keltan," I repeated. "My sister's husband."

"Of course," Craig said, smiling.

The awkward silence lingered on.

"Well, we should be going," Craig said. "We've got lots to do."

Heath only nodded tightly once.

"It was nice to meet you, bro," Craig said.

I couldn't speak so I offered a lame little wave.

A wave with my left hand.

The one that was suddenly heavier than the weight of my shame.

And I let Craig lead me away.

I DIDN'T EXPECT to see him again.

In fact, I'd been counting on it.

Counting on him keeping his promise and not saving me.

But he chose now to break his promise. Now being the last night in my old home before I made a new one with Craig.

When it meant the most and nothing at all.

"You shouldn't be here," I whispered, unsure why I was whispering since somehow the loft was empty yet again.

He didn't reply. He just stood there, staring at me, accusing me like he had at the store.

Just when the silence was too loud, too uncomfortable, too heavy.

He spoke.

He crushed me with his words.

"Does he tell you he loves you every day, Sunshine?" he asked, voice cruel. "Does he make promises about how he feels and what he'll do for you?" He stalked forward, not waiting for me to answer. "Yeah, I know that he does because I've seen him and he's the kind of man who makes promises, who tells beautiful girls he loves them. But he's not any kind of man for you."

He was close enough that the heat of his body singed at my skin while the ice of his gaze froze my veins.

"You don't need a man who's gonna tell you he loves you every day. Makes promises. You need a man who doesn't make shit, doesn't tell you shit. You need a man who shows you." His mouth was inches from mine. "Thoroughly."

I held my breath. I couldn't inhale him. I didn't trust myself.

Then he leaned back, eyes on my mouth. "He's trouble, Polly," he said, stepping back and folding his arms.

"You don't know him," I replied.

"I wasn't a good man when you met me," he said instead of arguing with me. "War makes it impossible to be a good man. There's no such thing as a noble cause when you have to kill another human being for it. Survival isn't noble, not when we get down to the crux of it."

He paused as if he sensed I couldn't breathe when he was shoving words down my throat so they could pierce my heart.

I inhaled,

Exhaled.

He continued.

"I wasn't a good man and I was at peace with that. Didn't come from a good place, good people, so it's not like I had the makeup for it. But somehow, taking the virginity of the one good, truly good woman I'd ever met and ever would meet—one of the worst things I'd ever done—turned a part of me, however small into a good man. And I carried that with me until I saw you and I wanted to be a good man for you. You turned me into a good man by givin' me everything and you turned me back into who I truly am by taking it all away."

He stopped with his words, with his attack and I gave myself two strangled breaths to recover. To realize it was time for an attack of my own.

"I don't deserve this," I whispered. "All of this blame because I didn't jump at the chance to be yours when you came back into my life after *years*, after leaving me to wake up alone after giving you *everything*." My voice was a low hiss. "Everything you took with you. I built my life around those days. I did it in a way that they stayed beautiful and untouched. Now you're back, they're not beautiful, because you're turning me into this villain because I'm not being who you want me to be."

"No," he argued. "You're not being who you want you to be, 'cause you're too fucking scared. If you didn't want this, like truly didn't want this, me, then I'd know, I'd fuckin' *see*. Because nothing's changed from that night. You still wear your heart on your face, and I see what it wants. Didn't think you'd be a girl to let her head get in the way."

And he walked away.

It was becoming common with us.

Him walking away.

Me being too cowardly to chase him.

And then I didn't see him until my wedding day.

And by then it was far too late.

CHAPTER SIX

Three Months Later

I WAS SHOCKED to see him. More shocked than having Rosie tackle me to the ground just before bullets started flying.

Yeah, seeing Heath for the first time after he'd tried to stop me from marrying Craig was more intense than being involved in a drive-by shooting.

Especially since I wasn't the one that was shot.

Rosie was.

I was too busy freaking out about that and the situation in general to notice Heath's presence until he was literally dragging me away from Rosie's bedside.

I would've fought him more if Luke hadn't been there too. Luke would take care of Rosie.

Heath wouldn't take care of me.

No, he might ruin me and my fragile state of mind.

He had me backed up against the wall in a secluded corner of the hospital before I could take him in. Before I could even inhale and exhale.

"Heath—"

"Shut the fuck up."

I flinched and did as he ordered. Because his words were a whip, slashing against my skin. Opening up barely healed wounds. His tone was cold, cruel, brutal.

As were his eyes as they ran over me top to toe.

Twice.

Though everything about him was cold, my body was on fire.

He was cataloging me. That's what he was doing, I realized. He was searching every inch of me for an injury.

"I'm okay," I whispered.

His eyes snapped up.

Another slash.

"You were shot at," he said flatly.

I nodded. "But I'm okay."

His jaw was hard. His hands were fisted at his sides.

He was different.

After only a handful of months, he'd changed. Everything about him was sharper. Colder. Tortured.

I'd done that.

My stomach lurched.

He'd disappeared after my wedding day.

In what was supposed to be happily married bliss I'd thought of him more than I cared to admit.

A lot more.

And in the two weeks since my happily married bliss became a nightmare, I'd consciously not thought of him. Of the huge fucking mistake I'd made.

I wondered if that's why Heath was here.

Because he'd heard.

Heard that I'd done the oh so Polly thing of leaving her husband after not even a year of marriage. He hadn't heard the details, obviously. Because no one knew the details. Except Rosie. And Rosie wouldn't tell. Plus, if he knew the details, he wouldn't be here, he'd be in prison for murder.

Though I reasoned he could murder someone without getting caught. Especially if that someone was my husband who'd decided to use me as a punching bag.

So he wasn't here because of that.

I wondered if he was going back on his word, on the promise he'd made on my wedding day.

"You're makin' a mistake, Sunshine. And I'm not gonna save you from it."

No, I wasn't wondering that.

A sick little part of me was *hoping* for that.

Hoping to be saved from it all. From myself.

But this wasn't that kind of story.

"You're back," I said when the silence had lasted for too long. Long enough for me to try and yank up a fantasy that toyed with my tortured soul.

His nod served as his response.

I itched to escape his empty stare. His cold presence. It was tearing at my skin.

But I also wanted to sink into that pain. Live in it.

I sucked in a breath. "Did you..."

"Hear that your marriage broke up after two months?" he asked, voice cruel. "Yeah, I heard."

I steeled against the pain.

"Not here to be the second choice," he continued. "Here because I was with Luke when he got the call. Needed to make sure you hadn't gotten yourself shot."

I was winded from the force of his successive blows. *"Gotten* myself shot?" I repeated on a whisper.

He nodded once. "Let's be real, Polly. Not like you haven't been playing Russian Roulette with your life thus far."

"And you know me well enough to hurl this at me?" I asked, my voice still a whisper.

His eyes stayed hard. "Oh, I know you, wish I didn't. But I do. You fucking know that. I've known you since that night four years ago."

"That night four years ago," I repeated, tasting the sweetness of the past on my tongue, then it turned rancid with Heath's stare.

I was done.

I had almost been *shot* today.

After hiding out for two weeks waiting for my bruises to heal. Bruises made by my husband. The man I loved.

Somehow still loved.

And now I was standing in front of another man. Who made what Craig and I had turn flat. Two dimensional.

But I was done with his accusations.

"That morning, when I woke up alone but for a slight stain serving as ugly evidence of something I'd thought was beautiful, I had two options. Only two." I made myself keep eye contact with Heath, struggled to keep my voice even, but I managed it.

I sucked in a breath and continued.

"Everyone only has two options in these kinds of situations. But because we're all different, there are a million different ways that these two options ultimately manifest. You make the decision from one of two organs. The brain or their heart."

I smiled, and I imagined it was full of melancholy.

"I used to think that was such a cliché, which is funny since *I was* the cliché. The idiot girl believing the man she was giving her virginity to thought it was special. And then he left, and I realized he wasn't of the same opinion."

I laughed, and I hated the bitterness to it. "But I realized I had two options, and whichever one I chose would serve as the roadmap for all future matters of love. Because it was pivotal, that moment. How I reacted would be how my thoughts about love and sex would be structured. My brain urged me to cry. Scream. Call my sister and get her and Rosie to track you down and get you locked up in a POW camp or something."

I narrowed my eyes at him. "The need for that was so strong, so hot, it was acid in my veins. And I almost did it. I was closer than I'd like to admit. But I remembered who I was. Listened for the whisper from my heart, separated it from the screams of my brain. So I didn't call my sister. I cried. But only to purge. Only to get rid of all that bitterness. And then I closed my eyes, wished you the best and believed that karma would teach you the lesson I wanted Rosie and Lucy to teach you. My lesson had already been taught. So I followed my heart. Let it lead me everywhere away from that ugly morning. And it led me to Craig. To something easy. Beautiful. Or so I thought, of course. I could lie and say that seeing you didn't urge me to throw myself into it that much more. But I won't. It's not my style. I followed my heart and it led me astray, but I won't regret it."

"That's a fuckin' lie," he hissed. "If you followed your heart, there's no way you would've walked down that fuckin' aisle. Said those vows. You did that because you were a coward."

I stayed silent.

I let him hurl those words at me. Let them spear into the places already radiating with pain. Let him create new ones.

Because in a way, I deserved it.

The pain.

The judgment.

He stepped back.

"You weren't brave enough to try something that didn't fit into your fucking fantasy. And now you've got your reality."

And then he walked away.

I sank down on the floor of the hospital.

I got back up eventually.

Two Years Later

The door closed with a resounding bang which beckoned silence.

Absolute roaring silence.

I paused, taking in the living room.

Nothing had changed, of course.

I had, though.

My hand was still fastened tightly on the handle of my suitcase. I was still standing in front of the door I'd slammed shut.

I was exhausted.

I'd been on ferries, buses, and planes for almost thirty hours, the grime of the trip and lack of sleep settling into my bones.

I hadn't eaten in as long because my stomach was too tied up at what I was doing in that thirty hours.

More specifically, where I was going.

Home.

After a year, I was back.

I hadn't told anyone I'd left, of course. Not until I'd landed in the AirBnb in Northern Italy.

People weren't exactly shocked since I was *Polly*. The unpredictable, flaky, flighty Polly. I did things like this.

Irresponsible things.

I modeled for a life drawing class because my boyfriend was a painter.

I decided I wanted to learn Mandarin.

Then I quit when I realized how hard it was.

I went vegan.

Then went back to vegetarian because I couldn't live without chocolate.

I dropped out of college with one semester to go because I had changed majors so much I didn't even know what my degree would be in, other than indecision.

I married a man I'd known for less than a month.

Then I divorced that very same man when he thought that punching me in the face was the best way to resolve an argument.

Then I was involved in a drive-by shooting. That wasn't *technically* to do with me, but chaos followed me everywhere. And I was with Rosie. Chaos was attached to Rosie's freaking *soul*.

And after getting punched in the face, I'd gone to Rosie for a safe haven, sworn her to secrecy and she'd saved me—again—and housed me until my bruises faded. And we left the house together when that happened, carrying around our mutual chaos.

Hence the shooting.

My mind thrust in what happened after.

Heath rushing in, the concern and terror painted on his face, the pain of that expression hitting me truer than any bullet could've.

I would've preferred the bullet wound. At least that would heal. There would've been a scar, but it would serve only as the memory of a pain now forgotten. Of how I'd survived.

But that expression, everything after that—heck, everything before that—everything that lay beneath it was a wound that would never heal.

Festering.

Bleeding.

Something I hadn't survived.

Something I was still struggling with.

And at the time, I couldn't handle that.

My sorrow and pain flew under the radar at first because of kidnappings, wars with human traffickers, Rosie's life.

And then when things quietened down, and my divorce proceedings began, my sorrow was misconstrued as heartbreak.

Which it was.

But it was also love.

The kind I couldn't handle.

Little Polly who worked on bubblegum dreams and fairy tales couldn't handle the truest and ugliest kind of pain otherwise known as love.

So after a year of fighting, pretending, bleeding from the inside out, I ran.

I told everyone I was 'finding myself' in Europe. When I'd really left all of me behind when I left *him* behind.

Because I was a coward.

Among other things.

My family thought this impromptu trip was to do with my then finalized divorce.

It was surely funded by it.

I hadn't wanted a cent of my ex's money at first.

"He made you bruise, we're bleeding him dry," Rosie had said.

I didn't agree. I didn't work that way, on revenge, on an eye for an eye. That wasn't my nature.

But it was in Rosie's nature. She, like the club that was otherwise known as my extended family, all but operated on revenge, on an eye for an eye.

Rosie herself was a force to be reckoned with. I could've

fought her on it. Maybe I might've been able to budge her, as hard as she looked outwardly, her heart was as soft and as big as I'd ever experienced—especially now she was with the man she'd been painfully in love with pretty much her whole life. But I didn't have the energy to fight the woman I considered a sister. I was already fighting an enormous, deadly battle with myself. And trying to hide it from everyone I loved.

So I yielded.

And Rosie was true to her word. I don't exactly know how she did it, Craig considered his money very important. I had to sign a prenup before marrying him, not that it bothered me. I had never been concerned with money, and I would never want money to come from the breakup of a marriage.

But then again, I didn't expect my marriage to crumble so quickly, just like that hollow love I'd convinced myself would fill me up.

There was no legal way Rosie could've gotten the money.

But she never exactly worked within the law. And her now-husband no longer enforced it.

It would pay for me not to know how she did it. Rosie just *did things*. You didn't ask questions if you couldn't handle the answers. And I wasn't too proud to say I couldn't handle the answers. I wasn't strong like her or my sister. I couldn't fight the world the way they did.

So I didn't ask.

And I was now a wealthy woman.

I most likely wouldn't have to work again if I didn't want to, considering my lifestyle wasn't exactly extravagant.

And I was wealthy enough to take the trip around Europe, flit around the continent like I didn't have a care in the world.

When in reality, the cares were cinderblocks I dragged around with me from country to country, from wonder to wonder. Luckily invisible in the many pictures I sent back to my no doubt concerned family. My carefree grin was firmly in place, mindful of the fact I loved them and didn't want them worrying about me doing something stupid.

Again.

So I *looked* happy. Joyous.

But my joy was only on the surface.

Even as I sucked down pasta in a little-known town in Northern Italy where I was all but adopted by a tomato farmer and his friends—wrinkled and leathery from a lifetime working in the sun, fond of grappa, not a word of English spoke between them, considering none of them had left their idyllic village in the hills. But they had kind eyes and large hearts.

I was invited to party after party when they realized the crazy American girl was on her own and that just wasn't okay.

So I was adopted.

I indulged in some of the most delicious food I'd ever tasted. The most vibrant company of people who didn't speak my language yet they somehow understood everything I didn't say. Everything I couldn't say.

But then, of course, I left.

Because the family and the happiness became sour on my tongue with the knowledge of my very own family half a world away. The delicious food was ashes in my mouth when my mind thought about another man a world away yet somehow right beside me.

So I ran.

Again.

Hopped through Spain. Ran with the bulls. Walked a week of the Camino. But that was too quiet. So I took a detour to Morocco. Rode camels in the desert. Learned to surf in a seaside town called Essaouira.

Went back upwards to Portugal. Did a yoga retreat in the hills for three weeks. I volunteered when I could because there was only so much wandering my feet could do before my mind followed suit.

Before my broken and bleeding, festering heart followed suit.

I kept busy.

Met people.

Had experiences that most people weren't lucky enough to enjoy in a lifetime let alone eleven months. And though outwardly I was enjoying every moment, I couldn't smile in my soul. Couldn't find the peace I thought an ocean and an ancient continent would give me.

So here I was.

Back in the apartment that Rosie had taken care of for me.

"I killed your plants," Rosie said one month into my trip over a crackling connection, after she told me about her wedding that I was going to miss. Not with judgment, but with understanding. She might not know the specifics of why I couldn't come back, but she knew I couldn't. "How I'm going to be a mother someday is beyond me," she continued. "But then again, a child screams when it's hungry. Plants just die quietly. So maybe plants are much harder to keep alive than a child."

So my apartment was devoid of all life that my houseplants had offered.

But it suited me at this point.

I stared at the apartment, unmoving even though my limbs were heavier than lead and my stomach was protesting painfully at the lack of food I'd given it. Usually, I took care of my body. I was a vegetarian, something that started because of a boyfriend who educated me on the horrors of eating meat and then I continued long after he was history. I became somewhat obsessed with taking care of what I put into my body because I hadn't taken care of who I'd let into my heart.

I drank kombucha.

I did yoga every single morning.

Meditated.

Took vitamins.

Surrounded myself with crystals that helped with spiritual growth and promoted clean and positive energy.

I lived mindfully and tried to do as little harm to myself and others as I could.

And wasn't that ironic since I'd harmed the person who I cared about more than myself. Broken his heart. Not because he'd broken mine. No, I didn't work that way. But I'd broken the both of ours because there was no other choice.

Not that he knew that.

He, like everyone else, thought I breezed through life on a whim and barely noticed the wreckage I left in my wake. And I left the broken pieces of us both eleven months ago, in this very apartment.

I let the weight of my pack settle on my back, sighing in relief as my body protested with the load. It was good to get something tangible on my shoulders to distract me from the true weight I'd been carrying around. That had brought me to my knees. At least I could stand under the meager physical reproduction of it.

I didn't pause to think about what I was doing. To have a wistful look around the apartment that used to be Lucy's, then Rosie's after Lucy got her ever after, and then Rosie got hers too so it was mine.

I didn't say happy ever after because despite what the world thought, I knew that endings, even the best ones—like what Rosie and Lucy got—they were never completely happy. Even when they involved love. Especially when they involved love.

I wasn't getting my ever after, happy or otherwise. The world had taken care of that. But I couldn't put my blame on the universe. No, the universe was not to blame for this.

It was me.

I didn't pause as I walked toward the door.

Didn't think about what I was doing.

I couldn't.

Because then I'd falter.

Then I wouldn't find myself at the airport.

I'd find myself at the door of the man I was running from.

And I couldn't do that.

I'd done enough harm.

And he'd made it clear that we were done. That there were no more chances for us.

As it turned out when I opened my front door, the universe had other ideas.

I sucked in a harsh breath when I was confronted with Heath. He didn't look like he was poised to knock before I'd opened the door. His hands were fists at his sides, his body rooted into the ground with such a force it was a surprise not to see chains on his ankles. Every inch of his body was taut.

His eyes were marble as they rested on me. Then they flared when they focused on my back. More accurately, what was on it.

"Going somewhere." It wasn't a question. It was an accusation.

I adjusted the pack on my back, suddenly it wasn't heavy enough to distract me from the weight of the blame settling on my shoulders with Heath's words, with his gaze, with his very presence.

I couldn't answer. I wanted to. I needed to. I needed to paint a smile on my face, needed to inform him of this wonderful adventure that I was going on by choice. Not by force.

"You're seriously fucking leaving?" he spat the words at me when silence had stretched on for too long between us.

I nodded once, still unable to say anything when everything I needed to say was clogging up my throat, my lungs.

More silence as his eyes turned cruel, hard and angry. It was familiar, since that was the way he'd stared at me since I'd announced I was marrying another man.

It wasn't present on my wedding day, of course.

No, it disappeared that day to show the vulnerability underneath.

But then I'd stamped on that, shredded it like I shredded my own heart and that horrible empty gaze was now permanent.

Because. Of. Me.

"Jesus," he muttered, shaking his head violently. Everything about him was violent now. It didn't used to be. Not on a night that turned into a weekend that seemed like a thousand years ago. The night that started it all.

He had a little violence in him then. Staining his skin. In a way that might just wash off, if things changed. If he found peace instead of the war he'd committed to.

But now it wasn't staining his skin. It was etched into his very soul. And I was adding to it. Because it seemed like every time we were in front of each other, there was another layer to his violence. Until it came with every movement, every glance, every breath.

And it was at its peak right now.

"You expect me to ask you to stay? To not let you leave?" he hissed. "To fuckin' demand you to stop running from this shit because it's evident whatever it is between us isn't gonna let us go, despite how fuckin' much I want it to?"

His words and the true frustration behind them hit me like bullets. It was a miracle I was still upright. Since I was expending all my energy just doing that, I didn't have anything left inside me to speak.

"Is that what this is?" He nodded to the pack. "You runnin' 'cause you want me to chase you? Because I'm not gonna do that."

He stepped out of the doorway, leaving it open to me.

"So if you leave, that's it. That's us. Finally fuckin' over. Because I won't chase you. I fuckin' can't. *One of us has to stop this shit. And I gotta do it for my sanity. I won't ask you to stay either. Because you do what you want, regardless of what I say. Of what I fuckin' beg. We both know that. And I'm still fuckin' standing here. It's the last time I will be. So what are you gonna do, Little Girl?"*

Something left his eyes when he uttered the last two words. Something that seeped into me. Tugged at all those frayed and torn threads in my soul. Teased me with a lie that maybe this could be fixed. Maybe like the two previous residents of this apartment, I might get an ever after.

But that wasn't my story.

I kept my lips pursed, somehow my eyes stayed dry and I walked out the door. I didn't look back. I couldn't. Every single inch of my willpower, my strength was going to putting one foot in front of the other, taking me away from the one man I'd truly loved with all of me.

The one man who'd broken me.

And then I'd broken him right back.

I blinked at the tears streaming down my cheeks. The tears I'd fought in this very doorway a year ago. Tears I'd battled with for every second after.

And they came with a force that literally brought me to my knees.

They beckoned me into the abyss.

CHAPTER SEVEN

"DUDE, ARE YOU DEAD?"

I jerked at the words because they were yelled at me. Like right in my ear.

I blinked rapidly, sitting up just as rapidly, the world spinning with a worrying speed and I panicked with a few moments of utter confusion of where the heck I was.

But then my seriously foggy brain caught up, and it caught up faster than most people since I was familiar with waking up in strange places. I was usually more panicked when I woke up in the same place for too long. The scream was familiar, as was the grinning face in front of me, and the apartment she was in.

My apartment.

The one I'd arrived in...however long ago.

The one I'd sobbed into unconsciousness on the floor of.

At some point, I'd obviously moved myself to the sofa, which was where I was now. I didn't remember this. But that wasn't strange. I was a sleepwalker—when I did sleep, that was. I had woken in all sorts of places I hadn't gone to sleep in. Hallways, gardens, once, somehow, my own car.

But this was likely more to do with being jetlagged and my zombie brain realizing it was uncomfortable to sleep on hardwood floors. I'd slept on much worse in my travels. I was a heavy sleeper when my brain let myself sleep. Could sleep through anything. And obviously, I had been sleeping through Rosie entering the apartment—which she would've done loudly because she's Rosie —and trying to wake me up in a slightly quieter manner than this.

I blinked grit from my eyes. It felt vaguely like I'd been hit by some heavy-duty vehicle. The last eleven months packaged into that vehicle.

No, the last *six years* packaged into it.

"Thank god, I didn't have to do mouth to mouth, it'd ruin my lipstick," Rosie said, this time at a more respectable decibel.

"How did you know I was home?" I croaked at her, my throat scratchy and crying out for any kind of hydration. My muscles ached. My stomach was cramping with the emptiness of it. My bladder was full.

I'd obviously been asleep for a long while.

Rosie tilted her head, obviously taking note of what a freaking mess I was. Of course, she was glossy and beautiful, wearing a bright pink knit dress, white ankle boots and her hair in messy curls around her face.

"Um, I have contacts at the border," she said as if I should've known this. I actually should've. Rosie had 'contacts' everywhere. "I had you under a red flag in like twenty-eight countries, just to be safe," she continued. "Color me disappointed that I didn't have to come and rescue you from some sort of cult again."

I frowned. "It wasn't a cult. It was a collective," I argued, speaking of my first residence in L.A.

"Anything that starts with C is a euphemism for cult, Pol," she said. "But whatever, I've missed you. And I would communicate this with a hug but you kind of...reek." She wrinkled her nose. "I'm guessing you haven't showered since some strange hostel in Belgrade?"

I blinked again. "How did you—"

"I'm me," she interrupted, again, as if I should know. Again, I should've. I'd known Rosie almost my entire life, and though she didn't share the same blood as Lucy and I, she was our sister. "Now, you get up, get showered and less scary and I'll make you food."

I raised my brow at her. "*You'll* make food?"

She sighed. "Fine, I'll order food. This is L.A., no one *makes* food." She narrowed her eyes. "And then I want to know everything."

My stomach dropped.

"Don't worry, not the stuff that made you leave in the first place," she said softly. "We'll get to that. But I'll hear about the rest until you're ready."

She patted my hand then yanked me up. "But first, hygiene."

I SHOWERED because as Rosie said, I did reek.

I let the warm water attempt to melt away the grime over the memories I'd been trying to escape. To try and loosen the tension from carrying around blame and doubt.

It didn't work.

By the time I'd gotten out and dressed, the smell of food had radiated through my small apartment.

Rosie had ordered enough to feed a small country. Despite how hungry I was, there was no way I'd eat it all. I made a mental note to run it down to Ed, the homeless guy who was usually down the street from my building.

Rosie was true to her word.

She didn't make me spill about what I knew she'd been curious about for over a year. Since things between Heath and I became too obvious to ignore. For everyone around us at least. I did a wonderful job of pretending to ignore what it was. How it was tearing us both apart.

"So," Rosie said, putting down her half-eaten cheeseburger. "Tell me everything about your trip. How many Italians did you romance? How many times did you almost get kidnapped?"

I smiled because she was being serious. Apparently you weren't "part of the awesome bitches club" until you got kidnapped.

"None," I said, opening my veggie burger with a rumbling stomach.

Rosie sighed. "You're young, there's still time." She paused. "Tell me everything else then."

And in between bites. I did. I told her everything about the trip and nothing about the truth behind it.

She was Rosie so she knew how much I was holding back. But she didn't push.

Because she was Rosie.

She left, eventually.

After promising she wouldn't get in touch with Lucy and tell her I was here yet. She was a loud person. So was I, on the outside of course. But Rosie knew when to keep quiet. Even when she didn't like it.

She'd been very vocal about how much she hated keeping quiet about how everything went down with Craig.

But she'd done it.

For me.

Because she was a good person.

The best.

"I know you don't feel like talking yet," she said in the doorway. "And I know there's so much more to the story than you've let on, and I'm absolutely *gagging* for it, I won't lie." She winked before her eyes went sad. "But I do know a little something about not being able to talk about things that have touched our souls. People that have done that. People that have destroyed our souls." She gave me a look, one that betrayed knowledge of things I hadn't told. "When those people are the people we see in the mirror."

I gaped at her. "What—how?"

She smiled. "No, I'm not a mind reader, and I have to clarify that because I know you believe in that shit."

I frowned. "It's not shit. It's people who are so in touch with the universe they vibrate on the same level in which we project our thoughts."

She raised her brow and smirked in that smile her and Lucy had reserved for me. The 'oh Polly's done or said something again, just grin and humor her and then set fire to the car of the latest man who has broken her heart.'

She leaned forward and kissed my cheek. "Honey, sometimes it's not about vibrations or the universe." She paused as she leaned back. "Actually, it's never about that. It's just the simple fact that we see in each other what we hide in ourselves."

The world moved under my feet at Rosie—my Rosie—uttering something as profound as that.

Then she winked again. "If you'll excuse me, I'm going to ravage my husband so he can't walk straight in the morning."

And there it was.

She blew me a kiss.

"Don't get into trouble. Not without me at least."

I didn't plan on getting in any.

No, I planned on somehow trying to make my life trouble free.

Peaceful.

Which was going to be a feat since I didn't know what peace looked like.

IT WAS three in the morning.

I was in the bath.

Mostly because I loved baths. I had every single kind of bath bomb imaginable, every bath product, I had a tray that could hold wine, books, and snacks that fit across the tub.

A speaker was shoved onto the small and cramped countertop, there was always music coming from it. Usually, it was peaceful piano.

Now it was ear-splitting rock.

Because I needed something like that to drown out the silence.

Silence was always loudest at three in the morning.

The witching hour.

It was the time many of my Wiccan friends believed that black magic was most powerful. It was the peak of supernatural activity. All of the demons and ghosts were most powerful.

And they were right.

But not the ghosts and demons that were tangible, that came from horror movies and great TV shows.

No, they came from the inside. Clawed their way up when our minds were trying to dream and woke us up brutally.

I had been jerking awake at this exact time for well over year. I had never been the best sleeper. My dad said it was because my mind was too busy to be clutched by dreams for too long.

"You dream while you're awake, baby girl. So you don't need to sleep like the rest of us."

He and my mom never tried to change me. Never told me to go to sleep when they found me wandering around a quiet house in the middle of the night. They accepted me.

I came from a loving and supportive home.

Had great friends.

My health.

A roof over my head.

Food in my belly.

I shouldn't have these demons.

Yet here they were.

Heartbreak was so much uglier than whatever movies portrayed it to be. There was no carton of ice cream, bottle of vodka, one-night stand and an amazing rebound guy type of combination that worked to cure that ache in your chest.

And it wasn't an *ache.* It was a sharp, stabbing, consistent *agony.* And it wasn't in the chest. It was everywhere. You ached for the person who hurt you. Who ruined you. Who broke down every part of what made you *you*. Craig did all those things and it was horrible and painful and so soul destroying that it took a punch in the face to make me leave, but still, there was the pain. The agony.

It was that much worse because now, I knew all of this, what a bad person he was and I still loved him. I couldn't just turn something like that off. The violence, the ugliness of his true character was enough to make me leave him, but that wasn't enough to make me forget him.

When you give your heart to someone, it remains in their

possession, at least a piece of it anyway, no matter what they do afterward.

So I was here, curled up in the bath, not cradling wine and listening to empowering music and reading *Eat Pray Love.* No, I was clutching my knees to my chest, curled up in the darkness of the room, sobbing violently and silently. Pain wracked every single cell in my body.

And in that moment, I wanted *him* to save me from this. Not Craig. Not the man who'd punched me in the face that I still loved with a part of me. But Heath, the man who'd punched through my soul when I'd torn his apart. Who I still loved with every aching cell in my body.

I stared into the water, my eyes swollen.

My fingertips trailed over the surface of the water, thinking about how such a thing could give us life, something we needed to continue living, could also kill us if we completely submerged ourselves in it.

Much like love.

My finger froze atop the water.

That had been my problem. Not just with Heath or Craig, with every man I fell in and out of love with since I grew boobs.

I had been looking for someone to save me. Not from dragons or villains, just from life. From loneliness.

And I hadn't realized there was only one person who could save me.

She was sitting in the dark in a lukewarm bathtub crying over the husband that beat her. Crying because she knew that she made a mistake on her wedding day. Walking down an aisle. Saying I do.

Walking away from a man who kept promising he'd never come back to her, but who always did, a little more broken and crueler than before.

"HEY DAD," I said into the phone, exhaling with the force my pseudo cheerful voice took to create.

"Polly!" he shouted into the phone like he had for the past year. Though every single conversation, the connection had been fine, he seemed to be of the opinion that the technology required him to shout so he could be heard across oceans.

"Where are you now?" he demanded. "I've had no pictures in days. You know the whole reason I don't go all Liam Neeson is because you send me my adventure updates."

I smiled.

"*That's* why you're not going Liam Neeson?" I teased.

My father was the furthest from Liam Neeson than any father could get. Yes, he was protective of me, of our entire family. But he didn't communicate this with threats of violence or curses.

I had no idea where Lucy got her genes from.

Plus, when it became apparent I was going to have a new boyfriend with every week, he didn't sit on the proverbial porch with the proverbial shotgun. He was actually nice to the "poor bastards," this was because "they are only going to get a handful of heartbeats with the most extraordinary girl on this earth because they're too ordinary for you."

It was safe to say he doted over me.

Because I was the youngest, obviously. And because I was a total daddy's girl. I adored my mother more than anything too, but it was a connection with my father that was something different. He got me. In a way most of my family didn't.

They accepted me.

But they didn't get me like my dad.

Never in my life had I seen an ounce of disappointment in his eyes when most parents would have an ocean of it.

Not when I changed colleges because of a boyfriend.

Or changed majors because of a different boyfriend.

When he had to loan me money because I'd loaned all of mine to a friend who had lost everything in a house fire.

Not when I'd dropped out of college and moved to L.A. and didn't tell him.

My mother had something to say about that. Not much, but something, because she was a parent and she loved me, and she worried about what future I'd have without that piece of paper that somehow said I was 'approved' to operate in the world.

But there was nothing from my father.

Nothing but support.

And when I'd announced my marriage to Craig, there was a slight wary glint to his eyes, but he still smiled and promised he'd walk me down the aisle.

And he'd walked me into the lawyer's office when I signed my divorce papers.

My mother had gotten me a cake. It literally said 'Happy Divorce' on it. And it was gluten-free and vegan.

Lucy had promised explosions.

"I have a very particular set of skills," my father said into the phone, still yelling.

I continued to grin. "Well, as much as I'd like to see those skills, I'm actually back stateside, so you'll just have to wait for the next great Polly adventure/disaster."

"You're home?" he yelled. This time I didn't think it was because of the connection. "Claire! Stop fiddling with that damn bread and come and talk to your daughter, she's home," he called to my mother.

There was a rustling as I imagined my mother getting on the other handset. Of course they still had a landline. My father hated mobile phones. He thought the government used them to track us. I didn't disagree with him. But I also knew I needed one. And he needed one to keep in touch with me and he'd begrudgingly bought it.

"Honey," my mother breathed into the phone. "You're home and you didn't tell us. We could've picked you up from the airport. And we could've used the trip to visit your sister. Oh, I'll cancel our plans this weekend and we'll come. How does that sound?" She didn't wait for me to answer. "Pete, what was the name of that place we stayed at in the city? That was nice enough, wasn't it? We'll book there."

"No," my father grumbled. "I didn't like the pillows. Too soft. The mattress was too firm. The valet was too expensive."

"It's L.A.," my mother sighed. "Of course it's expensive. I'm booking there because I liked the chocolates they left on the pillows."

"The *soft* pillows," my father interjected. "I'd rather sleep on the chocolates than the pillows, they provide better neck support."

"Oh stop being such a drama queen," my mother hissed. "That's your daughter's job."

It didn't bother me, that comment, because it wasn't made to wound. And also, it wasn't about me, it was about Lucy. She was the drama queen, a lot more uptight than the rest of our family, but utterly insane at the same time.

I didn't react to drama. I created it.

"Do you want me to call back after the pillow thing is sorted?" I asked dryly.

"Oh, no honey," Mom said quickly. "The pillow thing is sorted. Your father will bring his own. Now, I want to hear about everything."

She really didn't want to hear about everything.

Neither did my supportive and kind natured father.

Because it would break them.

And they'd only just healed from almost losing Lucy. Healed in a way that a bone wasn't set properly. It would always ache in those cold emotional climates that took us by surprise with the power of what could've been. You never healed from loss. Even when the person came back.

So no, my parents didn't need to know everything.

I just needed to pretend that I was giving them everything.

I'd only ever given one person everything before.

And he hated me.

And he didn't even know it all.

And he never would.

I WIPED my palms on my skirt for the thousandth time since I'd parked. I'd been sitting in my car for fifteen minutes. It took all of my strength in order to get out of it. To walk down the quiet and expensive street where the Greenstone Security offices were. It taunted me, that peaceful quiet that money could buy.

Money could buy anything in L.A.

Even peace.

Especially peace.

If you wanted to live in tree-lined neighborhoods, with gates and security guards, manicured lawns and no litter, you could. For a price.

I wondered if it was by Keltan's design to put the offices here. Because most of their clients were struggling with chaos. Violence. So he literally made the place they came to find respite somewhere outwardly peaceful.

I was sure he wasn't that deep.

And *I* didn't feel peaceful.

Because there were some kinds of chaos, of pain, that no amount of peace could quiet.

As I got to the top of the stairs that led to the double doors of the offices, I seriously regretted my decision to come here. But I'd already gone to Lucy's newspaper to surprise her only to find her desk empty. They'd laughed at me when I asked where she was.

"I can only tell you the place she almost never is these days," her editor said. "And that's her desk. I would fire her for that if she didn't write such great copy. And because if I weren't afraid her husband might kneecap me."

I laughed.

He didn't.

Obviously not a joke.

Keltan's offices may have been in a peaceful part of one of the most chaotic cities in America, but the man himself wasn't. Maybe a part of it was being from New Zealand, his persona was as rugged as his accent. I think it had a lot more to do with his past in the army. That was a thing that could steal peace.

I knew that because of what Lucy had mentioned. About him losing his best friend. I couldn't begin to fathom watching another human being die. Let alone someone you loved.

I also knew because of the shadows behind Heath's eyes before and after.

So it wasn't outside the realm of possibility that Keltan would break Lucy's editor's kneecaps if he fired her. Not that he'd need to. Lucy and Rosie would've likely already bombed something he lived in or drove. With no fatalities, of course. They didn't do harm, they sent messages.

Their words, not mine.

Since her editor had no idea where she was, and she wasn't

answering her phone, I figured her husband would know where she was. No, I *knew* he'd know where she was. Because ever since he'd held her dying on the street, he *always* knew where she was. And I loved that for her.

I didn't love that her husband employed Heath and in order to find my sister, I had to risk an encounter with him. My phone had died on the way out of the newspaper offices. I kept forgetting to charge it.

Everyone in my family had bought me portable battery packs.

And they were all fully charged, sitting in some drawer in my living room.

I wasn't someone who needed to be attached to my phone. I didn't have social media. Didn't like the spirit of it. The competition of who could make their lives look better, while behind the photos were problems and issues that broke people with the effort it took trying to hide them.

It was hard enough doing that in real life.

So I never worried about my phone too much. This was a time I cursed myself for not keeping it charged.

I could've gone home and waited until Lucy called me back. But I wanted to see my sister now my mind was cleared from yesterday. Especially because of the news she'd called me with two weeks ago.

"You're going to have a baby?" I whispered.

"I know, everyone has had varying degrees of shock since I'm not maternal, like at all," she said. " I can't be the only one to think that babies are ugly. Everyone's thinking it. When they're fresh, they're all wrinkly and red and look like aliens and they're just too small and breakable. It creeps me out. And now I'm growing one. Me. So shock is not surprising."

A tear trailed down my cheek. I quickly wiped it away. "No,

Lucy, this isn't shock. You're going to be the best mother. I know it."

There was a pause. I let Lucy take it. She didn't do emotions, so she had to collect herself.

"You're going to be the best aunt," she said, her voice husky. "Well, as long as you actually come back from your adventure before the baby is born. Because I'll kick your ass if you're not there to judge me about getting an epidural and lecture me on natural births."

"I'll be there," I said immediately. All of my pain, my fear, my heartbreak was not going to stop me. "And you know the dangers of drugs—"

"I'm getting the fucking injection, Polly," she hissed. "I'm pushing a human child out of my vagina. There is no way I'm doing that without drugs. You want to do that when you have your moonchild baby, more power to you. But it's not happening for me."

It was my turn to pause. Mostly because the breath had been punched out of my chest.

Lucy took this as disapproval. "The silent treatment isn't going to have me change my mind," she snapped. "I'm even considering a C-section because I like sex and I don't want a child I'll obviously love and cherish ruining that for me."

I sucked in a breath. "I'll support you with whatever you need."

"Wait, no way would you support a scheduled C-section, not without at least a few pointed comments," she said. "What's going on?"

Crap.

I forgot that my sister could read me, even across oceans.

"Oh, my phone's about to die," I said, not a lie. "I'll call you

later. I'm so happy for you, Lucy," this was little more than a whisper.

And then the connection was cut off as if my phone battery was giving out at the same time as my heart.

If only I could figure out a way to recharge the latter.

She'd be showing now. She'd have a bump. And my niece or nephew would be growing inside of her. I had taken last night to deal with my pain. And today was for my joy. I was anxious to let it chase away the worst of everything, hence me risking precisely everything by walking in the doors.

I should've taken more care of my appearance. I hadn't for the precise reason that in doing so I'd be tempting the universe into thinking I wanted to encounter Heath. Dressing up would be tempting fate.

So I had my hair in braids, messy because I'd slept in them after my bath. It was balmy in L.A., so I only wore a thin white tank, with strands of necklaces I'd collected on my travels slung around my neck.

My white skirt flowed down to my ankles where I'd put on heeled wedges that Rosie had obviously left and I thought were cute. My skin was a lot more tanned than usual since I'd spent as much time out in the sun as I could. Trying to warm my bones.

I'd lost weight because I had eaten barely anything since I'd booked my tickets to come home. Not because I *wanted* to lose weight or anything like that. I battled with Lucy all our lives with her obsession with food and weight. I ate what I wanted and didn't let society's notion of 'beautiful' dictate how I saw myself in the mirror.

It was my own actions that made it hard to stare at reflective surfaces lately.

I guessed I looked good.

Carefree.

Like the usual Polly.

Which was exactly what I was going for.

The cool, manufactured air of the reception hit me as I walked in, chasing at the beads of sweat that were forming in the middle of my chest. My body temperature tended to increase when I was nervous. Or when I was terrified.

I was both right now.

And I didn't even get two steps inside the reception before I stopped dead.

I had told myself the chances of seeing him were low. Miniscule. He, like Lucy, was barely ever in the office. He'd disappeared entirely before and after my wedding, apart from the day of the drive-by shooting when he shattered my fractured heart and disappeared until I left him standing in my doorway a year ago.

It wasn't a nine to five job, obviously. The offices were expensive and comfortable not because the employees spent a lot of time in here but because they needed to be welcoming to clients.

I wasn't a client, I was family. I should've felt welcome. But his presence was a ghost in these halls, so I didn't feel welcome whenever I came here, which was as little as possible.

And then the ghost turned tangible as the flesh and blood man strolled from the hallway into the reception. He was looking down at his phone so he didn't see me until he was halfway across the foyer. Getting closer to me.

When he looked up, he stopped his steps abruptly.

His gaze told me a lot of things.

One thing was a roar among the rest.

I was definitely *not* welcome here.

"You're back."

The two words were harmless in any other context. The

combination of them nothing that could be packaged or structured into something that would hurt.

And words could hurt.

Sticks and stones did break bones. But words broke souls.

I knew that better than anyone.

Because two seemingly innocuous harmless words did just that. Tore through the broken pieces jabbed at my insides for good measure.

It wasn't about the words.

It was the voice that spoke them.

The man that spoke them.

The man whose face I'd forced myself not to think of for an entire year. So naturally, it was the face ingrained into my memory like I'd stitched it there, sewn it into the fabric of my mind.

And I didn't recognize him.

Just like I didn't recognize that flat, cold, empty and dead voice.

I couldn't even say cruel.

Because cruelty required energy. Some sort of *effort*.

Nothing was there inside of that voice I pretended I didn't hear in my dreams. In my nightmares.

His gaze flickered over me blankly. With disinterest.

Not hatred.

Or longing.

It should've been anger.

I'd prepared myself for that. Prepared myself for the inevitable meeting that we'd have because of our mutual connections. I hadn't expected it to be so soon, but ripping the Band-Aid off was meant to be good, right? It was meant to make it hurt less. I'd known it would hurt, but I didn't think much could hurt more than what I'd already done to myself.

I'd reasoned it would kill me if he looked at me in hatred.

Oh, how I longed for that now.

Because that flat and empty gaze *ruined* me.

Right there on the spot.

I had to stay standing. Because we were in the middle of my brother-in-law's offices. There were people. People staring between the two of us like they might two bombs lingering near that fatal zero on the counter.

But there was no explosion.

Nothing.

I swallowed glass.

"I'm back," I agreed, my voice low, more than a squeak. I tried a smile, a Polly smile. That's what I did, after all, I smiled at people. Even the man I'd loved and run from—twice—the man looking at me like I was a stranger on the street.

Yes, I tried to smile at him because the only other option was sinking to my knees and falling apart right here in the modern offices of Greenstone Security, in front of the receptionist and my brother in law who had just appeared behind Heath, his face tight and fists at his sides.

I knew Keltan was worried. He was protective by nature. And I was a damsel by nature. But I would not be responsible for him feeling like he had to come to my aid by creating conflict with a friend. So I smiled, tearing my eyes from Heath and settling on the safer gaze of my brother in law.

But I feared my smile was something more than a grimace.

I wondered if I ever might smile again.

Like magnets, my eyes were drawn to Heath's once more.

I clutched onto that stupid, oh so very old Polly-like shred of hope I'd been carrying around like the tattered remains of a child's security blanket.

It was the hope that there would be something there, some

spark to hold onto, to feed me…something, despite the fact I didn't deserve it. Rage. Disappointment. *Anything* to hold onto.

But there was nothing.

The hope was a moth-eaten scrap of fabric, clutched too tight and crumbling in my hands.

Heath nodded once. "Good. I hope you had a nice trip."

And then he strode forward.

Toward me.

I held my breath as he gave me a wide berth—not wide enough since his scent, his very presence assaulted me with his nearness—and then strode out the door.

Like *left*.

I stayed there, frozen, unblinking.

I must've been breathing because I was upright and people that weren't breathing tended to be horizontal.

I couldn't believe we went through all of that, everything in the past, just to be strangers again.

That was the biggest tragedy of heartbreak.

When someone was your everything.

And then they were *nothing*.

He wasn't nothing to me, of course.

But I was obviously nothing to him.

And I couldn't blame him.

Not one bit.

There was only so much two people could go through before you had to call it, before someone had to back out, walk away. There was only so much two hearts could take. He was making the right decision turning us into strangers at worst, acquaintances at best.

There was pressure at my elbow.

"Polly?"

I focused on the source of the masculine concern.

Keltan was regarding me with pinched brows and a hard jaw. His eyes were soft, though. Because he was kind. And good. And he loved my sister more than anything on this planet and he took me as his little sister and did what everyone else did with me—handled me with a version of kid gloves, otherwise known as 'Polly gloves.'

I straightened. "I'm okay," I said.

I wondered who I was talking to, him or myself.

His eyes narrowed. "Didn't ask you if you're okay," he said, voice warm and low.

I blinked. "Oh."

"I know you're not okay so askin' would be a stupid question," he continued. "I don't ask stupid questions."

I paused, momentarily surprised at how astute the hulking New Zealander was. Then again, he was married to one of the most emotionally complex—some would say crippled—women on the planet, otherwise known as my sister, so he had to be on his game.

Also, it felt like I was bleeding from a thousand tiny wounds and I wasn't adept at hiding such pain and he was ex-military so he knew pain. He also had a tumultuous courtship with my sister, which ended in her bleeding out in his arms.

So yes, he knew pain.

And it was obviously painted on my face. It was certainly etched into my bones.

"Yes, you're not stupid," I said.

But I am, was what I left unsaid.

He frowned as if he could read my mind.

I paused. As Rosie had said the night before, I didn't completely discredit the ability for the right person in touch with the right energies to be able to tap into someone's thoughts, but I didn't think the muscled and tattooed man in front of me would've been able to do so.

Because if he did, I reasoned that his courtship with Lucy would've gone a lot smoother.

"I'm going to ask a question that's not stupid," he said, moving, still holding me by the elbow so I was moving alongside him too.

I let myself be directed farther into the offices that smelled faintly of lemon and mostly of Heath.

"Non-stupid questions are good," I murmured, my words distant from me as if they were coming from underwater.

I idly wondered if I was having a mental breakdown. I shouldn't have been surprised. My family likely wouldn't be either. They probably had brochures for all sorts of places 'just in case.' I hoped they were by the ocean. Or on a ranch. That would be nice.

We were in Keltan's office while I was thinking about the different retreats I could go to, to comfortably break down. Only wealthy people had the luxury to go crazy, and I was wealthy now and I'd just had my sanity stepped on by a man who barely blinked at me—though I deserved that—where was my cab?

"Wanna get drunk?" Keltan asked instead of asking me if I wanted to commit myself or have him do it.

I blinked again.

He was holding up a bottle of whisky.

I hated whisky.

"Abso-fucking-lutely," I replied without hesitation.

"KELTAN! WHAT IS THIS?" Lucy demanded from somewhere...upward.

"This is your beloved husband and your beloved sister, do you need to get your eyes tested?" a low and rumbling voice replied.

"You need to fucking get your head tested if you think that is an appropriate response," she snapped. "Really? You think that after not seeing my baby sister in a *year*, that *this* is the kind of reunion I'd want?"

Her voice was still upward, and I was still moving. Floating. Flying.

It was nice, I decided.

How cool would it be if I could fly?

"Well, I know this isn't *ideal*," Keltan said from above me. From what I could hear, he wasn't slurring his words, like at all. And he was still standing, carrying me if I wasn't in fact, flying. He'd drunk more whisky than me.

A lot more.

"How do they breed you in New Zealand?" I slurred. "Do you just get weaned off breast milk then straight onto whisky?"

A chuckle. "No, sweetheart, we go onto beer first, we don't get the hard stuff until we're at least able to walk and talk. After kindergarten."

"Keltan!" Lucy hissed. "You're not allowed to chuckle. Nor are you allowed to get my little sister this drunk. Not when I can't get that drunk too. I'm pregnant. You made me this way. I can't drink because it will stunt our child's growth."

A large thread of joy tangled through my drunk mind at my sister's words. But she wasn't drunk. Nor did she sound joyful.

"So it stands to reason I should be doing the drinking for you also. You're eating for two. I'll drink for two. A good compromise," Keltan decided.

We were still moving. How big was Keltan's apartment?

I wasn't as sure I liked flying anymore. I was reasonably

certain if I kept doing it much longer I'd throw up on Keltan, Lucy, or the floor of the apartment. And Lucy would *so* not be happy about that. Well, she wouldn't be happy about the latter two. Right now, it sounded as if she wouldn't mind me puking on her husband.

"A compromise is you sleeping on the sofa since my drunk and near comatose little sister is going to be in the guest room," she snapped.

Thankfully, we must've been in this mystical guest room and I was on the mystical bed. One I hopefully wouldn't throw up on.

"Thanks for the flying lesson, Keltan, but I don't think I'm suited for it," I muttered.

Another chuckle.

"Don't you fucking laugh," Lucy hissed. "Did you give her acid?"

"Jesus, no. Just whisky."

"That's worse!" Lucy exclaimed

"How is whisky worse than an A-Class drug?" Keltan asked, sounding amused and not at all drunk.

How could that be?

I knew he was close to inhuman because of everything I'd heard, but this was something else.

"It's worse because she's Polly and she doesn't believe in whisky."

"But she believes in acid?"

"She's *Polly*."

It wasn't entirely untrue. I *was* Polly.

And when I was really trying to figure myself out, I'd tried the stuff that everyone told me was a spiritual experience. Obviously nothing like heroin or anything that was going to ruin my life. I didn't do anything now, of course. But I had to say yes before I knew that I wanted to say no.

A slight tug at my ankles and the thumping of shoes hitting the floor caught my attention.

"Are these Rosie's?" Lucy asked. "I've been looking for these to steal for like an age. I'm glad you didn't vomit on them because I'm stealing them."

"Stealing is wrong," I muttered.

"Ah but day drinking with my husband instead of coming to visit me is totally and utterly fucking right," she returned dryly. She didn't sound mad. Not really. This was just another classic Polly move. She didn't get mad at Polly moves. She was used to them. It was why she loved me.

Or maybe she loved me in spite of it.

Whatever.

There was warmth and a soothing smell of lavender and Lucy's perfume as something soft and snuggly settled over top of me.

I sighed in relief.

I knew opening my eyes would result in the room spinning and then me likely throwing up, so I reached my hand toward where I guessed Lucy was.

A warm and dry hand circled mine.

"Lucy," I said, only slurring a little.

"Yes, Pol," she replied, her voice soft.

"I'm very happy to be here, to be safe with you. And I'm very much happy to be an aunt. I promise I won't feed the kid whisky or beer."

"Strictly acid?" she deadpanned.

I smiled. And it was a real one. Not even a grimace or anything.

"I love you," I murmured.

"I love you too, my little bug," she replied, squeezing my

hand. And then there was a nice sensation on my forehead as she kissed it and brushed the hair away.

"I love Keltan too," I sighed.

"Oh, you might want to wait until the morning until you commit to that," she said, smile in her voice.

"No, I know it all now. Even though I can't properly love anymore because I'm all ruined. I've got you guys."

There was a silence that may have meant more, meant a lot more if I was sober. But I wasn't, so I just sighed again and promptly passed out.

"GOOD MORNING, SUNSHINE," someone screamed in my ear.

I flinched but kept my eyes closed.

"Ugh," I said in response, even the small noise causing pain to radiate throughout my skull.

My mouth tasted like something had died inside of it, and my stomach felt like I'd eaten something dead and decomposed.

But no, just whisky.

On an empty stomach and a broken heart.

"Hold your hand out," Lucy yelled.

Or maybe she didn't yell and maybe it just seemed like it because breathing was the equivalent of a dull roar radiating from my lungs to my throbbing brain.

I weakly did so, my eyes squeezed shut.

Two small objects landed in my palm.

"Put them in your mouth," Lucy commanded. "Not something I'd ever thought I'd say to my baby sister," she added on what was supposed to be a murmur but worked as a screech.

I closed my hands around the pills. "What are they?"

There was a pause where I imagined my sister grinning.

"Honestly, Polly, since when have you asked what something was before taking it?"

"Since I saw purple butterflies talking to me at our kitchen table," I shot back honestly. It was enough to keep me off hard-core hallucinogenics for life.

"Well, this will stop the razorblades cutting at your eyeballs right now," she replied. "No butterflies."

Lucy would know. Where I didn't drink on the regular, she loved cocktails and partying. Which meant she had experience with hangovers. I had experience seeing her hungover and teasing her and generally riding around on my high horse.

That horse had thrown me off, left me in the mud and I was never going to get on it again.

I trusted my sister with my life, which was good since it felt like I was fricking *dying*.

I put the pills in my mouth.

Cool glass settled on my lips and I drank the precious water Lucy was offering to me. I suddenly realized my mouth was the Sahara. My fingers settled around the glass and I gulped until it was empty.

"You might not want to..." Lucy trailed off as the water reached my empty and protesting stomach.

I groaned at the pain of the liquid hitting it, seriously concerned about it coming right back up. If the sound of Lucy's heels retreating on the hardwood floors were anything to go by, she thought so too.

But I managed not to empty my stomach, more out of sheer force of will than anything else. There was a pause where I willed the world to stop spinning, and spearing me with flaming swords.

"You didn't barf, impressive," Lucy commented. "Though, I

guess you've got an iron stomach after gallivanting through Europe for a year eating god knows what."

The thought of food both disgusted and hungered me.

"It's *Europe*, Luce," I said, my voice little more than a groan. "They're kind of famous for their cuisine."

"Yes, but in the *nice* restaurants with tablecloths, wine menus and free bread. You likely were eating *street food* with *hippies*."

I pursed my lips.

She wasn't exactly wrong.

I wasn't the restaurant type of girl. I immersed myself in the culture, I ate where the locals ate, and it wasn't at places with pictures on the menu an English translations and rude waiters.

"Speaking of," she continued, snatching the glass from me. I imagined a scowl on her face while my eyes stayed firmly closed. "How is it that my little hippy sister did not inform me that she was coming home?" A pause. And I knew Lucy well enough this was more of an inhale before the screech. "Oh, right! How about the fact she didn't inform me that she was *motherfucking leaving* in the first place?" she yelled.

And I knew she properly yelled this time since it felt like my ears were bleeding on the outside and not just the inside.

I didn't speak, a little because I feared I might vomit if I opened my mouth, or my eyes for that matter, but mostly because I knew Lucy was not done. The sound of her heels pacing the floor in front of me told me that. She only paced when she was super pissed.

"And maybe you thought I might, you know, *want to come*?" she yelled. "I love pasta. I love Italian things. I know they make good shoes. I could've visited the birthplace of Manolos. Did you think of that?"

"You're kind of a newlywed, and Keltan took you to Lake Como on your honeymoon," I said.

"It was a *lake!*" she screeched. "It's nothing but a sea without the salt. Or beaches. Or sharks. Wait, are there sharks in lakes? If there aren't, *Lake Placid* had some seriously big plot holes." She paused. "But that is not the point. The point is you were going through a divorce and hurting and then you just left, and I thought you were going to join a convent or something. It was a traumatic time."

"I'm sorry," I murmured.

"Oh, I'm not done," she snapped. "And then when you finished your little Eat, Pray, Meditate Without Shoes On, you come home without telling anyone and then get drunk with my husband. Without even *inviting* me. I am much more fun to get drunk with than Keltan."

"You're pregnant," I pointed out, and I realized I hadn't even seen Lucy pregnant yet since I was pretty sure the conversation I had with her last night was all with my eyes closed. I itched to see her glowing with a new life inside her, hopefully with a little more meat on her bones, since I knew Keltan would not let her starve herself when she had a baby to feed.

I knew Lucy wouldn't do that either. Because I knew that she would love that little being inside her from the first moment she'd found out. All of her vanity was surface. Deeper down, she was one of the most selfless, brave and loving people I knew. She would do anything and everything to take care of her baby.

I didn't open my eyes because I was still sure I'd throw up if I did so. Not because I was scared I'd burst into tears when I saw her. That's what I told myself at least.

"I'm fun to get drunk with even when I'm sober," she hissed, unaware of the dark turn my thoughts had taken.

I was happy for her continuing tirade, it stopped the demons from doing too much damage.

"Because I'm *fun,*" she continued. "And I've missed my sister and I've worried about her more than I worried about my ankles looking like Kim Kardashian's."

The bed depressed.

A hand went to my forehead, it was cool, warm, and dry. Comforting for none of those reasons, but because it belonged to Lucy. My sister. My protector, best friend, and lecturer. The woman who burned down the cars of men that had broken my heart. Put them on terrorist watchlists and then fed me ice cream for the short period I'd considered myself heartbroken in between relationships.

I had no idea what heartbreak was back then.

Nor did I have an idea what love was.

Not until *him*.

I'd been so sure I'd been searching for it. That all-consuming, beautiful and fulfilling love, that I'd run from what I'd found. Because it wasn't beautiful. Or fulfilling. It filled me up only long enough to rip me apart from the inside out.

"Keltan told me why you drank whisky," Lucy murmured. "That you saw Heath. That it was bad."

My stomach clenched for different reasons than the aforementioned whisky, though it was still making sure I didn't forget about the after effects.

Heath's name whispered from my sister's kind lips was worse than any whisky induced hangover.

I swallowed hot ash, struggling to sit up without hurling and to blink without crying. "Yeah," I agreed on a croak. "It was bad."

It was now I found the strength to blink my eyes open. I immediately snapped them closed when a light that burned my corneas assaulted me. I took a long second before I tried blinking again. And I did it slowly, gave myself time to get used to the obnoxiously bright light obviously designed to give me some sort of brain bleed.

Lucy came into focus.

And I was right, she had a glow.

And not just because I was hungover and the light in the room had the power of the sun itself, despite the fact the curtains were drawn.

No, because she was *Lucy*. And she was beautiful no matter what. But she had changed. It was jolting for me, since the last time I'd seen her, she was still beautiful, but her angles were sharper, more severe in a gorgeous, runway model type of way.

But all those edges had softened. Her face was fuller, with a flush that was usually absent from her pale skin. Her hair was wavy, shiny, and messy around her face. And she was wearing a white tank and white silk pajama bottoms so I could see where her frame had filled out to what it had meant to be all along.

But it was the small but pronounced bump that got me.

That speared my heart with joy.

"You're pregnant," I whispered.

She glanced down, eyes bright. "Either that or I had a really big burrito last night."

I continued to stare. "Lucy, you're *pregnant*," I repeated, my eyes shimmering and not just because the light was causing my head to pound and stomach to roil.

Her hand settled on the swell of the bump, cradling it protectively. "Yeah, I am," she agreed.

"But you're hungover, and I feel like that's exactly the opposite of pregnant," she continued, blinking rapidly as if to chase away tears. But Lucy didn't cry.

Like ever.

"And pregnancy is a little more permanent than hangovers, lucky for you." She winked at me. "So I would like to talk about the reason for the hangover. And not my husband, though he is not the most popular man in the house right now." She scowled in the direction of the door and sounds coming from the kitchen. "But he's a man, he saw a problem, he saw pain and he thought rubbing alcohol works on the outside, so he tried to use drinking alcohol for the inside. That's not how it works." She paused. "Well, it's *sometimes* how it works. But it's with cosmos, or martinis, or margaritas. Not whisky."

My stomach lurched at the mention of all those alcoholic beverages in such a short amount of time.

"I'm never drinking again," I moaned.

"Oh, I doubt that," she said. "Because I've got a feeling this little thing is going to need a lot of rubbing alcohol and drinking alcohol." She paused.

Her eyes searched mine as if she were gaging whether now was the appropriate time to get the truth out of me.

Lucy didn't know the full story about Heath.

No one knew.

Which was in itself, strange.

I didn't do secrets. Not when it came to my feelings, good or bad—or my love life, good *and* bad. Lucy had secrets. A lot of them. So many that they seeped into her face sometimes, making her beauty something different and darker entirely. She didn't think I could see them. I was sure she—like everyone else—considered me too flaky and wrapped up in my own ridiculous fantasy world, dreaming of fairy tales and princes to be worrying about the dragons others fought in reality.

But I wasn't.

I saw them.

I wanted to help. More than anything.

I didn't want to be a princess, wasn't looking for a crown, I was looking for a sword, a freaking *butter knife* to help my sister slay her dragons. And Rosie, my adopted sister. But not even

Excalibur could slay the fire-breathing demons that darkened their doors.

And I had nothing on them.

My two brave heroines slayed the dragons they could and made friends with the ones they couldn't. Their hot hubbies had a hand in it, to be sure, but they did most of the work themselves, they were never damsels.

Me?

I was the damsel.

From pretty much the start of my life. And definitely from the start of the ending that was Heath and me.

"I don't think I'm ready," I croaked. "To...go there." It was a lame excuse, considering 'there' the past and I basically lived in it these days. I just pretended I didn't.

Lucy squeezed my hand. "I know, sweetheart." There was a comfortable silence.

Or what I thought was a comfortable silence until I remembered who my sister was, pregnant or not.

"No blowing up his car," I demanded.

Lucy gave me faux innocent eyes. "I wouldn't dare."

"Or his house," I added.

The eyes narrowed, and Lucy huffed out a sigh. "Fine."

She squeezed my hand again.

I almost felt whole.

If I ignored the gaping and jagged wound in my chest where my heart used to be.

CHAPTER EIGHT

One Week Later

LUCY HAD FORGIVEN me for getting drunk and then spending the rest of the day hungover at her house. We had an Audrey Hepburn marathon.

My sister had seen every movie at least twice.

And so had I, but I wasn't complaining since I was mostly trying not to barf the entire day. And cry.

Plus, I got to curl up on the sofa with the sister I'd missed fiercely, revel in her glow, her happiness and let it fill me up the best it could.

Keltan hadn't gotten off quite as easy.

But he'd disappeared and come back with grapes, Fruit Loops, and burrito and suddenly all was forgiven.

"Okay, I love you again," Lucy said, snatching the strange assortment of objects.

He was grinning as he leaned down to kiss her forehead and then her belly. "Again?" he teased.

"Or I've loved you all along, whatever," she said, ripping into the Fruit Loop box, grabbing a handful, then a handful of grapes and shoving them in her mouth.

I screwed up my nose not just because the food was offensive to my delicate stomach.

"Pregnancy cravings," Keltan explained, settling next to her and resting his hand on the small swell of her stomach.

My own stomach roiled, for reasons that had nothing to do with the hangover.

But then I met my sister's happy eyes and it settled again.

I settled again.

I'd figure out how to find my peace. Even if I didn't get it, the most important people in my world did and that was something.

Mom and Dad had come and gone.

Mom had looked through all my new travel purchases and tutted about me not buying enough. Lucy had echoed this.

My dad had taken me out to my favorite vegetarian restaurant while Mom and Lucy were baby shopping. He demanded I recount every detail of the trip. My dad had an adventurous soul just like mine. He soaked up all of my stories without judgments about how safe it was to take overnight trains through Africa or sleep under the stars by the sea in Italy.

I knew he worried, because he was my father. But he kept it to himself. Because he loved me enough to know that to try and stop me from doing these things was to stop me from being me. And he'd always nurtured my crazy soul.

Neither he or Mom mentioned Craig.

I knew they wanted to.

But they didn't. Because they were treating me with Polly gloves.

And that's why I was equal parts relieved and sad when they left. I adored them. But I couldn't take them handling me with that much care for any longer. Because when people handled you with care, it was impossible to forget just how broken you were.

I'd spent the rest of the week catching up with friends, learning about Rain's newest gig, helping out with some projects that my favorite charities needed extra hands on. Checked in with my favorite yoga center about what classes they had coming up.

I'd been determined to keep the week full, so I didn't think about the emptiness of Heath's stare.

I hadn't seen him since then.

But his ghost followed me everywhere.

I'd only just gotten back to the apartment from a yoga class when Rosie barraged in with snacks and a grin.

And then she'd dropped a bomb on me.

Not a literal one, it was important to distinguish with her.

"You're pregnant too?" I all but screamed after she'd detonated the verbal explosive.

"Yes, but I am not deaf," she replied, rubbing her ears. "Or at least I wasn't."

I ignored this and yanked her into my arms, happiness spreading through me with a purity that was rare these days. I wanted to hold onto it. Bask in the happiness for my sister who had gone through so much pain and turmoil and somehow come out of it.

"Stop squeezing me," she protested, pushing back. "The baby isn't meant to come out for like another five months."

"You're four months," I said, gaping at her nearly flat stomach. I hadn't even noticed the slight swell to it until now.

Rosie grinned. "I know, Lucy like *hates* me because we're only a few weeks apart and her ankles are already swelling." She flopped down on the sofa and lifted her stiletto-clad foot. "Still slim and beautiful on this end."

I walked over to the fridge to get wine for me and water for Rosie. She would likely hate me for drinking wine in front of her, but I needed it these days.

To dull the edges.

Even on happy days like this, everything was a little too sharp, the past prodding at me with enough force to draw blood.

"Did you guys plan this or something?" I asked, passing her water.

As predicted, she glared at me like I was offering her some kind of dead animal, taking it reluctantly.

"No, of course, we didn't plan it, we're not *that lame*," she replied. "I wouldn't put it past Luke and Keltan, though. Their bromance is going strong. Their cycles probably synced up or something."

I choked on my wine.

She grinned. "That's what you get for drinking wine in front of me. Ah, I love it when karma works instantly."

I rolled my eyes.

"Whoever invented the no wine rule with pregnancy was a douchebag," Rosie muttered.

"Um, medical professionals didn't invent it more so discover the side effects of alcohol on an unborn baby," I said dryly.

Rosie waved her hand in dismissal. "Yes but get this, Luke isn't letting me *work*. He thinks because I'm growing a baby I can't kick ass. I can kick ass until the day I pop this sucker out."

"He just cares about your safety, and the safety of his unborn child," I said.

"Whatever," she muttered. "He's got his safety to worry about if he thinks he can order me around."

"Love doesn't know order or peace, it only knows itself, which is both or neither," I murmured, sipping my wine.

I looked up after a considerable silence to see Rosie blinking rapidly at me, and only half of it was to do with the fact she was coveting my wine.

"Wow," she said. "That was really deep."

I smiled. "Yeah, it was something my yoga teacher said this afternoon."

She screwed up her nose. "That was a trap," she snapped. "I'm not supposed to agree with yoga teachers. I abhor everything they stand for."

I smirked. "What? Finding peace? Taking care of your body and mind?"

She scowled. "No, stretching your body into unnatural positions and not even getting an orgasm out of it." She paused. "Speaking of orgasms, when was the last time you had one?"

"Last night," I replied.

She narrowed her eyes. "One that didn't come from a battery operated device."

It was my turn to scowl at her.

"If you're giving me that look then it's been too long," she observed, correctly.

My last orgasm had come from my ex-husband.

But it had been almost unintentional on his part. He wasn't what I'd call a generous lover. He wasn't what *anyone* would call a generous lover. He cared mostly about his own orgasm and making the motions of caring about mine. But he was never really one to get assertive when he finished, and I didn't. Apparently, he didn't think both parties needed an orgasm, every time.

Thinking back on it, I realized it was somewhat of a metaphor for our whole relationship, an important example of the dynamics within it.

But back then, I was so busy throwing myself into him, into this falsified idea of love, I convinced myself that things like him not caring about my needs inside—and outside, if we wanted to be really honest here—the bedroom was not a big deal. And I excused the fact he pulled out, rolled over and didn't spend even a quarter of the amount of time I did ensuring my pleasure.

He loved me.

He said it.

He showed it, sometimes, when he was in a good mood. And there was good sex. Not often, but often enough for me to trick myself into thinking that if we stayed together long enough, it might become more frequent.

I'd tried to broach the subject to him, albeit after half a bottle of wine, so I didn't exactly articulate myself that well. Plus, it was an awkward subject to take up with the man you loved. I didn't want to hurt him. In fact, every decision I made, every word that came out of my mouth and everything I did was structured not to hurt him.

Again, hindsight tells me that this is almost literally the definition of 'walking on eggshells' and one of the red flags to the beginning of emotional abuse.

But love itself is emotional abuse, even the good versions of it. It's hard to separate that from a person that was using that love to manipulate and control you.

Which was what he did after I hesitatingly told him about the way his lack of effort in the bedroom toward me hurt me. First, I thought it might go well, with him being apologetic and loving. But then he turned. Then he talked about himself, and how sex wasn't the most important thing in a relationship and I was young and childish and too focused on shallow things to notice that.

I had immediately backed down, ended up apologizing to him, and then hating myself for not handling such a situation with my husband like a grown up. Another red flag signifying emotional abuse, the way another person can make you apologize for something *they've* done wrong. To make it seem like you're the one in the wrong.

It took him literally punching me in the face to see this.

I toyed with myself—more like tortured myself—with scenarios of what would've happened had he not snapped that day. If he'd continued landing emotional blows, instead of a physical one.

Would I have eventually found my strength, my truth and walked away? Or would he have whittled me down to nothing but a raw and exposed nerve, a shell of myself before I became too bad at hiding it and the people who loved me would've had to drag me out.

Save Polly.

Again.

Ever the damsel.

A snapping at my fingers distracted me from having to face the answer.

I straightened. "What?" I asked Rosie's fingers.

"I said, you need to get yourself laid," she decided, glaring at my wine.

"No, I don't," I said firmly.

Heath's hands on mine, his mouth on mine, him inside me assaulted my brain before I could stop it, and I had to squeeze my thighs together out of the pure need to awakened.

I had to stop wanting him.

It just wasn't healthy to want someone who legitimately hated you.

"S.E.X," Rosie enunciated. "You need to be having it." She held up her hand. "And even though I would be all about you doing it with Voldemort..."

"Voldemort?"

She sighed. "He Who Must Not Be Named. But I'm a badass like Harry and Dumbledore so I actually say his name."

I scrunched up my nose. "Is pregnancy turning you like, legit straight jacket crazy?"

"Of course not," she snapped. "I was *born* straight jacket crazy." She winked. "But you're obviously a little or a lot dense from lack of sex so you don't get that Voldemort was Heath and I was trying to save your fragile little heart by not uttering his name but now I have and furthermore I've made a big show of it, so I've likely made it worse. I'm going to soldier on because that's how I do." She gave me a sharp look that was also full of kindness. "So as much as I want you and *Voldemort* to sort your shit and do the nasty, I'm thinking that maybe this isn't one of those times that we're used to. Like the time when shit works out. And I'm going to tell you, it breaks my heart. Because of everyone who deserves to have their shit sorted with their person, it's you, my fairy-tale loving, yoga doing, mildly insane romantic."

She leaned forward to squeeze my hand, her eyes watering.

Rosie never cried.

Never.

And now she was crying for me and my utterly tragic non-ending.

"I'm still holding out hope because I had to wait thirty years for the man I loved to plant a baby in my womb, put a ring on my finger and make all these rules about how *unsafe* it is for me to build bombs with Gage while pregnant." She rolled her eyes. "There were a lot of times I lost hope. And by lost hope I mean I slept with a lot of guys. There is no such thing as staying chaste and noble waiting for that lost love. That shit only happens in movies. It's not healthy nor is it realistic to wait around with your legs crossed for the universe to get its cosmic shit together. So you, my dear are hot, young and I'm assuming great in bed, because Heath would not be doing his darnedest to become the world's biggest asshole in pretending he's not in love with you if you weren't." She winked to try and dull the blow of that sentence.

It didn't work.

I poured more wine.

That wouldn't work either.

But I still poured it.

"I'm not ready."

Understatement of the century.

I was crying myself to sleep every night, my fists clenched under my pillow to actively stop them from reaching for my phone. For reaching for someone who wouldn't want me anyway.

Just because he didn't want me, it didn't stop me from wanting him.

That's what was most tragic about Romeo and Juliet. Not the ending—that was just stupid and dramatic—no, not enough people focused on the real tragedy. Paris's love. Unreturned.

There was only one thing more painful than two people in love.

It was one person in love while the other moved on with their life.

That was the fricking tragedy.

Especially since people believed in time being the ultimate healer. I used to be one of those people. Until I realized that time stretched into forever, exactly the same amount of time I'd be yearning for Heath.

Tragic.

"Of course you're not ready," Rosie agreed. "Which is why you have to do it. *Everyone* does things before they're ready. All the best people anyway. Because if we waited until we were ready, we'd be waiting for death. And there's only so much heartbreak that you can wallow in without at least pretending you're moving on." She gave me a look. "Take it from someone who knows. Maybe one day you might not even be pretending." She shrugged. "Or maybe not. But not much can be worse than the way you're feeling right now."

Crap.

She totally had a point.

I chewed my lip.

"You know I'm right," she said smugly.

I narrowed my eyes.

Her own irises brightened. "Oh, a Polly glare," she marveled. "I thought they were a myth when Lucy told me of them. You are peace, love, and fucking tofu, I didn't think you had the ability to glare."

I gritted my teeth. "Well, I've changed."

Another understatement of the century.

Rosie's eyes dimmed slightly. "Yeah, honey. As much as I wished you'd stay our loving and cheerful Polly forever, there wasn't a shot in hell for that. The fact you lasted as long as you did is a miracle. And it wasn't even the asshole that punched you in the face that did that. It was the asshole of a different kind that punched you in the chest."

I didn't correct her.

That I was the one doing the punching.

Because Rosie was protective of me. She and Lucy saw me through rose tinted glasses. I was always the damsel. No way would they ever believe I was the villain of this piece, even though the evidence was pretty damning.

I married another man.

Divorced that same man.

Ran off to Europe for a year.

Yet they were sure that Heath played a part in this. That it was his fault. They didn't say anything because they wanted to protect me and talking about him was pretty much the most damaging thing they could ever do.

"Even if you're right—"

"I'm always right," Rosie interjected.

"Well even if you are, it's not like men are lining up at my door to date me."

She scoffed. "They would if they knew your address."

I narrowed my eyes. "Do not do something like hand out my home address to strangers on the street."

She scowled. "I wouldn't do that."

I raised my brow.

"Well they wouldn't be *strangers*, I'd ask their name, do a full background check and then give them your address," she relented.

"No."

"Fine," she muttered. "But seriously, you know you're a hot piece of ass. You'd get a date like that." She clicked her fingers. "Plus, you're not exactly new at the dating scene. You've had a boyfriend for every day of the week. You know where to find them."

"I knew," I corrected. "Before..." I trailed off.

Before what?

Before Heath?

Before Craig?

Before Heath...*again?*

Before I became horribly aware of how empty I'd made my life so I didn't have to face the depth of my suffering?

"Okay, well, just get one of those phone apps, it's what the kids do these days." She'd snatched my phone off the coffee table before I could stop her.

"Rosie!" I cried. "I'm not going to date a guy on an app."

Her nails clicked against the screen. "Of course you are."

And like most times, Rosie was right.

"SO WHAT DO YOU DO, POLLY?"

Crap.

I'd known this question would come up.

It was like the conversational blueprint in first dates.

What do you do? Where are you from? How many siblings do you have? What's your sign? What's the depth of your childhood trauma?

I'd had a lot of different answers to this in the past. Barista. Waitress. Dog groomer. Personal assistant. Sous chef at a raw food café.

I'd gone through careers like I'd gone through boyfriends, trying on different versions of life that never really fit.

But now I didn't have anything. Not when my very skin didn't feel like it fit.

Heath and I hadn't talked about things like that when we first met.

Well, I'd asked his sign because I was on an astrology kick at that point and it turned out that he was crazy compatible with me. He was a Cancer and I was a Capricorn. Opposites that fit.

But other than that, we didn't talk with that conversation filler known as the date blueprint. It was like the stuffing they put in purses when on display at the store. It made them look useful full so you could get the whole effect before you bought, but it was really useless once you brought it home and put all of your own stuff inside.

I wasn't meant to be thinking about Heath here.

Not meant to be *comparing*.

I hadn't done that after our first time.

I excelled at not thinking of him, in fact.

Where had all that skill gone?

Probably down the drain with whatever had been left of my childhood naivety.

"What do I do?" I repeated, fiddling with the straw in my margarita.

He'd made a comment about me not getting 'white girl wasted' when I'd ordered it. I think it was meant to be a joke.

I'd laughed.

It wasn't funny.

He nodded, his overly styled hair not moving at all as he did so.

"Well, currently, I'm volunteering at the St. Mary's Children's Hospital. And I also do work with a couple of homeless shelters," I said.

He inspected me, narrowing his suspiciously groomed eyebrows. Which shouldn't have been a surprise. This was L.A. Everyone groomed their brows.

Even men.

Especially men.

This was a city of images, of perfection, of success and failure. Of beauty on the outside of ugliness.

"But you don't have a *job*?" he clarified.

"Not one that pays actual money," I muttered.

He nodded. In L.A. it wasn't uncommon to not have a job and still not starve or go homeless. Not in the world of Instagram models, of rich boyfriends and richer fathers.

He opened his mouth, most likely to say something about himself. It was his favorite topic.

This was my second margarita and it was only *now* he was asking me what I did.

But the person storming up to our table kind of stopped that.

I was thankful until I saw who it was.

"You're on a *date*?" Craig hissed at me.

Crap.

It was the first time I'd seen him since I'd left.

I should've had to have court appearances and all sorts of things that required interactions. But I had Rosie. And Rosie had her connections. Hence this being the first time in over a year I'd seen my ex-husband.

He hadn't changed much.

He was slightly thinner than he had been, which was actually preferable than his unnatural muscles that I'd only found out after the marriage were thanks to testosterone injections more than lifting at the gym.

His suit was pressed, not as expensive as he usually wore, white shirt open collared underneath.

Clean shaven.

Eyes wild.

Full of hate.

How I'd never seen this was beyond me.

It was tempting to shrink back. To burst into tears. To run away.

But I straightened my spine. "Hello Craig, how are you? I'm well, thanks for asking."

He leaned forward. "How am I?" he repeated, spittle flying from his mouth, breath reeking of alcohol. "Well, considering my *cunt* of an ex-wife took me to the cleaners and almost everything I had, I've been better."

His fist slammed down on the table when he finished speaking, rattling the glasses. I reached out to steady my margarita glass. I had a feeling I'd be needing that very soon.

Ben was gaping at the situation and didn't seem too eager to jump in and save the day. Or even the date.

But I wasn't the damsel anymore.

Or at least I was trying very hard not to be.

"I think you need to go back to your table," I said, my voice firm. "This isn't exactly appropriate. Perhaps we can talk tomorrow. Over the phone. When you're sober."

He snatched my wrist, the one holding my drink, cold liquid sloshed onto the table and my fingers. "No, I'm happy to talk right fuckin' now." His eyes went to Ben. "You know what's good for you, I'd give me your seat and get the fuck away from my wife."

"Ex-wife," I corrected. The grip on my wrist tightened.

I wasn't a damsel, but I would've appreciated some kind of input from the man across from me. But he stood so quickly his chair screeched against the floor. "I'm sorry," he said to me. "I'm an extra on a soap and I can't risk anything happening to my face."

And then he ran.

Literally *ran* out of the bar.

Only in L.A.

Craig smirked at me in triumph.

"Let go of my hand," I gritted through my teeth.

He looked down, and then he squeezed harder. It was a cruel motion, to show me just how in control he considered himself. How weak and breakable he considered me.

But then he let go.

I snapped my hand back wiping the sticky liquid with my napkin.

I took a breath.

He rounded the table and took Ben's seat calmly as if the past handful of minutes hadn't happened.

"Excuse me, is everything okay?"

My head snapped up to see a waiter frowning at Craig then softening his gaze at me.

"Ma'am, is he giving you trouble?"

Ah, chivalry was not dead.

It just came from the guy who was paid to serve me drinks instead of the guy that didn't even buy them for me.

Craig raised his brow at me in challenge. He was daring me to be saved. To need saving. To admit that I couldn't handle him on my own. Which was probably true. I didn't handle his abuse on my own. The first thing I did was run to Rosie. And then she dealt with it.

"No," I said firmly, forcing a polite smile. "Thank you for your concern, but I'm fine. I'll be even better if I could get a fresh drink, we seem to have had an...accident with mine." I held up the now empty glass.

The waiter paused, looking between us, and then took my glass. "Okay, I'll be right back with another drink. And I'll be here, in case there are any more...accidents."

He gave me a pointed look and Craig a harsh glare before he walked away.

"Ah, I would've expected you to cry wolf again," Craig said.

I focused my gaze on him. "It's not crying wolf when you punch me in the face," I said. "It's called standing up to abusive pricks."

Something moved in his face. Something ugly, full of rage. And then it morphed. "Baby, I said I was sorry. I tried to explain. But I didn't get the chance. I've been going crazy without you."

I blinked at the change in his temperament. The way his eyes cleared, the way he sat back in his chair.

"I love you, Polly," he continued. "I've been thinking about you constantly, about what he had." He leaned forward. "And we had something, didn't we?"

"Yes," I said. Because I didn't have it in me to lie to him or more importantly, myself. I wished I could've said no, for the sake of my self-respect. Because admitting I had something with a man who thought violence was acceptable was embarrassing, to say the least.

But my heart wasn't controlled by such things.

So there was something with him. However small. I'd magnified it out of desperation. First, because I was desperate for something that didn't hurt as much as me and Heath. And then because I had no other choice.

I had a choice now.

"We had something, Craig," I continued. "But that was all shattered with you showing your true colors. And thank god that happened when it did. Before I could put down roots with you. Before it was too late. And it's too late for us, now. If we really ever had a chance." I observed him. "You might have a chance. If you get therapy. Explore the reasons why you feel the need to be violent toward women. Everyone has the power to change their direction in life. Even you."

Silence followed my words.

Maybe they took a second to penetrate Craig's alcohol-laden brain.

It was an instant change, the cliché flip of a switch version of a temper tantrum. Granted he'd come over here in one, but I'd thought he'd settled. Maybe sobered up. Wisened up.

And I still held something for him.

Because there was a part of him—no matter how small or false it may have been—that held me when I cried at sad movies, that got me the exact chocolate I loved when I had PMS, who went to restaurants he hated because he knew I loved them. He did all those things, whether or not he had an ulterior motive—to make me fall in love with him enough to make it so there was no way out.

He just underestimated me.

And the women around me.

All of whom hated him, obviously. Lucy and she didn't even know the full story.

They hated him because they loved me.

And they expected me to hate him too.

I'd discussed this with Rosie when she'd urged me on this disastrous date.

"I'm sending him love, and happiness, and I hope that he finds a way to have a beautiful life, despite the fact he has an ugly soul," I said, sipping my wine.

Rosie snorted. "Okay, you have fun with that peace and light bullshit, I'm sending him infertility in the form of a bullet to the dick, which I'll deliver personally."

The worst thing was, she was serious.

And though he purposefully and viscously caused me emotional and physical pain, I didn't want the same for him. I didn't work that way. I wasn't wired that way.

Which is what I told Rosie. What I didn't tell her was because my heart didn't work that way either. That my wretched and traitorous heart didn't know how to forget all of those little things that made me fall in love with him in the first place. It sure knew how to forget the bad.

It was always the way.

So that's why I'd softened slightly at the table. Not enough to want to ever see him again, let alone entertain any kind of cordial relationship. But enough to bask in the revisionist history that the heart created to explain why love didn't go away.

Then of course, the present tore through that.

Or more accurately, Craig tore through that.

And the table.

We were sitting there, in almost contentment—as much contentment as two ex-spouses—could be, and then he stood, flipped the table.

Like completely.

Glass flew everywhere.

And I stayed completely still.

It wasn't what one would expect. For me to calmly sit there while my ex-husband literally upended a table in the middle of a bar, with bulging eyes and a fury turning his handsome features ugly.

"You fucking self-righteous *bitch*!" he roared.

The man I'd promised to love forever, who I'd planned on spending my life with—however naive that was—and the man I'd been so sure who'd loved me, was now throwing tables around restaurants and screaming at me.

And I sat ramrod straight, my expression flat, blank, outwardly unamused.

Even on the inside I wasn't exactly freaking out. Which was weird, as he was now crossing the distance he'd cleared with his little outburst, with violence in his eyes.

People around had noticed. And were staring. But this was L.A., you could be literally bleeding on the street—as my sister had been two years ago—and the majority of people would watch like it was some live sitcom, they were that desensitized to violence.

Surely someone would come to my aid when Craig started hitting me. A quick glance to the side had me seeing my white knight waiter rushing around the bar with panicked eyes.

He wouldn't get here in time.

Not to save the damsel.

So I reached down into my purse, luckily my hand circling the object that I'd forgotten was in here since I hadn't used the purse in question for over a year, lifting it out and switching it on, holding it to Craig's body just as he reached me. He was still yelling, but when the taser hit his body, he stopped.

His mouth still moved and horrible garble stuttered out of it as his body stayed upright, jerking violently in a way that made me sick.

This was necessary. I knew this. But I didn't like it. Causing another human being harm. No matter he meant me harm.

But I couldn't always be the damsel. I couldn't keep expecting other people to dole out the violence.

He collapsed.

I dropped the taser beside him as if it were scalding my palm.

People still watched.

The woman across from me was filming on her phone.

As was the man in front of me.

Another woman at the bar sipped a martini, eyes on her book, barely fluttering her eyelashes at the scene.

The waiter arrived.

"I'm afraid I seem to have ruined another margarita," I said dreamily. "Maybe I'll just get the check."

He regarded the carnage. "How about a tequila shot and it's on the house?"

Only in L.A.

CHAPTER NINE

IT WAS after the promised tequila shot from the waiter that didn't save me that I made my way home.

No one called the police.

Because, well, this was L.A. The police had better things to do. And if the police went to every fight a couple had in the middle of a trendy bar, they'd never do anything like catch murderers and drug dealers.

I was thankful for that.

Because the cops coming would mean Rosie finding out at the very least. If I was lucky. If I was not, it would mean Keltan finding out which would mean Heath would find out. Not that he would care, I guessed.

He'd made it painfully freaking clear that he was making true on the promise he'd made me the day he left.

"You walk away from me now, that's it, we're done. Period. I don't know you, you don't know me."

I should've been more worried about Lucy finding out through Keltan. She might be pregnant, but she was scary. Especially if she found out what Craig had really done, instead of thinking my flight of fancy had expired, hence the reason for the quickie divorce.

It was her small and powerful strength that I was guessing was behind the banging of my front door, and I opened, bracing for Lucy fury.

I froze at what I got.

"You're opening the fucking *door*?" he hissed, pushing past me almost violently to storm into my living room.

I stared at the empty space he'd occupied for a moment, unable to fathom that *he* was here. And that another man I had been in love with was yelling at me for the second time in less than two hours.

I turned, my temper flaring in a way that was totally and utterly unfamiliar. "That's what I tend to do when someone is in danger of shattering the fricking wood," I hissed, folding my arms across my chest, partly because that's women did when they were pissed off, but also because it was a good way to hide how much my hands had been shaking before that.

Heath had been pacing the small living room, his boots hitting the floor with such force, I worried for Mrs. Alderson, my downstairs neighbor. But she was out of trouble when Heath stopped pacing to stare at me.

No, to *glower* at me.

"Why the fuck are you even still living in this piece of shit apartment with a door that has nothing but a deadbolt?" he hissed. "You've got money. A lot of it. From your *divorce*," he spat the word and coming from his mouth, it sharpened the word to a point so it speared through my skin. "You need to be in a better building, better neighborhood. Make it happen."

I blinked at him through the pain, trying to catch up. "Make it happen?" I repeated.

He nodded once, the motion violent and jerky.

"So let me get this straight, you came to my apartment, stormed in, yelled at me, to order me to move to a different neighborhood?" I surmised.

He didn't speak, maybe because I didn't give him time to, because I found that anger that had been absent when my ex had upturned a table in the middle of a restaurant and then presumably was planning on attacking me.

I was finding it because I was finding fear in front of Heath when it had been absent in front of Craig. Because Heath scared me more than Craig ever could. And he hurt me more than Craig ever could. The difference was he wasn't meaning to.

Or at least I didn't think he was.

He'd been a good man before.

A good man who'd wanted me.

But I'd brutally turned him down.

Did I break his heart?

I wasn't sure.

But I knew that a good man with a broken heart was almost impossible to distinguish from a bad one with a blackened one.

So he scared me.

And somehow with everything between us, my fear morphed in anger.

"In case you didn't notice this about me, I don't *care* about money," I hissed at him, trying to mimic that detached and harsh tone that he'd adopted. "And now I have more of it, it changes nothing. I *like* this apartment." I gestured around the small and cozy space. "I *like* this neighborhood. It's *me*. I *fit*. I certainly don't fit in some skyscraper downtown or a townhouse in Beverly Hills. And I'm proud of that fact. And I don't even know why I'm explaining this to you since it's none of your business. You made it very clear that *I'm* none of your business."

His eyes darkened. Blackened like the clothes he was wearing. "You're my business, Polly," he murmured, his voice low and dangerous.

My skin prickled.

"You're *always* my business. Primarily because my business is security and you're in desperate fucking need of it since you were accosted by your ex-fucking-husband two hours ago and he almost hit you, had you not fucking tased him!" He was not murmuring anymore.

"How do you know that?" I asked, voice flat, finding that strange calmness come over me in the face of Heath's anger as it had with Craig's.

But Heath's anger wasn't the same as Craig's. It wasn't full of menace, of the desire to hurt.

Well, not physically at least.

"How do I know?' he repeated as if I was a little slow and should've realized he was all seeing and all knowing. "I'm in the business of security, and about six different people posted the fucking whole thing online. We got our Amber Alert within fuckin' minutes."

I screwed up my nose. "Amber Alert? That's only with kidnapped kids."

He continued to glare. "And for three women from Amber who have a habit of gettin' kidnapped, shot at and stabbed," he bit out. "We're not too keen on havin' that shit become somethin' of a general occurrence, no matter how determined Rosie and Lucy seem to be about that." His face flickered. Something soft, something almost tender lay underneath his fury. For a moment at least. Like sun glare on a road, when you stared at it for too long, you saw it was an illusion. "But not you," he said. "*You're* not getting caught up in that shit. You're not like Rosie and Lucy."

I resisted the urge to flinch at this.

But he was right.

I wasn't like Rosie and Lucy. They were fighters. They were their own knights in shining leather—in Rosie's case, and in Manolos—Lucy's.

They were definitely my knights on occasion.

I'd always known this was true. I'd been okay with it. Because I knew it wasn't in me to fight like they did, not in my DNA. I'd accepted that.

Until I heard it from Heath's mouth. Until he faced me with the fact I was helpless.

Or at least in his eyes.

"I thought you never wanted to see me again," I shot back, impressed I was able to talk through the pain. I was using my yoga breathing. And sheer force of will.

His eyes emptied. "I didn't," he said flatly, the words themselves had enough of a point. "But I was the only one in the office when I got the alert, and Keltan is my friend. Didn't need him having to see this shit, having to deal with his *pregnant wife* dealing with it. You know who I'm talking about, right? Your *sister?* Don't you fuckin' think you've put her through enough? Gettin' married to some asshole after knowing him a couple of months, getting involved in a drive-by, divorcing that asshole then disa-fuck-appearing for a year."

He paused.

I struggled not to double over. He was hurling the truth at me like bombs. His aim was true. And fatal.

"I missin' anything?" he asked, voice cold.

He was.

He was missing a couple of huge fricking things. Some of those things Rosie knew about. And the worst of it, no one knew about.

Because he was right. The people in my life didn't deserve

another Polly disaster on top of everything else. Lucy had almost *died* a couple of years ago. Rosie ran off too, but I doubted it was to volunteer on an olive grove like me. Considering it chased her back here and kidnapped her.

Now they were happy.

Getting shot at a lot less.

Pregnant.

Heath was right, they didn't deserve more of the kind of thing that got them to their happiness. That wasn't going to lead me to mine, considering he was glowering at me with electric hatred.

He was right, but it didn't mean it was right to say.

"That's cruel, Heath," I whispered. I just didn't have it in me to raise my voice. To yell like Rosie and Lucy would have. I knew that they did a lot of yelling throughout their heartbreaking courtships.

They still yelled now, of course.

But it wasn't to disguise their pain.

But they were stronger than me. Heath was right.

So the whisper was almost beyond my strength.

He folded his arms, his eyes not betraying an inch of reaction at my broken tone. "The truth is cruel, Polly. You should know that better than anyone. You sure as fuck taught me that."

I flinched.

He didn't react.

Silence was heavy and uncomfortable in the small space between us.

"He hurt you?" he finally snapped, eyes roving over me, searching for injuries.

He wouldn't find any, of course, unless he had an emotional x-ray machine.

"I thought you didn't care," I replied, my response childish and voice much the same.

I hated that I was being reduced to such petty remarks. That whatever we had between us had been whittled, carved, broken and disfigured by time and circumstance. By my actions. The ugliest thing in the world is whatever love turns into when it doesn't work out. Something more than hatred. Something less.

I wondered if there was some weird parallel universe where all of that organic, lost and original love went. Where it flourished and didn't rot like it had here.

But of course, that was a Polly thought.

In other words, not something that would survive in the outside reality.

Heath didn't answer my petty question. Because he had all that strength and willpower not to engage in something that would turn into an ugly fight.

Or maybe he simply just didn't care enough to go to the effort to create a fight. Because I'd created enough little cuts in his feelings for me to drain out every piece of emotion he had.

"No," I said quietly. "He didn't hurt me...tonight."

It wasn't a lie. He hadn't hurt me tonight. Hadn't put a finger on me, in fact. But I was hurting now. From a different man who hadn't put a finger on me either.

But he didn't need to in order to crush me.

Something flickered in his eyes at my words. "Tonight?" he repeated, his voice low and almost feral.

Crap.

I totally forgot how perceptive he was. He had the ability to analyze everything I said, and what I didn't say. My young self had thought it was because of some crazy connection that had him in tune to my very emotions since we met.

The older and slightly less naive version of me knew it was because of his military background and because he was...Heath. He was an intense guy.

I didn't answer, because my aversion of a lie and the aversion from the truth was battling it out right now.

"Polly," he growled, stepping forward to grasp my forearms in his hands, the grip tight enough to bruise if he held on long enough.

Please let him hold on long enough.

"Did he fucking hurt you before tonight?' he demanded.

There was no longer a blankness in his tone, in his eyes.

No, there was murder in them.

I knew, beyond a shadow of a doubt right then, that Heath would kill Craig if I told him the truth. Of course that was not something that made sense. For starters, Heath didn't care about me anymore. He'd made that clear. And even if he had something left from our battered non-relationship, it wouldn't be enough to kill a man.

I knew he had enough in him to kill someone.

But still, it didn't make sense why he'd kill for me.

Not now.

Still, I knew that's what would happen if the truth came from my lips.

I didn't like Craig much. Or at all. But I'd loved him at some point in my life. And there was nothing I could do to change that. I didn't want him to come to harm. I didn't want anyone to come to harm. I didn't believe in capital punishment—an extremely unpopular opinion within my family, specifically with Rosie and Lucy—I hated any form of violence being used to solve a problem. Again, another thing that disgusted Rosie and Lucy. So I wouldn't want *any* human being to die because of a truth I'd uttered about them.

"No," I said, little more than a whisper, trying to focus on the situation and not the beautiful pain of Heath's hands grasping my arms.

"He didn't hurt me...physically, at least," I lied, trying to sound convincing. "He was drunk. Hurt. People do stupid things when they're hurt. Stupider things when they're drunk. The combination was bad."

He eyed me before taking a large step back.

My arms throbbed from the force of his grip, and from the absence of it.

"Seein' you on a date couldn't have helped that," he said, folding his arms and widening his stance as if he were anchoring himself to the floor so he couldn't move to touch me again.

His voice was back to that cold and foreign tone.

My mouth dried out.

"It wasn't a date, it was—"

He held up his hand. "Not my business who you fuck, Polly," he said.

I flinched again.

It wasn't the cursing that did it, I grew up around Lucy and Rosie for goodness sakes. And bikers. Swearing was not something that shocked me.

But I'd never liked that word used to describe the act of making love. I always found it so ugly and harsh. And it was all the more harsher and uglier coming from Heath's mouth.

"I'm not—"

"Not my business, Polly," he repeated.

The underlying sentiment was there.

I wasn't his business.

My vision blurred.

My throat burned.

Such a reaction was ridiculous. I'd *known* this. I'd actively *participated* in this. Heck, I'd *created* this whole fricking mess.

So why did it feel like my heart was being torn up through my ribcage, yanked out by Heath's blank stare, empty tone, and harsh words? Why was it mangled and bloody at my feet, taunting me with the truth of this mess?

He didn't speak. Didn't betray any ounce of emotion that he knew what this was. He just stared.

I stared back. A thousand things to say but nothing that would make a difference. Not now.

"I came as soon as I heard!" a voice all but screeched in the deadly quiet of the apartment, I jumped at a slamming of the front door.

My eyes went to Rosie.

"You tased him!" she shouted. "I brought cake to celebrate."

I looked to her empty hands.

Luke entered behind her.

She rolled her eyes. "Well, Luke is actually carrying it, because the pregnant woman cannot possibly hold something *dangerous* and heavy as *cake*. It's akin to lugging a nuclear weapon up eight flights of stairs," she said.

Luke didn't say anything, instead he placed the cake on the counter, moving to yank her into his arms and rub her small belly.

Rosie's body softened at the easy touch.

My throat burned with a jealousy so fierce it took me by surprise.

Rosie's eyes went between the two of us. "Shit, we're interrupting," she said. "We can go—"

"You're not interrupting anything," Heath said. "I was just leaving."

And then he did exactly that.

Without another word to me.

Without another glance at me or the mangled organ that he'd ripped out and laid at my feet.

The door slammed shut.

I stared at the empty air where he had been standing, blinking rapidly.

My face was wet.

I was crying.

"Fuck," Rosie whispered.

"I'm okay," I croaked to no one in particular.

Rosie snorted. "Yes, and Luke is an appropriately protective husband."

Luke might've reacted to this.

But I was too busy bursting into tears.

Rosie caught me.

Because that was what she did.

That was what everyone did.

Apart from Heath.

"WHY DO I always fall in love with men that don't treat me right?" I asked, spooning another sickening amount of ice cream into my mouth.

Yes, I was that freaking cliché.

Crying over the guy who you were in love with, who you lost your virginity to, lost him for half a decade, found him again, only to marry another guy and then have that guy beat you up so you divorce him and leave them all behind for a year and come home to a mess.

Okay, so maybe not *exactly* the cliché situation. Because I'm Polly. And I never do things the simple way.

Even heartbreak.

Especially heartbreak.

But maybe heartbreak was that simple for everyone, no matter how it's brought about. The pain is the same.

Excruciating.

And we try and cope with all sorts of different things, but women usually start with sugar and wine. We didn't have the latter out of respect for Rosie not being able to partake. But Luke had all but run out the door when I'd began crying and returned with a plethora of treats.

Rosie kissed him. "I knew there was a reason I married you and am now carrying your baby," she murmured.

He smirked. "So it wasn't just for my body?"

"Oh, yes, that's the rest of it. As soon as you let yourself go, I'm onto my next husband."

He shook his head, yanking her in for a rough kiss.

It was nice, seeing them like that, after years of seeing the mutual pain in their eyes. Agony. And somehow they'd made it to this.

It was enough to give a girl hope.

But for this girl, maybe I'd reached my quota on hope.

So instead I had ice cream.

Rosie squinted at my question as if trying to see the answer in the faded yellow wallpaper. "I don't know, I think it's nothing to do with them, but all about how we don't love ourselves enough to see we deserve better. To demand better. If we loved ourselves more, we wouldn't let assholes break our hearts because we would hold them too precious to give away to someone not worthy of them," she said.

I gaped at her as she sipped her soda.

She drained it and pushed up to refill her glass. She shrugged. "Also, because assholes seem to be prominently hot."

I thought of Craig. He was hot. Definitely. Not so much tonight.

But Heath was more than pure hotness.

And if their hotness was directly conclusive to their ability to break my heart, then it made sense.

But it didn't help.

Ice cream didn't help.

Words and support from one of my favorite people in the world didn't help.

Nothing did.

Maybe time.

But that was another cliché.

CHAPTER TEN

I STOPPED short at the entrance to the homeless shelter. Literally stopped in my tracks like I'd walked into a wall. And I had hit a wall. Just not one you could see. Or not one that other people would *feel*.

Not unless there were other people who were madly and horribly in love with the man in the black leather jacket with the perfect beard and hair tied into a bun at the nape of his neck.

He had to do a man bun, didn't he? It was like he was *trying* to torture me. And his expression underneath his glasses told me that he wasn't trying to do it in the good way. No, he was glaring at me like he didn't want to be near enough me in order to torture me.

I struggled not to drop my bags of groceries.

He didn't move.

He just continued to glare.

Another thing that gave me pause.

The old Heath would've moved. Would've snatched the bags from my hands and not let me carry such a load. He was like that.

But chivalry, in this case, was dead because I'd killed it.

"What are you doing here?" I asked when I recovered enough to speak if not to move.

His jaw ticked as his sunglass stare leveled me to the spot. "I'm here because no one else could cover you," he bit out like the words were acid.

I blinked, jostling my bags slightly, my arms were already screaming with the short trip from my car to here, and they were turning red at the fingers as I was sure I was cutting off circulation.

Not that I was going to ask for help. Not that Heath would give it.

"Cover me?" I repeated when I was sure I wasn't going to drop canned soup and vegetables everywhere.

He nodded once, still gluing me in place with his glare. "Yeah, we've got a team on you. Small, one-man tail, rotating basis."

I stared at him. "Is that supposed to be an answer to my question? Because I don't speak military man, Marine."

It just popped out. The name from the past I hadn't uttered since...since he was *inside me.*

Blush crept up my neck. My stomach dipped.

He stiffened, reacting to the word, but not in the same way I did.

"For fuck's sake," he hissed, pushing off the wall he'd been leaning on to stalk toward me.

I couldn't even scuttle back because I was afraid I'd lose my center of balance and me and all this food would go sprawling. I wasn't worried about my fate—I could survive a header on the pavement, hopefully— but this food was intended to feed people who maybe hadn't had a meal in days. I didn't want them having to wait because I couldn't handle myself in front of the man I'd lost my virginity to and almost left a man at the altar for.

A man I loved.

A man that hated me.

The bags were roughly snatched from my now numb arms before I could figure out what was going on.

He didn't offer me an explanation, didn't smile or even acknowledge my swift intake of breath that was a response to his presence, his arms brushed against mine for a beautifully painful split second.

Up close, his face, was, as always, more beautiful. But also it was harder. Crueler.

And then he turned on his boot and all but stormed into the shelter.

I stared after him.

He wasn't waiting.

He didn't leave the door open for me.

I didn't want to follow him. In fact, if there were a choice between eating a New York ribeye, medium rare or following him, I'd be cutting into a steak.

And I'd been a vegetarian for eight years.

But I had to follow him.

And not just because that dark and self-deprecating part of me was whispering in my ear, urging me to do so just so I could experience a little more pain. But because people inside that building relied on me. I made a commitment to them. And though people would be quick to say that I broke commitments like I broke hearts, it wasn't true. Not to these people, who had nothing but a hope to rely on strangers to keep their bellies full and their heads dry.

And I knew there was an opinion on why they were in that position and the fact that they should be helping themselves. I knew both Rosie and Lucy's thoughts on it. But it didn't matter *how* they got to this hopeless spot. Not to me. It just mattered that they needed help and I could try to give them some.

In someone's life, I could be the one saving them—even if it just came in the form of volunteering here and giving them things I strictly wasn't *allowed* to give. Like deposits on apartments, second-hand cars that a friend of mine didn't need anymore. New identities for battered women, courtesy of my friend Wire, who also organized new homes out of state. It was small. Minuscule compared to the things Rosie and Lucy had done—brought down drug dealers, did something I wasn't quite sure about with international drug traffickers, but something as terrifying as it was amazing.

It wasn't *anything* compared to that.

But it was *something*.

It was mine. It was all I had left to make me feel like I could do something for someone that was about making their life easier and not harder.

I walked through the doors.

I GOT to the kitchen to see my bags unceremoniously dumped on the stainless-steel counter, and Heath prowling around the industrial-sized kitchen like a caged animal.

I debated addressing his presence again, or more accurately, questioning it when he seemed like he'd be anywhere but here, but with his general demeanor, I didn't know how well that would go. I didn't know how well I would be able to survive it.

Plus, the whole point of this shelter was peace.

It was my favorite in the city.

I had volunteered at three before this one. All were run

badly, crammed in people, treated them like cattle at some kind of feeding trough, didn't clean the facilities and didn't offer any kind of help.

It wasn't the fault of the people running them—well, not entirely. Our system was not designed to help these people. The undesirables. We ignored them on the street, shook our heads without making eye contact if they approached us, held our collective breath in the hopes they wouldn't interrupt our lives.

Which was pretty much what the country as a whole did. Because homeless people were at fault for their own situations. Drug abuse. Alcohol abuse. Bad behavior.

It was not because they were in abusive relationships, or because they had mental health issues left untreated, or they were kicked out of a bad home environment, or because they lost relatively high paying jobs and the economy meant they couldn't get another one and they burned through savings and loans until they had nothing left.

No, that couldn't be right. Because that could happen to *anyone* when the circumstances lined up just so. And we couldn't believe that these people had one day been one of the collective mass walking past them on the street. So we made assumptions in order to keep ourselves sane, to lie to ourselves about how easy it would be to become the one begging for help instead of the one ignoring the pleas.

This place was different. Largely because Jay, the man who ran it, had lived on the streets for seven years before someone took a chance on him. He was now the CEO of some multi-million dollar company. Well, more than one. All very serious and businesslike hence me not ever remembering the specifics.

He could've easily left the streets behind. Especially because of the scars he'd left on his soul. Scars I only knew about because of one night with a lot of tequila. And because people seemed to talk to me.

I invited confessions.

Maybe because I never judged anyone. Maybe because it seemed like I lived life so honestly. So chaotically.

When in reality, I was the biggest fraud of them all.

Jay didn't know that.

So he told me the horrors he'd endured. The horrors that made him seem cold, cruel, and intimidating in ten thousand-dollar suits, five hundred-dollar haircuts, a handsome face. He wasn't warm. Didn't smile. He wasn't the face of the shelter. No, he was barely ever here.

We'd met on chance.

When he'd been at another shelter, looking about buying the space out for some kind of commercial project. I hadn't taken to this well, because no matter how poorly this place operated, it still operated. It still fed hungry people, it still gave beds to those without them.

And when I'd tried to speak to him, he'd turned on the ice.

I hadn't cowered away from him like I'd guessed a lot of people did. I smiled in the face of his grimace. I didn't let him scare me off with clipped answers and a cold stare. And I eventually somehow gave him the idea to convert another building he owned into a shelter if I helped pick the staff and gave him input.

He'd tried to pay me.

I'd refused.

"I don't do this for money."

"Don't be stupid," he said. "Everyone does everything for money. Or image. Which is the currency in L.A."

I smiled. "I guess you're right. But I'm not everyone *and taking money for doing this would go against* everything *I stand for. Helping human beings in need isn't something I should charge for. It's something everyone should do without expecting a paycheck."*

"You might be the only one in L.A. of that opinion, present company included," he said, pointing to his own chest.

I raised my brow in disbelief. If he didn't care about helping people, he could've shut me down, ignored me when I started lecturing him about the residents of the building he was converting into some condo space.

He wouldn't have offered another building and to provide staff and renovations.

I didn't say this because most people didn't want to hear the truth about their worst personality traits. Others, like Jay, who'd convinced themselves that they were some kind of cold and bad person, did not want to hear about their good ones.

So I stayed silent on that score.

And I'd taken him up on his offer.

We found a handful more people who didn't expect to be paid for helping others. I made sure they weren't people looking for something on their resume or their social media account. A lot of them were friends from the loft or at least people I knew ran in similar circles.

Jay was impressed.

Impressed enough to buy fancy tequila and get drunk enough on it to open up to me.

So we were as close to friends as someone like that could be. And he took my opinions, he let me contribute to the shelter. Now there were people that came in to help the residents get ready for job interviews, we partnered with charities to give donated clothes for these interviews. I ran a meditation class once every fortnight. There were separate dorms for women and children. Therapists for battered women. Drug and addiction meetings. Classes on things like how to get good credit, apply for an apartment. All the stuff high school never taught you. What parents were supposed to teach you.

Jay paid for it all out of his own pocket.

It was a deep pocket to be fair, but he didn't cut costs. The shelter felt more like a high-end dorm room than a homeless shelter. It was the most sought after in the city.

It was a warm and welcoming place, offered as much peace as these broken souls were able to grasp. It was that for me. When I finally found it. When I found I could help people even when I couldn't help myself.

And now Heath was here.

Dripping his hate and anger all over the place. Knowing him like I did, and all the men that had surrounded me since birth, I knew speaking to him, asking him to leave wasn't going to do any good. So I decided just to pretend he didn't exist.

A laughable concept when someone like Heath took the very oxygen from the room, from my bones.

But I managed to do so by unpacking the food, lining up what I needed, mentally thinking of a recipe since I didn't 'do' recipe books. I didn't like to follow rules.

Luckily more volunteers filtered in, offered me a bright hello and a questioning glance toward Heath, who offered them a slightly subdued glare.

"That's Heath, he's security for the day," I said with a faux bright tone, as if he wasn't glaring and my heart wasn't breaking.

Chester, the youngest volunteer, still in high school, who wore all black down to his eyeliner and nail polish, raised his brows. "Since when did we need security? We barely have stabbings anymore now that you've instituted that no weapons rule."

Heath's eyes bulged.

My smile didn't fail, but it did tighten. "Oh, Jay was just

trialing this new company, I don't think it's going to stick, though. They're very busy with high profile celebrity clients."

"Celebrities?" Chester asked. He might eschew a lot of traditional teenage past times, which led him to find solace here but wasn't exempt to being seduced by the celebrity culture.

"You don't know Unquiet Mind, do you?" he asked, enthusiasm leaking into his normally monotone voice. "For a mainstream band, they actually don't totally blow."

My grin turned real.

We did know the world-famous rock band, considering the lead singer was the daughter of one of Lucy's good friends, Mia, who was married to another one of Lucy's biker friends, Bull. But I wasn't one to name drop.

"How about you help me chop these carrots and we just treat Heath like part of the furniture?" I asked, cutting this off before Heath could be rude to a kind kid I respected and felt protective over. "He's not really a people person," I added, looking in Heath's direction, but not at him.

Chester sighed but didn't hesitate to do what I'd asked.

He was a good kid. A really good kid. His parents didn't know that because they took his outward persona to be his inside one. And they didn't understand quite how making oneself look black and dark on the outside might be a way to chase it from the inside. Plus, they lived in a gated community, belonged to a country club and drove a Range Rover. They were about image. And having a son like Chester, no matter how much they loved him, was a blow to them. So they tried to change him. Gently, of course. But trying to change a teenager from something they consider their solace, their identity was not a gentle process. One of the reasons Chester landed here. Not because his parents put him here, or because he wanted something for a college transcript.

He wasn't even going to college.

He just wanted to help.

"I figured a lot of these people are misunderstood. Misunderstood at first and then it turns into something else. And something else. And that's how they get here," he said on his second day.

I fell in love with that kid a little more every day. If I ever had a son, I wished for someone with Chester's soul.

I wished I could've said the rest of the prep passed in a blur. But it didn't. It was as if everything was in slow motion. The seconds dragged pieces of me through broken glass with Heath's stare. With the power of the distance in it. The lack of emotion. I forced myself to smile. Laugh. Make jokes.

I was Polly, after all. Chester made his persona dark and black so he could have something to cling onto. It was the same with me, only I was light and happy. I had to cling to it, because I was nothing without it. Nothing I was proud of, at least.

When it was time to open the doors, Heath pulled me aside.

My body reacted with his hand on mine, he seemed to notice this and immediately let me go. With his hand, at least.

"Stabbings?" he hissed.

I blinked.

Then I realized he'd held onto Chester's offhand comment from before, and of course he was Heath, so he wasn't letting it go.

"This is a homeless shelter, Heath. These are troubled people. They might come here to find peace, but they don't always bring it with them," I said, voice low.

He stared at me and I imagined that I saw something spark in those eyes. Something that wasn't indifference or anger or hatred.

"Greenstone is now handling the security for this place," he said in an indifferent but firm tone.

I sucked in a breath, mindful of the eyes on us and the fact I couldn't cause a scene. I had a no violence rule, after all. And I wasn't a violent person.

At all.

But Heath making decisions in the last place I had that wasn't tattooed in sorrow was awakening a rage inside of me I didn't recognize. "We don't need security."

"Stabbings," he repeated, folding his arms. "Plural."

I hated the way he talked to me. And not just with that cold and indifferent tone. No, in that way that was full of frustration and certainty that I needed protecting, my ignorance of the horrors of the world needed educating.

"Stabbings as in past tense," I said, slowly, purposefully enunciating. "As in we haven't had one since we've found a way to relate to our residents that doesn't require the presence of a scowling man wearing a weapon and exuding violence hovering around." I was surprised to hear my voice had a bite to it. Something flickered in Heath's eyes, something that told me he was surprised too.

But I wasn't done.

"These people come here from streets where they get stared at with indifference, hatred, cruelty on a daily basis," I hissed. "You want to look at me like that, fine, I can take it," I lied. I pointed out the doors from the kitchen where the sounds of plates and voices were carrying. "But you do not look at *them* like that. This is the one place they're treated like human beings, not trash on the streets, not criminals. I'll not have you changing that. I may not know why you're here, I may not be able to make you leave, but if you're going to be here, you're going to contribute."

I stomped over to the counter and snatched a plate of salad. Then I stomped back to him and thrust it at him.

He took it.

"So make yourself useful."

I then snatched a handful of plates and stormed out.

Heath did make himself useful.

He treated the people with kindness and respect. His version wasn't full of smiles and laughter because that wasn't Heath. It had never been him. Not even before the war had put shadows in his eyes.

So I focused on helping people find peace while he chipped away at the last of mine.

AN AFTERNOON of doing something that normally had me feeling as centered as someone like me could feel was finishing with me stopping at my car after Heath had said he was walking me to it.

This was communicated as "You got your shit?" No, wait for a response. "Let's go."

And the entire journey to the car was silent. He didn't even fricking walk beside me. He was two steps behind. Trailing me physically just like he had mentally throughout Europe.

It might've been funny if it wasn't so fricking tragic.

And I was done with tragic.

So I gathered my strength and turned to face him as we arrived at my car.

"This is the point where you tell me what's going on," I said. "As in, why are you here?"

Heath didn't move his expression. "What's going on is you're workin' in a fuckin' place that's had stabbings," he seethed.

I gaped at him. "You're still on that?"

He folded his arms and his veins were bulging. It was hard not to get distracted by how hot that was. His fury was pretty demanding of my attention. "Yeah, Sunshine, I'm still fucking on that."

I flinched at the name.

That gave him pause.

It almost looked like his face softened. That the corners of his mouth turned down slightly.

But I was beyond that, grasping at emotional straws, trying to feed off the scraps I pretended he was giving me.

"This is *my life,* Heath," I snapped. "I'm not going to stop helping people because there are others out there who want to hurt people. I'm not going to do that *in spite* of that. I'm doing *that because* of it. Because that's who I am. A lot of things may have changed since I was eighteen years old. But that hasn't. I could get stabbed right here, on the street." I pointed downward. "And you know what? My sister did." My voice broke. "So don't try to come and make me feel bad for something that brings me happiness. And how about you educate me on why you're here in the first place since it's glaringly freaking obvious you'd rather be anywhere but here."

I was breathing heavily after my final sentence. It felt like I'd run an emotional marathon.

"Your ex-husband accosted you in a bar while you were on a *date,*" Heath hissed.

I managed to hide my flinch at his harsh tone this time. I was getting good at it.

Hiding things.

"Yes, I am aware, I was *there,*" I said mildly. "And I was also there when *you* accosted *me* in my apartment about the incident so you being here is not to repeat the performance."

"No, it's not," he agreed.

Another hidden flinch.

"But he's unpredictable," he continued. "And he obviously

has no problem trying to get physical with you. Shit is obviously going down with him. And it's lookin' like there's gonna be blowback on you because he's an asshole with a bruised ego. And he lost you." Something moved in his eyes. "Losing a woman like you makes a man dangerous."

My stomach lurched. And in nowhere near a good way.

Heath's expression did not change. Not one bit. "We're looking into it. Until we are satisfied that shit can't blow back on you, Keltan's got a team on you. It was my rotation."

I digested all of this.

And it wasn't going down well.

Not just because this cold version of Heath was the one serving the news.

"You're *looking into* my ex-husband?" I clarified.

"Keltan is," he amended.

Ah, he needed to make it very clear that he didn't care enough to do such things, it was part of his job. This, being anywhere near me, my business with the man I'd married instead of him was definitely not his choice.

"It's not any of Keltan's business," I said, folding my arms. "Craig was having a bad night. He doesn't deserve—"

"You're fucking kidding me," Heath seethed, fury leaking onto his blank face. "You're *defending* the fucker?"

I didn't react to the pure judgment in his voice. "I'm saying he deserves to get on with his life without whatever Keltan and his team is planning on doing to disrupt it."

"He sure as fuck didn't care about disrupting your life," he countered.

I somehow held his gaze. "Love turns people into someone different from themselves. Heartbreak does that further still," I whispered. "Pain makes people change, Heath."

Heath's face stayed blank. My words were doing nothing to

him. What did I expect? There was only so much a man like him could take from a woman like me before washing his hands of it.

It had been years of pain. Of chaos. Of me toying with both of our hearts. I couldn't expect him to be holding on like I was. Especially when he thought I was the one that let it all go.

"You still love him?" It was an accusation, pure and simple.

But, like us, not at all pure and simple.

I could've lied. Most likely any other person in the world would've. You had to be crazy to admit to the man you'd loved since you were eighteen that you loved your ex-husband who hit you, yelled and you and was just an all-around dickhead.

But no one had ever accused me of being sane.

Plus, I was already telling enough lies to Heath, to myself, I couldn't stack something like this onto the pile.

"You want me to stop loving him because he's a bad person?" I smiled because these days it was either smile or sob. And I could only deal with my sorrow smiling. "It doesn't work that way. I fell in love with the man, it has nothing to do with what he's shown me now, that love sticks. So I'm not going to just shake it off and move on. Not care about where his life goes now. About what will happen to him if I don't at least try and stop Keltan from doing something because of me. Because that's not how I work. And if that's how you expect me to work, then we have nothing more to talk about. Because that means you never knew me at all. I don't want a man who expects a woman to let go of love so easily. Because that means he'll do the same too."

And then I got in my car and drove away.

I was proud of myself.

I didn't break down until I got safely inside my apartment.

CHAPTER ELEVEN

"CAN YOU BELIEVE IT?" I huffed after I told Lucy and Rosie the tale of my day and Heath's part in it.

They were around for dinner, at the place where they both used to live, no matter the fact that they both had much bigger, nicer apartments. It was girl's night. We'd had them regularly before I left, in the place where we could bask in the good and bad of the past, the simplicity of it, and the warmth of each other's company.

"Can I believe it?" Lucy repeated. "Um...yeah? Have you been absent for, I don't know, the whole time every alpha male we know has been drawing breath? Something dramatic happens to us and they turn up the drama and call it protection. I mean, there are more drama queens in that security firm than on all eleven seasons of *Ru Paul's Drag Race*," she said.

"To be fair, our track record does foster a *small* dramatic reaction," Rosie put in, pinching her thumb and finger millimeters away from each other.

Lucy scowled. "Since when were you ever fair?"

Rosie scrunched her nose. "You're right. Fuck 'em."

Lucy grinned, facing me.

"You need to tell Keltan to call Heath off," I told her.

Lucy laughed.

Like threw her head back and cackled.

"I'm not joking," I said.

She wiped a tear from her eye. "Oh, I know, that's why it's funny."

I scowled.

She squeezed my arm. "Sweetie, I do boast a lot of clout with my husband, especially since I'm the one that pretends I control how my legs open and close, but have you *seen* how hot he is?" Her eyes went dreamy for a second. "But it's not him that I have to convince. Nor is he in charge when it comes to you and Heath is involved."

"He was the one that ordered the security detail," I argued.

Lucy raised a brow. "And who told you that?"

I paused. "Heath."

She gave me a look, one that told me I should've figured something out.

"Heath did not have anything to do with this. In case you haven't noticed, he hates me," I argued with her look that tried to tell me this was all Heath's doing.

"He does not hate you, honey, and that's the problem," Rosie said. "He *wants* to hate you. But he can't. I'm going to guess he hates himself for feeling the way he does. Someone really has to sue Disney for unrealistic expectations of love and romance. If you lose your shoe at midnight, it's because you're drunk. And if it's a Manolo and you lose it, it means you're dead. If you fall asleep in a tower, there's no way a man is gonna get his shit together and fight a dragon then kiss you to wake you up. You know what wakes a comatose woman? The smell of fresh coffee."

She was rambling at this point because her words had hit their mark. And not just with me. Just because she and Lucy were married and pregnant now, did not mean their stories were over. And I knew that it haunted them, the pain it took them to get there.

It wasn't something you just forgot.

"Can we please just change the subject?" I pleaded.

"Gladly. Rosie, are you scheduling a C-Section or doing a natural birth?" Lucy asked.

Rosie widened her eyes. "My hair color is never gonna be natural and neither is the birth. C-Section locked and loaded. Why, are *you* considering pushing a human out of your body?"

"Women have been doing it for thousands of years, it's not some horrific act," I cut in.

"Have you *seen* birthing videos?" Rosie snapped. "*The Conjuring* has nothing on the 'beauty of natural birth."

And from there, it went on. Because it was Rosie and Lucy and they almost managed to distract me.

Almost.

"I KNOW what I want to do."

"For dinner?" Lucy clarified, glancing up from her phone. "Thank goodness, otherwise we'd be here forever."

I smiled. We had been known to take two hours to narrow it down to three different food options, and then we ended up ordering all three.

"Anything but Chinese. Or Mexican," Rosie interjected. She frowned. "No, wait. What am I, high? No, just pregnant. Mexican is always on the table."

"No, not for dinner, in life." I paused. "Well, not life in general, but a job."

Lucy blinked, her face carefully empty. I knew this look. This was his neutral 'let's humor whatever new thing Polly has decided is her calling.'

I didn't resent it. Because as many boyfriends I've had, I had about the same careers. The two were usually mutually exclusive. When I had the boyfriend who wanted to own a farm, I thought I'd make a great alpaca breeder. Or when I briefly—very briefly since he took himself way too seriously—dated a doctor I entertained some *Gray's Anatomy* fantasies and decided nursing would be amazing. Each of these new careers were met with that same blank face from both Lucy and my parents.

Rosie had no such reactions. She was grinning wildly. "Oh, can I guess this time?" She didn't wait for me to answer. "Lion tamer? No, chef at some raw food shop that doesn't even cook anything so you just chop and blend vegetables?" She paused. "Wait, you've done that. Please tell me it's something that'll give me some entertainment and excitement now I'm not able to chase after drug dealers and rapists." Her eyes were bright and wild like that of a child.

I smiled. "Well, I don't think this latest profession is going to give entertainment or excitement, I'm sorry to inform you. In fact, kind of the whole point of it is peace and calm."

Rosie rolled her eyes. "Yes, for anyone else. But it's *you*."

She wasn't wrong. I was me.

But I hoped she was wrong on this occasion. Peace and calm was exactly what I needed right about now.

"I want to be a yoga instructor," I said.

Rosie paused, screwing up her nose. "Wait, haven't you already done that?"

"No, that was a *Pilates* instructor," Lucy cut in. "They're different, right?"

"Yes they are different and no I haven't already done it," I said.

"Are you sure?" Rosie asked.

"Reasonably," I replied.

"Hmmm okay," she murmured, not sounding convinced.

"That's great, Pol," Lucy said, her voice only slightly more convincing than Rosie.

Slightly.

I sighed. "I know that I've had as many careers as I've had boyfriends, but this is something that feels right to me," I said. "This is something I've put thought into. I love the idea of helping people find peace."

"I thought it would mainly be about helping housewives finding ways to be more flexible to please their husbands who are already banging their secretaries anyway," Rosie said, screwing up her nose.

I laughed when Lucy scowled at Rosie with somewhat of a smile in her eye. She was trying to be my protector but also Rosie's best friend.

"I'm sure there will be some of that," I agreed. "But once I'm certified, I want to open my own place. Have it be about something other than a social media image and a place to wear Lululemon leggings or whatever. " I paused. "I just want to create...something that stands for calm. Even when my life stands for chaos. I'll use Craig's money."

Rosie gave me a knowing look. "Or you could use it to hire a hitman. I'd give you the five-finger discount since *I'd* be the hitman. But you'd still have to pay me because I need a new car. I'm thinking a convertible."

I narrowed my eyes. "You're not killing him."

She pouted.

"No," I said to the silent plea.

"Even after he accosted you in a bar?" Lucy asked. "And he ruined *two* margaritas."

Obviously she didn't know that he'd once ruined my face. Because Lucy would've actually killed him. I knew that.

"We aren't talking about him," I gritted out.

"Okay," Lucy agreed.

That was too easy.

"We're talking about Heath," she amended.

I knew it.

She held her hand up as I opened my mouth. "Before you talk about not being ready or try to brush off what it is that the two of you have, you know that's impossible now, right? There's only so much patience we can have on the matter. Two years is our freaking limit. And we're pregnant, you have to give us what we ask, right?" She looked to Rosie, who nodded.

"Yep, it's like law or something."

I raised my brow, my stomach curling in on itself at the knowledge that there was going to be no way to escape this one, because they were right, there was only so long I could keep silent. And I wasn't certain they wouldn't resort to waterboarding if I tried to keep them in the dark any longer.

"It's law to get you pickles and ice cream if you're craving them," I tried to stall because I had to gather up the strength. "Not tell you details about my private life."

Rosie waved her phone. "Um, welcome to the twenty-first century, hippy kid, there are apps for all of our pregnancy cravings. And husbands. So your job, as the aunt to these two, precious, precious children is to spill every sordid detail of your past with Heath. Including girth and tongue talent."

"My job as an aunt to your precious, precious children is

talking about girth and a man's ability to perform oral sex?" I clarified.

Lucy nodded. "You're catching on."

I sighed, long and hard. I couldn't say that there wasn't a part of me that wasn't itching to talk about this. To tell someone, anyone, what I'd kept inside for so long. And the two women in front of me knew me better than I knew myself. Plus, they'd been witness to my many stupid decisions over the years. They cleaned up my messes, and more often than not, made even bigger messes.

Keeping this large part of my life, my identity, from them felt like an ongoing and exhausting deception. And it wasn't just that Heath was a large part of my identity, it's what he made me learn about myself. How he taught me that I could be the ugly step-sister in the fairy tale.

How I could break hearts and ruin lives.

It was a heavy burden to carry alone. But this was one thing that my sisters couldn't save me from.

"Okay," I whispered, the word silencing Rosie and Lucy as they bickered over who I'd babysit for the most.

"Okay?" Lucy said, shocked. "You're going to tell us?"

I nodded.

And I told them.

Everything.

"HOLY. FUCKING. FUCK," Rosie breathed.

It was the first words she'd spoken it what felt like a lifetime.

I'd stopped speaking a full minute before she uttered them. I'd counted. Braced for their reaction. Their judgment.

They were shocked because I was sure that they didn't

expect the history of me and Heath to stretch back to when I was eighteen years old. Obviously we'd done a great job at convincing my family we were strangers.

I'd done a terrible job at convincing myself.

But there was no judgment, not even an ounce on their faces. Not that I had ever witnessed it. I'd thought this might be different. This wasn't me disappearing to the Dominican Republic and volunteering with my new boyfriend for three weeks.

This was years of half-truths, deceptions. This was me marrying another while breaking the heart of a good man. One both of these women respected.

"Holy fucking fuckedy fuck," Lucy whispered.

I nodded in agreeance.

"This is a lot," Lucy said.

"Even for you, this is *a lot,*" Rosie continued.

"For *us,* this is a lot," Lucy corrected.

"Okay, it's starting to get creepy you two speaking a run-on sentence," I said.

"Why in the fuck didn't you tell us?" Rosie demanded.

"Because I was ashamed," I whispered, looking downward. "Not at the start, no at the start I wanted it just to be mine. I wanted to keep that weekend inside me so nothing could corrupt it. Like some really old painting that just crumbles to dust if it's exposed to sunlight." I picked at my chipped nail polish. "Especially since I didn't think I'd ever see him again. I didn't even entertain fantasies about us meeting randomly sometime. I didn't let myself do that. So when I saw him, I didn't know how to react. I *couldn't* react. I made him into a stranger when moments before he'd been the most important part of my past. And then it got worse. Got messy."

Understatement of the century.

"It was a moment that everyone would've expected me to

grab with both hands if they'd known," I added. "The storybook moment when that first love comes back and everything is right and perfect and it happens how it should've the first time around. But it didn't happen like that. I didn't grab it with both hands. I used both hands to push him away because I'm a big fat coward."

I emptied my wine before looking to my sister, blinking away my tears.

"Everyone thought I was looking for the one. When in reality I was trying to find a way to lose the one." I sucked in a strangled breath. "I made a mistake," I whispered. "With all of it. All I wanted was the fairy tale." I blinked at my tears. "But I ruined whatever chance I got at that."

"You didn't ruin a fairy tale, my love, because fairy tales don't exist," Lucy said calmly. "Watching you grow up in your beautiful world, I thought maybe they might, for my peaceful and chaotic baby sister. I hoped that the ugly world would grant that small thing as to give you a fairy tale. But that's not how it works." She smiled. "Sometimes the story didn't follow the rules. The girl made the wrong decisions because she was scared and naïve and most importantly, human. We don't make the right decisions when it comes to love, when it comes to the real deal. We make choices to protect our hearts when they fuck everything up even more. Take it from someone who knows. I didn't get the fairy tale. But somehow I got the happy ending."

I smiled at her, a real one, even in the middle of my pain. Because I was always going to be happy that the two women in front of me got that. Got their happy endings even though they didn't get their fairy tales.

"I don't know if I'm going to get mine now," I whispered. "I think marrying someone else and running away to Europe after divorcing him has set fire to whatever future Heath and I could ever have had."

"Why did you marry him?" Rosie asked. It was a question neither of them had asked me until now, despite their obvious disapproval.

"Because I was a coward," I whispered. "Because he was someone that seemed safe. Easy. Because I loved him with the surface part of Polly that everyone knew. He would never know the deepest parts of my pain. Because I didn't think he'd hurt me." I laughed. "But it was me that hurt myself marrying him."

I didn't say more, even though there was more. More than even Rosie knew. I wouldn't say more. No matter what. They had yanked all the truth out of me I could ever offer. I wasn't going to say the rest out loud.

"And maybe, if I want to be really honest, I knew I didn't love him, not properly," I forced the words out. "And because I knew that what I had with Heath was real, and it was going to be a lifetime of pain, I wanted to take the easy way out. Because I'm weak."

That was it.

The truth.

And it wasn't pretty.

Neither was love. Maybe that's why I'd been running for so long. Because I'd pretended to be looking for love my entire life, the hopeless and scatterbrained romantic, playing the part so very well. When in actuality, true love wasn't pretty like I was trying to make it. Like I was trying to pretend, like some little girl in a plastic crown and a polyester dress pretending she was a princess. All those men were plastic crowns, polyester dresses. They fit, I could pretend with them, but they weren't real.

And I hadn't mourned them, not really.

It was onto the next one.

And if I had loved them, there would be no moving. There

would be a lifetime of mourning. There would be a huge gaping hole in my life that I couldn't cover up with anyone else.

And that's why I ran from Heath. Because it was ugly, what I felt for him. Unhealthy. Uncomfortable. Heavy. Like the weight of a real crown might be.

Lucy had moved at some point and now her hand was tight in mine. It was comforting. Healing.

Well, as healing as it could be.

No one spoke for a long time.

Until Rosie.

"Okay, so there are people that say that nothing is certain in life, I disagree." Rosie grinned, but her eyes were glassy from my words. "And not just because I like to disagree with people. But because there are things that are certain. Like your favorite lipstick will be discontinued the second you finish your last tube. It will start to rain the second you walk out in your new suede Manolos, or right after you've had a kick-ass blowout." She scowled at this, and then down at her shoes that looked perfect in my eyes but obviously weren't to her.

It had rained today.

She snapped her head back up. "You run into Chris Hemsworth on the street after a workout, makeup-free and scarier than that Stephen King book with the clown," she continued.

And then her face changed. Turned a little more serious. A little more kind to me. "And, this is the biggy, you'll always fall in love at the wrong time. Most likely with the wrong person. Then you'll fuck something up. Or he will. Shit goes down. Because life likes to screw with us, babe, whether it's ruining eight hundred-dollar shoes, or sending us the perfect man in the most imperfect—sometimes seemingly impossible—of circumstances. But here's a secret, we're not people. We're kick ass bitches." She looked to Lucy, then to me. "And just because you don't literally kick ass like we do, 'cause you're into, like, peace, or whatever." She rolled her eyes. "Doesn't mean you don't *kick ass*. I refuse to hear yourself talking about yourself the way you would never talk to us. To the people, you love most in this world. You were there for both of the disasters that were the beginning of the relationships. And I don't think it's presumptuous for me to say we both fucked up. A lot." She looked to Lucy for confirmation.

Lucy nodded. "A lot."

"But you didn't judge us," Rosie said. "You didn't say one thing about a wrong decision, a cowardly one made by our brain in an attempt to protect our heart. You understand because you're Polly. You love everyone, are kind to people even when they don't deserve it. But the person who deserves the most love and kindness right now is yourself."

Lucy nodded. "And Heath is not a blameless saint in all of this. Not from where I'm standing. You both made wrong decisions. And he has no fucking right to treat you the way he has, riding around on his high fucking horse." Her voice was pinched in fury.

"Do not blow up his car," I said suddenly, wiping a tear from my eye.

Lucy widened her own in a faux look of innocence. "I wasn't even considering it."

I raised my brow.

"I might've been considering it," she amended. "But Keltan doesn't let me handle explosives anymore so you're safe."

I wasn't.

I was the farthest from safe I'd ever been in my life.

CHAPTER TWELVE

I SHOULD'VE BEEN GETTING MORE ACCUSTOMED to seeing him.

But I had the same reaction to him outside my apartment building the next morning as I did to seeing him outside the shelter. In the Greenstone security offices when I got back from Europe. Seeing him outside my door before I left to Europe. Seeing him standing in front of me while I was wearing a wedding dress and he was telling me to run away with him.

Pain.

And a sense of strange relief in that pain.

A safety.

His gaze was the same as it had been since I left him on my doorstep.

Blank.

I guessed I deserved that.

No, I *knew* I deserved that. Despite what Rosie said the night before.

I was trying to be kind to myself. But I also had to be honest with myself.

Me lying to myself was what got us here in the first place. I had to own that blame.

"What are you doing here?" I asked him when he pushed off the wall and moved slightly toward me, but sure to keep distance between us.

"It's Thursday," he said by response, by greeting.

"I'm aware." I was getting almost good at mimicking his cold tone.

Almost.

Or I was failing utterly and completely.

"You read to the kids at St. Mary's on Thursdays," he said.

I froze.

He didn't rush to fill the silence. In fact, he didn't fill it at all.

So it yawned on until I was recovered enough to speak.

"How do you know that?"

His face didn't change. "Work at a security firm. It's my job to know shit."

It was his *job*.

"Right," I whispered. "And I suppose there isn't much shouting or sassing or cursing I could do to stop you from this ridiculous security detail?" I asked, realizing with everything that happened with Lucy and Rosie last night, I had not been able to further plead Lucy to work her wiles on Keltan to back off.

I made a mental note to call him.

Because this could not go on. Forget Craig doing me any kind of harm, *this* would kill me.

Something rippled underneath Heath's glasses at my words. "You don't shout, sass or curse."

"I might if it would make a difference," I shot back, if only to fight the fact he knew that simple yet intimate fact about me.

"It wouldn't," he said, voice iron.

I knew as much. Rosie and Lucy *did* shout, sass and curse during the times they had been tangled up with males who wanted to protect them.

Regularly.

I knew it didn't make a difference. But then again, their stories were a little different than mine. They definitely didn't involve them getting married to another man and having the man who they'd rejected tail them around after the fact.

The men they shouted, sassed and cursed actually *cared* about them.

"Right," I repeated, this time slightly louder than a whisper.

Despite the facts, I should've been arguing this. That was what pretty much every other woman I knew who was involved in a somewhat similar situation did. Granted I didn't pay a lot of attention to the now infamous Sons of Templar courtships. Mainly because I was always falling in and out of love, out of majors, and always into some form of trouble.

But I did follow them intently. Because they were the real-life version of a fairy tale. The stories weren't pretty. Each of those women and the men had gone through types of pain no fiction writer could reproduce and certainly not market to children. The kind of pain that made a version of a happy ever after seem impossible.

But they got it.

All of them got it. And it filled me up with all sorts of hope and notions of love that no other book or movie could do.

But no way in heck did I want any of that for myself. There were explosions, kidnapping, all sorts of violence. Battles. The Sons of Templar lived for violence, so it stood to reason that it would be involved in their courtships.

As much as loved that it all worked out in the end, I didn't want that for me. No matter what people might think, I had no need for dramatics in my love life. It seemed like it on the outside, what with the revolving door of boyfriends.

But I didn't want that violence.

So it was why I was reluctant to fight Heath when he fell into step with me as I walked to my car. Because I knew him. Or I knew who he used to be. And back then, before the world had chipped away at each of us, he was stubborn, alpha and protective. He'd changed a lot. But that hadn't. It had only intensified.

If I tried to fight him on this, I'd lose. I forced myself to breathe through the pain of his physical nearness and emotional distance.

He didn't try to fill the silence as we walked to my car. He looked straight ahead with a tight jaw and his eyes hidden by sunglasses. I was glad of this. I didn't want to look into his eyes. I couldn't see the blankness in them this early in the morning.

I got to my car. And realized I didn't have my keys in my hand. This was something that happened every morning when I didn't leave them on the coffee table in the apartment, of course. I'd have thrown them into my bag and then spent five minutes digging through it to find them again. It didn't bother me when I was alone, I was never in a rush anywhere, anyway. Even if I was late. Because rushing when you were late was a sure-fire way to somehow make yourself take twice as long to do everything like find your keys in your purse. I wasn't usually bothered by the extra five minutes looking for my keys.

But five minutes more in front of a silent Heath was about as appetizing as five minutes of waterboarding.

In fact, I would've preferred the waterboarding.

"So, you'll forgive me if I don't know the procedure for something like this," I said, looking into my purse, desperate to fill the silence. "Are you riding with me or...?"

I dragged out the question in a prayer. I could not handle being in an enclosed space with him. The clutter of my car was nothing compared to the emotional junk of our past rattling along through L.A. traffic.

"Fuck no," he clipped immediately.

My flinch was hidden by jerky movements to look for my keys. My hands finally felt the fabric of my keyring. I clutched them but didn't yank my hand out of my purse, or lift my eyes. I didn't trust myself to do that.

"I'll follow you," he continued. "I'd appreciate it if you don't drive like a maniac in order to make it easier for both of us."

I almost laughed. Easier for the both of us would require Doc Brown and an industrial amount of plutonium.

"I don't drive like a maniac," I said, finally lifting my eyes up and pulling my keys out of my purse.

He was staring at me with folded arms and the designated 'tough guy' stance with slightly widened legs. An eyebrow raised from beneath his sunglasses was his only response.

I huffed, hating that yet another thing he somehow knew about me was that I'd failed my driving test three times. Because I'd told him, in the middle of the night, or the day, in that everlasting weekend we'd spent tangled up in bed and in each other.

"Whatever," I snapped. "I'll endeavor to do everything I can to make this easier for you." The attitude in my voice surprised me.

It must've surprised Heath too, because something flickered in his expression. He opened his mouth like he was going to say something, finally step all over the emotional eggshells we'd been pretending to be walking on. He closed it again. Took a visible breath.

"Much obliged," he said and turned on his heel and walked toward his black SUV.

I watched him for far too long, checked out his ass when I shouldn't have and then I got in my car.

"YOU SAID you weren't gonna drive like a maniac," a voice clipped at the same time my driver's door was wrenched open.

"I didn't," I protested.

Heath stepped back in order for me to get out of the car. It was almost comical how much unnecessary distance he put between us in order to make sure there was no accidental brushing of our skin.

"You almost hit three cyclists, two buses and a BMW," he said, voice tight.

I sighed. "*Almost*, but did not hit," I clarified. "Maniacs *hit* things. Therefore I am not one."

He did not appreciate this. "You ran three red lights."

"They had an orange tinge."

I locked my car, banishing my keys back into the depths of my purse and then bracing myself for another day—another moment—of Heath.

A grip on my hand paused my movements. Paused my fricking heart. Because it was *Heath's* grip. Heath's hand on my arm. And it wasn't gentle, it was tight and almost violent, as was the movement that yanked me around to face him.

At some point, he'd shoved his sunglasses onto his head. The unobstructed view of his eyes hit me square in the chest. There was fury in them. Pure and utter rage.

"You drive like you bowl through life," he accused. "Full of *almost* hitting things, near misses, almost disasters. You've been lucky, so far, Polly. But no one is lucky forever. The world doesn't give almosts forever. One day, you're gonna fuckin' crash. I'm not gonna let you do that to yourself. So get your fuckin' shit together and drive like you actually value your fucking life."

"I do value my life," I hissed back.

"Could've fooled me."

I yanked my hand back from his, despite the fact his grip felt like home. "That's the problem, Heath, I can't fool you."

And I pretended I didn't see the emotion on his face before I turned around and stormed toward the hospital entrance.

WE DIDN'T SPEAK for the rest of the day. Which was good, since I didn't know if I'd surprised another verbal assault from Heath.

He wasn't pulling punches.

Wasn't being gentle with my feelings.

But then again, I hadn't been gentle with his when I'd married another man. So maybe I deserved it.

He had followed me silently from the car. He was my ghost in every sense of the word. Apart from the fact he was flesh and blood, of course.

But it didn't really matter, he could've been incorporeal for all the difference it made. It's not like I was going to touch him, kiss him, ever again.

So why was that all I could think about today? Even when I was reading to my kids in the rooms of the hospital? Even when I spent longer holding Ella's hand—the little girl with leukemia who was still too ill to gather with the rest of the children in the reading room.

Even when I went out to get my favorite nurses donuts and the good coffee because I knew that their breaks weren't long enough to leave the hospital. They were barely long enough to suck down bitter, scalding hot vending machine coffee and slurp some instant noodles.

I was supposed to be finished at the hospital at three, but it wasn't until six that I was walking out the door. That *we* were walking out the door.

Heath had been a silent shadow.

Until the kids talked to him and every ounce of his ice melted with them. He smiled, he laughed. Told jokes. He transformed.

It was utterly beautiful.

And it somehow turned ugly and rancid on my insides. Not because I was jealous of those little children getting a part of Heath I'd never get, no, I was glad they got that. No, it was for an entirely different reason.

A reason that sent a conversation from six years ago hurtling into the forefront of my mind.

"Can I ask you something?"

"I thought we'd discussed that you don't have to ask me to ask a question," he replied, voice light and teasing.

I smiled into his chest. "Oh, yes, well my mind has been somewhat occupied since then."

The tenderness between my thighs served as a beautiful reminder of this.

I didn't think anyone in the history of the world had been introduced to sex as thoroughly and as often as I had in the course of this weekend.

I was talking to try to chase away the ever lighting of the previously pitch black sky. I usually liked sunrises. Loved them. As a girl who slept little, I was usually always up to see them, to welcome a new day, a new adventure.

I didn't want a new day.

And no adventure could top the weekend I spent with Heath.

I didn't want it to.

But it would.

Every day had a sunrise. And it just so happened the one coming in a handful of hours was going to signal the end of something bigger than the fricking sun itself.

To me, anyway.

Hence me trying to distract myself. Trying to fill myself up with as much knowledge about this man as I possibly could.

"Does everything you went through as a kid make you not want one?" I whispered.

His arms tightened around me. "Fuck no," he said. "My parents controlled me when I was helpless. Until I got old enough that I didn't let them. They don't get that. They don't get to take that shit away when they've already taken shit from me to turn me into what I am now. I want kids. Want a chance to be the father I never got. Give my sons and daughters the mother I never got. Want a family, 'cause I never had one. Want to make a life I never had. Not gonna continue any fuckin' cycle."

I blinked away tears at his words. That didn't work. They fell onto his bare chest.

He clutched my chin, bringing my head up to face him even though he couldn't see me in the dim moonlight. His thumb wiped at the wetness on my cheek. "You don't need to cry for my past, Sunshine. 'Specially when my present is this fucking great."

I swallowed roughly. Present. That's what I needed to focus on. Not that empty future that dawn would bring.

"How many kids do you want?" I asked, deciding to give myself a luxury I'd never have after the sun came up.

A fantasy of the future. An impossible future. One where Heath finds his way back, finds his way back to me. He doesn't look at me with fresh eyes and decide that I am just a girl that gave him distraction on a lonely weekend. He tells me this weekend carried him through the years.

We pick it up where we left off.

There's marriage.

Children.

A family.

Ours.

And every morning is spent waking up in Heath's arms.

"However many I can fit into a minivan," he said.

"You would drive a minivan? Isn't that like humanely impossible for a man like you?"

He chuckled. "A man like me?"

"Yes, a manly, strong, Marine type man."

"Well, this manly, strong, Marine type man would happily drive a minivan if it was full of my kids. My family. Manliest thing I could ever do, I'd think."

My heart swelled the size of Jupiter.

I imagined myself sitting next to Heath in a minivan. It was a comforting thought. Even though before then, the idea of any kind of conventional, cookie-cutter 'American Dream' sickened me and every decision I made was purposefully done to move me as far away from that life as possible.

But I wanted the dream with Heath.

A lot had changed about Heath since that conversation in the early hours of the morning. I had been responsible for some of the changes. But the harshness of his path was responsible for the rest. He may have looked different, sounded different, spoke crueler, acted colder, but he hadn't changed that dream. For a family.

It was unmissable in the way he interacted with those children.

It was still haunting me as we walked out into the crisp air of January in L.A.

Though January in Antarctica had nothing on Heath's

demeanor toward me. "You headin' home now?"

I shook my head. "My friend Rain needs me to help her move. And then I've got to run lines with Bobby, he's got a big audition tomorrow and he's worried he doesn't know how to play a straight man."

He stared at me for a long time. "You're serious?"

"Why wouldn't I be?"

"Because you've been at a hospital all day, feeding children joy, feeding overworked nurses coffee and donuts, doing all sorts of shit that I'm guessin' goes above and beyond the job of volunteering. You've barely sat down, and I know for a fact you've only sipped tea and not eaten a fuckin' thing for eight hours. Now you think it's appropriate to go and help someone move after all of that? And then go and practice lines with someone else? And you didn't sleep last night."

I blinked at him. "How did you know that? And I swear, if you say anything about it being your job, I'll scream right here."

He seemed to gage my words. My utter truth. Because I had been feeling like screaming. And there was only so long I could keep it in for. Only so long before I exploded.

"Know it, 'cause I know you," he said. "And know that you've had trouble sleepin' since you were a kid. You're good at hiding the signs, your body doesn't even show any hint of it now, it's so used to it. But I notice because I know what to look for. More importantly, I know what's missin'. That spark, that extra light. So, no, it's not my job to know, I just do."

It took me by surprise. The words that should've been spoken softly, because the meaning behind them was soft. But they were delivered in Heath's same cold and emotionless tone.

It was the first time he'd referenced our time before since I'd gotten back from Europe.

I didn't know what to say.

But he didn't want me to say anything.

"You're runnin' on empty, and despite the fact you're used to it, empty's empty. It's gonna hit you sometime," he continued. There was a pause. "You let too many people in," he accused. "It's giving the world more chances to hurt you."

Something lay beyond that accusation. Something I couldn't let myself hope was concern. I'd promised myself no hope when it came to Heath. It was a luxury I couldn't afford.

So I straightened my back and forced myself to meet his eyes.

"I give people the ability to hurt me, yes," I agreed. "To break my heart, to ruin me. But I don't think that's a *fault*. Because that means I'm willing to let people in. I invite heartbreak and pain, yes, but I also give myself the possibility for joy. And I think that's worth that, don't you?"

His façade flickered for the longest and shortest moment. "I think it's not worth you even attempting to do any of this shit that I'm not gonna be able to talk you out of unless you eat," he said. "So you're eating."

"I had planned on eating," I said defensively. "I'm not an idiot. I do know to feed and water myself. I'll stop and get a salad on the way."

"No," he decided.

"No?" I repeated. "You just told me I needed to eat and now I said I'm eating and you're saying no.

"A salad doesn't qualify as eating," he all but barked. "We'll go somewhere. I'm fuckin' starving. And I know a salad won't satisfy me. Since you're my job, you're comin' with me."

I blinked. "*We'll* go somewhere?" I picked the most important and most dangerous part of that out of the sentence.

Heath nodded.

"Is that a good idea?" I asked.

"No fucking way," he said, voice still harsh. "But we're going anyway."

I WAS SHOCKED when we pulled up.

In separate cars, of course. Just because we were going to dinner together did not mean anything had changed. Did not mean that we would be able to fit all of our baggage in my small and cluttered Toyota. Or even in his large and most definitely not cluttered SUV.

Nothing had changed inside Heath's eyes when I got out of my car either.

He was waiting for me.

But he didn't open my door for me.

Because that would be sending the wrong message.

Then again, the place we were eating sent all kinds of messages.

"You remembered?" I asked, whispering as I stared up at the small, fading script above a crumbling set of double doors.

Heath didn't answer.

Because obviously he had remembered.

Because we were here.

The place I'd told him about in amongst all the other things I'd told him in those two nights. One of the most mundane things I'd told him. About my favorite restaurant that no one knew about. No one knew about it because they banned phones. Even back then, before Instagram was at its peak, the owners seemed to recognize how such things could bastardize places like this.

I'd found it by chance and I wasn't put off by the shabby exterior or the initially rude staff.

"Polly!" Lukas exclaimed as I woodenly followed Heath in.

Heath had dumped his phone in the bucket by the door.

I had done the same.

It was half full.

And somehow, no one ever took something that wasn't theirs. It was part of the charm of this place. It was a little pocket of something, just like our loft had been. A little pocket where greed and image didn't creep in. Somehow couldn't.

I hadn't taken Craig here.

For whatever reason.

Lukas yanked me into a warm hug. He smelled of garlic and olive oil. Of comfort.

He'd been rude to me on my first visit. They were rude to everyone on their first visit. It wasn't a case of the customer being impressed enough to come back. It was a place where you had to impress Lukas enough to *let* you come back.

He didn't invite food critics. He told everyone to sign a verbal contract saying they weren't some kind of "hipster food blogger."

It shouldn't have worked since the food was out of this world, Lukas was amazing—once he approved you, of course—welcoming and one of the best chefs (and people) in the world.

"We haven't seen you in a year," he exclaimed. "I was worried about you. Was going to call your sister!" He was holding me at arm's length and yelling like he did when he was happy. Or angry. "But of course, I told my Maria you'd be out adventuring, exploring the world." His eyes went to Heath. Then to me. "Ah," he said, quiet, almost a whisper.

Lukas didn't whisper.

"You did a different kind of exploring," he said, voice still soft.

"No," I said quickly, not able to have this man think of Heath and I like that. I'd never be able to come back here.

"Thank you, Lukas," Heath interrupted me. "You know Polly, she's got about a thousand places to be and she needs fuel."

I was jolted at the familiarity in Heath's voice and the fact he didn't seem to want Lukas to know that we weren't what he thought we were.

Lukas nodded rapidly, grinning. "Of course, of course." He looked up. "You!" He pointed to a couple that were just getting their drinks. "You move, over there." He was pointing to the only other free table in the joint.

Free only because it was slightly dark and closest to the restrooms.

"But—" the man began to argue, betraying the fact it was his first visit.

"But nothing!" Lukas yelled. "You wanna eat, you move."

No one else at the other tables looked up from their food. Obviously all regulars. Most people were regulars.

The couple moved.

Lukas clapped his hands. "Right. One vegetarian. One meat. Sit. Sit. I'll bring drinks."

He rushed us to the newly vacated table.

There were no menus.

You told your waiter about allergies—"real ones, none of that gluten-free bullshit"—and vegetarianism and they gave you food. Whatever Lukas decided to cook that night.

And whatever it was was mind-blowing.

Sometimes it was Tagine.

Or moussaka.

Or Irish stew.

You would never know, but you would never be disappointed.

One of the things I loved the most about this place was that every single table was talking to the people surrounding them. They were engaged. Present.

Because everyone's phones were in a bucket at the front door.

It was rare, almost impossible to truly enjoy a meal, good company with just the people in front of you. You were always competing with whoever was more important on the screen of a phone.

Craig had never been separated from his phone. But his work, which I didn't know much about, required him to be 'accessible.' Being accessible to everyone else meant that he was inaccessible to me.

Heath had never glanced at his phone.

Even when I wished he would, wished he'd stop giving me so much of his empty attention.

So yes, it was one of the things I loved about this place.

Until now.

Because I wished there was something here to connect us to the world, disconnect us from each other.

But we were already disconnected.

Because Heath didn't speak.

Didn't make an effort to do so.

No small talk.

No polite mutterings.

Nothing.

Because it was all or nothing with us.

I'd made sure all wasn't an option.

"You come here?" I asked when I couldn't stand the silence and the chill in one of the loudest and warmest places in L.A.

Heath nodded.

"Since when?"

His eyes hadn't left mine since we sat down. "Since I got back."

"Why?" I whispered.

He was silent for so long I didn't think he was going to answer.

"Was trying to keep something alive," he said finally. "Trying to kill some other things."

Don't cry, I commanded.

Because I couldn't stand the thought of Heath, emerging from the war, damaged, tortured and alone, coming to the place I'd told him about while we were naked and in each other's arms.

We didn't speak for the rest of the meal.

Because there was nothing to say.

Because there was everything to say.

CHAPTER THIRTEEN

One Week Later

ONE WEEK.

One week had passed since we'd silently eaten the best food of my life in one of my favorite places on earth.

None of the warmth from the restaurant, from Lukas, from the past, seeped back into us. No, if anything, it chilled Heath more. He was more withdrawn than usual, if that was even possible.

He was still accompanying me to the homeless shelter four times a week. To the children's hospital. But he barely spoke. And then I spoke too much. About where I was going. Who I was seeing. How Tim, the young man who'd been living on the street for three years had gotten a job, an apartment, and a girlfriend.

I didn't say that I'd gotten him two out of the three.

I spoke so I didn't have to hear the roar of the silence. Not that it changed. Not that Heath responded.

I wasn't speaking now, though. Hadn't since I walked out of the doors of St Mary's. Heath hadn't come in this time.

He had 'shit to do' in the car.

I was glad. So fricking glad that he wasn't in there when...it happened. When I'd had to witness the single most ugly thing I'd ever experienced.

Though I'd come to crave the pain of his presence, there was no way I could've wished him standing inside a hospital room watching a little girl quietly and devastatingly leave the earth.

Ella had been holding my hand when she died.

I'd sat there, frozen, unblinking and holding onto a dead little girl's hand for a long time before I moved. Before I reacted. And I didn't cry, throw up or sink to the floor.

No.

I laid my lips to her cold forehead and leaned over to press the call button.

Then the nurses came.

I left quietly before Ella's parents could arrive.

No way I could handle that.

I'd walked straight to the car, needing Heath's empty stare, his cold indifference.

I needed the agony of it. Something to distract me from the horror I'd just witnessed. Just lived.

If he noticed my change in demeanor, he didn't mention it, not while he walked me from my car into my building and up the stairs.

I stopped abruptly in the hallway, two doors down from my apartment.

He didn't slam into the back of me, though he'd been close behind. He had good reflexes.

Then again, that I was kind of the point, I supposed.

I didn't turn to face him and he didn't utter anything about my abrupt stop.

"I can't tonight," I whispered to the hallway in front of me and the ghost of a man and his love behind me. "I know you're going to have something to say, something to accuse me of, something to shout at me about, but just not tonight, okay?" I sucked in a breath. "I just..." I trailed off. "I just can't."

Silence hung heavy in the hall but heavy was what I was used to now, my light, carefree life a thing of the past, and when I thought about it, a thing of fiction.

Pressure at my elbow turned me around.

I jerked at the contact.

My ghost was touching me.

Willingly touching me. And not to drag me around to face him and then let me go like my skin was fire. No, it was a gentle probing for me to turn, and when I did so, he kept his hand there and his eyes were on mine.

I sucked in another strangled breath.

They weren't empty, or cold or cruel.

It was like the utter hopelessness in my voice had somehow chipped away at something I'd considered immovable.

He didn't say anything.

He didn't need to.

"Everyone expects me to be Polly all the time," I whispered. "To be happy, to be cheerful, to see the world through rose-tinted glasses. And I am. And I do. As long as I'm not looking in a mirror. I've created this image for myself that gives me no room to be the opposite of Polly. Like I am now. The nothing. The blow-up doll version of me that's deflated, flat, sad and up close, not at all living up to what was promised. I'm just so tired." My voice hitched then cracked.

A tear trailed down my cheek.

"I'm so fucking tired, Heath, and I know if I sleep for a year I won't be rested. And I ran away for a year because I thought if I was somewhere where I don't have to 'be Polly' for everyone around me, maybe I'd be able to find some rest."

Another tear trailed down my cheek.

"But I didn't realize that the person I had been killing myself being Polly for was me," I whispered. "I can't fall apart because that's not what Polly does. And if I'm not her, I'm no one."

That's when another tear fell.

And other.

And my body started to shake with sobs so powerful I wondered if they'd shatter my teeth.

I wanted to run, to not let Heath see me in this way. Not expose all my fragile and broken pieces for him to grind away to dust with his indifference.

But he didn't.

He yanked me into his arms without hesitation, without any of that chill that had been present for what seemed like forever.

He smelled the same.

I clutched the fabric of his tee and his arms cocooned me in his warmth.

I sobbed harder.

He kissed my head.

"You don't have to be Polly with me," he whispered against my hair.

"I know," I choked out. "And that's the worst part."

He didn't say anything as my sorrow wouldn't let me communicate beyond strangled and uneven breaths.

He just held me.

For what felt like a lifetime.

He had every right to walk away from my tears, to leave me to marinate in my mistakes that had affected him. But he put all of that aside to hold me when I was breaking down because he knew that I needed it.

In my sorrow, we found a pocket of simplicity that we'd never have outside of it.

And for that reason, I hoped my tears, my pain, my sobs, wouldn't stop.

But nothing lasted forever.

Not the bad.

Not the good.

Or anything in between.

"DO YOU WANT TO, can you, will you...come inside?" I asked, lifting my head from where I had soaked his tee with my tears.

His hands tightened around me.

His eyes were still hard.

Cold.

I braced myself for the no. For him to let me go, to step back and to adopt the persona that was becoming so horribly familiar.

But he didn't.

"Yeah, I fucking want to," he said, voice rough.

And he did.

We didn't speak when I unlocked the door.

Not when I led us through the living room, dumping my purse on my sofa.

Not when we entered my bedroom.

I didn't turn on the lights. Because that would make it impossible to avoid the look in Heath's eyes. The truth. Reality.

"Can we live in a fantasy, just for tonight?" I whispered. "I know we need reality tomorrow. And the next day. That it makes it impossible for a fantasy to last longer than tonight. I just..." I trailed off. "I just really need it."

I paused.

"I just really need you."

There it was.

Me speaking the truth that I'd been stuffing down for years. Me exposing that raw nerve that he'd been prodding at, damaging.

He could crush it now.

I wouldn't blame it.

But he didn't.

There was a lump of his boots hitting the floor. A squeak of the springs on my bed.

"Get into bed, Sunshine," Heath ordered quietly.

I didn't hesitate. Didn't wait for him to change his mind.

I climbed into bed. Into his arms.

Into the fantasy.

And in the morning, he was gone, replaced by reality.

"YOU DON'T HAVE to walk me up to my door," I said, fiddling with my keys.

I had come prepared with them out of my purse the entire walk and elevator ride with Heath at his prescribed distance.

The distance that betrayed nothing of the night before.

Like it never happened.

Like it wasn't even real.

Maybe it wasn't.

Maybe *I* wasn't.

No way did I want to prolong this feeling. But even in pain, I wanted to be around him. It wasn't for me that I wanted to speed up our separation. It was for him. Because I knew how much he didn't want to be here, near me. How miserable it made him.

The last thing I wanted in this world was for Heath to be miserable.

Especially when my mere presence was the reason for it.

"Yes, I do," he said. "It's—"

"Your job," I finished for him. "Yeah and let's talk about that." I stopped at my door, facing him. "Because this is getting beyond a joke. Your job is to protect people that are in danger. I'm not in danger. Craig saw me by chance, he was drunk. And he reacted. It was not part of some grand plan. Some threat to my life. It certainly doesn't warrant this." I waved my hands between us. "And even if it did, it does not require you to do it. I'm assuming Keltan has other men in the office who don't have...your *distaste* for me."

Something moved behind his eyes. "Why? You asking for another man so you can find your next husband?"

I flinched. There was no hiding the reaction to a blow that obvious. That painful. It was a punch that he didn't pull, didn't care to mind my feelings for. He wasn't holding back.

I'd been punched in the face by a man I'd thought I loved. And it hurt. Both the physical act and the emotional knowledge that he could do that to me.

But it didn't hurt as much as that comment coming from Heath. Heath could always hurt me more than Craig. And that meant he was the only one I really loved. Because only people you loved completely could ruin you so efficiently.

"That is brutally ridiculous, Heath," I croaked out.

He didn't look affected by the pain in my voice and what I was sure was agony in my expression. "You want to know what's brutally ridiculous? This whole fucking situation. You." His stare was a thousand knives and a thousand different wounds, and I couldn't look away. "You ran," he accused, his voice cold and hard and so full of judgment it hit me bodily.

My instinct was to cower. To hide from this. Escape it. But I'd done that once. I'd tried to do that once. And I'd failed. There was no going back now. No hiding. So I jutted my chin up.

"What you felt between us was real and visceral and you couldn't fuckin' handle it," he spat. "So you ran. You ran into the arms of a man that hurt you. That doesn't respect you. That showed that in a fucking restaurant when he was about to *hit* you."

"That's cruel," I whispered.

Nothing moved in his eyes. "You've made me cruel, Polly. You've made me fuckin' *crazy*. It was one thing to watch you fuckin' marry someone else. It was a little death. And a lot of big ones. Every fuckin' day I woke up with the knowledge that you weren't in my arms 'cause you were wakin' up with your fuckin' *husband*." He hissed the word. "And it was all I could do to get through that day thinkin' you were happy. I hated it wasn't with me, but fuck I got through the day because I guessed you knew yourself enough to give yourself happy. And then I figure out you were wakin' up with someone who had the world in his arms and he was ready to put his fucking *hands* on you? That wasn't a little death. Or a big one—that was fucking annihilation."

His hands were fisted at his sides as the blank and emotionless mask he'd been wearing started to slip, to give way to anger, to something else.

"You tried to put an ocean between us. A whole fucking continent." He stepped forward, and I backed up right until I slammed into a wall and I couldn't retreat any farther. He didn't pause, didn't show mercy at my obvious fear.

He didn't have mercy because there was no room for mercy between us.

He boxed me in until his hands came against the wall, either side of my face, his body lightly pressing into mine.

His gaze ripped through me.

"So, Little Girl, did it work?" he murmured. "All that distance? That ocean? Did it wash us away from you?"

I blinked at him. "You know it didn't," I whispered.

The words had barely come out of my mouth until his lips crashed onto mine. Brutally. Painfully. Exquisitely.

It was everything I'd craved but pretended I didn't need. Pretended I didn't need because I was sure I couldn't have it.

But now that I did, now Heath's hands were tearing through my hair, yanking my body to his, and then my legs were suddenly wrapped around his hips, I couldn't imagine taking another breath in a world where this wasn't a part of it.

I'd run out of reasons to fight this. To fight us. To pull back. To run again. There was no more running for me. No, there was Heath. Finally. Kissing me. Me, finally getting my shit together.

Just as quickly as he started kissing me, he stopped. He was across the hallway in one heartbeat.

My hand went to my lips, trying to extend the sensation of his kiss.

"Fuck," he growled into the empty air.

I focused on him.

He did not look like he was ready to stop fighting. To continue kissing me.

No, he looked like he was about to run.

But he didn't run, of course.

He gave me one last glare and turned on his heel and walked purposefully out the door.

"DUDE, do you know you've got a hot guy following you?" Rain stage-whispered as I met her at the doors to our favorite bar.

Well, it was *my* favorite bar and I took her here one night and she, therefore, decided to was 'our favorite bar' since then.

It was mine and Heath's bar.

It was dangerous. The emotional version of self-harm to come here at all, let alone the night after...everything that happened last night.

I hadn't slept.

Not a wink.

How could someone sleep with those words bouncing off their skulls? Off the walls? They were louder than any chaos in L.A. could reproduce.

So I just lay there, replaying the words. Replaying the kiss.

And then it was morning.

I expected Heath to be waiting outside the building.

But he wasn't.

There was a man, he had impressive muscles, leaned with the appropriate alpha stance, but he was not Heath. He was slightly shorter, he had short blond hair and a much kinder expression than what I was used to.

It was his kind expression that almost brought me to my knees. It was the fact he was there at all. The morning after Heath had kissed me and walked away.

He'd given up on me.

Finally.

It was all I could do to continue walking toward the man supposedly responsible for my safety.

"Polly," he said, grinning. "I'm Duke."

He extended his hand and I took it, smiling back because it was reflex to smile at someone who smiled at you so easily and openly. His hand was dry and warm and welcoming, just like everything about him.

I liked him.

I knew he'd be easy to be around, he wouldn't make it hurt to breathe. To exist.

But I missed Heath physically nonetheless.

"I'm guessing you're my next victim?" I asked, walking toward my car.

"Victim? You a serial killer?" he asked.

I smiled. "Not that I know of. But I'm wasting the time of someone who I'm guessing has much better things to do."

He grinned, snatching my keys from my hand in a gesture that managed not to be rude and opened my door for me after unlocking it.

Heath didn't open doors anymore. Sometimes he looked like he wanted to jam one of my fingers in one.

"Hanging out with a pretty lady who I've heard is crazier than her sister in all the best ways is not what I consider a waste of my time." He winked, closing my door.

Before I knew it, the passenger door was opening, and the large man had folded himself into it. He threw a yoga mat into the back seat and two paperbacks.

"You're riding with me?" I asked, though he'd put his seatbelt on so it was pretty obvious.

He nodded. "Heard you're a maniac driver and I haven't had time to head to Disney this year so I'm lookin' forward to the thrill."

Again, I couldn't help but smile. "I'll do my best to recreate Space Mountain."

"All I can ask for."

Duke had been easy all day. Offering help when needed at the homeless shelter and even volunteering to teach self-defense classes once a week when he'd talked to a couple of bruised and skinny girls who were barely out of their teens.

All of his pleasant and joking manner had disappeared when he'd finished speaking to them. I knew why. They were under the thumb of some asshole pimp who preyed on girls with bad home environments. He showed them a beautiful life for just long enough to get them committed, tied. Then he took down the façade, trapped them in an ugly life.

Not unlike how Craig had with me.

I just had people to run back to.

These girls had no one.

I'd been trying my best to help as many as I could. Using Craig's money, I'd managed to rehome a lot of them out of state, and Jay arranged everything out of his own pocket when I'd told him about it. Wire did his thing and they disappeared. But for every girl I got out, another ended up in her place.

I knew that Rosie had a side business for people like this. That I could've told her, and the problem would've gone away with the life of the man spreading all of the violence and pain, ruining innocence along the way.

But as much as I hated seeing those girls like that, it went against everything I believed to make a call to end someone's life.

Now Duke knew even a little bit—and those men gossiped like high school girls—I wondered how long these girls would have under the control of that ugly man.

The thought simmered at the back of my mind but disappeared for the rest of the day until I informed Duke I was meeting a friend and that he didn't have to come.

"She has a taser, pepper spray, and brass knuckles. I'm covered with her. And it's Friday night. Surely you've got something better to do."

It was one thing having Heath follow me around. And that

was uncomfortable enough. It was quite another with Duke having to stretch out his day protecting me from a threat that didn't even exist.

"I can honestly tell you there's nothing better than meeting a woman that owns brass knuckles," he said seriously.

I laughed.

He came with me to the bar.

And Rain obviously drank him in as we approached.

"Seriously," she said. "Do you know that he's like, right there?" She held up her hand and pointed into it, in a false attempt to hide the pointing.

I smiled. That was Rain. As subtle as a two by four to the face.

"Rain, this is Duke, Duke, this is Rain," I said.

She shook his hand. "Nice grip." She grinned.

"Ditto," he replied.

"You two are going to be trouble, aren't you?" I asked.

Rain grinned. "Oh, no more than usual."

But trouble was on its way.

And it had nothing to do with two good people.

It had to do with a lot of very bad ones.

"I THINK it's my turn to drive," Duke said, deftly taking the keys I'd unearthed from my purse.

I nodded. "I think you're right," I agreed, not slurring my words, but I was almost singing them. A sure sign of a tipsy Polly. Because one of the things I never did when sober was sing. I was considerate of people around me, and wouldn't subject them to my tone-deaf tunes when sober. So, despite the fact I'd only nursed two beers over the two hours Rain and I had gone over six years of pain—Duke had sat at another table for most of the night, and that meant I had to spill the reasons why, reasons that ended up into the whole story—I was tipsy.

And tipsy meant no way was I driving.

Drunk driving was something I was violently against. Not just because if someone crashed, and killed themselves, it was their families and friends that had to suffer through a preventable death. But because it could kill someone going about their life, completely sober, doing everything *right.*

The person doing wrong usually walked away.

Duke opened the door for me and he was in the driver's seat in what seemed like a long blink.

"You know, there's really no excuse for drunk driving," I said. "Not with things like Uber. Or, you could just do what I did, get married to an a-hole, divorce him, not see him for a year and then have him accost you in a restaurant so your brother in law gets his security firm to cover you."

"Agreed. But it is a heck of a long game to play for a free and sober ride home," Duke said, smile in his voice.

"Yeah, Uber is most likely much easier. And it won't ruin your life."

There was a long silence after my words.

"Could you take me somewhere?" I asked.

"You got a hankering for a cheeseburger?" he asked knowingly.

I shook my head. But I did kind of feel like one. Veggie burger, of course. "No. Do you by any chance know where Heath lives?"

Another pause. Duke was grinning.

"Yeah, I do by chance know."

I STARED up at the building in awe. "This isn't where Heath lives now."

"Well I sure hope it is since I've been pickin' him up for our workouts every Saturday for three years," Duke said dryly.

I continued to stare. "He's still here," I whispered.

I was looking at the same apartment building I'd lost my virginity in years before. The exact same one.

I'd assumed now that Heath was out of the Marines, he would've made a home, a real one. I knew Keltan paid his employees well, so Heath could've afforded a condo in a nice area, even in L.A.

But he was still here.

I wanted to cry.

But I didn't.

I turned to Duke. "Thanks for bringing me."

"Thanks for asking me to bring you," he said.

I furrowed my brows in question.

"Heath's a buddy. We don't talk about shit 'cause...well, we're guys, and we don't talk about shit, but I know he's hurtin'," he explained. "Know he's *been* hurting. And I know it's never as simple as it seems on the surface, so I don't judge you even a little bit for holdin' back. Understand it, in fact. But I'm thankful you're here." He nodded to the building.

"Well, you might be the only one," I said, sobering instantly at the reality of what I was doing. And being faced with the fact that Heath might not want me here.

That Heath might not be alone.

The mere thought filled my mouth with bile.

He had every right to have someone else in his bed. I'd married someone else, for Christ's sake.

"Whatever you're thinkin' about, you cut the shit right now," Duke commanded. "He's gonna be thankful you're here. You trust me on this. Fucker can't get out of his own way, 'cause, well...he's a fucking guy and we can't swallow our pride at the best of times. This ain't the best of times. But I've got a feelin' it might be able to turn into that, you get outta this car and stop overthinking shit."

Overthinking.

No one in my life would've ever accused me of that before.

But that's what I was doing.

I leaned over to kiss Duke's clean-shaven cheek. "Thank you."

"Didn't do anything, but I'll take the thanks." He winked at me. "Now get outta the fucking car, babe."

I did as I was asked.

But I stopped to lean back in before I closed the door. "Will you stay, just in case he slams the door closed in my face?"

"He won't."

"But will you stay, just in case?"

"Sure, babe."

I decided that I loved Duke.

The walk into the building and the ride up the elevator was strange, because it was familiar and foreign at the same time. I'd unwittingly replayed the night Heath and I first met tonight, well, sans Heath. I wished I'd had more beer since sobriety was coming as fast as the numbers on the elevator climbed.

The doors opened, and I stared at the empty hallway for a long time before I stepped out. Long enough for the doors to almost close, to almost save me from making a dangerous decision.

But this was a time I didn't need to be saved. I didn't *want* to be saved.

So I found a strength that had a lot to do with Dutch Courage, but more to do with Heath and I walked out into the hallway, all the way to the door I remembered in stark detail. It was a plain door, of course. But plain things become extraordinary when connected to the memories of someone we loved with all of our being.

Before I could let the thought of him not being alone inside the tiny apartment poison my mind anymore, I knocked.

My hand was shaking as I did so. My heart was in my throat. My breathing was shallow.

Luckily since the apartment was small, I didn't have to wait long for Heath to open the door.

He opened the door shirtless.

Shirt. Less.

My mouth dropped open.

I couldn't help it. I had memories of his torso. They etched into my mind with as much definition as his abs. So I'd known his body was good.

And though he'd been clothed since I'd seen him lately, I know he'd gained more muscle. *A lot* more. And I did fantasize about what exactly the muscle looked like when I was alone at home with my vibrator.

But the reality far exceeded any fantasy.

He was wearing sweats, slung low on his hips, so I could see that delicious 'V' that pointed down to an equally delicious appendage.

My core pulsated with need. Hunger. It had been to years since I'd had sex. I couldn't stomach any kind of romance while I was gone. Not like before, when I'd used some form of lust to pretend I wasn't heartbroken. The mere thought of another man's hands on me was sickening. Plus, I was too busy trying to figure myself out to even give someone unimportant my energy.

And every man who wasn't Heath was unimportant.

I snapped my head up, realizing I was staring at his crotch, not speaking after I knocked on his door at almost midnight.

"I don't know why I'm here."

His eyes were dark and not and all blank how I'd come to expect them to be. There was a glimmer of hunger as he roved his gaze up my white sundress, cowboy boots, and denim jacket. My hair was plaited into loose pigtails.

"Didn't ask why you were here," he said. He didn't say anything else.

Neither did I.

We both stood there, staring at each other silently.

I knew this was a moment that Heath was deciding what to do. If he stepped aside and let me in, it was more than in the literal sense, it was a tiny glimmer of hope that he might let me into places other than his apartment. Or if he closed the door, it was the final and heart shattered close to what had turned into a saga between us.

I expected him to close the door. I deserved him to close that door.

The seconds yawned in like years.

He stepped aside.

I WAS awake for a long time before I opened my eyes. I didn't want to open my eyes. Because then the person whose arms were tight around me would know I was awake and most likely his arms would not be around me and then I'd have to abandon the fantasy that this could be every single morning.

"Know you're awake, Sunshine," a throaty voice said.

Obviously my tactics were extremely flawed.

But his voice wasn't cold, cruel or detached.

So I opened my eyes.

I'd been using his chest as a pillow, my leg cocked up at his hip and sprawled across his body. Barely any of my body was actually on his mattress.

He didn't seem to mind since both of his arms were tight around me, clutching me to his body. They loosened slightly so I could move my head to meet his eyes.

"You sober?" he asked.

He caught me off guard, so it took a couple of moments to answer. "Yes."

"You hungover?"

A strange question, but I took stock of my body. I had a slight headache that was likely more to do with dehydration than a hangover. I'd drank enough to get me tipsy, to give me the courage to come over here, but not enough to take me out of my head. Or to make it throb the next day—though it was still the early hours of the next day.

My memories of the night before were stark and lucid.

After he'd let me in he hadn't spoken, he'd taken my jacket, his hands ghosting over the bare skin of my shoulders.

My entire body shivered with the simple contact.

Because nothing was ever simple between Heath and me.

I stepped inside the apartment. Barely anything had changed since the last time I was here. There weren't any photos in the living room. He'd upgraded his television and sofa. The coffee table was the same black glass top. It had a couple of neatly stacked paperbacks on top. There was a laptop open on the sofa.

His kitchen had a couple of new and expensive appliances. The counters gleamed. There was a beer sitting on the breakfast bar. Nothing else. Because it was Heath and he was all about order.

The differences between his stark, empty, clean apartment and my cluttered, mismatched and messy one were comical. Or they would've been if they weren't metaphors for the differences between us.

"Beer?" the offer echoed through the empty apartment.

I turned to see him watching me wander around his living room, looking for something to grasp onto, some sign that he had finally found a home. Found peace.

"No," I said, my voice a little more than a whisper. "I've had enough."

"You drunk?" he asked.

I shook my head.

He nodded once.

I wanted to say more. To say everything, but even with this empty apartment, there wasn't enough room for it all. I didn't have enough energy for it all. Weariness settled suddenly on my shoulders and I struggled to stand under it.

"Tired?" he asked, seeming to see the wave of tiredness that had hit me.

I nodded.

He drained his beer, rounded the kitchen, threw it in the trash and then came to stand in front of me.

"Let's go to bed then."

And we did.

Went to bed. To sleep.

He handed me a tee. I went to the bathroom to change and brush my teeth with his toothbrush.

He was in bed when I came out. We didn't speak. The covers were set aside for me. His eyes held invitation that he didn't articulate.

I didn't hesitate to curl under the covers and into his arms.

"Home," I whispered.

He jerked.

But he didn't speak.

And I fell asleep.

"No," I said once my mind had finished going over the events of the night. "I wasn't even that drunk—"

I didn't get to finish since Heath hauled me up his body, grabbed the back of my neck and wrenched my mouth down on his. I should've worried about morning breath and about how scary I looked with my curls escaping from the braids and wild around my face.

I didn't think about anything but his mouth on mine and the fact his tee had ridden up, like all the way up since my legs were splayed on either side of his hips and my panties were grinding against a definite hardness between his legs. He let out a fierce growl into my mouth as I moved against him out of instinct out of pure hunger, out of desperation.

He pulled my head back to stare at me in a way that had wetness pouring into my already soaked panties. "I'm not gonna be able to be gentle, Sunshine," he rasped. "Not now. Not even the second time around. I can't promise you I will be able to fuck you gentle for a long time."

My stomach jumped as my pussy clenched at his words. "I don't need you to be gentle," I said. "In fact, I couldn't stand gentle right now."

My words were swallowed by another brutal kiss and his tee was no longer covering me. Heath's hands were everywhere all over my naked torso, and then his mouth was right there, right on my nipple. I cried out as his teeth grazed the sensitive nub, my orgasm threatening to bowl me over with his mouth alone.

Just as it became too much to bear, his mouth was gone.

"You're gonna ride me, Sunshine," Heath growled, yanking at the sides of my panties. "And it's not gonna be sweet. There is no sweet left for us, Sunshine," he said. "There's no more of that kindness left for us. Because we've chipped away at us, at this, until there was only the truth left. And the truth isn't kind or sweet. But sweet doesn't fill you up, babe, no matter what you tell yourself. I'm going to fucking fill you up."

The tear of the fabric echoed through my brain like a roar. It mingled with his words, the literal enforcement of his words. Of the truth in them. The beautiful, ugly, *fucking hot* truth. He had just *ripped my panties from my body.*

I struggled with his sweats, desperate to free him. Desperate to free the both of us from all the shackles that had been strangling us.

He lifted me enough to pull them past his hips. His gaze bore into me as he hovered me above him. "You ready, baby?"

"You know I am," I whispered, my voice throaty and low.

"Don't you take your fuckin' eyes off me," he commanded.

As if I could.

He didn't move me and my blood ran hot through my body as the need for him to be inside me drove me wild.

"Tell me you won't take your eyes off me as you ride my cock, Polly," Heath said.

My pussy clenched. "I won't take my eyes off you," I said.

His eyes darkened with a command.

"As I ride your cock...*Marine*," I finished, the last word barely out of my mouth as he slammed me down.

Slammed me down on his cock and he filled me up.

Completely and utterly.

White clouded my vision and I cried out. I was primed and ready for him, of course. But the angle, the tightness of my pussy, my wild need for him had me almost blacking out.

Heath's hands were tight on my hips, maybe to the point of pain, but I could not feel pain, not at this moment. Pleasure was the only thing in my system.

Heath was the only thing in my system.

I blinked away stars.

I focused my gaze on Heath, whose jaw was hard, veins protruding from his neck with the force he was keeping himself still. I placed my hands on my spot, on his chest. And then I moved. And then I rode him.

"Fuck, Sunshine," he ground out as he yanked my head down, pressing our foreheads together.

I continued to move.

Continued to slam into him.

"My Polly," he growled, his voice guttural.

My orgasm was about to take me over, snatch all my sense and words. "I was always your Polly," I whispered, my voice fractured. "And I always will be."

Then I shattered.

And I'd never felt so whole in six years.

I DIDN'T REMEMBER GOING to sleep.

I must've, since I was waking up.

And I must've gone to sleep with Heath inside me since the last thing I remembered was him growling his release into me, his mouth on mine. His eyes devouring me with a hunger and an intensity that I'd been certain was gone forever. That I'd been certain I'd killed inside him.

I'd been ready to carry that around with me for however long it took me to get over him. In other words, forever.

It was almost too good to be true to have it back. But then again, it's not like things had been easy up until now. So maybe I needed to be like the old Polly, take the good without bracing, without believing the worst. Because when you believed the worst, the worst tended to happen. If you believed the best, better things came.

Law of Attraction and all that.

An ethos I lived by.

I stretched out like a cat, my muscles delightfully sore with evidence of just how much time was spent getting biblically reacquainted with each other. And getting reacquainted to this new roughness between us. To this new violence. Because Heath was right, there was no room for sweet between us anymore. And me, the hopeless romantic who read Nicholas Sparks books should've been disappointed with that. But there was no way in hell that I could be disappointed with what happened last night.

It turned out I didn't want sweet. I liked sour. Bitter. Because that's what it was. That's what we were. But it tasted like ambrosia.

I was surprised I wasn't using Heath as a pillow, surprised that his arms weren't tight around me, as they had been in the short periods Heath wasn't fucking me last night.

I was even more surprised that me stretching out didn't encounter warm and hot naked and muscled flesh.

I was also very disappointed with this.

"Heath?" I called, my voice croaky with sleep. I creaked my eyes open to find an empty bed. The sheets were rumpled with the evidence of last night. His scent still clung to the cotton, mingled with the smell of sex.

My core pulsated with the pure memory of it.

Even though I was aching in every area in my body, I needed more than a memory. I needed Heath to show me that last night wasn't a dream. That it wasn't a one-off. Because it was more than sex. It was *always* more than sex with us.

That's what started all the trouble.

All the pain.

I knew that the trouble and pain wasn't over. It was never going to be over. Not with our history. Not with the things Heath knew and, more importantly, the things he didn't know.

My heart clenched at one specific thing. The specific thing that had me fighting everything since my divorce.

I pushed it aside.

For the morning at least.

I sat up, the sheet falling with me to expose my naked skin to the morning light.

The curtains were open. As they had been all night. Because Heath knew that little detail that I didn't like sleeping with curtains if I could help it. I liked looking upon the beauty of the universe in the night sky—what little I could see in L.A. anyway—and I liked the soft rays of the sun waking me up on the rare occasion I wasn't awake already.

The sun was high in the sky, and I wasn't one of those people that could read the time like a fricking sundial, but I knew it was late. That was something. I didn't sleep late. Even though I was up most of the night and I should've slept late to compensate, I didn't. My body didn't stay unconscious when there was a new day, a new adventure. A new escape.

But in Heath's arms, where I was having an adventure, when I'd stopped looking for an escape, I finally gave my body the sleep it needed. Never had I felt so well rested.

But there was one problem.

"Heath?" I repeated, this time louder, though the size of the apartment that if he was here, he would've heard my low croak.

Something settled in my stomach. An unease with the knowledge I was naked and alone in Heath's apartment.

"Don't believe the worst, Polly," I muttered to myself, getting up and snatching Heath's tee from the floor, smelling it first. The scent of him and I mixed together was calming. "He's probably gone for muffins or tea," I continued muttering to myself, looking to the bedside tables for a note.

Heath was a man who left notes. Because he was also the man who had an alarm clock directly in the middle of the bedside table, despite the fact he woke automatically at dawn. Well, he had before. I assumed that something they took such trouble to drum into you at basic training was something that was hard to shake.

And that's because who Heath was.

He wasn't as ordered or groomed on the outside as he had been in the Marines, but his apartment told me he still was on the inside.

Hence me looking for the note.

There was no note in the bedroom.

I padded into the kitchen, guessing it might be tacked on the naked fridge. But that didn't even have magnets to pin it on.

Who the heck didn't have *fridge magnets*?

The counter was clean, wiped down, mail stacked neatly to one side.

Again, no note.

That uncomfortable feeling settled in my stomach as I snatched my purse from the sofa I'd dumped it on last night.

I scrolled through my numerous messages and voicemails. Something that was the norm for me since none of my friends operated on the same timeline.

Nothing from Heath.

I sucked in a breath.

Was he doing it again? Was this his final revenge for everything I'd done to him? To use my body and soul and leave me the next morning without a goodbye, without anything?

I deserved it.

But Heath wasn't that man. To do such nasty things.

Craig was that man.

Heath wasn't one to act. Last night couldn't have been an act, what we'd shared. It was too bone shaking. Too visceral.

Craig was the one who perfected acts.

But then again, Heath had perfected the hatred toward me since I'd been back.

I couldn't even call him.

Because I didn't have his freaking number. I'd had it before I met Craig. In one of our many arguments about us, he'd snatched my phone, programmed his number into it and demand I use it "when I got my shit together."

I would lie in bed at three in the morning after hours of staring at that number, wishing I could get my shit together and press call.

You'd think I would've memorized it by now.

Heath would've had the same number. Because Heath was not like me and did not lose phones at least once a month. So even if I hadn't deleted his number when Craig and I had gotten engaged, I wouldn't have the same phone to call him on. I could've called Lucy or Keltan to ask for it. But then of course, they'd realize what me asking for his number would mean and they'd make a big *thing* of it.

And it was a big thing.

I hoped the biggest of all things.

But I wanted to keep it small for as long as I could. Small enough to hold onto. Treasure. Keep to myself.

I stood in the middle of Heath's living room holding my phone and my heart. I really hoped that the latter wasn't going to get broken again.

CHAPTER FOURTEEN

Heath

HE HAD LEFT HER. Without a note. Without waking her up.

He'd done so because she was dead to the world, she hadn't even exhaled roughly when he moved her off him. Fuck, he loved that. The way she clung to every inch of him in her sleep. No way in fuck would he classify himself as a 'cuddler.' Ever. But he found that Polly attached to him, sleeping deep and peacefully—something he knew was rare for her—was something more than cuddling.

It was fucking *everything*.

Knowing how little sleep she got, seeing how finally at peace she was in his arms was what made him not wake her up. Fuck, it had almost stopped him getting out of bed at all. But this was *their* morning. This was a fresh fucking morning.

A fresh fucking start.

Yeah, there was shit to sort.

A lot of shit.

Because clean slates were well and good in practice, but they didn't work in reality. And he wanted them to be in reality. Not some fantasy where they could go on from everything they'd been through without mentioning it.

Heath *didn't* want to mention it.

He didn't want to even think about her marrying another man. Building a life with him. Then breaking it apart.

He hated the thought of her with someone else. So bad he wanted to rip the skin from his body.

But what he hated more than that was the thought of her in any kind of pain. And that's what got him through when she'd actually married the fucker. That she wasn't in pain. That she was with someone else. Happy. It killed him that it wasn't with him, but he could breathe knowing she was happy.

But when it ended, he hadn't felt relief, not immediately. He felt dread, utter bone-deep dread at the thought of Polly going through pain. Because she put her whole heart into everything she did. And he knew that whatever everyone else thought, she wouldn't jump out of marriage as soon as she jumped in for no good reason.

And a good reason involved a fuck load of pain for her.

Then he'd turned cruel and bitter and contributed to that pain. He hurt her because he was hurt himself and he didn't deal with that shit well. Or at all.

Then that kiss.

That fucking kiss.

Every kiss with her was spectacular. Beyond anything. But every single one was something different. Because it meant so much more than a kiss. Ever since the first time she'd pressed her lips against his.

"I just wanted to see what it was like to kiss you."

The open honesty, the beauty of it hit him in the cock and

chest cavity simultaneously. And he knew then, in that shitty bar, in what he thought was going to be a shitty night—a shitty three days—that he'd found her.

Her in the sunflower dress and fucking pigtails.

Far too young for him.

Too good.

Too naive.

But he took her anyway because he'd known he couldn't have her forever, even if that's what he itched for. She was *it*. She was fucking *his*. And he wouldn't be able to have her. So he'd been greedy, needing to have as long as he could to carry him through the years.

That's why he reacted the way he did when he saw her again.

Like a fucking crazy person. Trying to claim her like the years hadn't passed. Because to him, they hadn't. She was still his. She was still *it*.

He wouldn't have come on like he did had he not seen it on her too. Because she wore her heart in her eyes, in the effort she put into hiding things from her sister. He saw that she wanted him too. And as a man who'd made an art out of controlling everything in his life, the fact he couldn't control the one thing that mattered drove him crazy.

So instead of being gentle, trying to see where she was coming from, he treated it like a battle, a war, reasoning he'd get through to her and then get her.

He'd tried to use a battle to get the girl who lived for peace.

He was a fucking idiot.

And he shouldn't have been surprised when she had another man. One that he hated instantly on principal and also because there was something off about him. But then he'd searched for evidence, a shred of it to give him a solid reason to kill the fucker.

He knew Lucy and Rosie were doing the same. No one found anything.

And Polly had her heart set on this. No, she had her *mind* set on it. He saw that. So he had to step aside. Let her work through it.

He hated it, but he'd gotten it.

He did not expect her to fucking *marry* the fucker. For him to push her that far away. Yeah, that fucked him up. He wanted to hate her just so he could stop wanting her.

But he didn't hate her.

Not when she walked down the aisle looking utterly beautiful but not like her.

Not when she left the man two months later. Not when she walked away from him for a fucking *year*.

And not when she came back.

But he acted like he hated her because he couldn't act like he had before. Because he was scared that he'd push her into the arms of someone else.

He'd hurt her acting like that. He'd seen it. Because he saw *everything* with her. And he wanted to stop, but he fucking couldn't. Because his coldness was the only thing he could control. Even if it was fucking bullshit.

He'd been driving her to hate him, so maybe he wouldn't love her so much. But every day, seeing how much she gave to everyone around her, even when it meant taking everything she had, watching her doing it with a brightness and that outshone the sun, he loved her more and more each day.

Yet he continued to hurt her. Even when it wasn't necessary. He didn't need to be following her around every day on some bullshit protection detail. He was worried about that fucker of an ex, but not enough to warrant the constant surveillance. He'd used that as an excuse to be with her every day. It was a shitty thing to do, even shittier because he treated her like dirt.

But she'd still fucking kissed him.

Walking away from her after that kiss was the hardest thing he'd ever done. No, leaving her after only forty-five hours of knowing her, of taking the most precious thing she had to give and taking it with him to get bloodied and dirtied by a war zone, *that* was the hardest.

Walking away after that kiss was a close second.

He'd done it because he knew she'd give him everything, even after the way he'd treated her. And he was mad as fuck with her for it all. But she didn't deserve the brunt of his rage. He knew that Craig had done something ugly to her. He didn't know what. But he knew it was something. Something she was hiding.

And he'd turned into a bad person. *She* hadn't turned him into that. Not on purpose. It was *them*. He'd been of the opinion that he wasn't going to make her forgive another man that didn't treat her right.

Him.

He was trying to be too fucking noble by walking away and he'd regretted it. But he held firm because that was who he is. He stuck to decisions. Even stupid fucking decisions.

He would've broken at some point. Maybe that very night. Since Duke had texted him and told him the name of the bar he'd damn near driven over there. Reading that had been a punch in the chest.

She went *there*.

After everything *he'd* done. Everything *she'd* done.

She fucking went there.

And then she came to his place.

Slept on his chest.

Rode his cock. Hard, fast, beautiful, fucking perfect.

And that was it. She was gonna be his. She was gonna *stay* his.

So he'd gone out to provide for his woman because he didn't have shit in his fridge to eat. 'Cause he'd been here as little as possible. Living here was his version of torture. Because it was full of her. It was all he fucking had of her.

And it was pathetic. His home that wasn't a home. No pictures. No personality. But she had seeped into the walls, and no way was he moving when that's all he had left. He could afford a bigger place. He could buy one.

Cash.

Keltan paid handsomely, he lived simple.

But what was the point?

Now there was a point.

He was making a mental note to hire an estate agent while loading his cart full of that healthy shit Polly loved. She took care of what she put into her body.

He liked that.

Even if it confused the shit out of him. What in the fuck was a chia seed pudding? He didn't know, but he had ten because he knew she ate them.

And didn't eat meat. That would be a transition since he was a carnivore. But he'd give up meat in a second if she asked. She wouldn't ask. She'd fry him a tenderloin every fucking night if he asked.

That was her.

His phone had rung as he was deciding between almond and oat milk. How the fuck did someone milk an almond? Or an oat for that matter? Throwing both in the cart, he'd answered.

"Need you in the office, now," Keltan clipped.

Heath was on alert the second he heard the tone of his friend's voice. Shit was going down. And when shit was going down, Heath was there. Because he had nowhere else to be and work was where he found his peace. Even if peace was helping Rosie chop the balls of a rapist when her husband was busy.

Or when her husband didn't know she was doing it since she was now pregnant.

"Can't come in," Heath replied.

There was a pause.

Heath knew why.

Because he'd never said no to Keltan. Not since he said yes to the job when he came out of the Marines.

"What? You on your deathbed, missing a limb?" Keltan demanded.

"Busy."

Another pause.

"You're never busy unless...fuck," Keltan muttered, putting two and two together. "Well, then you definitely better get in here."

Heath froze with some shit called kombucha in his hand. "What?"

"It has to do with Polly, or more accurately, to do with *Craig*, and it's not fuckin' good."

He left the cart and went straight to the office.

He should've called Polly, but he didn't. Because he assumed Polly would sleep most of the day away—she sure as shit needed it and he made sure to exhaust her—and he'd be back before she woke up.

He didn't plan on it being any other way.

Didn't plan on his whole fucking world blowing apart.

Lucy

Being pregnant *sucked.*

I didn't care what all the movies and books said about it being a glorious and beautiful time of growth and new life, it was utter bullshit.

I had a backache. I'd already thrown up three times today and it was barely noon. I could be sure I'd throw up at least another three times. Whoever coined the term 'morning sickness' was full of shit and I would've sued them if I could.

I had heartburn hotter than Satan's fireplace. My ankles were starting to look a little puffier than usual and I had to wear an *elasticated waist.*

Yes, I loved that Keltan's child was growing inside me, and the way he protectively placed his hand over my bump at every moment, but the rest of it was *bullshit.*

Especially since I was pregnant everyone decided that I was now an invalid. Keltan included. I wasn't allowed to do anything *fun.* Not blow things up. Not investigate the latest string of women gone missing from L.A. in disturbing numbers. I'd tried to, of course. But my editor had snitched on me. My editor who had been held in contempt of court for not divulging his sources gave into Keltan. The United States Court system he hadn't bowed down to. But somehow he was my husband's errand boy.

And my husband has taken me off the story.

Then he'd used emotional blackmail to keep me off when I protested.

"I watched you bleed out on the fucking street for a story," he hissed. "I almost lost you. You've got my whole world inside you. My baby, your lungs, still drawin' breath. So you're not doin' a story that could threaten that. You want to threaten that, Snow?

Obviously I'd look like an asshole if I continued doing the story behind his back.

So I relented.

Only because I'd gotten the next best reporter at the paper on it and giving me updates. Which was allowed since I wasn't technically *on* the story. And also Keltan didn't know. Which was good, since pregnancy was making him as insane as it was making me nauseous.

He'd tried to take heels from me. *Heels*.

At least Rosie was in it with me. We hadn't planned being pregnant at the same time, but it was pretty fucking awesome. Or it would've been if I had someone to suffer with. But the bitch didn't have *any* morning sickness and my hormones were making that in itself seem like a reason to cut off all ties and never see her again. And also snitch to Luke about her taking cases behind his back. But that would mean that I'd have to tell him Heath was involved. Then he'd kill Heath. Then Polly would get mad.

And no matter what was going on with them right now, Polly would care if Luke killed Heath. Because things would work out. They had to work out. Polly deserved it. And despite my low opinion of him currently, so did Heath.

Keltan had to go into work early for some emergency. Which meant I didn't even have morning sex to perk me up. Now *that* was a good thing about being pregnant. My sex drive was ramped up like a thousand percent. And if there was one place where Keltan was willing to stop treating me like I was going to break, it was the bedroom.

I was tired, cranky from decaf coffee, vaguely thinking I'd be throwing up again soon and praying that my feet wouldn't become too big for Manolos. I needed cheering up. So I was going to Polly's.

I was thinking she might cheer me up. Since Duke had the

biggest mouth in the office and he'd informed me—under only the smallest amount of duress—where Polly had been dropped off last night.

And no one had heard from her since.

Or Heath.

Fine-fucking-ly.

Before this, I was starting to get scared. That my beautiful, kind, caring, hopeless romantic sister was going to be the exception to the alpha male rule. The rule that said when an alpha male found it—the mystical *it* that lived in the woman perfectly imperfect for them, the mystical *it* that was *that* woman—he didn't let go. He wouldn't stop fighting.

I started to fear he'd stopped fighting.

That there would not be some sort of grand overcoming of the obstacles between them.

Granted they were a lot different than what we'd seen, but Heath loved her. It was painfully obvious. And just plain painful.

Because it wasn't a beautiful, storybook kind of love. No, it was the kind of love that you saw chewing at his very insides. Like leading up to the wedding. Polly's short marriage. Her divorce. Her disappearance to Europe. Her reappearance.

And when I saw my sister, I saw the pain there too. Nothing that had ever been on that face of hers before, despite being 'in love' more times than I could count. She'd been in love but never truly miserable until Heath. Which meant she'd never been in love until Heath.

Hopefully they'd boinked each other's brains out and all was well.

I'd known that Heath would've gotten called into this emergency meeting so I was deciding to chance the fact that Polly was home and was going to give me all the details.

And that she'd be smiling.

Really smiling.

But when I got to her door—which was ajar, not unheard of for Polly, since she sometimes left it like that when she'd lost her keys—she was not smiling. Because she was unconscious and bleeding from her head.

And there was someone standing over her.

That fucking *prick* of an ex-husband.

I rushed toward her on instinct, my hand reaching into my purse for my gun, until I realized it wasn't there.

I realized that right at the same time Craig—the fucking asshole—punched me in the face. Then I joined my sister on the ground, the punch not enough to knock me out so I twirled in the air to best protect my baby.

Such a twist did not protect my head which whacked against the floor with enough force to knock me out.

Keltan

He had been prepared for Heath to come storming into the office. Anything to do with Polly had him storming, swearing and almost murdering Duke moving some file in his anal as fuck office.

This was under *normal* circumstances. Or whatever circumstances passed for normal when Polly was involved.

He loved his sister-in-law, not just because of her connection to the woman he loved more than anything in this world, but because Polly was completely and utterly unique. Because it was impossible not to love her. She was sunshine in a fucking person. Everyone saw that. But you can't bottle sunshine, can't own it. Can't hold it down. Many poor fuckers tried.

And watching a man he respected and liked try, and fail, it was fucked. More so when he saw that Polly wanted that man too. And for reasons known only to Polly, she married another man. Maybe because what was between the two of them wasn't sunshine.

He'd been quietly hopeful about recent events bringing them together.

Especially since Heath had stormed into the office the night Craig accosted Polly and demand they put a rotation on her.

"As much as I wanna keep Polly safe, and I do, no matter how impossible that job is, I don't think he's a threat," Keltan said, *planning on paying a visit to Craig. Or more accurately, his fist taking a visit to his face.*

But, by the looks of Heath's knuckles, that had already been done.

"He's not a threat? He overturned a fucking table in a restaurant in public. Would've put his hands on her if Polly hadn't tased him," Heath yelled.

Heath didn't yell. He was cool under pressure. In normal circumstances. In extenuating circumstances.

But not with Polly.

Keltan wouldn't have believed Polly willingly tased someone —even her husband advancing on her with violence in his eyes—if he hadn't seen the video for himself.

She was all about 'do no harm' and all that shit. It was comical that she was Lucy's sister since Lucy had suggested they castrate Craig the second she learned about the divorce.

Keltan had been more than willing.

But both him and his wife and held back because of Polly. Because they loved and respected her and hurting anyone she still cared about would cause her pain. And she still cared about the fucker. Remained tight-lipped as to the reasons for the divorce and did not say one bad word against him.

Not one.

So yeah, it had hit Keltan when he saw the video.

"He's a man scorned," Keltan said. "He saw Polly on a date. He was drunk. You're telling me that *was an accident?" He nodded toward Heath's knuckles.*

"No way it was an accident," Heath clipped. "It was violence directed nowhere near Polly. I don't have a good feeling about this guy, Keltan. Haven't since the start."

Keltan raised his brow. "Haven't since you found out he was marrying the woman you loved?"

Heath didn't reply.

Of course he wasn't going to reply to that shit.

But he also agreed with him. Keltan hadn't liked him either. He was too polished. Too charismatic. Too all over Polly. And not in a way that he didn't want to stop touching her because he loved her. No, because he wanted to communicate possession. Ownership.

You couldn't own sunshine. Keltan knew the fucker would get educated on that. He just hadn't expected it to go as far as the wedding. Granted he'd been distracted leading up to the wedding since his wife had been recovering from the stab wound that almost killed her.

In fact, there was no almost about it.

It had *killed her. Twice.*

She'd come back.

And he thanked the Lord every fucking day. Thanked her. Since it wasn't a lord that brought her back to him. It was her.

So he was distracted when Polly had brought Craig into the fold.

Not distracted enough not to do his job—protect Lucy. And he'd failed on a sidewalk weeks before. He didn't plan on doing that again. Protecting Lucy meant protecting Polly.

"We did a background on him. Found nothing two years ago," he reminded Heath.

"I don't care. She needs a team."

"Okay, I'll put Duke on it," Keltan relented. He would admit he'd be at ease knowing someone was keeping an eye on Polly.

He worried for her.

"No fuckin' way. I'm on it," Heath clipped.

Keltan raised his brow. "Didn't think you'd want to be anywhere near her."

Heath gave him a hard look. "You want to be near Lucy?"

"Every fuckin' second."

"Then I'm on her."

And that was it.

He kept it quiet when Polly assumed he was responsible for the detail. Better to let things happen organically.

And they had happened, last night, if this morning's conversation was anything to go by.

And the timing could not have been fucking worse.

"We found something on Craig."

Heath froze.

He didn't speak since he knew Keltan wasn't done.

"Still waitin' for more info, but there's intel to tell us he's been seen with The Sixth Street Gang. Who had been low-level assholes until recently. Now, they're connected to Fernandez."

Heath's eyes turned to granite. "The human trafficker Rosie tried to bring down?"

Keltan nodded. "The one that we're working with the Sons to end. Smartly."

Smartly meant patiently. Meant they had to play a long fucking game. Which frustrated the fuck out of them, Luke most of all, since the fucker had kidnapped his wife. And it fucked with all of them since the fucker was responsible for trafficking women all over the world.

Taking him down was on top of their list.

But he was smart. He knew that people would want to end him. He had all sorts of fail-safes in place in order to destroy anyone who tried. So they couldn't try. They had to succeed.

They would.

But while they were playing their game, Fernandez was playing his.

"How in the fuck did we not catch this earlier?" Heath demanded.

"'Cause we thought that he was clean, and we looked deep. But didn't know to look for this kind of shit," Keltan said. "Encrypted shit that Wire is only now trying to decipher. Craig never did face to face shit. All his money came legal." He clenched his fists. "Or places that *appeared* legal. Convincingly so. Enough to hold up against an FBI investigation. Didn't think to look in places Wire is finding now he knows where to look. And by chance I had a man on him, he snapped the photo. Caught the connection."

Heath's fists were clenched against his sides. The only sign of him losing control. But that sign meant a fuck of a lot. Keltan knew this because it was the last point before he stopped clenching his fists and started using them. "Okay, we'll end him, make sure Polly doesn't find out, of course," he said evenly. "But I don't think this qualifies as a reason to take me away from the one good morning I've had in years."

Keltan sucked in a breath. "There's more."

Luke and Duke took now as the moment to enter the room. Good thing too, since they might need all three of them to lock him down.

Heath's eyes didn't move from Keltan's. "More enough to think you need Luke and Duke to lock me down," he said, reading Keltan like he always did. Fucker noticed everything. Came to every conclusion.

"They're here because we need the team on this," Keltan said. They hadn't been briefed yet, but both of them looked grim. Keltan focused on Heath. "Need you to make sure you handle this. First, I'm guessing Polly is at your place?"

Heath nodded once.

Keltan exhaled. "I'll get Lance over there."

Heath stiffened further. He knew what it meant if Keltan was sending Lance right now. Lance was relatively new, but he was good. Quiet. Ruthless. And would protect any of their women with his life. Mostly because he didn't seem to value it that much.

They'd all been through shit.

But Lance had been through *shit*.

"You need to tell me what's goin' on right now so I can get my ass over there," Heath clipped.

"My man didn't just see Craig talking to this guy," Keltan said, speaking slowly, carefully. But then how careful could you be when you were tearing through a man's world? "Saw him handing him something. And it just so happens he's got a good camera and was curious why he was handing him something physical when everything is done virtually now." Keltan sucked in a breath hoping that Heath didn't break the furniture. Not that he blamed him. "It was a photo of Polly."

Duke sucked in a harsh breath.

Luke swore.

Heath had no response whatsoever.

"You're tellin' me that Polly's ex-husband—who you fuckin' told me wasn't a threat—handed over a photo of Polly to someone connected to the biggest human trafficker in the world?" Heath asked, voice mild.

"Brother—"

"Where is he now?" he asked, voice still mild.

"Got my man on him," Keltan replied, the rest of his response drowned out by the ringing of his phone he glanced down. "That's him."

"Well get him to give me an exact location," Heath demanded. He glanced to Luke. "Also get in contact with the man Rosie uses to cremate her bodies. He'll have a job soon."

Luke nodded once, getting up to do so.

It would've been funny, the prior police chief organizing a body disposal. The fact he did it semiregularly with his wife. It would've been had it not been for the dread that had settled in Keltan's bones since he found out about the photo.

It only increased when the man on the other end of the phone spoke. "What the fuck do you mean, *lost him*?" he demanded.

"I don't know, man," Ron said. "I had him. Thought he was too fucking dumb to even notice he had a tail let alone lose one."

This fucker had them all fooled. And Keltan hoped it wasn't a fatal mistake. "Where did you lose him?" he demanded. The fact he lost Ron was big. He was one of the best. Ex Secret Service. It was no small feat to shake his tail.

"Beverly Hills," Ron said. "But I just got signal in the tracker I installed. He's nowhere near there."

"Where is he?"

Keltan's blood went cold the second he told him.

And it turned to fucking ice when he hung up and saw the message Lucy had sent him that he'd somehow missed.

Snow: *I've thrown up three times. Yes, this is too much information but you put the baby in me and you don't have to*

experience this first hand so you at least have to know what you're doing to me. Plus you left before morning sex. That's cruel and unusual punishment.
I'm at Polly's. I think she got laid last night. Hopefully she'll distract me from wanting to barf.
Get home quick so you can distract me with sex.
I promise I won't barf.
Not until after.
Kisses
xxx

•

KELTAN'S CHAIR smashed against the wall with the force he'd pushed out of it.

Duke and Heath were on alert. But he didn't even spare a second to talk to them. He was too busy running out the door. Because the place they had Craig's signal was where his pregnant wife was.

Polly's apartment.

Lucy

"I didn't have my gun," I said woodenly.

Keltan's hand was on my belly, eyes on mine. Neither his eyes nor his hand had moved since I woke up in his arms on Polly's floor.

The expression on his face was only slightly less dire than it had been then. Now we were in a hospital and both me and the baby had been cleared, the only injury the bruise I'd have on my face from the punch and the lump on the back of my head from where I'd hit the ground.

I didn't even have a concussion.

I'd had much worse. But because I was pregnant everyone treated it like the end of the world. When really the end of the world was the fact the last time I'd seen my sister she was bleeding from the fucking *head.*

"What?" Keltan asked, obviously confused at my words.

I blinked against the pain in my head. It was manageable. The fear running through my veins was not. "I didn't have my gun because you took it off me so I couldn't shoot the man who made my sister bleed from the head and *who has her now*. A man that is obviously not afraid to hurt women. Pregnant women."

Keltan flinched at this, but I didn't have it in me to care. Or at least to show that I cared. All my caring was taken up for my sister.

I stared at my husband coldly. "Now, someone has to be really fucked up to hit a pregnant woman."

Another flinch.

I continued. "But to hit a creature like *Polly*..." I trailed off, unable to get that image of her lying unconscious out of my mind, "that's like shooting a fucking *dove.* Someone that does stuff like that is capable of a lot of things, Keltan."

Now pregnancy had nothing to do with my sudden urge to vomit.

"Things that Polly should never even *hear* about let alone *experience,*" I choked out. "And he has her now, this monster with a stupid fucking name because I didn't have my gun because *you took it off me* because apparently being pregnant makes me more *volatile.* When volatile was *exactly* what I needed to be to save my little sister. But I couldn't. Because of *you.*"

"Lucy," Keltan said softly, not even blinking at the cruel

misplaced blame I was hurling at his feet. His hand moved up to lightly cup my bruised face. "We're gonna find her. We're gonna kill him. I'm gonna kill him with my bare fuckin' hands for layin' a hand on my family. Riskin' my whole fucking world."

He paused abruptly, his eyes going to the heartbeat monitor as if he needed to make sure it was real, that the baby was okay before he kept going.

"We'll kill him then we'll find Polly. In one piece. Because she's *Polly*. And you know she's one of the strongest people you know. In a way that's different than anyone around us. If anyone can survive a monster, it's Polly." He laid his lips to my temple. "But right now, I want you to control what you can control. And that's taking care of our baby. Because you know how much Polly loves it already. You know how protective of it she is. And when we find her, you know she'll be more worried about you and that baby than she will be about herself."

A tear ran down my cheek. "You'll find her? In one piece?"

He kissed my tear away. "I promise," he said, even though we both knew it was a promise he couldn't keep.

"You'll kill that fucker, Craig?" I prompted, knowing there was no way he'd let me do it myself.

"Yes, babe," he all but hissed.

And that was a promise he could keep.

I just prayed to every single god out there that they found him before he killed that beautiful innocence that was inside of Polly.

Heath

Three Hours Missing

The elastic on his wrist snapped at a steady rhythm that was designed to calm him. Or more accurately, the demons inside him.

It was some shit that the military shrink had suggested to him. All of the other stuff she spouted was bullshit, but this one thing seemed to work for him when he was about to go dark side.

The elastic snapped.

It was safe to say it wasn't working for him now.

"We got anything?" he demanded the second Keltan closed the door.

He didn't school his tone. It was savage, rough and aggressive. Just like his fuckin' soul.

He should've taken the effort, taking in Keltan as he sat at his desk. The fucker was carrying the weight of the world on his shoulders. Considering his woman was his world and her sister was a big part of hers, it was a load. Especially considering what he'd gone through to make her his wife. Especially since they'd rushed into Polly's apartment to find his pregnant fucking wife unconscious on the floor next to a pool of blood.

What they'd found out later was Polly's blood.

He saw it on his friend's face as he dropped to his knees, cradled his pregnant and unconscious wife in his arms, murmuring to her about breathing, about staying still. It was remnant of when he almost lost her on a sidewalk two years ago.

And now there was this shit.

Keltan was one of his closest friends.

They'd gone through shit together.

Shit you never talked about once you got home, once you stood on soil that wasn't stained with the blood of your brothers, of those you'd killed. Because if you talked about it, you had to really question the reasons your brothers in arms were killed, why their wives were widowed and the children fatherless. Then you had to question those people you'd killed, someone else's brothers, fathers, husbands. Then you might have to face the terrifying fucking reality that they were all savages, killing each other for no reason other then the orders of the men above them.

So they didn't talk about it.

And it was in their silence that they found solidarity. As much peace as they could.

Which was why Heath had jumped at the chance to work in his security firm. He was doing shit he wasn't proud of before. Chasing violence because that's all his soul knew. All his soul craved.

No, that was a lie.

His soul craved a blonde haired, peace-loving, chaos-bringing girl who'd turned into a woman with his dick inside her.

Yeah, he fucking craved her.

If he was honest with himself, it was her words that managed to roar over the gunshots coming from his piece when he was ending the lives of other human beings. It was her face he held onto when he was presented with the charred remains of one of the first men he'd met upon arriving in the fucking desert.

It was her touch he remembered when a bullet tore through his side, when he had to continue even though his side was on fire, blood was pouring from the wound, as he was certain he'd fucking die if he kept running. Kept fighting.

But there was a starker truth that he'd die when he stopped running. Stopped fighting. So he held onto the image of the woman who told him she fought for peace when he fought for war.

And it was that woman's face he held onto to stop him from ripping the skin from his fucking arms, because he had to hold onto that smile, that peace that she told him she lived by. He had to fucking kid himself thinking it wouldn't be that penchant for peace that would kill her.

He almost fucking threw up his breakfast on that thought. Would've if his breakfast was anything more than black coffee. As it was, it came up enough to burn the back of his throat.

Because he'd been planning on having breakfast with her. Even eating that healthy shit. He'd been planning on having her pussy for breakfast first. He'd been planning on having her all fucking day.

And the day after.

He could still smell her on his fucking skin she was that close.

But he also couldn't get the vision of the small pool of her blood on the floor out of his mind. Best case scenario, that was all the blood that was spilled. But it was hers. Even in the best case, she was *hurt*. She *bled*.

Worst case...Heath didn't even have the strength to think about.

So he focused on Keltan and Keltan's answer on what the fuck they were doing to find Craig since he'd disappeared into thin fucking air. With Polly. He'd left the ride they had the tracker in the parking lot. Left it like he left that little puddle of blood and a bruised, unconscious, pregnant Lucy.

Fucker was *taunting* them.

"Got the Sons on it too," Keltan said, his very words a sigh, but every inch of him was held tight. Taut.

Heath was one of the few who knew just how dangerous, how fucking ruthless this fucker was. Of course, you had to look at him to know that. His muscles weren't for the gym. Weren't pumped up with fucking chemicals.

No, they were for a purpose.

To hurt and end human beings.

But it was something beyond that.

Especially after he'd lost his best friend. Heath hadn't been there when it happened, but he had been there when Keltan had to be forcibly removed from Ian's body.

Keltan broke that day. When you see your brother in everything but blood, mangled flesh, and bone for a war that meant fucking nothing but money and power, your view of the world gets warped. Or maybe you see everything for how fucking ugly it is.

And it fucks you up. In a way that most men come back to their families and a life that's not about surviving by killing and they can't handle that. Because no one *gets it.* That's why so many eat a bullet. Yell at their kids and their wives until they scare them enough to leave. Then they find a bottle, if only to forget how fucked up everything is.

The great fucking system.

Keltan was lucky.

He had a woman that showed him the world wasn't all pain and ugliness. Or maybe it still was, but he didn't give a fuck because he had her. Lucy had saved him, and Keltan was man enough to admit it.

Polly had saved Heath.

And he had not been man enough to admit it.

Because he had been angry.

Still too angry at the fucking world, and that meant he didn't understand her. Because *she* wasn't angry. She found joy in the world.

And because he couldn't fucking understand that, he'd fucked it up. He'd hurt her. Because she'd hurt him. And he was trained to hurt people that hurt him. He was trained to destroy him.

He hadn't even had a chance to truly show her that he was going to put her back together if it took the rest of his life.

The rest of both their lives.

His hands fisted atop the table.

"They get shit?" Duke asked, glancing to Heath, knowing he was holding it together by a thread.

Duke hadn't been with them, he was deep Special Ops. He didn't say shit about what he'd done. Uncle Sam probably made sure he'd rot in a cell for the rest of eternity if he did so. But he didn't need to say shit.

He was an intelligent motherfucker, as well as deadly. His smile was a front for something much darker.

"Their hacker has something," Keltan said, glancing to Heath too. They didn't know the full story with Polly.

They didn't even know half of the fucking story.

But they knew enough.

Keltan had known enough to let him go when Polly had got married. Respected him enough to give him nothing but a clap on the back and not a single question when he returned.

They knew that Polly was his.

And now she was *gone.*

Keltan knew what that was like better than anyone else.

So did Luke, who was silent across the table.

He was fighting shit too. Because his woman was like a sister to Polly. And his woman took shit hard. Because she'd seen and done shit that made her worthy of a place at the table with these men.

She was battle worn in a lot of the ways they were. And a lot of the ways they weren't. Heath didn't scare easily, but that woman could be downright terrifying. And just as dangerous as every single man at that table.

She could handle herself.

But Luke did everything he could to handle shit so she didn't have to. Which was, of course, a constant battle with someone like Rosie.

Though now she was pregnant it was one Luke won.

Only after he'd physically dragged her out of a drug dealer's house.

Heath only did missions with her because he knew she'd do them alone and he figured it was better for her to have backup. And he knew that she loved her child more than anything, she wouldn't put it in danger. He'd planned on putting a stop to it when she started to show.

But she had done that herself.

"It better be the location of that fuck, and more importantly, Polly," Heath said through gritted teeth.

It had been three hours.

Three hours.

A lot could happen in three hours.

And it wasn't death.

Death could happen in three seconds. That wasn't the thing drawing poison through Heath's system.

It was all the other shit that would kill all the beauty in Polly's soul. It might not take three hours to kill it all, because she was strong. But even killing a fucking inch of that was enough to haunt Heath for the rest of his days.

"Not yet. But he's got intel on someone who might now."

Duke stood. "On it."

Heath wanted to go too. But he couldn't trust himself not to kill the man before they got the right information. And making someone wish they were dead, think they were dead without killing them was Duke's specialty.

He trusted that man with his life. And with Polly's. Which were one in the same.

SIX HOURS MISSING

He was about to crawl out of his skin. He was ready to tear it apart so he could feel something that wasn't the utter fucking helplessness that was sitting in this fucking room not being able to do shit to help Polly.

Not being able to kill the fuck who made her bleed.

Duke was still working on the man.

But he was deep in the business, and they were trained to withstand torture. If he didn't break soon, Heath was going to break him, if only to fuel his need for violence, for death.

Keltan had been in and out, checking on Lucy, who was in the bedrooms in the other wing of the offices. He'd only let her discharge herself because they had an on-call doctor with her.

Fucker wasn't taking any chances.

Neither would Heath.

Ever a-fucking-gain.

It was just him and Luke now. Luke had been exhausting all his contacts in and out of the law enforcement. They'd put APBS out on Craig. On women matching Polly's descriptions. Were running any cars that were stolen from the same area Polly was taken. Running all of Craig's cards.

And they were coming up with shit.

The door burst open.

"Are you fucking *kidding* me?" a female voice demanded.

Luke moved the second the owner of the voice stormed into that room.

She held up her hand to her husband. "Don't you come near me," she hissed. "You don't get to come near me when I have to find out from one of my sources that there's a missing person's alert out for Polly. My sister. And then my other sister, who is pregnant, *got punched in the face* by Polly's total fucking *asshole* of an ex-husband." She pointed at Luke as he opened his mouth and tried to move forward. "I. Am. Not. Done," she seethed. "I am also armed. And I wouldn't normally shoot the father of my baby, not even to get on Jerry Springer, but this qualifies as extenuating circumstances." Her voice shook, from what most people would've thought was fury, considering she just threatened to shoot her husband.

But Heath knew her, saw more than most people. And she was holding on by a thread. And her voice was shaking with terror. It took a lot to scare Rosie.

"You decide to keep that shit from me when I could've fucking helped," she hissed.

"You had an ultrasound," Luke said, voice soft. "They were checking to make sure you didn't have placenta previa. If you did, anything upsetting, anything raising your blood pressure will risk *you* and the fucking *baby*."

"And you think my blood pressure is nice and steady right now?" she screeched.

Keltan entered the room, upon seeing Rosie, he muttered, "fuck."

She raised her brow. "Fuck is right."

"Sit," he said, nodding to the table.

"Are you telling me that because I'm pregnant and I couldn't possibly stand just like I couldn't possibly handle the news of Polly being kidnapped as soon as it motherfucking happened?" she demanded.

"Rosie," Luke murmured.

"Nope," she hissed at him.

Keltan rounded his desk and sat. "I'm telling you to sit because we need to talk." He gave Heath a look. "All of us."

"Whatever," Rosie muttered, sitting beside Heath.

She reached across and squeezed his hand.

That was Rosie. She was hard as nails but was soft where it counted.

"Wire just gave me some info," Keltan said once Rosie had quietened enough for him to speak, she was glaring at her husband and he was glaring at her.

"You remember the shooting that you were involved in with Polly last year?" he asked Rosie.

Luke stiffened.

As did Heath at the memory. But not for the same reason as Luke. Or maybe for precisely the same reason, because someone tried to tear through their whole world with bullets.

"I vaguely recall it," Rosie said dryly.

"We assumed it was to do with your shit because, well, you're you," Keltan said.

"Aww you're so sweet," Rosie said, forcing a grin.

"Let me guess, it was aimed at Polly?" Heath said, the words acid coming out. He needed to remind himself that none of those bullets hit her then. But that was hard as fuck to do when he had no idea what was hitting her *now*.

Keltan nodded.

The room turned wired.

"Okay, it's fine to shoot at me, but at Polly?" Rosie said.

"It's never okay to shoot at you," Luke hissed.

"Not the time," she muttered back.

"It was some kind of threat to Craig, as much as we know," Keltan explained. "Apparently he was getting in deeper when he'd only been low level at the start. He was causing enough shit that they sent him a message. Obviously they didn't know they were separated by that point. Which I'm still confused about." He looked to Rosie. "Is the reason she divorced him because of that?"

Heath knew that wasn't true. Because Polly wouldn't have protected him if she knew he was at all connected in human trafficking. No matter her views on peace or feelings toward him.

He knew what it wasn't, but still, he had no fucking clue what it was. He had been planning on gently probing it out of her in the periods he wasn't fucking her today.

He'd thought they had time.

He was a fucking hopeful idiot.

Rosie's expression changed. She pursed her lips.

"Now is not the time to protect Polly's secrets," Heath clipped. "Not if it could be the reason we fucking find her."

"It won't," Rosie said.

"You can't know that," Heath replied.

She didn't back down. "I can."

"Rosie, they need to know this shit," Luke said, his voice soft as if he were trying to protect her. Heath didn't give a fuck about protecting Rosie's feelings right now.

"No, this will only distract them from what they need to figure out. Which is where Polly is," she said.

"Just fucking tell us!" Heath roared.

Rosie jumped. And not because she was jumpy at all by nature. She was harder to shock than Duke. But Heath didn't yell. Not at anyone. Especially not at women.

"He hit her," she said, voice small, a contrast to Heath's roar. The three words silenced the room.

Keltan's face drained of all color.

Heath's body drained of oxygen.

He hit her.

He hit her.

He couldn't stop the words from screaming in his mind.

"That's why she left him," Rosie continued. "She swore us to secrecy because she knew how much it would hurt Lucy." Her eyes found Heath. "How much it would hurt you."

"Of course, she's the one whose husband hits her, and she worries about how that'll hurt everyone around her," Heath spat.

Rosie flinched.

Luke glared at him.

He didn't give a fuck.

Because Polly had carried that around for two years.

This fucker didn't hesitate to hit her when she was with him when he had her as his wife. Now he didn't...

"Rosie's right," Keltan clipped cutting off Heath's toxic thought. "As much as that makes me wish we'd castrated him when Lucy first suggested it, it doesn't change anything now. And there's more. These fuckers have had their eyes on her since the divorce. Probably since the marriage. They trailed her around Europe."

Heath stopped breathing.

"Only reason they didn't snatch her because she moved so often, so erratically, they couldn't pin her down."

"You're telling me that Polly unwittingly evaded some of the most ruthless fuckers on in the world just because...she's Polly?" Rosie asked in disbelief.

Keltan nodded proudly, trying to grin. It didn't work. "Yeah, that's about the size of it." He moved to eye Heath. "Seems I owe you an apology since if we hadn't started her security detail, they likely would've snatched her if we weren't a constant and visible presence."

An apology didn't mean shit, especially since they snatched her anyway.

An apology wouldn't save her.

Sure as shit wouldn't save him.

CHAPTER FIFTEEN

Polly

Eight Hours Missing

IT WAS SHOCKING to be kidnapped.

I was a lot more shocked than I should've been, considering my family's history with such things. Rosie had been kidnapped. International drug dealers had tried to kidnap Lucy but failed. Then they stabbed her in the middle of the day on the street and almost killed her.

My stomach roiled with that thought, that memory.

She's safe, I chanted to myself.

She's safe and she got out of that which means you will get out of this too.

Even though it hadn't actually hit me that *I was in this.*

That I was in a dated, obviously cheap and thankfully clean hotel room, and chained to the bed. With a black eye. Well, I didn't know for sure that it was actually black. It felt hot, it was throbbing, and the skin below and above my eye felt tight and swollen.

The back of my head was throbbing too, and it felt sticky and hot. From me cutting it as I hit the floor.

That was from Craig punching me in the face.

I'd told myself, I'd *promised* myself that he wouldn't lay a hand on me again. But such things weren't exactly within my control when he turned up at the door and said hello—and goodbye—with his fist.

I'd come home from Heath's after deciding I couldn't wait in that apartment for a second longer. Not like I did last time.

Last time I spent the whole day there, entertaining the fantasy that Heath didn't get on a plane, he came back, picked me up and we spent a life together, on the run. From war. From peace.

Of course, my sister had called frantic that I'd been in some kind of "Vegan Coma"—her words— and I'd had to leave.

I couldn't stay like last time, nurturing a hope that might get shattered. I forced myself to get an Uber home. I was still wearing Heath's tee. I hadn't showered. I smelled like him. Like us.

I'd answered the door smiling because I thought it was him.

But it wasn't.

It was Craig. Smiling wickedly, coldly and then...nothing.

And I woke up here. Chained to a bed.

I wasn't quite sure it was just the punch and the head wound that had knocked me out, because there was a heavy and blurry quality to my thoughts that hinted that I'd been injected with something.

Since drugs could knock me out for an hour or a day, I didn't know how long I'd been here.

Though in addition to my throbbing eye, my arms screamed

from their position above my head, my wrists felt raw from the rubbing of the cuffs, my bladder was uncomfortably full—to the point of bursting—and my stomach was painfully empty.

I would hazard a guess to say I'd been here for a while.

And I couldn't even fathom that I was actually here. Sure, that break from reality probably had something to do with whatever chemicals were coursing through my system, but a lot of it was pure naive disbelief.

Because although violence and kidnapping were somewhat of a regular occurrence with my extended family, it was something that never happened in *my* life. My life was designed around peace. Chaos, too, but a peaceful kind of chaos. The chaos that had me deciding to camp in the desert with four friends for five days, not the kind of chaos that would get me chained to a bed with a bruised face.

And there was surprise that Craig would actually do this. I shouldn't have been surprised, considering he had no qualms hitting me in the face when I was his wife, so it stood to reason that kidnapping me and hitting me in the face was not a problem now that I was his ex-wife.

But I was still surprised.

Because there was something off inside him, something broken.

But I had been under the impression that there was still *something* inside of him. Something that he'd shown me to make me fall in love with him, something human and vulnerable and something that somewhere along the way had been ruined and broken by someone else.

It wasn't a thought process I was proud of. But I liked to believe the best in people. The world did enough for us as a society to expect the worst in everyone. Our very media was saturated with human brutality, with fathers killing children, women killing husbands, with senseless violence, genocide, war. It was so much so that it was our default to brace against the brutality of our race.

Because we were never shown the kindness. Never shown the woman who spent her time and money volunteering in children's shelters after she'd lost her only child to cancer. The couple that had been together for fifty years and died within minutes of each other because they couldn't stand to breathe in a world where the other didn't exist.

Kindness didn't sell newspapers.

Because people didn't *believe* it. They were conditioned to expect, consume and crave violence on some level.

And I rebelled against that.

My entire life.

I was lucky I had a family that nurtured this belief, even if they didn't completely agree with it.

I missed my family with an ache that was bone deep right now. I wondered how long I'd been gone. If they were worrying. If Lucy was worrying so much that it hurt the baby. I prayed no one had noticed I was gone, if only to save them from that.

Wait, I needed them to notice I was gone. Since I needed them to rescue me.

"Oh Polly, ever the damsel," I muttered.

I MUST'VE DOZED off to sleep at some point because the slamming of the door jerked me awake.

I had a moment of panic and confusion at the fact my hands wouldn't obey me and every one of my muscles screamed. The panic was not because of the burning and immobile arms above my head, or my screaming bladder, or empty stomach. No, it was because I had no memory of why they existed.

I blinked Craig into view and it all came rushing back.

"You're awake," he said, rather sheepishly, not holding eye contact.

He looked bad.

His eyes were bloodshot. Shirt was wrinkled and stained with something that looked like coffee. His hair was a mess.

Sweat beaded on his forehead.

"I need to pee," I said.

Not the first thing that a victim should've said to her captor/ex-husband. I should've asked why he was here, or why *I* was here, what he planned on doing with me and if he could please not kill me or do anything else unimaginable and just let me go.

But my bladder was straining to keep under my brain's control, and I was not going to wet myself on top of everything else.

Craig paused, obviously surprised at my words.

He rubbed the back of his hand over his mouth as if he were pondering whether he was going to grant me the right to meet my basic human needs. It was jarring and humiliating to have someone in control of whether you let go of your bladder while chained to a bed or whether you would be allowed to use a toilet.

Something glinted in Craig's eyes as he ran them over me, something like satisfaction in that control, something ugly and vile that sent ice into the base of my spine.

He paused long enough for me to think he was going to make me wet myself just for his cruel entertainment. Then he walked over, dug his hand into his pocket and retrieved a small pair of keys.

"Don't try and run," he warned, eyes dark.

I shivered at what was behind them. Not a threat. A promise. But there was something mingled with that. Not pure malice. There was a panic. A kind of hopelessness. I knew he was a bad person. But what turned a bad person into an evil person was that hopelessness. With nothing left to lose, evil bred.

"I'm not going to try to run because I'm currently trying not to wet myself," I said truthfully.

It was funny how something as seemingly simple as needing to use the bathroom could surpass needing to know the reason for one's kidnapping and the fate of one's life.

He inspected my words and the desperation behind them and nodded once, lifting the keys.

My hands were lead when the metal came off.

They literally thumped onto the mattress, not at all under my control.

I tried to use them to push off the bed, but they wouldn't hold my weight, they barely twitched in response to my brain's command. I desperately scooted with the rest of my body protesting at the use of muscles that had long since locked up having been in such an unnatural position for so long. I worried that even now that I was free, I wouldn't be able to make it from the bed to the bathroom.

My knees buckled when I put weight on them. I half limped, half ran to the bathroom, my arms still hanging uselessly at my sides. I didn't even have the strength to close the door behind me. Nor could I spare the time.

I had been married to the man in the other room, after all. I'd shared all sorts of things with him. Then he'd hit me, broke me, kidnapped me. So him seeing me pee wasn't exactly going to be something I was going to dwell on.

I managed to make it to the toilet with great pain.

And the relief itself was so painful I almost cried.

But I reasoned I'd have plenty of reasons to cry as I hobbled back into the bedroom. Craig was sitting on the other twin bed, head in his hands. It popped up as I entered the room.

"I got you food," he said, nodding to the grease-stained paper bag I hadn't noticed him carrying.

My stomach growled audibly at the mention of food and spotting the water bottle next to it. I only now realized how painfully dry my mouth and throat were.

I should've refused the food and water. That's what the strong and plucky kidnap victim did, right? Refused to consume anything given, tried to escape at any given moment.

And I was in a given moment right now. I was standing. I wasn't cuffed. My bladder was no longer in danger of exploding.

But my arms were still little more than useless, it had been an effort to even get my panties down, I was thankful for the fact I was only wearing Heath's tee.

I didn't know if my weak legs would enable me to run. My arms certainly wouldn't allow me to fight.

Craig was watching me. He stood, striding to the bag, snatching it, along with the water and moving toward me.

I instantly backed up, my face throbbing in warning.

Something crossed over his features as he did so. He stopped advancing.

I didn't stop retreating until my hip bumped against a side table painfully.

He placed the bag on the bed then backed off.

"It's vegetarian," he said. "Probably half cold. Not great, 'cause there are not many options, but it's something." He shrugged as if the food was the only thing he had to be sheepish about.

My eyes went from him to the bag.

My stomach contracted painfully once more. My tongue

expanded in my mouth.

The paper bag was in my hands before I quite knew my decision had been made and I struggled to try to stuff the fries into my mouth with one almost useless hand while unscrewing the water bottle with the other.

The cold greasy fries hit my stomach and it was both glorious and painful as my body didn't quite know what to do. The same happened with the water, but I didn't throw up, so that was a positive.

I ate the veggie burger in silence, trying not to notice the fact that there was no tomatoes or ketchup in it because Craig knew I didn't like tomatoes or ketchup.

It was a strange thing to have this man treat me so brutally and then do something as considerate as to make sure my burger didn't have the condiments and vegetables I despised inside.

He was silent as I ate.

"Why did you do this, Craig?" I asked quietly balling the paper bag up and putting it aside.

He jerked as if he didn't expect me to speak.

Or maybe he didn't expect my voice to be as low and soft as it was.

He stood, snatching up the handcuffs.

"Sit back," he ordered.

The thought of being chained back up like that, hopeless and helpless panicked me immediately. My arms still burned, still throbbed and were already red and raw.

"I won't run," I lied. "You don't have to cuff me."

He was on me in two strides, he brutally snatched my arm and dragged me up the bed so hard I was sure my shoulder popped out of the socket. The pain was white hot and blinding, it was only the click of the cuffs that told me I was chained to the bed again.

"Why do you have to make everything so hard?" Craig hissed in my face, his breath rank.

I didn't answer.

I was too busy trying not to cry from the pain in my wrists and my shoulder.

Craig scowled at me and straightened.

He started to pace. There was an erratic, panicked quality to it. One that prickled at my skin. Because there was a desperation to *him*. People did uncharacteristic things when they were desperate. And punching me in the face was one of Craig's characteristics. I hated to think what he'd do to me in the clutches of whatever this was.

He stopped to stare at me.

A stare that crawled up my spine like a deadly spider, waiting to strike.

"If that *cunt* hadn't bled me dry, none of this would've fucking happened," he hissed, eyes bulging and face red.

It took me a second to realize the ugly word was being used to describe Rosie.

"She ruined fucking everything," he continued. "*You* ruined it. Why did you leave me? I fucking *loved you*!" He was screaming now.

"Because you communicated your love with violence," I said evenly, both surprised and proud at my even response. "That's not love."

He glared. "Oh, perfect fucking Polly is against violence," he mocked. "But you didn't have a problem in sending that cunt after me and taking everything I had."

I stiffened. "I'm against violence, but I won't stop her from committing it against you if you use that word to describe her again," I said my voice chilly. "And she *will* find me. They all will. And at this point, they're likely not going to listen to me when I tell them not to hurt you. And I'll tell them that, despite you hitting me, chaining me to a bed and calling Rosie that vile word. Because you still have a chance to get out of this. But it's getting smaller by the second. You know my family, Craig. You know my sister's husband runs the most successful security company in the city, if not the state. You know they'll find me."

They'll save me.

The damsel.

Again.

I pushed away the self-hatred that came with that thought.

The damsel was not all it was cracked up to be in fairy tales. In fact, that was the only place it belonged, in fiction. I needed to learn how to save myself. Which would, of course, start after I was inevitably rescued from this situation. I didn't like my chances of escaping handcuffs. I would try, of course. But it was good to have a backup.

Because I was Polly.

And I screwed up.

Again.

Craig was scowling at me. "Yeah, I fucking know your family, I know that they meddled in our shit, they didn't like me from the start. *They're* what kept us apart."

I was surprised at his delusion. Yes, he had shown himself to be an asshole, but I at least thought he was a lucid one. "No, Craig," I said. "As I mentioned before, it was your fist in my face that kept us apart."

He started pacing again. I guessed he wasn't going to acknowledge or apologize for this. Not that I expected an apology. One didn't kidnap his ex-wife if he planned on apologizing to her.

"It's all fucked up now," he muttered. "I need it, the money. I knew if I separated you from them that you'd give it to me." He faced me, his expression now soft and kind and familiar.

This was the man I'd fallen in love with.

And he wasn't even *real.*

Because he wore that expression like a mask that didn't fit quite right. If you only glanced, not knowing any better—like I had before—then maybe you could be convinced. But upon closer inspection, you could see where it didn't quite cover the hardness in his eyes, how it was a little too perfect to be genuine.

"But you," he said, in that perfect soft voice that matched that perfect soft face. He stepped forward. "You, my kind little idiot, you will understand. You'll give me the money back. Because you don't want me to get hurt."

He had made it to the side of the bed and was now gently caressing my face. His hand was soft and gentle over the throbbing bruise he'd created with that same hand.

I flinched inwardly, not able to physically do it because I was afraid of the quick transition from kind to cruel. I knew how fragile his hold on calm was. It was just a precursor to violence based upon my reactions.

"You don't want me to get hurt, do you?" he asked sweetly.

He didn't wait for me to answer and suddenly the grip on my face was no longer gentle, it tightened, and my throbbing eye screamed as the pads of his fingers pressed onto the damaged skin.

"And I know *you* don't want to get hurt," he continued, the false veil over his voice slipping. "Because the people that will hurt me will try to do it first by hurting my pretty wife who I love so very much. They will do *horrible* things to you." His eyes roved over my body and it was now I realized that Heath's tee had ridden up high on my hips. And that was the only thing I was wearing when I opened the door because I thought it was Heath,

I'd hoped he'd find me wearing it and we'd pick right up where we left off.

Craig's gaze told me he had something in the same vein in mind. But something that would be brutal, horrific, jarring against the beauty I had last night. It would pollute and taint every touch that was still a shadow on my skin, disappearing by the moment.

My stomach lurched with the gaze and the knowledge of how very helpless I was. Another horror I hadn't imagined would happen to me became actualized with Craig's leer. It was tangible. It was real. The brutal act had the possibility to become reality based on the actions and decisions of a man who hasn't hesitated to hurt me in the past.

My physical wellbeing was now dependent on him. And my emotional wellbeing. Because if that leer became physical. I'd scar. I'd break. On the inside. And I wouldn't heal like the bruise on my face. I could still recover if this was all it was. I wouldn't be quite the same, but I'd recover. I'd still recognize myself when I looked in the mirror.

But there was a cold knowledge with the fact that if he did...*that,* then I wouldn't be the same. That something would shift inside me and I would never be able to be the person I was before. That I wouldn't even *resemble* her.

His eyes yanked themselves back up and I exhaled slightly, I wasn't stupid enough to think the end of the stare would be the end of the possibility of rape.

"They will do u*nthinkable* things," he whispered, his other hand trailing lightly over the exposed skin of my leg. "Things that *I* used to do to you out of love. And you did love them, didn't you?"

A cold sweat settled on my temples as his finger moved higher.

"You did," he murmured. "You l*oved* it."

It wasn't exactly true. The act itself was meant to communicate love, but it was only physical with Craig. With Heath, it was everything. Every cell in my body responded physically. And every facet of my being emotionally and physically.

Craig's hand stopped moving and clenched the skin on my thigh roughly, painfully. "But you won't love this," he said, voice cold and cruel again. His eyes had that malicious grin that was becoming more and more common as his hold on his façade loosened. "I promise you that."

Bile crept up my throat.

He let my thigh go.

His face cleared. "Of course I want to protect you. Because I still care for you. You're such a *gentle* soul," he said it like a threat. "So very *breakable*." His hand relaxed on my face and the release of pressure was almost as painful as the grip itself. "I don't want you to be broken. You don't want to be broken, sullied, *dirty*, do you, Polly?"

I swallowed. "No," I croaked.

"Good. It's decided."

He stood, and I sank into the bed as it sprung up with the release of his weight. But there was still an immovable weight on my chest.

I watched him move to a bag on the armchair by the window.

He pulled a laptop out, went to sit across from me on the other bed and opened it up.

The tapping of the keys echoed in the room.

I wondered if I'd be able to hear the tapping of laptop keys again and not be reminded of this moment. But that would be a blessing, I told myself. Because that would mean this moment was in the past and I was okay, whole in the future.

"I'll need your bank login details," he said, glancing up from the screen. "And then we can arrange the transfer."

I blinked. "The transfer?" I repeated.

He sighed, long and exaggerated as if he were a tired parent dealing with a sullen child. "Yes, Polly," he said. "The people I told you about, the ones who want to hurt you. They need money. Money I don't have because your stupid fucking..." He stopped himself from saying the word that I guessed was his label for women he couldn't control. "Because I lost it in the divorce," he said after a beat, his voice shaking from the effort it was taking him to keep it even and pleasant. "Now you don't *need* that money. It's one of the things I love about you. You're so *low maintenance*." He worded it like an insult. "So it's not hurting anyone by transferring the money. In fact, it's *saving* the hurt."

The threat was painted in the air.

But he didn't need to keep reminding me. It was carved into my bones.

"Okay," I breathed. Then I rattled off my bank details without hesitation.

He was right.

It was only money.

What did I care?

Money was fluid. It wasn't necessary. The abundance or lack of it wasn't something that changed the core of who I was. But what would happen because of my abundance—I thought of Craig's stare—that still might happen regardless, was something that would change the core of who I was.

I hoped it was as simple as money and then I could be released. Wouldn't that be lovely?

There was more tapping.

A loaded pause as Craig's eyes darted over the screen.

His face changed again.

It was scary, terrifying to see a person change so quickly from one identity to the other. Scarier too when it was someone you thought you loved, someone you once promised to love forever.

But there was only one person I'd love forever.

The man who I'd been forcing myself not to think of because if I did, I'd break down. Because we'd finally, finally, maybe gotten toward where we should be, after all the pain. And now there was this. I knew he'd know I was gone by now. And I knew it'd be torturing him. I thought I was done torturing him, inadvertently or otherwise.

But with love, and with me, it seemed, the torture was never done.

"Where's the fucking rest of it, Polly?" Craig asked quietly.

"The rest?" I mimicked.

He looked up. His eyes were cold. "Yes, Polly. The fucking *rest.* I don't want games. If you've hidden it, I'll find it eventually. It'll be the whole amount, but I can't promise you will be quite as whole at the end. You had over three million dollars in the divorce, there's fifty measly fucking grand in here, where the *fuck* is the rest of it?"

"There is no rest of it," I said quietly.

He blinked. Then he laughed. Like really laughed. Like we were across from each other at a restaurant and were sharing a joke that only two people in love could really understand.

Instead, it was two people who had both pretended to love each other, both for very different reasons. Me, because all of my love was used up, spent on another man. Craig, because he was obviously some sort of creature, some sort of *monster* not capable of such an emotion.

"Yeah, like you could spend all that in one go," he said, still speaking in that false jovial tone. "I know you've been away. But I also know that you barely spent anything on your trip. You volunteered. You stayed in *hostels,*" he spat the word. "You're still in that piece of shit apartment. You're still driving a piece of shit car. So I know you didn't spend it. Not my Polly."

"I didn't spend it," I agreed. "I donated it. Half to a charity providing for battered women and half to St. Mary's Children's Hospital." The rest was used to help the people at my shelter find jobs, homes, peace.

There was a silence after my words.

A roaring one. One that rang in my ears.

Then the laptop was no longer on his lap. It flew through the air and then smashed against the wall.

And he was up.

And then he was hitting me.

There was pain then.

For a long time.

And then I broke.

Broke, as Craig promised, in a way that meant I'd never be whole again.

Heath

Twelve Hours Missing

He had gone through a packet of rubber bands.

He was now on whisky.

Though he was limited to two glasses since no way in fuck would he let his faculties be impaired when they got news of where Polly was. When he went to get her. And when he'd find her safe and fucking sound and unharmed.

He snorted as he finished the second glass, slamming it down on his desk hard enough to shatter it. Glass shot in all directions, creating a visible mess in the stark order of his office.

He barely noticed it.

He wouldn't have noticed if a hurricane flew threw and ruined all the order he'd thought was so important.

Only one hurricane mattered. The one who'd tore through the order of his life, of his fucking soul. The one who believed in peace, even when the world showed her violence. Who believed the best in people even after they'd shown her the worst. Polly who gave everything to the people around her, even when she had nothing left to give. Polly was the one that everyone thought believed in the fairy tales, yet here he fucking was, clinging to one because he was too fucking weak to handle the truth.

That being the chances of Polly being unharmed were slim.

He was a professional. He knew what happened to kidnap victims. Especially when the victims were kidnapped by abusive spouses. Especially when abusive spouses were connected to a human trafficking ring. Especially when the victims looked like fucking Polly.

He squeezed the glass, forgetting it was broken. Warmth spread onto his hand as a jagged edge cut the skin. There was no pain of course. He was in battle mode. It was the state in which he'd trained himself to switch off all human faculties that could be considered weakness in order to do his job without hesitating. Physical pain was a weakness. As was mercy.

He had gotten through a fucking war with ironclad control over this state.

But sitting in his office, with nothing to do but wait and imagine what was happening to Polly right now, he was losing his fucking shit.

His door opened.

His chair was falling to the ground immediately, with the force in which he stood up.

Keltan eyed him, then the whisky bottle, then his hand.

"Gonna need stitches," he commented.

Heath didn't reply.

"We got something."

He pulled the glass from his palm, standing.

And he prepared to go to war. The most important one he'd ever fight. To find his peace.

He hoped to fuck that his peace wasn't shattered.

Because that would mean Polly was.

THEY HAD SET up the conference room and the large computer screen in the middle of the table showed a skinny, ungroomed man wearing a Sons of Templar cut. He was in a room full of screens and discarded energy drinks.

"Craig owes a lot of fucked up people a lot of money," Wire said dispensing with pleasantries and small talk. Heath was glad as fuck for that. He didn't have the patience, the fucking strength for that shit. "And since our girl Rosie bled him dry, he can't pay up." Wire grinned at Rosie, who managed a weak smirk back. "These are not the kind of people to forgive unpaid debts. Unpaid debts are cleared with blood and pain. By the looks of it, Craig can't handle either, unless of course he's doling it out to defenseless fucking angels like our Polly."

Heath clenched his fists at the rage in Wire's tone. The truth in it. And the emotion. Everyone was affected by this. They'd been through shit before. A lot of shit. Both the men at this table and the men wearing the cut that Wire had on his back.

But this was different. *Polly* was different. It was unexplainable, but everyone knew it. She was separate from the world that she'd grown up in. She was separate from the fucking world she was born in.

That world shouldn't have been able to touch her. To fucking hurt her. But it did.

"So he took her to pay a debt," Keltan surmised, jaw tight. He was composed because the fucker had a poker face that had cost Heath a lot of money over the years. But he saw the cracks emerging with every hour she wasn't back.

He saw it because he felt them in himself with every passing second.

Wire nodded. "He owes them a cool two point five mil," he said, his keyboard tapping.

Heath wondered if he'd be able to hear that previously asinine sound without attaching it to this moment. This fucking nightmare.

Maybe he'd be able to handle it when he'd touched Polly. When he cataloged every inch of her body to make sure it was unmarred. Then he cataloged every inch of her soul to make sure it wasn't broken or bruised in any way.

Maybe then.

But maybe fucking not.

Because horrors did not get erased. They became memories. Visceral and dangerous and they were always stark and fresh. Heath knew that better than anyone. If he let himself, he could smell the charring flesh of his commander. He could feel the warm stream of blood coming from a suspected insurgent he'd gunned down.

Suspected.

There was no nobility in war. And there sure as fuck weren't confirmed enemies. He didn't know how many of the people he'd killed deserved to die. It didn't matter. Orders were orders. There was no place for moral reflection in a war zone.

That was for when you got home.

When you stared at a handgun and a half-empty bottle of

whisky and wondered how many families were torn apart because of you. Wondered if you'd ever stop feeling the blood or smelling the death. Wondered if it would be better if you pulled a trigger one last time, ending it all.

For some reason, the tapping of that fucking keyboard seemed worse than all of that shit right now.

"Probably thinks that she's still got it," Wire was saying.

Heath straightened. "What do you mean *thinks* she's still got it?" he demanded.

Wire glanced up from where he'd been staring off-screen.

"She got all of his money in the divorce," Heath said. He knew it all because he'd tortured himself with every fucking minute detail of it. "She hasn't bought shit, she went on her trip and volunteered most of the time. The fanciest place she stayed was an AirBnb. Money doesn't mean shit to her."

Everyone was looking at him and he didn't give a fuck.

"No, money doesn't mean shit to her," Wire agreed after a beat.

Heath hated that he knew that about her. It was fucked up and selfish. She gave herself to everyone freely and without expectation. He fucking *loved* that about her. But *he* wanted to own those things. That knowledge. He didn't want anyone else knowing shit.

"Which is why she doesn't have it anymore," Wire continued.

"What the fuck do you mean?" he gritted out.

Wire glanced to Rosie and then back to him. "Dude, she donated almost all of it to charity pretty much as soon as she got back Stateside. Used a shitload of it to help home people from her shelter. She kept enough to fund her training. Live humbly on. It's never been about the money for her."

There was silence.

Well, until Heath threw his coffee cup at the wall and it

smashed.

No one reacted.

Because everyone else was digesting what the fuck this meant.

It meant the chances of Polly coming out of this shit unharmed just when from abysmal to impossible.

"How in the *fuck* could you be so stupid?" Heath shot at Rosie, pushing free of his chair, laying his palms on the table and leaning forward. He'd missed a piece of glass and it was pressing into the flesh of his skin.

Luke stood immediately. "Watch yourself," he clipped, face darkening.

Heath paid him no mind. "You bled him dry, knowing that the money didn't mean *shit* to Polly."

Rosie put her hand on her husband's arm, presumably to stop him from attacking Heath like he was poised to. Heath didn't give a fuck. He was out for blood. Luke was his friend, but at that point, it didn't matter. He'd give him a decent fight, something to distract him from the cold and visceral dread that clawed at his throat.

"Money didn't mean shit to Polly," Rosie agreed, glancing from Luke to Heath once she was assured her husband wasn't moving. "But it meant shit to *Craig*." She made a face as she said his name. "And he took something from her. Something she could never get back, something that should not have been taken from someone like Polly."

Heath's heart clenched now he had the knowledge of how much he took from her. How he put his fucking hands on her. That knowledge would be taken to his fucking grave. Along with the guilt of how he'd treated her in his ignorance.

Rosie wasn't done. Because when that woman was on a roll, she was on a roll. Every one of her words were bullets.

"And she because she is who she is, I couldn't take anything more valuable, like say, his dick so his money was the next best thing. And I knew Polly wasn't going to keep it. Because she's Polly," her voice wavered slightly. "I knew that she'd likely hand it all over to the old man that she walks to the bus stop every day or the young kid she'd been helping with his college payments ever since she met in a Starbucks one time. I knew that because that's who Polly is. She'd literally carve out her heart and hand it to someone just so they could have two more heartbeats than they needed."

She gave him an accusing look.

"Than they *deserved*. So don't you try and lay the blame for Polly's asshole ex snatching her out of the comfort of her own home on me, because I won't let that fly. You want to look for someone to blame? How about you go find a fucking mirror then ask it why she was sitting at home, alone unprotected, most likely thinking about the man who broke her heart. And I'm not talking about the one who is currently holding her captive right now."

She was yelling at this point.

"You think about that while you go all manly and smash perfectly good mugs and perfectly good, kind and giving fucking hearts."

She stood up quickly, flipped him the bird and then stormed out of the room.

HEATH WAS STARING at his bloodied hand, wondering if he was wearing more or less than Polly was wearing. If she was in more or less pain than him. Wondering how many marks she was wearing on her perfect body. The body he'd had in his arms this morning.

Was it only this morning?

And he'd gotten out of bed with the intention of a fresh start. With the intention of never letting her go again.

He wondered if his bloody and torn hands would ever hold her again.

His door opened and closed and his head snapped up, instantly alert, instantly bracing.

"No news," Lucy said quietly, knowing that's what Heath was surviving on. Scraps of information that might lead him to her.

He flinched at the growing bruise on Lucy's face. On the pain in every part of her.

Keltan followed behind her, hand on her lower back. Of course the fucker wasn't gonna let her walk the short distance from the bed to Heath's office.

Heath didn't blame him.

If—no, *when* he got Polly back, she wouldn't be walking from the bed to the kitchen alone.

"You okay?" Heath forced himself to show concern for Lucy. Because Polly would want him to do that. Because Polly showed concern for everyone, no matter how much pain she was in.

Lucy raised her brow in response.

"Yeah," Heath agreed.

Lucy sat down across from him.

Keltan stood behind her, hands on her shoulders.

There was silence.

"You love her," Lucy said finally.

Heath didn't hesitate. "More than anything on this fucking earth."

She smiled. "From the start?"

"From the second I saw her in that bar, and every second after that," he said.

Lucy lost her smile. "She's not the same as us," Lucy said, voice quiet. "And I don't mean this in a bad way. It's in all the best of ways. Because there was something special in her, something soft and precious and something that I've always considered my duty as her sister to protect. Everyone that encounters her and loves her considers it their duty. To make sure that Polly continues to experience the world exactly how she sees it. And now that's gone. I can't protect her anymore. And even in the best case scenario, it's going to break my sister."

Heath didn't flinch with the words. Though they cut him. Speared him. As did hearing the absolute sorrow in the tone of one of the strongest women he knew. Lucy had more of a poker face than half the men he'd served with. He'd seen it for himself.

But this wasn't like anything they'd experienced.

This was Polly.

And she was so fucking different than them in all the best ways, which meant that this was cutting them to the core in all the worst ways.

"You're wrong," Heath said.

Keltan stiffened as he spoke and leaned forward as if to spring. Heath didn't doubt he would if he didn't like the next words coming out of his mouth.

"She's stronger than you think. Than you know," he continued not giving a fuck about Keltan's glare. "She isn't going to let the ugliness of the world break her."

His words sounded certain, sure.

But they were little more than a prayer.

No one normally listened to his prayers, but Duke burst into the room.

Heath stood.

"We got her," Duke said.

CHAPTER SIXTEEN

Polly

Sixteen Hours Missing

YOU GET RESCUED in the nick of time.

That's what happens in those fantasies in the head you pretend you don't have. You know, the ones where something crazy happens and wakes up that person that you've been thinking about forever and then they come and save you, right in the nick of time.

Then they hold you in their arms and you're safe and warm. They whisper to you about how they'd never leave you, how you were safe now.

It would've been *nice* if that happened.

But this seemed to be the period of my life when the universe had to educate me on the fact that fantasies didn't play out here in real life.

Not mine at least.

So I was not rescued in the nick of time.

Or at all.

The back of the truck was uncomfortable, to say the least. My hands bound awkwardly behind my back contributed to that. As did the uneven terrain we seemed to be traversing on. I guessed it wasn't a main highway from the number of times I went flying forward, back, up, down.

I had opened up a cut on my cheek.

It was from Craig's wedding ring.

I hadn't noticed he was still wearing it until it tore at my skin when he was beating the crap out of me.

I wondered why he'd worn it for so long. It can't have been out of love. Because even deluded and ugly love didn't let a person do what he'd *done to me.*

I wasn't thinking about that.

It wasn't going to help me.

It wasn't going to help *anything.*

I was careful to keep my mind very blank as the journey continued. I took in the large area I was being jostled around in. Not too much, mind you, because I was shackled to something on the edge of the truck. It was considerate. Chaining me up to the side of the truck. So I wouldn't go flying all the way across the truck. Without my hands to break my fall I could break my neck.

That might be nice.

Quick.

But I couldn't wish for death.

That was so utterly *selfish.*

Heath's words haunted me.

"You drive like you bowl through life. Full of almost hitting things, near misses, almost disasters. You've been lucky, so far,

Polly. But no one is lucky forever. The world doesn't give almosts forever. One day, you're gonna fuckin' crash."

I wondered how much satisfaction Heath would get knowing he had predicted the future. I didn't crash, literally, of course. But my body and soul was shattered into a thousand different pieces and that was pretty much the same thing.

The words bounced around the empty expanse surrounding me, hitting me now and again. It hurt. Which was surprising. I'd thought I'd stopped feeling pain.

I was in a large truck. Like a big long haul one. It was designed for large amounts of cargo. It had a strong smell of off milk. Maybe yogurt?

But it wasn't refrigerated.

Maybe that's why it went off.

Maybe that's why it was used for transporting humans.

Or just one lone human.

I couldn't go off, could I? But my insides felt like that's what was happening. They were rotting, decaying, turning into something rancid and not at all pleasant.

It was off-putting.

But there was not much I could do about it, was there? *It* had happened, and I was here. Most likely there was worse in store for me. Or at the very least more of the same.

The thought provoked that lust for a quick death I had brushed away because of the people it would hurt.

My family.

I wondered how they were. I wondered how long they'd look for me until they gave up.

Never.

I knew that Lucy would never give up.

Neither would Rosie.

Them and their respective husbands would tear apart the

earth for me. Because that's what they did. They might find me, rotting in a shallow grave. I hoped not.

I smiled thinking about their babies. They'd have them in sorrow, of course. And I hated that I would involuntarily have a part in that. I wanted so much joy and love for them. Because they deserved so much of that. I wanted to meet my niece or nephew. Wanted to cradle the new warmth of life in my arms, and feel my heart grow with love for such a tiny being. I wanted to babysit when Lucy and Keltan were sleep deprived and going crazy. I wanted to save Luke from Rosie murdering him when he didn't let her go back to work immediately.

I could've been that cool aunt. Because I'd never be a mother, even...if *everything* didn't happen.

But everything *did* happen. I was wearing the evidence, body and soul. I should've been in pain. A lot of it.

And I was, somewhere amongst the layers. But I'd sunk down to someplace inside of me that was rather quiet and vacant and at peace with all the horrors that I'd gone through. Or maybe in denial. I knew it was a temporary place. One I'd likely get wrenched out of the second the truck stopped and my life—as I knew it at least—stopped too.

And my death might start.

Craig had sold me.

Sold. Me.

Like I was a commodity. Something that he had the right to throw at men, half-conscious and sullied and talk about being 'even.' As if my life, my soul was something that weighed just the right amount to even whatever scales he'd disrupted in the first place.

I couldn't muster up the appropriate disgust for this right now. Because underneath the layers my emotions were muted. My panic. My sorrow. My fear. All still here, but manageable.

They were quietly eating away at my insides, but it wasn't as unpleasant as before.

Yes, before had been *unpleasant* if there was ever a word for it.

The truck stopped.

My breath might've too.

But no, I was still awake and alive when the truck doors opened, so I was breathing.

A pity.

I waited for them to climb in. Unchain me. Maybe hurt me. They hadn't done that yet. It'd just been Craig so far. But the way they'd handled me was not giving promises to gentle treatment. It was a precursor to abuse.

But no one climbed in.

Because people started yelling. There was a flashing of lights. A thump of bodies against bodies. Grunts.

Ah, I must've been dead.

Or at the very least hallucinating.

Because this was it. The scene when the damsel is saved. But the scene was too late. Because the damsel wasn't meant to go through...*that*.

If I was going to be saved, it would've already happened.

That was how it *worked*.

I read that people constructed different kinds of reality when the real one suddenly became too horrific to live through. That must've been what I was doing.

It made sense.

I was Polly, after all, wasn't I? I excelled at creating realities different from the ones I existed in.

The doors were wrenched open.

Light stabbed at my eyeballs and I flinched away from it. I

didn't like that. It was too bright, too real, too urgent, it tried to tug me away from all my layers.

I squeezed my eyes shut.

"Fuck," a voice clipped, the one curse full of pain and relief.

It was familiar.

Too familiar to be real.

Steps across the interior. Hurried. Urgent.

I kept my eyes squeezed shut, making sure there were no crevices where the light could come in. I didn't want the light anymore. Not ever.

"Oh, baby, *fuck*." The voice was still a murmur. It was soft. Broken.

Just like me.

Hands went onto my body.

I couldn't remember if I still had clothes on, but a bare hand went onto my bare skin and that was *not okay*.

I flinched away violently, even though the hands were familiar like the voice. Because it wasn't really those hands touching me. No, I was just pretending. Obviously, there were rougher, dirtier hands on me right now and I couldn't handle that, so I was pretending it was the one I wanted.

Needed.

"Polly," he whispered, voice strained and full of pain. "Polly, baby, I'm going to uncuff you now, that means I'm gonna touch you."

There was a pause. An exhale. It sounded like he was struggling with something. Struggling to breathe. Struggling to keep himself together.

Ah, I knew how that felt.

"I'm not gonna hurt you, baby," he whispered. Again, the words were broken. Fractured. Bleeding. "I promise you, you're not gonna be hurt anymore."

I didn't reply.

Even if no one laid a finger on me for as long as I lived, it didn't matter. The way I'd been hurt couldn't be erased, and worse, it wouldn't dull. It would continue to stab at me forever. I knew that.

There was more touching. I kept my eyes squeezed shut through it.

My hands were free now.

They fell down like lead.

I imagined they, along with my body, might've hit the ground.

But he caught me.

His body was warm. Hard and soft. He smelled like blood and death and comfort.

I wanted to nuzzle into him.

But it wasn't really *him.*

So I stayed still.

He cradled me in his arms. I felt lips on my head and he began rocking me back and forward. "Baby," he choked. "Polly, *fuck*. I'm sorry baby, I'm so fucking sorry."

I didn't reply.

What if I spoke and my words fractured this beautifully ugly reality?

"You're okay, you're okay," he chanted.

But I didn't believe it.

And I could tell that he couldn't either.

We stayed like that for a long time. I wondered what was really happening, outside of this reality I'd constructed. Was someone really holding me with this love and tenderness, rocking me back and forward and clutching me like I was encased in a cocoon?

Of course not.

But it was *nice.*

I couldn't move. It might tear this reality. Disappear it.

But *he* could. And he did. In one fluid movement, he was standing. We moved across the truck.

There were more voices. They were familiar too. Smells. Burned rubber. Smoke. Blood.

I would've thought blood didn't have a smell before. But I'd scented my own against my pain...before, so I knew it smelled coppery and wet. Like rancid meat and old pennies.

"Heath, is that—" someone began, and then his voice broke, I imagined as we came into view.

As I came into view.

I imagined I looked bad on the outside. Even if it betrayed an ounce of the hurt of the inside, it would've been *bad.*

"No," the voice murmured. Or maybe pleaded.

I should tell him that didn't help. Pleading did nothing but chip away at your dignity while everything else was carved off your body. Your soul.

"I'm gonna hand her down to you, Luke," Pretend Heath said.

"Yeah, brother," Pretend Luke said, voice quiet. Kind.

Luke was always kind.

The arms around me tightened just a little. A kiss on my forehead. "I'm gonna let you go for just a second, Polly, I can't climb down with you in my arms. I don't wanna hurt you. Luke's gonna take you. He won't hurt you, 'kay?"

It was nice he was talking me through it.

This was all so very *nice.*

Well, nice amongst the horror, of course. But I didn't focus on the horror. I focused on the nice.

The arms squeezed tighter, but not actually tight. Like someone trying to hug an egg without breaking it. I guessed maybe he didn't realize I was already broken. Maybe in this reality, I wasn't broken.

That would be nice too.

I was jostled slightly, and the move sent a pain so sharp and so visceral it stabbed through all my layers and got me in my safe place. Or what I thought was a safe place.

I didn't cry out. Or even flinch.

Interesting. I didn't have a good tolerance for pain normally.

But normal was dead. Buried. Never to be resurrected.

My eyes were still squeezed shut but I was in new arms. They felt different. Still warm. Still safe. But they didn't smell so much like death. Maybe clean linen and the ocean. Clean would've been nice.

But I'd never be clean again. Not even if I scrubbed my skin from my body.

"I've got you, honey, you're okay," a voice murmured.

"Thank you, Pretend Luke," I whispered, still staying still.

I knew it was a risk to talk in my faux reality, but I felt Luke needed thanks. He needed something. He sounded so hopeless.

His arms flexed with my voice. I didn't blame him. It was raw and ugly. I guessed I must've been screaming at some point.

"Give her back to me," a voice growled.

There was a pause. "Brother," Pretend Luke warned. "We need to check her over. You gonna be able to hold it together? She *needs* you to hold it together."

"I'm holding it together. I know what she needs. And I need you to give her to me."

Another pause.

The air was wired.

A strange thing to have in my pretend world. Wasn't it meant to be easy and lacking that conflict that was the thing I was escaping? The pain?

There was a lot of pain here. Not inside me, I was thankfully still numb to that. But on the outside. In the air. In the way both of these pretend men spoke.

In every syllable that Pretend Heath seemed to rip out from his very soul. It was very strange I was able to construct such pain. I had a powerful imagination, everyone told me that, but not *that* powerful. But maybe it was that powerful because now I knew pain really well. Intimately. That must've been it. Before I injected happiness and love into my fantasies because I was lucky enough to know it very well. Now it would be pain and ugliness.

No more happiness and love. Not ever again.

Yes, that was it.

I decided it just as I was jostled into another set of arms. They did that thing where they squeezed me like an uncracked egg. But I was already cracked. Shattered, leaking out through the broken pieces.

Gravel crunched under boots.

My eyes flickered as I decided it might be time to open them, because this might be the last time I was strong enough to create a fantasy this strong, this real, and this might be the last time I could see Heath. So I should feast on him before I get taken away from my mind.

"No, Sunshine," he murmured. "Keep your eyes closed."

He must've been watching me, staring at me pretty hard to see the tiny movement under my closed eyelids to signify that I was about to open them.

I kept them squeezed shut. If he didn't want me to open my eyes, it was for a reason. He was protecting me from something, maybe. I let out a little giggle at that. He was protecting me from something when there was nothing left to protect.

We stopped.

"Fuck."

The third male uttering that word and somehow using it as a cry of sorrow instead of a curse.

More familiar.

This was Keltan.

"Set her down, we need to see her injuries."

"You can see them from here," Heath hissed.

"Brother, you need to let her go." Keltan's voice was gentle, tentative, like he was trying to talk a man off a ledge.

"Letting her go is what got her here in the first place."

I sensed this might go on for awhile. Again, this puzzled me as to why my pretend reality might be full of such things. Something tickled the edge of my mind, tried to coax me out of my layers with the seductive thought that maybe this was a reality. Maybe *this* was the true one.

Maybe they were really all here, wherever here was, and maybe I was getting saved.

Much too late of course.

This thought and the men's argument was cut off by the sound of tires.

"You've got to be fucking *kidding me*," Luke's furious voice clipped out from somewhere near.

A door closed.

"I told you to sit fucking tight," Luke said, his voice almost a shout.

"And since when did you think that what you told me to do is what I'm going to actually do?" a woman's voice asked.

Familiar.

Too familiar.

She began to yank me out of the thought that this was all pretend. Because if I was imagining this, I would never bring *her* here. No, I would never want her to see me like this. I would never hurt her like that. I was already hurting, scarring the man I loved beyond belief. But I didn't have the strength to save him, because I needed him before I was lost altogether.

"Since you're four months fucking pregnant," Luke continued, voice hard.

"I waited until you stopped the killing." The voice was closer. "Which I could've done. Viking women gave birth on the battlefield, Luke, and I'm much tougher than they—"

She stopped speaking at the same time the gravel stopped crunching when her voice got nearer and nearer.

It was an abrupt knife through her words, the ensuing silence. I guessed it was when she saw me.

The pain was coming back quickly now because I was beginning to sicken with the realization that this was real. How was it that I was having a more violent reaction to being saved than when I thought that I was still being tortured?

"Baby." Luke's voice immediately softened, all of the previous anger leaking out like my soul did through the cracked pieces.

His voice was broken too.

I didn't want to open my eyes now.

Because his voice told me he saw something on Rosie's face.

Pain.

Because of me.

"Polly," Rosie croaked.

More gravel crunching.

I smelled her perfume.

My hair moved and a soft hand trailed across my forehead.

It took all of my strength to open my eyes.

The pain came back then. With Rosie's tearstained face.

All of it.

The outside and the inside.

I looked behind her, not at the people around her. No, at the yawning desert around us. It was dusk or dawn. Did it matter if the day was ending or beginning? Maybe it used to.

Not anymore. Endings and beginning were the same now.

Meaningless.

"We're in the desert," I whispered. "I've always liked the desert. It's a nice place. A nice place."

And then I was gone.

One Month Later

Heath

They were in the conference room.

The one he couldn't walk into without the chill of what felt like someone was walking over his grave.

But every step in a place that he'd existed in before was a step over the dead remains of his life a month ago. Before he'd died the second he opened the doors to that truck. Saw her chained, bloody, brutalized beyond belief, beyond comprehension. Wearing his torn fucking tee shirt. And wearing *nothing* on her face.

The woman who wore her heart on every inch of her body, in her expressions was wearing *nothing*. That hit him as hard as her physical injuries. And they hit him pretty fucking hard.

He hadn't lost that much of himself in those two seconds in three tours in the desert.

No war could take from him what those moments took from him.

And though she was back, she wasn't back. No, he couldn't even find comfort in the fact she slept in his arms every night and he woke to her every morning because it wasn't her. Not really.

So everywhere he went, when he had to leave her, when he forced himself to leave her, it haunted him with what was there before.

The conference room was the worst because that was where they got the news. That's where they finally got her location and he hoped, like a stupid motherfucker that they'd find her.

Whole.

That was the last place he entertained the idea of an unbroken Polly.

So it was fucking torture to sit at the same seat he'd sat in one month ago.

But he did it. He welcomed torture. He needed pain, he craved more of it. Because he could never go through in a lifetime what Polly lived through.

They met here once a week. Well, *all* of them did, the women included. But the men met every single fucking day since it happened, usually with a member of the Sons of Templar either by Skype or in residence.

The whole club had come when Polly had been found.

As a show of solidarity more than anything else.

They'd been out for blood, of course, but Heath and Keltan's men had spilled it all. Including Craig's.

He'd wanted to make it slow, painful. Agonizing. But he couldn't waste time killing someone when it was more important to bring Polly back to life.

It hit the Sons too, what happened to Polly.

Scarred them.

And they had renewed motivation to try and end Fernandez.

The energy Heath had left to spare was spent on that.

But this meeting with the women was for everyone to coordinate their shifts. Their shifts with Polly.

She had not been left alone since *it* happened.

Not even for her benefit, she hadn't made a show of not being able to be alone, hadn't made any kind of show, hadn't shed a fucking tear. But not one person who knew and loved Polly could stand the thought of leaving her alone.

Her friend Rain was with her now.

Every single person she'd helped, she'd given to, had been around. Dropping off some scary and meat-free food. Crystals. Prayers. Affirmations. All sorts of shit. People who loved her, whose lives she'd touched wanting to show her she wasn't alone.

Heath had hated how much she'd given to people before, because he was selfish. But he was so fucking glad of it now.

"She's handling it well," Keltan said as he sat his wife down on his lap.

Quite a feat, considering how pregnant she was, but the men didn't seem to willing or able to let go of their women these days.

"That's just it," Lucy whispered. "She *shouldn't* be handling it well. No one handles *this* well. Handling it well means that she's not handling it at all. It means it's eating her up on the inside and she's too worried about preserving the outside in order to save everyone around her. She's always done that. She's always going to try and save everyone before she saves herself," she whispered, but it was a roar in Heath's ears. "She would sacrifice every part of herself if it means someone she loves is saved even an ounce of pain. And that's what she's doing now. She's sacrificing all of it, whatever's left, whatever *he* didn't take and ruin, and she's holding it together on the outside because she knows how much we love her."

Heath hated the words. Hated the pain in them because it showed him the depth of his own. Hated them because they were fucking true.

Apart from the night where she'd screamed bloody murder at

being taken to a hospital, she hadn't reacted to what happened to her.

But that reaction was burned into his brain. Her breaking, falling apart right before his eyes as she pleaded, fucking *begged* to not be taken to a hospital.

She needed a hospital.

Fuck did she need one.

But no one could say no to Polly. Not before. And surely not fucking then.

So they'd made her a hospital in the security offices. Pooled all their collective contacts, Luke's, Rosie's, Keltan's and the Sons of Templar.

Got her better treatment than a hospital would ever offer.

Physically, at least, she was almost fully healed.

Not the best doctor in the world could stitch up the wounds that Heath saw, that cut him to the fucking bone.

He couldn't do that, though he'd carve his own heart if it would repair hers.

But she was the only one person who could do that.

And it fucking terrified him, the knowledge that she might not. That the dead in her eyes and her soul might be permanent.

"GIVE ME A SECOND WITH HEATH, BABE," Lucy said, kissing Keltan.

Keltan paused, hand on her belly and nodded.

He clapped Heath on the back on his way out, closing the door.

"How has she been sleeping?" she asked the same question she asked every week.

"Good," he said.

Lucy's face pinched. With most people, being able to sleep, not having the nightmares of the past reality keep you awake was a good thing. Polly was not most people. She didn't sleep much because she had too much light, too much life in her to do so. She didn't like missing out on life, she wanted to suck as much out of it as she could.

But lately she'd been eager to curl up on Heath's chest and lapse into unconsciousness. It didn't mean he didn't *like* the weight on his chest. He did. He barely slept himself because he couldn't give in to a world where he couldn't *feel* her.

"Has she told you what happened to her yet?" he asked, dragging the words from his throat was a physical exertion.

Lucy blinked away the pain on her face. Or attempted too. Her hand went to her swollen belly, rubbing it for some kind of comfort.

"No," she whispered. Her eyes shimmered and she focused on him. "Has she said anything to you?"

He resisted the urge to openly scoff. Not just because he respected the fuck out of Lucy, liked her, considered her a sister already, and doing such a thing in the face of her pain was callous even for him. But also because he didn't even have the energy to acknowledge the dark humor of it all.

"No," he said. "And you know what?" he found himself saying. "A tiny part of me is *glad*. I want to know, I'm consumed every fucking day with not knowing. But I also am glad I don't know yet because..." he pushed his hand through his hair in frustration and shame. "Because, fuck, I don't know if I can handle hearing it, not from her. What kind of coward does that make me? I can't even handle the *thought* of *hearing* it, and Lucy, she had to fucking *live* it. And she still does. She's fucking good at hiding it, so good it scares me, but she's not that good. So she lived it once and she'll continue to live it for the rest of her life. And whether she's handling it badly or not, she's fucking handling it. And I'm not."

Lucy was across the room, putting her arms around him the best she could with her belly.

He wasn't one for physical contact that didn't come from Polly or didn't come from violence. But he found himself putting his arms around Lucy, kissing her head.

"She'll get through it," she whispered. "And she'll get us through it. Because she's Polly."

He didn't answer because he was fucking terrified that was a lie. That she wasn't Polly anymore.

CHAPTER SEVENTEEN

Polly

THE DOOR SLAMMED SHUT and I jerked awake, sweat both cold and hot on my forehead, my heart in my throat as my nightmare still held onto me and taunted me with the thought that the bang of the door was the sound of it being brought into reality.

"Okay," Rosie sang, her voice ripping through thoughts of violence and confinement.

Rain had only just left—or had only just left before I nodded off—and now I was getting sure that they were rotating on some kind of shift. Rain had arrived just as Heath was leaving. Though I knew he didn't want to, leave that was.

I knew that because for the first week, he didn't leave my side. Not once. Granted, for the first two days I was drugged up and barely conscious. That had been nice. All my wounds dull at the edges, the pain only a nagging ache. And I could almost pretend that it wasn't *that* bad. That it never even really happened.

My only constant, the only solid thing had been Heath's grip on my hand. His presence. The utter pain in his eyes. That had made it impossible to believe it never really happened. His mere presence was the reason I couldn't sink into a fantasy. Couldn't escape.

I didn't tell Heath that his presence, his pain was a reason I couldn't escape mine, even for a second. Because if I did, he'd leave. Even though no one could make him move from my side the first week and it seemed like a physical exertion every time he did it now, he'd leave in a heartbeat if I told him the truth.

Because he cared for me.

I'd been so dumb, so blind to it before because he was so good at acting like he didn't care about me. But no one put that much effort into an act if they didn't care.

I was too caught up in my own pain to truly see that.

Or what I'd thought was pain before.

Now I was drowning in pain, getting choked by it, I saw how much Heath cared. How much he loved me. Just in time to see how much that love was torturing him. And if he knew it was torturing me too, he'd leave. And though my mangled, bleeding heart was barely beating, I wasn't going to completely destroy it with Heath's absence.

It was selfish of me. So fucking selfish. I needed to push him away. Needed to somehow get him away from me. From the pain my presence, my healing bruises, cuts, and broken soul caused him.

Caused everyone around me.

My parents didn't know.

That fight had been almost as big as the one about me not going to a hospital. I'd needed a hospital. I knew that. I knew the extent of my injuries. I'd lived them. Every single one was lined up in a neat and tidy list in my otherwise messy mind. The list was long. But I wouldn't survive a hospital. That clean, stark environment. All sorts of strangers' hands on me.

No.

I could barely stand the kind doctor who had worked on me in the Greenstone Security office.

She was the only one that knew every single one of my injuries. I couldn't quite remember how she'd gotten Heath out of the room to examine me. There was shouting. Swearing.

Her voice had stayed calm and constant.

And she'd managed the impossible, to out-stubborn Heath.

So she *knew*.

And respected my wishes to keep my filthy, tarnished and dirty secret. On the proviso I let her examine me once a week. Let her talk to me.

Heath wasn't around for that, of course.

No one was.

But the rest of the time, there were people.

Always people.

People I loved.

Adored.

Even Jay turned up.

Heath had not reacted well to the attractive, cold and dangerous man in a suit at the door. I was sure he'd been bracing for some assassin. Even though I knew the danger was gone. In other words, everyone was dead.

That should've bothered me more than it did.

But I was still focused on the fact that the danger wasn't gone. And they couldn't kill it. Unless they wanted to kill me. Because the danger was inside me, my memories, my waking nightmare.

Hence why I slept so much. To escape the nightmare when I was awake.

And Jay had been affected seeing me. It was a small softening of his eyes, a working of his jaw, but to him, it was everything.

He reached forward and squeezed my hand, ignoring Heath's clenched fists. I held my breath not to flinch from the touch since I knew what a big deal such a simple touch was to him. And if I showed an inch of discomfort, Heath would be there, trying to protect me with violence. I'd had enough of that.

"I'm sorry, darlin'," Jay murmured, voice still cold but eyes as warm as they'd ever be.

I'd smiled at him like I smiled at everyone. One hundred percent fake.

"It's okay. I'm here. I'm okay."

He inspected me, picking apart the lie with a practiced eye.

He didn't call me out on it. Just squeezed my hand once more before leaving.

He checked in every day. The calls were brisk, almost businesslike, but damn near warm for him.

And warmth was all around. Chester brought banana cake. It should've been funny, the goth kid bringing banana cake he'd baked himself. I'd made it seem like I found it appropriately funny. Laughed and joked with him as he pretended not to be shocked with my bruises and cuts.

But like everything else, it was surface.

My friends came in a steady stream so not once was I alone.

Never.

It was a blessing and a curse.

Because I would've thought that seeing the love, the light I had around me would chase away the worst of the demons, when really it invited them in.

Because I couldn't escape my pain in people's eyes.

I didn't tell them to leave, didn't say no when many of them asked if they could visit. Because I knew that they needed to. For their own peace of mind. Peace was lost for me, but I could give it to the people I loved even if it caused me pain.

It wasn't broadcast, my kidnapping and...everything else. But good news traveled fast, bad news traveled everywhere. Luckily, my parents were switched off to our L.A. lifestyle and news had been carefully kept from them. Lucy understood this, better than anyone, but she didn't like it.

We'd agreed we'd tell them an extremely sanitized version of the story when I was healed enough. That Craig had lost it and hit me then disappeared.

They would not know the ugly truth.

No way would they ever know that.

I would do everything in my power to make sure *no one* knew that. Even Heath. Especially Heath. But he saw more than everyone else. So he'd see soon. I'd be unable to hide soon. I had to stop it before it got to that point. But I couldn't. His was the only touch that I could handle without wanting to throw up. Because he seemed to know that I couldn't handle a lot of it. Even though he didn't know the real truth. If he did know, I'd know, because the pain on his face would be something more than was already there.

He didn't know *that*, he knew that he needed to be careful touching me too much, even though he needed to. I'd seen him reach for me multiple times, down the street, in the car and then snatch his hand back right before he made contact as if he'd seen the way my skin prickled with revulsion. With fear.

Not from him, from the shadows, the demons crawling underneath it.

Before, I'd been a touchy person. Expressive about my love. Even our short time together had shown Heath that.

But he understood that something inside me had been fundamentally changed and that wasn't me anymore. I knew that he expected this to be temporary, like my cuts and bruises.

It was not.

I felt temporary. But also horribly permanent in this temporary state.

And Heath was the only one who made me feel real. Falling asleep in his arms every night, waking up to his eyes, his scent every morning.

And he hadn't pushed me for anything more.

He laid his mouth on mine gently, closed mouth kisses when I knew he couldn't stop himself. I fought against pleasure and revulsion as he did so.

But that was it.

He didn't push.

For whatever reason, I was glad. Because if he pushed, then he'd know. He couldn't know. Which was why I needed to make him leave before he found out. I wasn't strong enough to push him away because I wasn't strong enough to be without him just yet.

I needed to figure that out.

"I come bearing gifts," Rosie said, jerking me back into the present and proper wakefulness.

I sat up and hastily put on a smile that I hoped wasn't wonky. The last thing I needed was Rosie to take on my demons. She had plenty of her own, they were quiet now, and no way was I going to be the reason her life got loud again.

Well, any louder—she was Rosie.

Luckily she wasn't focused on me, she was placing three plastic bags on my kitchen counter.

"I got all sorts of treats for us, I'm getting good at knowing what to buy post-kidnapping." She gave me a look that was carefully structured to look jaunty, easy, light-hearted. "Of course, every woman is different, just because I crave tater tots in the month after I've been taken captive does not mean you will." She pulled out a bag. "But I got them just in case. And also, I feel like tater tots. Plus, a plethora of other things, and don't worry," she made a face, "they're all *vegetarian*."

She began to pull items out at random.

"I do have one sure fire thing that every woman I've encountered post-kidnapping—that being all of my best friends and sister-in-law—has been in agreeance helps." She yanked up a bottle of tequila, frowning at it. "I would drink it with you, but they frown on drinking while pregnant."

I smiled, then focused on the bags. "Plastic, Rosie?"

She paused with the tequila still cradled in her arms. "Oh, no, here we go," she muttered.

"I got you reusable bags," I chastised.

"Yes, but I forgot them," she moaned.

I narrowed my eyes. "They sell them at the store."

"Yes, but they charge like five bucks for them," she replied defensively. "That's simply exorbitant."

"How much was your purse, Rosie?" I asked sweetly, eyeing the distinct double C on the leather.

She scowled at me and stroked the aforementioned purse. "It's the principle of the matter. And what is this, the Spanish Inquisition? Here I am trying to do something *nice* for you and all you've got is negativity. That's not the Polly I know and love."

The words were light, full of joking and love.

But they hit me. With darkness and pain.

"I'm not that Polly, Rosie," I said, the words slipping out before I had the chance to catch them, stop them from causing the pain that I knew they would inflict.

The truth hurt, after all.

Hence me lying to everyone in my life for a month.

But I couldn't do it anymore.

She froze, her smile slipping right off her face, evidence of the fact it was a mask, just like my own.

"I always knew I'd get a story sometime," I whispered my words falling out like blood from a wound. "Even with the marriage, the ensuing divorce." I waved my hand. "And all the other stuff. I had a little hope I'd get a story. After all, you got your story and it only took two decades."

I smirked, it was fake, but it suited the moment.

Rosie smirked back. It was fake too.

"I didn't know it would be this *hard*," I continued. "But I accepted it, you know? All the best heroines go through trials. Pain. It's spiritually building. Through pain comes growth. And I've known that. But I just didn't think there would be so much pain," I whispered. "I just didn't think my story would be *this* dark."

A tear rolled down my cheek. "I don't think I was meant to grow *this* much. I don't know if I can handle it, Rosie."

She had gathered me into her arms the second my voice broke.

It was awkward with her belly, but she managed it and I burrowed into her chest, she clutched my head and pressed her lips into it.

I expected myself to start sobbing. I felt like I was cracking, breaking apart, and it hurt. It was agony, actually. But I didn't. That one tear that was dried on my cheek was all that left my eyes. I just stayed there, smelled Rosie's perfume, felt the presence of her strength. The comfort in the moment.

"No one was designed to handle this," she whispered. "Not you, most of all. But that doesn't mean you can't handle it." She pulled back so I could see her eyes. "I *know* you can handle this, because you *are* handling it, my beautiful Polly. You still smile.

Even if it's only because you want to try and hold us together. You're somehow still you, even though the holes that fucker put in you should've made your spirit leak out onto the ground. I've seen it. I know it. One of my best friends is forever scarred from it. But she wasn't exactly light and sunshine and rainbows before." She grinned through tears and I knew she was talking about Lucky's wife, Bex. "But now there's no chance of light or sunshine, she's just found a home in the darkness, and it suits her soul, the way it was before. But yours, you don't have a soul designed for darkness."

I didn't have a soul designed for darkness. But darkness didn't mind the design of a soul. It just destroyed it.

I didn't say this of course.

"I like to think everything happens for a reason," I whispered. "There is a plan for everyone. And maybe some kind of deity made it up, I don't know. But this world is far too weird and wonderful to not have a plan for people, you know?"

I sucked in a breath.

"But I guess I just don't really know what the plan was here."

Rosie kissed my hair. "I don't know either, Pol. I really fucking don't. Maybe to show us that the strongest of us all has the softest and most beautiful heart?"

I didn't say anything because Rosie was grasping at straws more than anything.

Plus my heart wasn't soft or beautiful. It was hardened. Calcified. Ugly.

But she didn't need to know that.

No one needed to know that.

I WAS WAITING for Heath when he got back.

He had a key, I didn't ask him how he got one since I hadn't given him one.

Then again, I'd never locked my apartment before.

Nor did I have the three separate locks on it before either.

But that was before my ex had waltzed right up and kidnapped me.

But he was gone now.

And now I had all those new locks. As if someone else might waltz up and do the same thing all over again.

I didn't think that was the case. But Heath was looking for something he could control, looking to put some order in this, so I didn't say anything about the extra locks, the key, the fact I always had a babysitter.

"Hey," I said, letting myself exhale with whatever small safety his presence offered.

There was pain in it, in his gaze. The way he braced when his eyes met mine. Jolted a little with both relief, presumably that I hadn't been kidnapped again, and something hard and agonizing to look at.

Love.

That was it.

He frowned at me.

Or more accurately what I was doing.

He was in front of me in less than a second, mostly to do with the short distance between the front door and the stove, but also because he was Heath. He didn't hesitate to cross the distance between us after a long absence.

Or what had become a long absence in this past month—a handful of hours.

When before all of this, we'd gone years.

"Baby," he murmured, hand at my neck, searching my eyes.

I counted to five for the sickness from his touch to go away. It did. He chased it away. It was nice now. I just had to get through the horrific five seconds when it wasn't him touching me.

He didn't speak for a beat, his eyes running up and down me. I was used to this by now since it happened every time he saw me. He needed a moment. To touch me. To see me. As if he needed to make sure this was real.

I let him because I needed that too.

Even if sometimes—most of the times—I wished this wasn't real, those moments when he held me in silence, in prayer, I was okay with it being real.

Then he jolted with the sizzling coming from the pan.

He moved me with a gentle touch to my hip that sent heat to my stomach and a chill to my bones. My body battled between its instinctive reaction toward Heath, and then its instinctive reaction toward touch.

I was tucked into his shoulder as he took over cooking.

"Baby, you shouldn't be cooking this," he said, voice hard.

"Why? You like steak."

It was true. He loved steak. He told me this right after I'd told him I was a vegetarian. We'd laughed about it. It was pure, that laughter. Easy. I'd never appreciated just how rare and complex such easy laughter was.

It was lost to me now.

I might laugh again. Surely I would. But not like that.

Heath loved steak but hadn't eaten it in the whole time he'd been here. Because most of my friends brought food. And my friends knew me. So all of the food was vegetarian, healthy plant-based.

Heath was the only one who'd eaten without complaint. Rosie and Lucy had protested loudly about the "health of their babies," but they'd eaten it too.

For me.

I'd decided that Heath was not going to be doing that anymore.

"Baby, you spent an hour telling me, in detail, how a steak is produced, and what an animal has to go through for me to have my New York Strip," he said.

"Yes, and I do not eat meat for that reason," I told him as I moved from his arms to get plates and salad. I ate more out of habit than anything else, not hunger. I was never hungry. Most of the time I had to force the food down without retching.

But I did it.

Because Heath watched me like a hawk. As did the rest of them. Me not eating, me fading away to skin and bone—like I urged to do—would hurt them.

So I ate.

"I'm not going to deprive you of something you love because of my beliefs," I continued, pouring us both wine.

Wine was something that I didn't have to force down. I did have to force myself from chugging a bottle of it down in one sitting, though. It dulled everything beautifully.

Heath turned from where he'd gotten my eggplant bake from the oven, placing it down with an intense gaze.

Though all of his gazes were intense.

He placed both glasses of wine down and yanked me into his arms with a roughness that told me he'd forgotten about our unwritten touching rules.

I held my breath.

"Sunshine, the only way you're gonna deprive me of something I love, the one thing that matters, is if you stop breathing," he rasped. "And you're not gonna do that. Not anytime soon. I'll be making sure of that. So I'll handle the eggplant and the cauliflower for the rest of my life, happily. What I won't do is have you doing something that you hate. Like supporting the cruelty and brutality of the meat industry."

I wanted to smile at the way he was parroting my words from six years ago back at me. My mouth might've twitched. But I was still trying to hold my breath at the contact.

Something moved in Heath's eyes as if he were realizing just now that he'd pressed his beautiful and hard body against mine. His grip loosened and he stepped back, clutching his glass of wine and handing me mine.

"Well," I said, exhaling. "That particular steak was grass-fed, organic, and the kindest version of murder I could find. So I'll bear cooking it."

Heath looked at me. Then he smiled.

And then he chuckled.

He didn't laugh.

Because I suspected he didn't have that ability anymore either, but he chuckled, and it was real.

I smiled in the face of such beauty. It was real too.

"What?" I asked, sitting down as he served the plates on my small dining table.

I learned that it was impossible to try and help Heath, and he liked doing little things like these, so I let him.

He placed the food down in front of me and kissed my forehead before sitting. "Only you, my Sunshine, could talk about the kindest version of murder in regards to my steak," he said, still smiling. "But, baby, I don't want you to just bear cooking. Or just bear life with me." He lost his smile now. "I want you to find joy in it again. I'll do anything and everything I can. Anything. And right now I know that means understanding that bearing things is all you can do. Just want you to know I'm gonna be making sure that changes. I'll be here to make sure that changes."

I blinked at him. This was the most he'd said about the elephant in the room since I'd come home.

He was making promises.

All kinds.

Kinds that were too heavy for my delicate emotional state.

He squeezed my hand. "Your eggplant is getting cold," he said, voice soft. "And considering on what that shit tastes like hot, I'm thinking you better eat it now."

That was his version of telling me I didn't have to respond. Deal.

So I ate.

And so did he.

And we both tried to ignore the big elephant in the room.

And we both failed.

Three Days Later

I had planned on telling Heath to leave the night of the steak. It had been a big thing. I even had a speech rehearsed

But I couldn't do it.

Not after the meal when he topped off my glass and did the dishes while I read. Especially not when he bought the bottle, a tub of my favorite ice cream then turned on our new favorite show—yes, we had a favorite—pulling me into his embrace and settling us in.

No, I couldn't do it then.

And then I'd fallen asleep.

And I couldn't do it the next night.

Or the next.

It had to be tonight.

Because this was getting bad.

Because it was getting permanent. We had a show. We had a routine. Everything I'd wanted before. Nothing I could have now.

I was working on getting my life back together. Or at least fractured and chaotic like it had been before. Of course it would never be like it was before, but I could make it look that way. And when it looked that way, people would stop having to babysit me on rotations, stop having to hide the pain in their faces, just stop all of it. I needed to get my life back to its version of together so everyone around me would be okay with getting their lives together too.

Rosie and Lucy were having babies. They needed to be excited about that. Yelling at their husbands for trying to make them drink decaffeinated coffee and stop shooting people.

I spent three days preparing.

Making calls.

Making plans.

Procrastinating the one big thing I needed to be doing.

And I was forcing myself to do it today.

My stomach was roiling when Heath walked in the door, when his shoulders both sagged and tightened, when his eyes fastened on mine. When my soul relaxed, just the tiniest bit when he did.

"We need to talk," I said before he could say "baby" in that soft, rough tone of his and melt my resolve.

He was instantly on guard.

Not that he wasn't always.

But he was more so now. Because he was Heath and he saw most things in other people and everything in me.

Almost everything.

I was pacing.

I did that in moments of extreme loss, I was noticing. I'd done it when faced with losing Lucy. Now I was doing it preparing to lose Heath. The last part of myself.

He moved, watching me, and he stopped in front of me.

I stopped pacing and held my hand up as a barrier to stop him from coming closer.

In the past, he might've ignored that, yanked me into his arms anyway. Not that we'd had enough time together for me to form such opinions, but it seemed a very Heath thing to do.

But he didn't.

"Sunshine," he murmured.

I flinched at the word. At the meaning behind it. Every time he said it was torture. But there was enough comfort in the pain that forced me to handle it.

"You remember how you said I light up a room?" I asked. "When we first met?"

"Yeah, babe, I remember," he replied, body tight.

"I don't mean to sound narcissistic, but I kind of knew I did that," I said, looking down because I couldn't meet his eyes. "Not because I think of myself as being overly brighter than anyone else, but because everyone else mutes themselves, who they truly are because they think that's what they're meant to do. They need to blend in. Not stand out. And I know I stood out. Because to me, blending in was a little death. It was a disservice to the meaning of life. I like to think I made things brighter because I made people realize that they could be who they were around me. Made it okay for them to let their light out." I peeked up at Heath. "I know it's stupid—"

"It's not fuckin' stupid," he ground out.

I swallowed the power of his words. The passion in them. I didn't let it stop me. "Well, I used to be a little proud of that," I continued. "Most of my life I didn't have it together. I didn't really have a lot to contribute, I didn't have a skill like Lucy has for writing and Rosie has for...chaos. I never let the fact I didn't have a 'thing' get to me because I kind of thought of that as my thing."

I sucked in a ragged breath against the power of Heath's stare, knowing if I met it again, I'd crumble. So I kept talking.

"But now, I don't have it anymore. I don't light up a room. I suck all the light out when I enter. Like the people who love me most are afraid to be happy around me. I can see it in their eyes, that forced brightness. They're ashamed to truly be joyous about their lives because how can they possibly be with poor, broken Polly around?"

Heath had gone still, absolutely still with my words, but I had to keep going. For his sake and mine.

"It's because they love me so much, I know that," I whispered. "But it's because I love them so much that it kills me a little inside to be around them." I said them when I meant *him*.

I finally got the courage to meet his eyes. "To be faced with just how draining I am, it's exhausting. My light's gone out, Heath. And I don't know who I am now. Don't know *what* I am now." I sucked in another breath. "I can't even begin to figure out who I am now when I'm wondering what we are."

"There is no wondering about what we are," he said. "We just are. After fucking everything. We *are*."

I struggled against his words. "That's not an answer," I whispered. "After everything, that's not an answer."

His eyes didn't leave mine. "Yeah, babe, it is. After everything, it's the only fucking answer."

Something that should've made my heart soar, would've in any other circumstance, suddenly made my blood boil. Anger, intense and unfamiliar surged through me.

I narrowed my eyes, finding it much easier to meet his stare that way.

"So what, now I'm the damsel again, now I need protecting, fixing, *that's* what brought you back?" I hissed, the words cruel and unfair. "*That's* what makes you think that we can work on this now that I'm hopeless and weak and you can be strong and heroic?"

Heath didn't react to my anger, my venom. Not in the way I expected him to. With that cold and ruthless exterior that had been absent for this last month. The exterior I was trying to call forward to make this easier, somehow.

But this was not meant to be easier.

So Heath's eyes softened at my ugly accusations.

"No, babe, it's the exact opposite of that," he said, voice equally soft, gentle. "What happened did not make you a damsel. And it sure as fuck didn't make me strong." He moved as if to step forward, he saw my entire body stiffen so he held himself back with a tight jaw.

His eyes ran over me with reverence. "It made you into something I don't understand," he continued. "Turned you into a survivor. But not like most people. Because those who survive, lose parts of themselves, big parts, important parts. Those who survive lose a little of what makes them human. And you haven't lost an ounce of it. Your kindness. Your generosity. It should've made you hate the world. Hate everyone. When you're showing everyone just the same amount of love that you have before. More, if that's possible."

I wanted to scream. Actually scream in the face of his words. I ached for cruelty because it was bearable. But he was giving me this.

"You hated me," I whispered, desperate to probe that out of him. "Just because I got kidnapped and whatever manly testosterone-fueled emotions were sparked from that, doesn't change that, Heath. You're not obligated to stand by and protect me. To coddle me or watch and make sure I don't go off the deep end." I paused. "Again. Lucy has already lectured me about joining cults or folk bands. I'll be okay. You don't have to do this."

"Didn't hate you," he murmured, eyes and voice still frustratingly and beautifully gentle.

I raised my brow.

"Was angry with you," he said. "I was furious with you. Fuck, I wanted to hate you." He ran his hand through his hair. "But I couldn't. Hate you. I could never. Not for as long as I walk this earth. Nothing you say here, while you're trying to push me away is gonna make me do that, Polly. Say what you need to. But it's not moving me from my spot. From this spot."

My vision became blurry and stark all at the same time. Heath's energy swallowed up all that anger that had been so visceral before.

"I realized I never thanked you," I said finally, wrenching my eyes up to meet his.

"For what?"

"For finding me. Saving me," I whispered.

His eyes hardened. "You're not thanking me for shit. Especially when I was too fucking late."

I didn't say anything. I couldn't. Because he was right. It was too late.

"It's not your fault," I said finally.

"Not yours either," he said fiercely. "I know you're toying with the past. With yourself. Trying to lay some kind of blame where it doesn't belong. So I'll say this now and I'll say it every day, every moment until you believe it."

His fingers lightly grasped my chin to move it upward so my eyes could drown in his gaze.

"This was not your fault," he declared, throwing each word into the air with force.

Maybe he was right. Maybe it wasn't my fault. The kidnapping, the brutality.

But it was my fault if I harmed more people than needed to be harmed.

People being Heath.

"I'm not the same girl as I was when I was eighteen," I said, deciding to go for a different tactic. "Not even the woman I was eight weeks ago. This is not the story where there's the happy ever after. This is what happens after the damsel is saved," I whispered. "They never show you that because that would ruin it all. Wreck it all. Because the damsel isn't really saved in the end. Not this one at least."

"I'm not tryin' to save you, Sunshine," he said, taking me into his arms as if he was. "Just lookin' for *you.*"

"Are you really looking for *me,* Heath?" I asked, grasping at emotional straws. "Second chance romances don't work. Or in our case, third chance," I said. "Of course in movies and books they do because they're written by some heartbroken artist who is hoping to create their future, that impossible happy ending. And because most of us are lost, heartbroken souls, we rework those stories to fit our situation. Which isn't hard, because heartbreak is always the same. And we always want the same thing, either for it to stop hurting so much, or it to hurt more when the person comes back. So we watch those movies. Read those books. Imagine, pray that those stories will come to life. It's nice."

I smiled.

"Really nice to do when things are dark and ugly in the present and you can find some solace in the marriage of an embellished past and am impossible future."

My smile failed as I focused on him.

"It's lovely and nice, but it doesn't *work*. Not when years have passed, and the world has changed around us, and we haven't." I paused. "Changed, that is."

I roved my eyes over the outside changes that had nothing on the inside changes.

"Life is still the same, but it's intrinsically different. That feeling, that..." I trailed off in order to find the courage. I met his eyes. "That love survived the years, but only because it's attached to a memory, it will not survive when we try to attach it to what we are now."

What I am now, was what I didn't say. What I couldn't. I didn't need to anyway. It was the elephant in the room, pressing on my lungs. On my heart.

He was silent for a long time. It was something I was getting used to, but it still made me uncomfortable, a person who always reacted, spoke, laughed, cried, jumped immediately, on initial reaction, on instinct.

Heath worked on instinct too. But it was a warrior's instinct. Analyzing all the options, all possible threats, all ways to attack, to defend, to survive. I wondered if it was a throwaway from the war. But I thought about the war as something that required action without thought. Wasn't that the whole point of basic training? To drum out those pesky unpredictable personality traits in order to promote the appropriate split second predictable responses in a soldier.

I found another yawning gap in my knowledge of the person who had consumed my mind and heart for so long. I did not know what lurked in those pockets of silence. When he just stared, silent, intense. Was something yanking at him? Something from before? Something horrible I couldn't fathom? Couldn't imagine, let alone live through?

I found myself utterly desperate to pry open his brain and

dive into that darkness I knew I couldn't handle. That I knew would wreck me. For the simple fact it might close that gap between us. I wanted to live his horror so I could find a way to give him peace.

But there was no way to pry open a human being's memories without doing damage to them. And I would not do any more damage to Heath. Not even for my own peace.

Especially not for my own.

Heath yanked me closer to him, brows furrowed slightly as if he could read my thoughts the way I wished I could read his.

His hands fastened on either side of my neck. "I don't know about all of that, baby," he murmured. "Know my love for you has survived a lot and it sure as shit hasn't made it through everything just to die when I've finally brought it to life." His eyes searched mine. "But even if you are right, I'll fall in love with you all over again. I'll learn about what's changed in you, I'll make sure there's never a moment when you don't remember that the past is nothing but the past and our future is together."

I blinked. "You love me?"

He blinked back. "Come on, babe. Everything we've been through, everything you see in me? You can't see that?" In the midst of this moment, Heath's voice held a hint of teasing.

"We've never said it to each other," I whispered.

He narrowed his eyes. "Yes, we have."

And I knew what he meant. That every look, every fight, every moment from the night in the bar was saturated with it. It didn't make sense. To love someone after a collection of chaotic moments.

But with me, wasn't my life just a series of chaotic moments?

But wasn't love supposed to bring you peace?

"Love doesn't have to be peaceful to bring you peace," he murmured, showing me I'd said that last thought aloud.

Heath laid his lips gently to mine.

And I wasn't overcome with fear, panic, and revulsion. All that was there, of course, but not as overwhelming as before.

"I'm not going anywhere, Sunshine," he promised. "'Cause I'm looking for peace in your chaos too."

CHAPTER EIGHTEEN

I CAME out of my room and was no longer surprised to see Lucy and Keltan standing there bickering over the harm it would do Lucy to have one sip of coffee.

"Not happenin'," Keltan said, folding his arms.

And of course, he thought the subject was closed, because these males—still after being married to women like Lucy and Rosie—thought that a firm tone and a crossing of muscled arms somehow cemented a decision.

"Fine," Lucy said, and I blinked in surprise.

Maybe pregnancy had finally mellowed her.

And we had approximately six weeks to enjoy that mellowness.

"I'll just have a glass of wine at dinner." She folded her own arms, albeit awkwardly since her protruding belly was in the way.

Or maybe she wasn't mellow. Like at all.

"How in the fuck do you go from thinking one sip of coffee won't hurt the baby to one glass of wine?" he demanded.

"Well, the baby's already grown, so I'm sure it's fine anyway. It's really just...marinating. But you will get hurt if you keep this up, buddy."

I could've watched this forever. It made me warm in places that were now almost always cold. Reminded me of the reasons not to let it win. The darkness. Because of my sister. Because of her happiness. And that little baby.

I wanted to watch it forever and warm myself up in front of their lives and pretend for as long as I could that my coldness wouldn't come back as soon as I stopped watching.

But I couldn't pretend around someone like Keltan.

"Polly," he said, yanking Lucy to his side and kissing the top of her head. His palm settled protectively over her belly.

She scowled at him but relaxed into his arms.

I braced myself for her smile. Because it was forced, full of sadness. It was ice water to my bones. Lucy didn't know she was doing it. It would break her heart if she did. It was a smile she put on for me because she was scared I couldn't handle anything else from her. I was still to be treated with kid gloves and Polly gloves.

It hit me when her eyes dimmed a little, losing the brightness they'd had moments ago.

It hit me. Right in the chest. But it wasn't hard since there was a constant gaping and bleeding hole right above where my heart should be. Despite the beautiful words and promises Heath made last night. Despite the fact I fell asleep in his arms and woke up to his lips on my forehead and him murmuring goodbye, promising to see me soon.

It would've been nice if such things could heal that big bleeding hole.

It only dulled the edges of the pain.

So obviously I turned on a megawatt smile to hide it.

"Don't you two have like, jobs or homes to go to?" I asked

cheerfully, walking toward the kitchen and snatching my reusable coffee cup from the counter.

"I don't have a job since they kept sending me home," Lucy huffed.

"Babe, you couldn't fit behind your fuckin' desk," Keltan said dryly.

"Make one more remark about my size," Lucy shot. "I dare you, soldier boy."

I smiled as I filled up my cup with hot water and tea.

There was a pause.

"Yeah, I thought so," Lucy said. "Keltan owns his place and the whole point of owning a business is so you don't actually have to go to work."

"Not the point of owning a business, at all, babe," Keltan cut in.

"How is it that you have the bravery to continue baiting a pregnant woman with access to a knife?" she asked curiously.

Keltan chuckled. "Lucy, I confiscated your knife about three months into your pregnancy when you threatened to slash the tires of the guy who cut in front of you at Taco Bell."

I fastened the lid and grinned at Keltan. "Good call."

He grinned back at me.

He was one of the only people whose grin was almost genuine. Maybe because of what he'd experienced from war. Because there were parts of him that had been broken and he knew that there was no healing them by treating me like glass. I was sure Lucy and Rosie knew this too, since they had experience with pain, but they didn't want to admit it.

Lucy rolled her eyes at him. "Whatever, dude," she muttered. "If this kid's a girl then I'll be sure to hide all of the firearms on her first date, see whose laughing then."

Keltan's eyes darkened. "No fuckin' way is my daughter dating until she's forty," he hissed.

I laughed.

It was almost genuine.

"We're here because we thought we'd take you out for breakfast," Lucy said, deciding to go back to ignoring her husband. "This new healthy vegan place just opened in Santa Monica and it's supposed to not actually be terrible."

Right.

This was just one in a long line of excuses that had one or both of the two of these people at my door.

It was part of the 'wait for Polly to fall apart' schedule.

I didn't blame them. Firstly, they loved and cared about me. And second, I was Polly.

So there were impromptu breakfasts, shopping trips to decorate nurseries, movie dates. Lunch dates.

And in Rosie's case, a day at the gun range. Or she'd planned it to be a day, but it had to get cut very short when I refused to touch a gun.

"As much as I love a good vegan restaurant, and I love watching you trying to eat vegan food without insulting someone's fashion choices, and I do," I smirked at Lucy, "I've got a class to go to."

Lucy's pretend smile dimmed immediately.

"What?"

"A yoga class," I clarified, moving across the room to strap my yoga mat across my shoulder. "It's part of my teaching certification."

"No, you can't go to yoga," she said.

"Why not?" I asked, meeting her eyes. "Because I'm meant to be passed from one person to another, to be coddled and protected from the very world that has already done the damage?" I smiled. "No, Luce. As much as I appreciate and love you for everything you've done, and I do, I need to get back to my life."

I hadn't told Heath about this.

Not because I didn't think he'd let me go. I knew he'd support me moving back toward my old life, even if I was just going through the motions. I hadn't told him because I was scared of where that conversation would lead. Terrified it would lead to somewhere I couldn't control my emotions. Somewhere too close to the truth, the past.

"There's no rush," Lucy said, stepping forward. "I know you're Polly and you've been in a rush to do everything including leave the womb six weeks early, but this is something that you do not need to rush." Her voice was only slightly more than a whisper when she took my hands in hers.

"I do," I whispered back. "Because rushing was my life. It kept me sane. Kept me, me. Staying still doesn't work for me, Luce. It works for you and it warms my soul that it does, but if I stand still for much longer I'll scream."

Lucy gauged my words. With shimmering eyes and pain in her face.

She squeezed my hands again.

"Okay. I get it," she said finally. "I don't get the whole yoga thing, it sounds fucking insane, but I get the rest. And I do kind of get we've been hovering. I know it's selfish of us to suffocate you like that."

"It's not suffocating," I argued.

She leaned in to kiss my forehead. "But it's not helping. Not really. I should've seen it earlier. You need people around when most people need space, so it stands to reason when most people need company, you need space."

"No," I whispered. "Just peace."

As if it were as simple as leaving the apartment and teaching yoga.

But it was a start.

I SHOULD'VE EXPECTED Heath to be waiting in the parking lot for me.

I didn't. Because even after a month of having him come home to me, fall asleep with me and always be there, I wasn't used to it. I wasn't letting myself become used to it.

Not when it was temporary.

My muscles ached slightly from the class, the instructor pushing us past our limits because "you're not going to be able to take your students from your comfort zone if you're still residing in yours."

I liked it. Challenging myself in a safe environment. Even if I was prodding at doors that rattled when I opened my mind up in the practice. I knew the more I practiced, the more dangerous it would be. Yoga was more about the discovery of the mind than the stretching of the limbs, after all.

My skin prickled at that realization.

If I continued doing this, I'd have no choice but to face my demons. Luckily, those thoughts didn't find traction, since Heath was pushing off his car—which he was leaning on very well—and striding toward me.

He didn't give me a moment to speak before he pulled me into his arms with a gentleness that was characteristic of the way he touched me now. It was funny, people only tended to treat others with tenderness after they'd been broken.

His lips pressed to mine, gentle too, but with a slight hunger that I wanted to respond to. To feel. I almost did. I felt it, somewhere. The need for him. But it was buried in shame, in filth, in pain.

"Did Lucy call you?" I asked when he released me slightly, hands still resting on my hips. He was touching me more often now. It was getting easier to bear. Only with him, though.

I wondered if I'd ever get to a point where there wasn't five seconds of revulsion to bear before relaxing—as much as I could—into Heath's arms. If I'd be able to hug my sister without wanting to tear the skin from my bones. If I could shake someone's hand again without having to run to the bathroom and scrub my own.

"What do you think?" Heath asked in response to my Lucy question.

He was good at that, yanking me from my mind the second things got too…prickly.

I looked into his eyes and let them hold me in the moment. "I think she called you the second I left," I replied with a slight grin.

He nodded in response.

I let out a sigh and relaxed into Heath's arms on instinct. His eyes flared at this since it was something I hadn't done before, but otherwise, he didn't acknowledge it.

"And do you agree with her rant that she no doubt repeated to you?" I asked. "Do you think it's too soon?" I nodded my head back to the studio, waving to my instructor as I did so.

He waved back and inclined his head into a small bow.

Heath gave him an oh so manly chin lift.

I was surprised he was here *after* the class if Lucy called him so soon. He was all about protecting me. And I would've thought he was on the same wavelength as Lucy, poor, broken Polly couldn't get back to her life yet. Not when she hasn't shed a tear. Spoken a word about what happened to her.

They were waiting for that.

But they weren't going to get it.

Heath's eyes darkened. "If you don't think it's too soon, then, no," he said quietly, running his hands along my jaw lightly. There were no bruises there anymore. But his eyes followed the roadmap of pain that was only showing on the inside now the marks had faded.

"As much as I'd like to keep you close within touching distance so I never have to relive those sixteen hours again, I can't," he continued, eyes meeting mine. "'Cause I want you free. Want you to be Polly."

"You want me to be Polly," I repeated, the words ashes in my mouth.

His eyes searched mine. "Always."

I paused, chewing on those simple words that were not at all simple. I couldn't say I'd never be Polly. That Polly was lost and there was this...imposter in her place. No, I couldn't say that out loud because I was afraid of what else I'd say.

So, in the middle of a parking lot, I said something else.

"We haven't addressed this, not really," I whispered.

Heath furrowed his brows, obviously not expecting this response. "What?"

"Us," I clarified. "We only...reconnected...before." That almost hunger sparked again at the memory of that beautiful time in his apartment and Heath's hands at my hips flexed.

I sucked in a breath as panic chased that warmth away with the reality of what happened after. I tried to focus on that night. The night before everything was shattered. But it was hard to hold onto beauty when ugliness clutched onto your soul.

"There was no talking," I continued my voice rough. "No going over everything. No going over *anything*. And then we're here. And it's like, we're..."

"Exactly where we're meant to be," he finished for me. "It wasn't meant to be. Not how we got here. I'd change that if I could. Would give anything to change it. But I can't. So I gotta take the small favors where I can." His thumb brushed over my lips and I shivered at the contact.

And that almost hunger sparked up again. Teased at the bottom of my stomach. Fought against the ugliness residing there.

But it was a fight that it'd never win.

And I didn't want every touch, every gaze to be a fight with Heath.

"My whole life has been chaos, Heath," I whispered. "Granted, most of it has been self-imposed." Heath's eyes hardened at this, but I continued. "But now, after..." I trailed off, unable to finish that sentence. I took a breath. "After what happened, I've realized it, I know what I need. I need peace. And I can't get that from you. From us."

It was a lie. Kind of. I could get everything from us. But not without taking everything from him. Not without my ugliness draining all that was good inside him.

He regarded me for a long while. "There's a problem there, babe. With that peace. You're looking for quiet amongst that chaos you think is such a bad thing." He smiled, and I hated that there was so much sadness and pain in that smile. "Your chaos is the single most beautiful and defining thing about you. You live life wild and loud, babe. I'm not talking about sound. I'm talkin' about the way you smile, the way you enter a room. The way you *love*."

I'd been so certain that the cruel way he'd talked to me before was what hurt me most. What made my insides bleed. But it wasn't cruelty that was breaking me worse than ever before. It was his kindness. His love.

"My love isn't sunshine anymore, Heath," I choked out. "You know that better than anyone."

He flinched, actually flinched at my words. "No, I fuckin' don't," he hissed. "I know that standing here in the middle of a parking lot on a cloudy day, in a fucking cloudy point in our lives, all I can feel is sunshine. That hasn't changed. That's something that'll never change. And I'm promising you that." Something flared in his eyes. "Remember, Polly, I'm a man who keeps his promises."

He pressed his forehead to mine, his thumb wiping at the single tear I'd let escape.

"I'm not inside your head, baby," he murmured. "I don't know how to help you, though I wish to fuck I did. I would give anything to be able to know exactly what to do, what to fucking say to make it..."

"Better?" I offered, I hated how cynical, how cold my voice sounded after the warmth of his words.

He rested his head on mine for a moment longer, then he straightened, hands still on my hips. "I'll settle for bearable," he said. "And I'm not meanin' for me, or for your sister, or for Rosie, 'cause I know how fuckin' hard you're trying to make it bearable for everyone else. I can see it in you. You're exhausting yourself helping your family deal with this. Helping *strangers* deal with other shit. And I honestly don't give a fuck about them. I give a fuck about you being able to smile without it taking every ounce of your energy to make it look like something you think it should look like. But you gotta give yourself a chance for that, Sunshine. You're the most selfless person I know, but I'm going to request you be a little selfish in order to breathe again. 'Cause I know you're suffocating, even if you won't admit it."

The lump was bigger now. As was the hole in my chest. He

saw it. He saw all of it. I thought I'd been doing so freaking well. I'd thought I was excelling at my performance. I should've known Heath saw more.

Saw the ugly.

He lived it, after all.

"I can't," I choked out. "I have to stay busy, to help people with their horrors, to understand them, because I have a visceral need to understand their nightmares, so maybe I can understand mine one day."

His jaw was hard, was iron with even my small admission. So I knew there was no way I could ever utter the big one.

He pressed his lips to mine hard and quick. "Well, I'm here, Sunshine. I'm here 'til you understand it. And I'll be here after too."

It was another promise.

I shouldn't have let him make it.

But I did.

Three Weeks Later

"Can I ask you a question?"

Heath's eyes lightened with my words. Ones that called up images from the past. I hadn't consciously chosen them. No, especially considering my question. I didn't want those beautiful memories in the proximity of the words that I was going to utter next. But here they were, ready to be tainted like everything else was.

Of course, on the surface, it didn't look that way.

I was getting close to becoming certified as a yoga instructor since I'd done some training...before. I was back to volunteering, with Heath at my side, of course.

I was back to helping Rain with her latest move—the girl couldn't keep an apartment to save her life—to helping my friend Dave with his new role on a soap, running lines with him when I could.

I read to the kids at St. Mary's. Every Thursday.

My timetable was full. Bursting.

Just like before.

But nothing was like before.

People weren't babysitting me anymore. They were still bracing, but they were trying to get back to something resembling normal. Lucy was yelling at Keltan for getting her the wrong flavor La Croix. Luke was yelling at Rosie when she was still at the gun range.

The nurseries were being decorated.

Life went on.

Kind of.

I was still sleeping through the night, in Heath's arms. He still treated me gently. Still wasn't pushing. Though he could walk down the street with my hand firmly clasped in his and I didn't feel the urge to yank it back. He could kiss me more often. Close-mouthed and quick, of course, but he could do it more. Obviously he did. Often.

As soon as he sensed I could take more, he gave me more. Another touch, another gaze, more murmured promises of the future.

Our future.

Our impossible future.

I should've tried to stop it again. But I was Polly, I never did what I should've.

So we were curled up on the sofa, watching *Stranger Things* and eating peanut butter popcorn. Heath had screwed his nose up the first time I put it in our cart—yes, we were grocery shopping together now—but then he tried it and we had to buy four packets to last the week.

My head had been on Heath's chest, I had been almost content.

So of course that's when the demons in my soul chose that moment to strike. That's why I lifted my head and spoke. Heath paused the TV, turning to give me his full attention. He did that. Gave me his full attention. Always. I always got all of him. And I gave him tattered scraps of me.

"You're askin' to ask me a question?" he clarified, voice holding a bit of teasing. Only a bit, because the man he was now wasn't capable of the light teasing, the light happiness of the man he was before.

I was largely responsible for this.

"What did you do with Craig?" I asked, deciding to plow right through with the emotional bulldozer.

My words worked to wipe that light teasing right off his face. Like right off. I *hated* that I had the ability to do that.

"I'm not strong enough for all the details," I said quickly. "I'm not like Rosie or Lucy or the old ladies in the Sons of Templar. I don't need to know everything. *I can't* know everything. It's not in me. But I need to know at least, is he breathing or not?"

I had a hefty amount of shame admitting what I couldn't handle. The whole truth. I barely knew anything about how they found me, though I knew it had to do with the Sons of Templar and Wire since he had been there during the first horrible days of my recovery. Physical recovery at least.

But I didn't know what was going on with the larger picture. The men who Craig had tried to sell me to. It was something I should've asked about. But I didn't.

Heath was silent for a long time.

Long even for him.

I guessed by the way his fists were resting on the tops of his knees, the steady and forced breaths, he was trying to calm himself down.

Because of course, I needed to be treated with care.

I ached for him to not do that. To explode.

Because at least that was honest.

"Does it matter?" he said through clenched teeth. "He's never going to hurt you again."

"It matters as to whether he's never going to hurt me again because he's banished to Siberia or whether he's in a shallow grave and you have his death on your soul," I said.

Heath's jaw ticked. "I have plenty of death on my soul. That one is not gonna haunt me for a *second*."

The blow was physical.

"You killed him," I choked out.

He didn't reply.

Which was a reply.

"You had no right to do that," I said, my voice broken.

"I had every fucking right," he hissed, voice chilling by the second. "It was the only thing I could do to punish him." He paused. "There were a lot of things I wish I could've done to punish him."

My skin prickled with his cold and foreign tone. His ruthless tone. His war tone. "He didn't need punishment," I said quietly. "He needed forgiveness."

My words brought about silence. Tense and dangerous silence.

And Heath's fury tore through it.

"Are you fucking *kidding* me?" he exploded, jumping from the sofa.

I stood too.

There was no more care, not now. No more Polly gloves, I found myself strangely relieved.

He started to pace. "The fucker hit you. *Kidnapped* you. Hurt you."

As if his words brought back the reality, he stopped pacing to stand in front of me. His hand ghosted over the spot that was now healed and unblemished.

"Not just on the surface, but on the parts of you that don't heal as easily as a bruise. That is a crime punishable by death." His hand fisted beside my face and went to his side. "And you want me to believe, to fucking accept the fact that you think he deserved *forgiveness* instead of death?"

I smiled at him. Which of course, caught him off guard. When he got like this, like the man who had to use his anger to get him through the hardest of times, when he had to hurl his words out, pepper them with profanities in order to continue on the road he'd chosen, I doubted he often got a response such as this.

"I don't expect you to understand it, Heath," I said. "Nor am I going to try to convert you to my own state of belief. Because that's not how I work. And even if it was, I should know that no one is going to convince *you* of all people, to change a pattern of behavior."

I paused, wanting to touch him. Needing to touch him. I almost did. But the past stopped me. So I sucked in a breath.

"But I do want you to accept it. Certainly believe it," I murmured. "Because if you know me half as well as you tell me you do, then you will *know* who I am."

His gaze was softening, draining of that visceral fury as I spoke.

"So many people walk around with anger in their hearts," I

whispered, my eyes going to his chest, then back up to his eyes. "And that anger is warranted, of course. Because the world hurts every single person who walks across it, in some way or another. Some worse than others. And if you want to find one, there is a reason to be angry every single day. Every single *second*."

That anger was creeping up my throat, even as I spoke. It was an effort, a great fricking effort to swallow it.

"People are going to walk around with anger in their hearts and I will not blame them or judge them," I said. "We all deal with what we're given the best ways we know how. The ways that we know will keep us standing, keep us inhaling and exhaling. For you, that's a lot of profanities, yelling on occasion and a lot of intense and brooding stares." I smiled sadly. "Even death threats. Violence," I continued, no longer smiling. "You know me, so you know that I don't believe in this. But I *accep*t it. Because that's what's got you here, right here in front of me. Exhaling."

I lifted my hand up to trail his beard, it was soft and scratchy at the same time. It was comforting.

He jerked at the contact, the first I'd initiated between us.

"For me," I whispered, "it's forgiveness. Because I can't carry the weight of anger or hate. For me, I can't stand underneath that. I have to forgive, or I can't move forward. I can't exhale." I moved forward to touch my lips to his. "And right now, I'm really fricking glad to be inhaling and exhaling."

He was taut, shaking with his exertion to let my lips move slowly against his. To let me control this kiss. The first one I'd initiated. It was gentle. Tentative. Slow. Sweet.

It was goodbye.

I stepped back, and he let out a sound of protest at the back of his throat.

"Why'd you do that?" he demanded.

I smiled at the proximity of the past right now. It was something I needed. "I wanted to see what it felt like to kiss you," I whispered.

He jerked again. Like I'd stuck him. His eyes were on fire with heat, with everything. "No, Sunshine, wasn't asking why you kissed me," he growled, hands fisted at his sides. "Askin' why you *stopped*."

My stomach dipped at the way his words caressed me. The way they demanded attention from parts of me I thought were dead.

I ached to step forward again, press my lips to his, let the kiss chase away the horror. The truth.

But I wasn't eighteen anymore. I couldn't do that.

I had to invite the truth. In all of its horrible glory.

"I was pregnant," I whispered, the words barely breaking the air that was rumbling from energy between us. It was like they screamed at me, roared in the hollows of my skull. The hollows of my heart.

Through those roars, I saw Heath go still.

Go completely and utterly still.

He waited a long time. Presumably for me to speak more, or maybe for him to get himself under control. I wasn't sure which.

But I wasn't ready to speak more. I wasn't sure if I could.

"Say again?" he murmured, voice shaking.

I sucked in air, and it settled in my lungs like concrete. "I was pregnant," I whispered again, my eyes darting downward. "I didn't tell anyone, not even Lucy. Not at first. Because you're not supposed to tell anyone until twelve weeks. And imagine, *me*, following the rules in that one thing when I break all the others." I tried to smile, but it didn't work. So I shrugged instead. "I honestly don't know why I didn't tell her. Or anyone...even *Craig*."

I almost choked on his name. I saw Heath's jaw twitch from the way I uttered it.

"It wasn't the reason he asked me, he didn't know the, neither did I, it was too early." I sucked in a horrible breath. "I loved him." I chewed my lip, unable to lie to myself any more after everything that happened.

I surely couldn't lie to Heath.

Even if that admission was acid in my soul right now.

"Maybe, I loved him," I amended, unable to believe that statement, that feeling after everything I'd gone through.

"The part of him that he pretended to be, at least," I said. "The part that seemed so easy and right when things between us...weren't. I found out not long after we got engaged. Not long after we saw you that day. After you left. After my feet started to get cold. My soul started to get cold."

I'd never admitted that to anyone. My reservations leading up to the wedding. I certainly didn't admit it to myself. But it was time. Beyond time. I had too many secrets in my soul. I needed to let some of them out.

"I knew that I didn't have to get married in order to have a baby," I continued. "I didn't *have* to stay with Craig. But, I've lived in chaos, in constant motion for so long, I knew the second I saw that plus sign that I wanted peace for my baby. That normal life that I pretty much rebelled against, since, well, ever."

I smiled.

"Because when I think about my mom and dad, the life that they gave Lucy and me, how happy I was, I wanted to reproduce that. If I hadn't have met you, I would've been so *certain* about that. But there was hesitation, when I was holding a stick telling me I was carrying another man's child...there was you." My voice was a broken whisper and I didn't have the courage to meet Heath's eyes so I continued to look at the floor.

"If it was just me..." I trailed off. "I don't let myself torture myself with those 'ifs,'" I rasped. "Because then I would think about if I didn't lose..." I choked, literally choked on the words right as they were coming from my throat.

If I didn't lose my baby.

"Polly," Heath said, the word seemingly yanked from him, torn from his very throat it was full of that much pain.

Pain for me.

More pain.

That's what we were now.

I held up my hand. "I need to finish," I whispered.

"You need to fucking *look* at me," he demanded.

I sucked in a breath, counting the scuffs in the hardwood. "I can't," I said to the floor. "I can't because I see myself in your eyes, I see my pain in your eyes and I'm scared I might not be able to stand if I see that."

Whether he had been respecting the distance I put between us, or maybe he'd just been unable to move until now I wasn't sure.

All that I knew was there wasn't distance between us now.

Heath's hand was on my hip, yanking his body to mine, steadying me, even when his touch weakened my knees. His other hand went to my chin, gently moving it upward to meet his gaze.

I flinched.

Because there was pain there.

Agony.

Of what I'd lost.

Of what *we'd* lost.

A life.

Peace.

"You don't need to stand under it, Polly," he murmured. "Not when I'm here to hold you up."

A single tear trailed down my cheek.

He didn't wipe it away.

He just watched me, waiting for more.

And there was more.

With us, it seemed there was always more.

"I planned on telling everyone...after the honeymoon," I continued. "I would be exactly twelve weeks then, and I wasn't really showing. Craig didn't notice, apart from a comment about me eating more donuts than usual. I should've taken more notice as to why he wanted the wedding to happen so quickly. Not because of him loving me and wanting to marry me as soon as possible." I laughed. "No, because there was only so long he could keep up the act. The human mask itches the monster underneath. But I was distracted. I'm always distracted about something. But this time I was distracted about the fact I was going to be a mother. I was growing a baby inside of me. And I didn't let myself think of you and what could've been because I felt like I was betraying that little life that had become more important than anything else in the world to me. It was her peace that I had to think about not my own. I thought I was making the right decision. But I was wrong."

I sucked in a raspy breath.

"That day, right before the wedding," I began.

"Fuck, Polly," Heath started to argue.

"No, I need to finish," I said. "Standing in my wedding dress, chosen for another man, with that same man's baby inside of me, I was close. I don't like to say how close I was to giving up my baby's peace for you. But I couldn't do that. You're a good man, Heath, despite what you think. Good enough to raise another man's baby if it came to that..."

"It fuckin' would've come to that," he growled, cupping my face. "Anything grown inside of you, half of you, I would've loved it with all of me."

Another tear trailed down my cheek.

More pain.

"You know what I said about ifs," I whispered. "They're dangerous. Fatal. Especially since there's more." I steeled myself. "I lost my baby exactly one day into my honeymoon. Not the best way to start married life. Craig was understanding, kind, of course. Took care of me. But now with hindsight, there were moments that he was...*irritated* with it all. But I was too deep in sorrow to care I guess. I don't know. It was blurry. But what the doctors told me after wasn't. That I likely would never conceive naturally again. That I'd never carry to term, even if I could. That I would never be able to give the gift my parents gave me to a child of my own."

I let the words sink into the air. They were heavy. I knew this since I'd been carrying them around with me.

Dragging them with bloodied and broken fingers.

"I decided I didn't want to tell anyone. Craig agreed. He said he didn't want kids anyway, so it was okay with him. *Okay*. Me literally losing my baby and any possibility of another one."

Okay.

I remembered hating him in that split second.

Absolutely *despising* him.

But I let go of that because I had to.

"I made myself okay. Because there was no other choice. I couldn't say it out loud, Heath."

I sucked in air and it raked down my throat like broken glass.

"I physically couldn't reproduce the sound of my dreams shattering in that cold and no-nonsense tone like the doctor did. I couldn't spread the utter agony and loss around my family like a plague. So I kept it. Let it infect me. Because I knew I'd survive it. Because I managed to do things like breathe and blink and walk after they told me. Then I managed to pretend to smile. Laugh like I almost meant it. Throw myself into life with Craig that was so different than how I expected."

I blinked to glimpse into the past. "Sometimes it was nice. Good, maybe. And then I remembered that I did love him, so I made excuses for those cold looks, those strange and cruel comments that I didn't understand, and he apologized for later. I made excuses right up until his fist in my face was too big of a thing to excuse...and you know the rest."

That was a lie. Even telling the ugliest and painful truth I'd been nurturing for two years, there was the ugly, decaying lump of truth inside of me that I couldn't purge right now.

Couldn't purge ever.

Heath didn't speak.

He was still holding me, frozen in the pain from my words. Likely torturing himself for one reason or another.

For me.

"You want kids," I said, more than a whisper. Barely. "You told me that. You want to make a family you never had. You deserve to make the most beautiful family there ever was. You deserve a son with your courage, bone structure, and strength. A daughter with your eyes and your heart. I can't give you that, Heath. I can't give you the one thing you want above all else."

"Stop," he said. The word was harsh. Painful. Because he'd yanked it up his throat with a force that hurt to hear. "*You* are what I want above all else, Polly. *You.*"

He shook me roughly in his arms as if to bring home his point. As if to remind himself that I was still there.

His eyes burned into mine. "Your fucking *sunshine.* Your smile. The fact that you wander around the house at three in the morning because it's some sort of witching hour and you want to suck up the 'positive energy.'"

I jerked at that because I hadn't done that in the two months we'd been here.

Because there was no positive energy for me to suck up. I slept past the witching hour. Slept past the nightmares.

Heath knew this somehow, like he knew everything about me.

And he wasn't done.

"You who won't eat meat but who will cook me steak with a wrinkled nose because she knows I like it," he growled. "You who constantly loses phones, keys, remotes, but never forgets a birthday, an anniversary, a commitment to a friend. You who smiles at strangers because that's your first instinct. You who sleeps tangled up in me and uses my chest as her pillow."

He cupped my cheek in his hands. "*That's* what I want above all else. I didn't have a home, a family, until *you*. You carry home around with you. You make a family everywhere you go because you attract people who want to be involved with you, connected to you, dedicated to you. So if you think that what you lost, what breaks my fucking heart, is going to make me lose you, then you're fucking *wrong*."

As if he couldn't help himself, he leaned forward, kissing me hard and brutal in amongst his gentle words.

"I'm not going to lose you," he murmured against my mouth. "Not going to walk away. Never. Because you're my *family*. Even if it's all I'll ever have, it'll be enough. More than enough." He paused, searching my face.

I blinked at him, unable to digest his words.

He waited. For the words to tear through me. To settle.

And then he fed me more.

"Being part of something like this," he murmured, tightening his hands around me, "is something special. Sacred. And when we started, I didn't treat it that way because there was no fucking way I could. You were still in fucking *high school.* The only reason I didn't run away was because I knew you were legal, that and I couldn't fucking resist you." He squeezed again.

That hunger that had been only teasing, weakly fighting against the rest of the vile filth inside me, it sparked again with that squeeze. With the desire in Heath's eyes.

"I couldn't resist taking you even with the knowledge of knowing I'd have to leave you," he murmured. "Because you're the beautiful girl who wants peace but fucks like it's war."

My thighs clenched at his words.

Heath's eyes flared in response to the desire I must've been wearing on my face. "You're the woman who deserves a smile on her face every day and a man that doesn't have demons that makes that impossible," he continued, voice raw. "So that's why I left at first. Because I knew I was gonna be in a war fighting demons and creating worse ones in their place. Knew I was going to sacrifice whatever parts of me would've been able to give that beautiful little girl her smile. I did the wrong thing that morning to do the right thing in general."

"I know that," I whispered.

His eyes flickered. "You know that?" he repeated.

I smiled. "Of course I know that. I used to live in a fantasy, most people will tell you that. But I lived in that fantasy to save myself from pain in the world. If I'd held onto fantasies into regards to you, then I'd be in insurmountable pain when they never came true."

We were laying it all out here, with talks of murdered ex-husbands, lost babies, lost loves. Lost lives.

"I know that you leaving was the only option," I said. "I knew that the second we kissed. When you took my hand and dragged me from the bar. I knew there was a time limit. An expiry date. That's why I fought so hard, before," I said. "When you came back. Because I couldn't stand our love having an expiry date."

"It fucking doesn't," he promised. "It never fucking will."

I smiled. "I think I'm getting that now."

Something moved in his eyes. "Not quite. But I'll prove it to you."

CHAPTER NINETEEN

One Week Later

"YOU NEED TO GO," I murmured against Heath's mouth.

"I know," he responded.

But instead of letting me go, he yanked me closer, melding my body against his and laying his mouth against mine.

I responded. Completely. With all of the hunger I had for him, with all of the fear that pulsated through my body with his touch. It was a battle, every time he kissed me like this. But it was worth it.

I moaned into his mouth as his hand palmed my ass, grinding my body into his.

He let out a growl at my response, the first audible one I'd had to his touch since...then. The single thought was like ice water and I froze, my hunger retreating as the demons won again.

Heath noted the instant change. He always did. Because it was becoming the norm. Every time we got further, every time we nudged at the desperate hunger I knew was hiding in between both of us—that Heath was physically restraining—my ugly memories fought back.

He released his grip on my ass, moving one hand to my hip, the other to cup my jaw. His eyes roved over my face with concern. He didn't ask me if I was okay.

He never did.

He knew I wasn't.

"I'm sorry," I whispered.

He jerked as if I'd struck him, his hand flexing at my hip, his jaw hardening. "You don't apologize, Sunshine," he clipped. "No fuckin' way do you apologize for kissin' me like that, for giving me that when I know what it takes from you." He kissed my nose. "I'm the fucker that should be sorry. Sorry I'm pushing you."

"No," I interrupted. "You're not."

And I was right. He wasn't pushing me. I was pushing myself. Because he'd made it apparent he wasn't going anywhere, no matter how hard I tried to push him away. And I didn't want him going anywhere.

So if I wasn't pushing him away, I needed to push myself back. Back to somewhere we could try this. Somewhere we could make this work.

His eyes searched mine. "Polly," he said, voice tender but tentative. He inhaled, and I knew it was coming. The moment when he asked me, straight up, what happened.

He was yet to do that.

And I was thankful. Because he seemed to know how impossible it was for me to utter it. And how impossible it was for me to lie to him.

But there was only so long a man like Heath could wait. Could withstand the torture of not knowing.

I braced.

But then the door opened.

"I didn't barf today!" Lucy announced to the room.

Heath and I both jerked back, well, I did. Heath moved enough to tuck me into his side.

Lucy looked between the two of us with a shrewd gaze. "Oh, am I interrupting?" she asked, sweetly.

"No," I said at the same time Heath snapped, "Yes."

I smacked his shoulder.

Pain radiated through my knuckle as it encountered pure marble.

"Damn you and your iron type shoulders," I hissed, rubbing my hand.

He snatched it and laid his lips gently on it. "Oh, did my shoulder hurt your fist?"

I scowled at him but did not snatch my hand back.

"Okay, this is so sweet I could vomit," Lucy interrupted, throwing her purse on the sofa and doing her best to sit down gracefully.

An impossibility since she was eight months pregnant.

"I could vomit, but I won't," she continued. "Because I didn't vomit today," she said, grinning.

"Congratulations," Heath said dryly.

She glared at him. "I know you're being sarcastic, but I don't even care. Because I've been vomiting, every day, at least three times a day for eight months. And now I have not." She rubbed her belly. "It was kind of an asshole move to make me sick until the last month of pregnancy, but your father is kind of an asshole, so it makes sense," she muttered, talking to her belly.

I inwardly flinched at watching the moment, hating the envy I had for the sister I loved. Heath squeezed me a little tighter, kissing my temple as if he sensed my thoughts.

"I've gotta go," he murmured against my hair.

"Yes you do," I agreed.

He turned me to face him fully, Lucy still talking to her belly.

He cupped my cheek. "You need anything?"

Apart from a time machine?

The ability to kiss my boyfriend—if that's what he was now—without wanting to crawl out of my skin?

To not look at my glowing and pregnant sister without feeling jealous that I'd never get that?

I shook my head.

He laid a kiss on my mouth. "I'll be back at three."

I nodded once. It was Friday, after all.

"I'm teaching a class at one, so I'll be at the studio."

"Well then, I'll be there," he amended. "With that horrible green shit you like to drink afterward."

Warmth spread through my belly. "It's good for you."

"I sure hope so," he muttered.

I smiled. And it was real.

"There it is," he murmured, kissing me again.

I melted into it.

He stepped back, hands fisted at his side.

"Bye," he said.

I waved because my vocal cords weren't working.

"Bye Heath!" Lucy all but yelled, grinning from ear to ear.

"Bye Luce," he muttered. "Congrats on the no barfing."

I watched him leave.

He paused at the door for one last glimpse.

I blew him a kiss.

And then he was gone.

"Oh my god," Lucy uttered.

I snapped my eyes downward. "What is it?" I rushed forward in a panic. "Is it the baby? Is it coming? I was six weeks early you know."

"Chill," she hissed. "No, can I not be dramatic about things with my appropriate amount of flair anymore?" she said, scowling.

I relaxed at her scowl, sitting on the chair across from her. "Not until after you push the baby out."

She scrunched up her nose. "Don't remind me I have to do that."

I nodded to her belly. "That's not reminder enough?"

"Well now I can't have a C-section, it is reminder enough," she snapped. "But I was getting delightfully distracted by the Heath and Polly show and then you had to go and remind me."

I grinned. I was getting better at them now. "Well, I apologize."

She rolled her eyes, then they turned serious. "You don't have to apologize for being happy," she whispered. "Is that what you are? Happy?"

I thought about it. I considered lying to her. It was certainly kinder to lie to my pregnant and worried sister. But she'd also murder me if she knew I was treating her with anything resembling care for her pregnancy. "Almost," I said. "Sometimes."

Lucy's eyes shimmered. "You need to talk to someone, anyone, about this," she said gently.

I nodded. "I know."

She blinked. "You *know*? But I had a whole speech drafted. You kind of stole my thunder."

I grinned. "Do you want me to protest so you can perform the speech?"

She waved her hand. "No, the moment's ruined." She narrowed her eyes. "So you know you have to talk."

I nodded. "There is a group that one of the women in the shelter told me about. I go every week."

She gaped at me. Openly gaped. "You go *every week*?"

I nodded.

"For how long?"

I thought on it, back to when I started going. Back to when I told Heath, and he hadn't hesitated to tell me he'd drive me every Friday. He also hadn't asked questions. Hadn't probed. Not when he dropped me off or picked me up. "Like three weeks?"

"*Three weeks*!" Lucy screamed. "How does Heath not know?"

"He knows," I replied mildly, hoping she wouldn't induce labor with her hysterics. But then again, her being calm was out of the norm, so that was more likely to induce labor.

"He knows?" she hissed.

"Are you just going to repeat everything I say?" I asked, standing to get my things ready. "Because I'm going to be late for my class."

"You're always late to everything," Lucy countered.

"Well, yes, that's true, but since this is the first class I'm teaching, it would be a bad look."

It was my first class.

Heath knew this.

Because he was Heath.

But he didn't make a big thing about it, because he knew that I was nervous, and him making a thing would make it worse. So he was Heath, and it calmed me.

Lucy stared at me, didn't move, I could see her considering using her considerable size to bar me from leaving until she got the truth out of me. I also saw the fear, the pain in her eyes if she did get the truth out of me. My sister, the bravest woman I knew, the woman who took on drug dealers and won, was scared of me.

Of my truth.

She stepped aside. "Fine," she huffed.

Then she reached forward and squeezed my hand. "But just so you know, you're loved, you're not alone."

I smiled. "I know that," I whispered.

But I was alone.

Of course I wasn't going to tell anyone that.

I LIED TO LUCY.

Something that was rare for me before but it had become the norm now. I used to think badly about untruths and omissions. Used to strive to live an honest life. Because I thought that honesty meant doing no harm.

I really had been living in a fantasy.

It wasn't a huge lie. But lying was lying, right? I did go to the meetings. That was correct. Heath dropped me off with a kiss on the forehead, a tortured look in his eyes and a promise to be back in an hour.

I wasn't sure if he even actually left. I had a sneaking suspicion that he just sat at the curb. He didn't probe about the meetings. Didn't push me to talk. He'd just kiss me again when we got in the car and let me have my silence, maybe thinking I'd had enough talking for the night.

There was talking at the meetings.

Just not from me.

I sat there, was insulated against my own horrors by hearing those of others. No one judged me in my silence. I certainly wasn't alone in it either. I wasn't alone in my pain either. That was the thing that had me coming back, even though my skin crawled every time I walked through those doors. Every time I faced a pale, gaunt, haunted woman who was trying to repair herself, recognize herself. Because I was forced to face the entirety of my own pain then.

I knew I had to. In order to heal, I had to embrace the pain. I taught that to my new students. To embrace the discomfort, for it's only through discomfort that we grew. These meetings were me trying to practice what I preached.

But I couldn't bring myself to talk. Physically couldn't. A lump settled in my throat as soon as I walked through the doors. Again, I knew what this meant. I wasn't getting the flu. Didn't have mono.

I studied physical manifestations of spiritual imbalances in college and then got farther into it as I began my yoga courses. Not for everyone. "More new age horse shit," were Lucy's exact words.

But I believed in them. And there was no hiding the evidence. Technically, I was in perfect health. Until I walked through those doors and it was almost impossible to swallow. The entire class, my throat was sandpaper. It was about my throat chakra and my inner truth. It was the link between my heart and my head, and the harder I tried to suppress my emotions, the bigger the lump grew to.

But this afternoon it was worse than it ever had been. I could only take a strangled breath around it. I knew that meant I had to speak the unspeakable.

I waited until almost the end of the class. Because I was a procrastinator in everything in life, obviously it would work tenfold for having to vocalize something I'd previously kept quiet with a ferocity that my life depended on it.

And it did, in a way.

But I knew that this silence would slowly kill whatever was left in me.

I stood on shaky legs, wiped my sweaty palms on the thighs of my yoga pants.

"My ex-husband said that it wasn't rape when I'd willingly 'let him in there' before," I said, my voice flat and clear and scarily detached. "My screams, my pleads, my struggles, *that* still didn't make it rape," I continued. "Not even when he punched me in the face so hard that he fractured my cheekbone."

I touched the smooth skin that had a small mark, slowly fading, sinking into the skin to join the scars on my bones.

"It wasn't rape even though he'd kidnapped me because he wanted money." I laughed. "*Money*. Three million dollars was the price of whatever was left of my innocence. My faith in the goodness of the world." I paused. "No, that's not right. I still have faith in the goodness of the world. I just lost faith that *I* would get that. Because apparently there is a dollar amount where the man who promised to cherish you and love you, decides to brutalize and violate you." I paused because I had to. Because images were assaulting my mind with a stark reality that made me blink rapidly to bring the room back into view and chase away the shitty hotel room.

Chase away the squeak of the bed.

The rough breaths in my ear.

The pain of being split in two.

I forced myself back into reality.

"Of course, his ability was always there, with or without the money," I continued, voice hoarse. "Maybe he would've done it anyway. If not to me then the next woman to fall in love with that mask he wore. It's a lot of maybes, and I'm not allowed to work in those." I looked at the faces around the room. They were full of kindness. Understanding. Pain. "Because then I go into dangerous territory. Maybe I hadn't left Heath's. Maybe I didn't answer that door. Maybe I fought when he uncuffed me to let me use the bathroom, and I escaped. Maybe I died in the back of that truck."

My voice was still cold. Still empty, even though I was filling all of my haunted and tortured thoughts into it.

"Or maybe I didn't marry him in the first place," I whispered. "Maybe I went with a man who promised me the world and not the fantasy that Craig had constructed to hide my nightmare. Maybe I didn't lose my baby, maybe I made the right decision for once."

A tear trailed down my cheek, which was weird since I didn't feel sad.

"So I'm not allowed to play maybes," I said. "It happened. And despite what he said, it was *rape*." The word was ash on my tongue. "And I've been feeling so *ashamed*. Of his actions. I've been feeling like it's *my* shame to hold onto. To let rot my insides. When it's his shame. This is not something I should hold inside because it makes me feel dirty to admit to the world, let alone myself. It's not my fault. It's not my fault, but that doesn't mean anything. Because it happened. And I'm here. And I'm lost."

Heath

"Hey dude, you feel like fucking up some drug dealers?" Rosie asked cheerfully, entering his office belly first.

He glanced up. "I do not feel like getting murdered by your husband, so no," he replied dryly.

She scowled at him. "No one's any fun anymore," she moaned.

"I would've thought Polly and an excessive number of tacos would've cheered you up."

She frowned. "Yes, Polly and an excessive number of tacos would cheer me up. Where is she? I'll call her. No, her phone is probably dead, and you've put some kind of tracking device on her in her sleep, right?"

Heath had been frozen the second she started speaking. "You haven't been getting tacos with her."

It wasn't a question.

But Rosie answered anyway. "No, as you so shrewdly pointed out, tacos put me in a good mood. I'm not currently in a good mood," she snapped. Her face dropped. "Why do you think that I'm getting tacos with Polly?"

He stood. "Because she fucking told me you picked her up from her meeting three hours ago."

"Meeting?" Rosie parroted.

"Fuck," he hissed, stabbing at his phone.

He got voicemail.

Of course he did.

"Keltan!" he all but roared into the intercom.

"Oh fuck, what now," Keltan sighed.

"Polly's missing."

There was a pause. "Fuck," he hissed. Heath heard that goddamn tapping of keys again. "On it."

His mind went to that night in the desert.

Every inch of his skin went cold.

He couldn't handle that shit again.

He fucking *couldn't.*

No matter what shit he'd handled in a desert world's away, on a fucking battlefield, it had nothing on opening the door of that truck and seeing her. Holding her and having her feeling so light, like someone had just scooped everything out of her. After they'd beat her bloody, that was.

"If Fernandez has her, I'll kill him, fuck the plan you idiots have and fuck the fucking pregnancy," Rosie hissed.

She was pacing.

It made him nervous.

She was fucking pregnant as fuck, she shouldn't be pacing like that. The baby could just fall right out or something. Both her and Lucy were close to delivery. And that scared him more than he cared to admit. Not just because he might be the fucker who had to deliver the baby like Cade had with his wife in the Sons of Templar clubhouse.

No, because he knew what it was doing to Polly. He saw it, every time she looked at them. The joy in her face for her sister. The love. He saw it because she wore that love like she wore those fuckin' dresses that drove him wild.

It fit her.

But sometimes it moved. Just a little so no one but him could see it. The sorrow. The pain so deep it speared through his bone.

She wouldn't get that. She wouldn't grow big with his baby, feel it inside her.

And it fucking killed him. Not because he felt like he was losing out on something. No, with her he had everything. But because of what the world was taking from her. The girl that radiated sunshine and love, who gave everything. The woman who would be the best mother on the face of the planet. And she didn't get that.

It was too fucking cruel to bear.

She'd get that, though. He'd make sure of it.

He'd already been looking into adoption agencies. Sure, it might be too soon, but he wanted to be prepared, ready. Because Polly was getting back to Polly.

Slowly.

But she was getting there.

And he knew when she got there—and she'd fucking get there—she'd be ready to jump into things. When that day came, he wanted to be able to be ready for whatever she wanted. Which was why he'd been carrying a ring around for a month. One that he'd gotten from some obscure, vintage jewelry store, that only sold antique shit. And the ring was Polly. Simple. Understated. And mind-blowingly beautiful.

He knew she'd want a ring with history. With a story. Because she lived for stories.

And he was going to give her one.

Give her everything.

Hence him researching adoption agencies. Pulling every string he had to make sure that they could get on the list as soon as she decided. If that's what she decided. It would've been easier if they were married.

And they would be married.

Heath was gonna make sure of that.

But no way would he rush her.

They had forever. And as long as she kept falling asleep in his arms, he could handle her not having his ring on her finger.

What he couldn't handle, was Rosie pacing. No, what he couldn't fucking bear was the fact they were back in that room, in that horrific fucking room and Polly was missing again.

"Rosie, Jesus Christ," Luke seethed as he entered, face tight. "I told you to stay off your feet, and what? Now you think it's a good idea to pace holes in the carpet?" He placed his hands atop her belly and looked down. "In fucking heels? I thought we talked about that."

Rosie narrowed her eyes. "You talked. I did not listen since it was utter madness, and not the good kind. You get me out of heels, you get me out of this marriage."

"I'm gonna interrupt here because this because my fucking woman is missing," Heath hissed.

Luke's gaze snapped to him. "We got her," he said.

Heath almost fucking throttled him for the fact that was not what he led with. Yes, concern about his pregnant wife was pressing. But she was right in fucking front of him. Heath had no idea where Polly was.

And the last time he had no idea where she was, he'd found her broken, battered and half fucking dead in the back of a truck.

"We've got a tracker on her phone," Luke continued. "Lance was closest. He's got eyes on her." He paused. "She's okay. Physically."

Rosie stopped pacing. "It's happened?" she whispered. "It's finally hit her."

Luke nodded once, face tight, bracing for his woman's pain.

"It's hit her," he agreed.

Heath was halfway out the door.

Because shit wasn't hitting Polly. Not without hitting him too.

Polly

I wasn't one hundred percent sure how I got here.

I had left the meeting, feeling empty and full at the same time. Like I'd released something but also like I was stretched so tight I was going to snap.

I must've left early, because Heath wasn't waiting.

And Heath was always right on time.

I also must've texted him, because I didn't want him to worry. That was the last thing I needed. On autopilot, I'd told him Rosie had picked me up for an impromptu taco run.

He'd responded immediately.

And he hadn't been surprised.

Because Rosie was kind of wildly obsessed with tacos at this stage in her pregnancy.

I was impressed my fractured mind was able to conjure such a watertight excuse. I must've spent all my excess brain power since I couldn't think of anything else to do. So I started walking.

I was only wearing sandals so it wasn't exactly comfortable

after the first two miles. But that was good. I liked the discomfort. After another two miles, some of the skin was opening up on my feet and blisters were forming. That was better than good. Tearing on the outside was great, so I didn't feel like I was going insane just tearing on the inside.

I wasn't counting the miles, or the hours, or even the pain.

I was just walking.

The only reason I knew that I'd walked almost nine miles was because I got to the park. I'd mapped the distance from Atwater to Wildwood Canyon when one of my friends was training for a marathon. So I knew how far it was. I'd unwittingly followed the trail I used to run with her. Not because I was training for the marathon, or because I particularly liked running. She needed the company. The motivation.

And I'd always liked the destination.

This park.

It was pretty late by now, the sun kissing the horizon, bathing the city in a warm glow that made it look like it was magical. That down there, it wasn't full of pain and lost dreams.

I liked that.

"Ma'am, you okay?" a kind and scratchy voice asked from above me.

I realized I'd sat down at some point, on the slightly damp grass.

The man who'd spoken had tangled hair and an unkempt beard. His clothes were dirty, and his shoes had holes. He was holding a paper bag with a bottle top peeking out.

He had kind eyes.

I smiled. "Yeah, I'm okay."

He frowned. "You don't look it."

"I know," I agreed.

He paused for a beat longer. "You shouldn't be out here too

late, pretty and troubled lady like you," he said. Then he pointed to a copse of trees. "I'll be over there, watching out, make sure no more trouble comes to you."

And then he wandered off.

It was nice to think someone was watching out for me.

Even if all the trouble had already come and gone.

"SUNSHINE?" an urgent voice called into the ever-creeping darkness.

"Heath?" I replied immediately.

"Fuck," he hissed as he emerged from a curve in the hill. He was on me in two strides. I was in his arms, the warmth surrounding me, showing me just how cold I'd gotten.

Not from the ever-retreating sunlight.

No, from the memories I'd finally let in.

Heath's arms squeezed me tight enough to make my bones protest. I didn't say anything, because the pain in my feet had retreated, so I needed the pain of his embrace to make myself feel real. He kissed my head, rocking me slowly in his arms before he released me enough to look at me, to take stock.

I knew he was looking for injuries.

I hated myself a little bit for making him have to do that. For putting the worry and fear on his face.

"I'm not hurt," I said.

He paused for a moment, then he pressed his lips to mine. "Yeah, baby, you are. And it's okay to hurt. To show you're hurt. I can handle it," he promised.

"I just felt like walking," I whispered against his mouth. "And then, maybe I thought why don't I just keep walking for a little while. Maybe get a little lost. Because maybe I might find myself again."

He stood, and gathered me into his arms. "Let's get you home," he said.

I glimpsed up at him through my tears. "I am *home*. I'm sorry that it's taken me so long to realize that. That I've been fighting it because I loved you so much I didn't want you to have the pain of loving me. I'm sorry I disappeared again because I couldn't realize it without doing something so utterly Polly-like like walking ten miles in Birkenstocks."

Heath smiled. "The only thing I care about is my wild, beautiful, strong woman is back. That she's mine," he said as he began to walk back to the parking lot.

"Wait!" I cried out.

Heath stopped immediately.

"Put me down," I ordered.

"No way in hell."

"Okay, well take me over there," I gestured to the copse in the trees.

To his credit, Heath didn't even ask questions, because he knew me.

The man was still there, sitting slightly straighter when Heath pushed through the small shelter to reveal his home. There was a littering of candy wrappers, empty bottles, tattered blankets. A pillow. Newspapers.

Heath stiffened at the man.

The man stiffened back, then his eyes went kind as he focused on me.

"See someone found you that's gonna help you with your trouble," he said, voice throaty.

Heath relaxed slightly. Even he could hear the kindness in the man's slightly slurred words.

I moved so I could retrieve my phone which was now dead. "Heath, give me your charger," I demanded.

I knew he carried a portable one everywhere. Not for him, because his phone was always fully charged, but for me.

He sighed and jostled me effortlessly to retrieve it.

I kissed his bearded cheek and then stretched my arms out, with both the phone and the charger in it.

The man in front of me just stared at them.

Another thing that showed me his heart. He didn't snatch. He just looked at what I was extending with confusion, as if no one had offered him something before.

"Take it," I said softly.

He bent down to put down his bottle, then straightened, taking the items gently from my hands.

I smiled. "Now, it's not charged, because it's my phone and I keep forgetting to do that. But my man always has a charger." I nodded to the second item in his hands. "So you can charge it with that. And then you can call a man called Heath." I nodded my head. "That's Heath."

"Pleased to meet you," the man muttered.

"Likewise," Heath replied.

"Oh, and I'm Polly."

The man smiled. "Course you are," he muttered. "Spence," he added.

"Well, Spence, I'll answer Heath's phone since it's now mine until I get another one since that's yours now." I held up my hand as he began to protest. "And I'll hear no arguing because if I didn't give it to you, I would've lost it in a few weeks anyway," I said. "So you'll use it. Call Heath. Then we'll talk about this awesome place, where, if you feel like, you can visit me. I can cook a mean veggie lasagne, and you could even stay for awhile, you know, if you felt like it. No pressure."

I was going easy because I knew a lot of people were insulted when well-meaning people tried to help them off the street.

"I'm asking this for mainly selfish reasons," I continued. "Because a lot of people would've ignored me before. And if they didn't ignore me, they were less likely to treat me with kindness like you did. So I want to thank you," I whispered. "So if you call, if you come down, you'll be doing me a favor."

Spence was silent for a beat. "On one condition," he said.

"Anything."

"I want lasagne with real fuckin' meat. Who eats veggie lasagne?"

I laughed then.

Actually laughed.

I would've thought such a thing was impossible in proximity to my horror. But I did so.

Heath's arms tightened around me while I did.

And then I figured maybe I might be okay.

Maybe I might be able to go back to Polly.

A version of her, at least.

CHAPTER TWENTY

HEATH HAD CARRIED me up to my apartment.

The apartment that I realized was now *his* apartment.

How it took me two months to realize was beyond me. Then again, I hadn't been known for noticing such things. But it was hard not to notice the fact that I fell asleep on Heath's chest every single night. He came straight home from work to the apartment every night. His clothes were in my closet. Aftershave neatly placed amongst the clutter of my various beauty products.

"You live here now," I whispered as he sat down on the sofa, me still in his arms and he positioned me so I was in his lap. My stomach jumped as I brushed right against his crotch, the fabric of my leggings far too thin to work as any kind of barrier.

A small spark of carnal hunger came with that contact. One that I hadn't felt in months not without something else tainting it. One I didn't think I'd ever be able to feel. It was mingled with something off, something rancid, something that would always be there, tainting me. But there was something else. That need. That want. For Heath.

The way his eyes flared and his hands settled on my hips a little tighter than he usually touched me these months told me he felt it too.

"You just notice I live here?" he asked, voice thick and a little rough as the flame grew with his hardness pressing against me.

"Well...yeah," I said, my voice throaty and breathless.

"That a problem?" he asked, eyes searching mine.

I searched his right back. "Is it permanent?"

Heath's hands moved to the side of my neck, pulling me down so our foreheads touched. "Baby, it's *us*. You know it's permanent."

My stomach flipped for a completely different reason than our current position.

"That scare you?" he asked.

"Yeah," I admitted. "But after months of feeling fear that what was inside me, eating at me, it's a *nice* kind of fear. It's a good kind."

His face changed, a mixture of joy and dread.

"You wanna talk about what made you walk today?" he asked, voice soft.

I swallowed. "I haven't been talking," I whispered in response. "At the meetings you take me to. I haven't been talking. I haven't been strong enough to talk."

"You're strong enough to walk through those fuckin' doors," he hissed. "You're strong enough to carry the weight of the world." His hand tightened. "You're strong enough."

I smiled. "Today I was strong enough to talk. To tell the truth. What I haven't told anyone. Not you, not myself, not really. I've just been pretending it wasn't real, and if I didn't admit it. Didn't vocalize it, maybe it would decay my insides."

Heath knew. I could see it in his face, the way his entire body braced like someone would seconds before a car accident. "I could lie and say that I haven't pushed you to tell me because I wanted to handle you with care."

His grip relaxed as if he was now just realizing he'd been pressing his fingers into my skin hard enough to bruise.

He brushed a curl from my face. "I could lie and say I wanted you to feel safe enough to tell me when you were ready," he said, voice rough. "But I can't fucking lie to you, Polly. Not after everything. Not even to protect you from my weakness. And that's what it was. I was too fucking weak to handle the truth. And that's my greatest fucking shame because you handled it for yourself, and everyone else."

Pain ricocheted through my body as a tear trailed down Heath's cheek.

A tear.

For me.

The strongest man I'd ever met was being brought to tears.

Because of me.

"You're so strong," he rasped. "You're the strongest person I've ever fuckin' met."

I framed his face with my hands as his words became strangled with the depth of his emotion. "No. You're strong. Because you *knew,* Heath. I know you did. I lied to myself and said that you didn't. But you knew. You knew even if you didn't admit it to yourself. Because you know me. Every inch of me. Every inch of me is yours. And *he* couldn't take that. It's taken me a long time to see that."

I brushed at his cheek, wiping the tear away.

I didn't have to say that ugly word that I'd finally uttered aloud today. Which was good, since I didn't know if I could pass it through my organs without it tearing them. Because Heath knew. He knew without me having to say. His tears told me that.

"I'm ready," I whispered, leaning toward his mouth, my eyes not leaving his. "I'm ready for you to show me I'm yours again."

I subtly moved against him, touched my mouth to his, my intention clear.

Heath froze.

"Sunshine," he growled against my mouth. "We don't have to. I'm willing to wait 'til you're ready. If it's too soon—"

I shut him up with a kiss.

A real one.

He was hesitant at first. Not because he didn't want me, no the hardness pressing through my leggings was evidence of that, but because he was worried I was doing my Polly thing, jumping into something without thinking. Jumping into something that might damage me, us in the future.

This was the one thing I was sure about. It wasn't jumping blindly when I knew Heath would catch me.

My tongue slipped into his mouth and that's when he responded. That's when he unleashed his hunger. A low growl vibrated through his body and into mine as he clasped the back of my head and tore into my hair.

My grinding became a lot less subtle.

In fact, it could only be described as desperate.

Violent.

Heath was standing, still kissing me, hands still tearing my hair from its ponytail. I instinctively wrapped my legs around him, my entire body jerking when his hardness pressed against the thin fabric of my leggings.

He moved, and every movement was torture, creating a new friction, building a new fire, driving me wild.

He didn't stop kissing me.

Not until he put me down on shaky legs, my calves pressing into the side of the bed.

He stopped touching me.

Moved away from me so his back was to my dresser.

"Heath," I whispered. "What—"

"Take off your clothes," he ordered.

I froze.

Well, I didn't truly freeze, since my heart was in my throat and my breathing was rapidly trying to find room around it.

Fear was a living thing running over my skin.

But my thoughts froze as the words echoed from the past into the future. The words spoken in a different apartment, when Heath had been pressed against an entirely less cluttered dresser, I'd been pressed against a bed with military corners, and I'd been a different Polly entirely.

But he was giving me something with that command.

The past.

He was showing me how much had changed.

But also, how much hadn't.

His eyes were still bursting with fierce desire. His fists were clenched at his sides communicating the force of his restraint.

He still wanted me now like he did then.

Even though my body had been defiled, my soul ransacked. He still wanted me, exactly how he'd wanted me when no one had ever touched me.

"Take off your clothes, Sunshine," he murmured, voice gentler.

I didn't hesitate this time, though my hands were shaking when they grasped the bottom of my tee.

The air whistled through the open wounds that were hidden by my skin when the tee fluttered to the floor. I ached to cover myself, my wounds, the dirtiness on my skin.

But Heath's gaze stopped me.

His harsh intake of breath stopped me.

I'd been very careful to change in the bathroom. To wear his tees to bed, and leggings underneath them, since I always sprawled my body all over his. I didn't want to risk bare and broken skin being exposed for him to see.

Because I was scared of his reaction.

No, I was terrified of his *lack* of reaction. Of him seeing that filth etched into my skin, of it disgusting him. Of not seeing the want, the need for me that he used to have.

But I saw it.

I saw more of it than I'd ever seen.

So I kept going.

I peeled my cropped sports bra off, exposing my aching nipples to that same air. The air Heath owned.

"Fuck," he hissed when my breasts were exposed fully to him.

He was shaking with the force he was keeping himself in place.

I was shaking with my need for him. For him to touch me. Worship me.

"You're so fucking beautiful, Polly," he murmured.

I didn't reply. I couldn't. Instead, I hooked my fingers around the fabric of my leggings, pulled them down and stepped out of them.

Again, I ached to cover my body, only standing in front of Heath in my panties and my pain.

But I didn't need to cover myself. To protect myself.

Heath's stare did that.

So I went to do it. The big and terrifying thing. Step out of my panties.

"No," Heath hissed, crossing the distance between us, his hands on top of mine at my hips.

"Your memory fails you," he murmured, inches away from my mouth. "That's my job."

My stomach clenched with the sex in his voice. The promise of what was to come.

"Lie down," he ordered.

I did so immediately, the comforter rubbing against my bare skin.

Heath knelt at the edge of the bed. Lifting my leg up.

Then he focused on my foot. The one I'd forgotten about. The one with torn skin and open blisters.

He froze.

Ah, great way to ruin the moment, Polly.

"Baby," he demanded, voice full of concern.

"They're fine," I said.

"They don't look fuckin' fine," he hissed. "You need me to take care of them."

He started to stand.

"No!" I cried.

He froze with the desperation in my voice.

"I need you to take care of me first," I said. "Please."

His jaw was hard as he cradled my feet gently. I knew it was cruel of me to ask. Knew all of the protective and alpha cells in Heath's body were crying out for him to try and heal the things he could.

"That can wait," I pushed. "This can't." I moved my hand down the center of my chest to trail the tops of my panties.

Heath let out a low hiss. "Fuck," he rasped circling my ankle and yanking me forward so he came face to face with my aching core.

He breathed me in then focused on me. "You're gonna be the end of me," he hissed.

"You're the beginning of me," I replied.

He paused at my words. Then he moved.

Then he ripped my panties right off.

I flinched from both pleasure and pain at being exposed to him, so exposed. All of my scars, all of my damage. I struggled with that. The panic rising in my throat, with the brutal way he'd ripped off my panties.

He wasn't to know that's what...he did.

My stomach roiled.

But I forced myself to look at Heath. To remember that *he* wasn't the first one to do that. It was Heath, the night he gave me my first time. The first night he gave me his heart. And no way could Craig take that.

Heath was watching, waiting, bracing for me to fall apart. I could see that concern mingled with the desire in his eyes.

But then he saw me relax, I knew he saw it because his eyes moved.

And then his mouth moved.

Right *there.*

My hands fisted the covers and I cried out in pure pleasure as Heath tasted me. As he devoured me.

Worshipped me.

I'd thought my first climax...after would be hard. It would take work. Concentration in actively not thinking about...before.

But there was no work.

No concentration.

Just Heath's mouth on my pussy.

And my climax was not hard. It was soft, warm, and then it was an explosion.

It melted me. Completely and utterly melted me.

I didn't even realize that I'd blacked out until Heath pulled me up the bed and his weight settled on top of me. His naked weight.

I frowned. My hands trailed his pec. My spot. "That was meant to be my job."

He grinned, it was full of dark desire. "Yeah, well, you were otherwise occupied," he growled. And then he pressed against me. *There.*

I jerked, because I was sensitive and because I was thinking.

Remembering.

Heath cupped my face, hands gentle, grin gone. "Sunshine," he demanded. "Don't go there. Don't go anywhere." He pressed his mouth to mine, coaxed it open, kissed me gently, achingly. "You're here. That's the only place you ever need to be." He kissed me again. "And we don't need to do more. Not if you're not ready. Tasting your pussy..." He trailed off. "Fuck, babe, that was heaven. I don't need more."

My thighs jerked with his words. "No, I want to give you more," I replied, my voice husky. "I want to give you everything."

"You already do."

I wrapped my leg around him, pressing him harder against me.

He hissed through his teeth.

"Fuck me, Heath, please."

He growled. "As if I could say no to you."

And then he did.

He didn't go slow, gently. No, like last time, like the first time, he surged into me.

And like the first time, there was pain.

But not just physical.

No, there was a searing emotional pain that threatened to tear me in two.

"Polly?" Heath demanded. "You're here. With me."

His words chased away the worst of it.

Then he moved.

And there was still pain.

There always would be.

But we both found pleasure in it.

A lot of pleasure.

Heath

It was three in the morning.

Heath knew this not because he glanced at a clock, he couldn't even if he wanted to, Polly didn't keep clocks in the apartment. Something that should've bothered him since his home had always had clocks in every room since he'd become a Marine.

It didn't bother him because he hadn't had a home until this cluttered, colorful, chaotic, clockless apartment.

He didn't glance at his phone to know either. Polly did not allow phones in the bedroom.

"We're too connected. We should be allowed to have a sanctuary where we're not accessible," she'd said, snatching it from his hands the second week he'd been staying here after her kidnapping. Her face had still been bruised, swollen.

And it killed him every time he looked at it.

But he did his best to hide that.

Because he knew his pain at her injuries would add another bruise to his beautiful Polly, just one he couldn't see.

"Plus, the light's bad for your eyes right before sleeping," she added.

Then she'd stomped into the living room, placed his phone in the fruit bowl, next to a banana and her own phone, stomped back, climbed into bed, rested on her spot and promptly fell into unconsciousness.

He didn't tell her that he needed his phone handy as part of his job. He didn't have set hours. And if he did, they would be closer to midnight till four than nine till five. He didn't tell her that because no way in fuck was he saying no to her in any way shape or form.

He'd quit his fucking job if she asked. If it meant he'd get every single night of her laying on his chest and sleeping.

He planned on getting every single night.

But as she healed, as they got into a routine, he'd had to gently tell her about the need for his phone.

"Well, you'll have a separate ringtone for work emergencies," she decided. "One loud enough to hear from the living room. And though this apartment isn't as small as yours, we'll still hear it," she decided.

He agreed.

Because he'd agree to anything with her, to get her back to her.

He didn't tell her that 'his apartment' was no longer his. He still had the lease, of course, but was planning on breaking it. He wasn't planning on sleeping another night in that fucking place. And not because he couldn't physically sleep another night without Polly in his arms.

Because this was *home.*

No matter how broken it was right now.

Polly was home.

And now, things were a little fixed with that agonizing truth actualized. Burned into his brain like acid. It was something that he'd never get over. Forget. It was a wound that cut him to the core.

But he had Polly.

And she'd get him through.

In little ways like waking up at three in the morning to an empty bed.

He pushed out of bed and found Polly doing yoga in the moonlight.

Yeah, she was healing. She didn't think she would be the same, she didn't think she could be fixed. But the fact she was here, awake, not willing to give in her life to sleep anymore, it meant a little piece slotted back into place.

She came up from a forward fold—he was learning the terms because it was important to Polly and he didn't give a fuck if that made him a pussy—and caught his eyes. She didn't jump in surprise, she smiled, openly and warmly.

His heart clenched in his chest.

A broken piece inside him slotted into place with that smile.

"Couldn't sleep, and it's a full moon," she said, looking out the window. "It's a shame to waste it."

Only Polly would think that not getting up in the middle of the night to do yoga and charge her crystals—he saw them on the windowsill, and knew she did this every month—would be *wasting* a full moon.

She was back.

He crossed the room and yanked her into his arms.

"Does it count as wasting the full moon if I fuck you in front of the window?" he rasped.

Her eyes flared with hunger. "No," she breathed. "No, it doesn't."

So he did just that.

Polly

Two Days Later

"I think it's time I called my parents," I said sipping my tea, and perving at Heath as he got ready for work.

He froze, looking up from his belt.

"I'm not telling them *everything*," I said quickly. "Or even half. I just...can't. I'm not putting that on them."

"This isn't about putting it on them," he said immediately. "This is about you doing whatever you need to heal. You needa stop worryin' how that process is gonna hurt others. Because it won't. Only way it does is if someone who adores you—list is long with me at the top—thought you were hurting yourself to save them. Don't know your parents, but know the kind of women they've raised, so I know they will be of that opinion."

I blinked at Heath's words. I wondered if I'd ever get used to the way he spoke. His beautiful honesty. And his ugly honesty too. All mixed up together.

"I know that," I said. "I know that it'd hurt them more if they found out I'd been keeping things from them. But, sometimes there are things you have to keep from your parents. This is one of those things."

Your ex-husband kidnapping you, raping you and then selling you to human traffickers was definitely a thing to keep from your parents.

Heath watched me for a long time, testing the truth in my words.

He nodded once and crossed the room to snatch me into a kiss. "I trust you, babe. Trust that you know yourself well enough to make that decision. Not gonna make you change it. But I'm gonna make sure you know I'm here when you call them. When they come. Because my place is at your side. It has been since you were eighteen years old. Now I'm here, I'm not going anywhere. Sooner your parents, and you, realize that, the better."

Tears ran down my face.

"You trust me?" I repeated.

He frowned. "Of course I fuckin' trust you. I love you. With everything I am. Fucking adore you. You might deal with shit different than anyone else, you might deal with life different than anyone else, but that doesn't mean it's wrong." He kissed me. "Means it's the only thing that's right in this fucked up world. You're the only thing that's right."

More tears trailed down my face.

"I love you," I murmured.

"Good, 'cause I plan on growing old with you, it helps if you love me," he said dryly.

A strangled giggle merged with my sob.

I was able to do that more and more now.

Laugh.

And Heath was able to tease me.

I'd thought that was lost.

But we just needed to find each other first.

I toyed with his belt and his body went instantly taut.

"You really need to go to work...now?" I asked sweetly.

I squealed as he yanked me into his arms. "No fucking way do I need to go anywhere but inside your pussy," he growled.

And he did.

Twice.

CHAPTER TWENTY-ONE

I CALLED my parents later that morning.

Much later.

My hand was shaking as I dialed, but I was sitting in Heath's lap, borrowing some of his strength.

I managed to dial.

To speak when they answered.

The second I'd gotten the words—the lies and half-truths about that day almost two months ago—out of my mouth, my parents were getting ready to get in the car.

They arrived hours later.

Mom was still wearing her slippers.

She full on sprinted at me in the parking lot of my apartment building. I collapsed in her arms. We both would've collapsed if Dad hadn't caught us both.

I'd been so sure that I could handle not telling my parents. That it'd be somehow okay. But there was no way to heal without your parents to hug you. To cry with you. It wouldn't heal me fully. Or even half. I knew this.

But I wouldn't have gotten anywhere near back to something resembling me without the smell of my mother's perfume, without my father's lips at my head.

"It's gonna be okay," he murmured into my hair.

And I believed him the only way a daughter believed her father when he told her it was all going to be okay.

Because it wasn't, not really, on the outside of all this. But inside my dad's arms, it was.

DAD AND HEATH had gone out to get some burgers and beer for dinner.

I didn't get how it took two of them to do so, but it was likely some sort of male bonding thing. And it was definitely my father trying to protect me.

But then again, he'd taken to Heath almost immediately.

Not that Heath made an exact good first impression, with his beard, muscles, cold demeanor. But Dad looked between us, or more accurately looked at the way Heath had pulled me into his arms, wiped a rogue tear from my eye and murmured, "You okay, Sunshine?"

My father was a shrewd man. He saw things. I knew he saw things about Craig, but he was a good father so he kept his reservations quiet.

And because he was a good dad, the best, I knew he was going to carry that around with him, blame that didn't belong on his shoulders. And that hurt. Added to the pile of pain I was carrying around. But I didn't focus on that. I focused on the way he was with Heath, and it warmed me. *Heath* warmed me. Every day, every new wound I exposed, he stayed, he made roots. Made sure to tell me, to show me that this was permanent. Even when he knew I was broken. No longer that bright and happy girl he'd fallen in love with.

He was showing me that he was falling in love with this new Polly.

And I was falling in love with him all over again.

"You want the veggie burgers from the place that has the preacher out front or from that place that plays that weird music?" he asked, resting his hands lightly on my hips before they left.

My heart almost broke with that simple question. Because nothing was simple between us. And him knowing the places I got my veggie burgers from depending on my mood and cravings—and willing to travel thirty minutes out of the way to get them—was more than a simple question. It was everything.

I smiled. I couldn't help it. And it was well and truly real. Not an original Polly smile. But a new one. Maybe slightly less bright, a little less naive, but it was real.

"The preacher," I whispered.

He stroked the edge of my jaw, looking at me in what could only be explained as awe. "Been plannin' a lot of shit to get that smile back to me," he murmured. "Didn't think it would be from getting you veggie burgers. They're gonna have to be on the menu every day for the rest of our lives."

Then he kissed me hard and fast on the mouth.

In front of my *parents*.

I expected my father to be thin-lipped when he released me. But he was smiling. *Beaming*.

My mom's eyes were misty, but she was smiling too.

"Right," Dad said, clapping Heath on the back. "Hamburgers, and the shit the hippies try to sell as hamburgers."

I grinned.

Whatever Dad said about it, he always drove me to every

health store in the area since I'd decided I was vegetarian, without much complaining.

Because he loved me.

That was the secret. People who loved you didn't have to believe in everything you did. Didn't have to agree with it. But the fact they'd go out of their way for something they didn't believe in, for *you*, that was saying a lot.

It was saying everything.

Heath gave me a long look before him and Dad walked out the door.

I pressed my hands to my lips, still smiling.

"Well," Mom said to the room, her voice shaky. "He's the best yet."

I looked at her. "Yeah, he is," I whispered.

She searched my face in a way only mothers could. "He's the one, isn't he? The real one?"

I nodded.

Mom's shoulders sagged, like some sort of weight had just been released.

But then they tensed again.

"There's something I need to tell you," Mom said, dabbing at her eye. She took a breath. "Something I should've told you a long time ago. But I wished I wouldn't have to burden you with the hard truth when you seemed so beautiful and soft."

She crossed the room to take my hand and sit us both down on the sofa. She squeezed my hand. "Not weak, just to clarify. I *never* thought of you as weak. But you are my Polly. My little dreamer. And I thought maybe I could preserve that dream. That I could save you from a truth that would only harm you. But now I see you need that truth so maybe it might heal you."

She paused like she was bracing for something. For impact. "I was married, before your father."

I blinked. That was a surprise. A shock, to be more accurate. My mom and I shared everything. She knew when I lost my virginity, obviously not the whole Heath story, but she knew that it happened. I told her about bad boyfriends. Bad friends. She did the same. I thought we shared mostly everything, and I felt guilty for beginning to hide things from her the older I got, the uglier the truth got.

But having a marriage before my father was a pretty darn big thing to hide.

I understood it, though. I might not have three years ago. But I did now.

Because sometimes, some truths were too big to share.

"Holy crap, Mom," I said.

She nodded. "There's more." She looked strange, her face pinched and wary. Dad always said I got my 'open face' from Mom. We could never hide how we felt.

"Some people wear their heart on their sleeves, you wear it on your beautiful face."

She almost looked...scared? Guilty?

"My first husband, he was not a good man," she said. "If you knew him, were friends with him, worked with him, you would disagree with that. Because he was polite. Handsome. Charismatic. For all intents and purposes, he was the ideal husband and father. On the surface. But when he closed the door and loosened his tie, put down his briefcase, he was no longer burdened by the surface. And I didn't realize this until I married him." She took a long breath. "Until I got pregnant."

The words hit me with enough force to take my breath away.

Mom saw this, but she kept going. Because there was obviously more.

"And it started to slip, his mask, after your sister was born," she said. "And I should've seen that, should've done more. But I couldn't. For a number of reasons. Mostly because I had been so blindly in love I gave him control over everything. He counted on this and made it so I couldn't leave with anything. By this point, I had you as well. And it didn't get bad until you were talking. It was bad, don't get me wrong. Bad in a way no man should scream at his wife the way he did with me. Treated me the way he did. But I was in love and I made excuses and I thought that loving someone was forgiving them for their ugliness. Until his ugliness was all there was and he felt entitled to my forgiveness. And then he started to get violent."

My stomach dropped. Literally dropped.

I had to put my hand on it to make sure all of my organs are still in place, that's how violent of a reaction I was having to the mere thought of someone hurting my mother.

My *father* hurting my mother.

My biological father.

"And he was sorry, and he loved me," she whispered. "And he had brainwashed me into thinking that it was my duty as a wife to forgive him. I won't make excuses because I don't need to." She squeezed my hand again and more tears trailed down her cheeks. "You know what love for the wrong man can do to the right woman. It's a soft heart that gets manipulated by hard souls. I was making plans to leave. Saving. It was taking time because I had no one to lean on. He had made sure of that. To slowly isolate me from my support system, from people that might've seen the signs, tried to help me had I not shut them out at his gentle probing."

My stomach lurched again.

Because Craig had done that.

He had tried to do that. With subtle comments about my family, about them stifling me. Not understanding me.

It might've worked not on a weaker woman, but on weaker

bonds. As it was, no one was ever breaking the connection I had to my family. Though he did fray it. More because when I loved someone, I wanted to give them my all. Life and breathe them. But Lucy was used to this, as I'd been doing it on and off over the years.

And she understood it.

And never judged me,

I wondered what it would've been like for me if I hadn't lost my baby, if Craig had managed to separate me from my family.

"It was you," she murmured, jerking me out of that dangerous game of 'would've beens.'

"What?"

"You were so tiny," she whispered, eyes watering. "You had figured out a way to escape your bedroom at night, because you liked to explore. And you were bad at sleeping even then. You never cried once you figured out how to get yourself out of bed. You didn't need attention in the night. You were just curious."

She smiled through her tears.

I gripped her hand so hard my knuckles were white.

"I had burned dinner that night," she said. "Or maybe I didn't iron a shirt correctly." She tilted her head. "I don't remember now. It's funny, it seemed so *important* at the time. Like it would be etched into my mind forever. But it faded. It took time and love and a life that I've been blessed with to make it happen, but it faded."

I struggled with my tears.

"Whatever the reason, what won't fade, what can't ever fade is seeing your wide, beautiful, curious and pure eyes fixated on me on the floor. My nose was bleeding. You wiped it with your security blanket. The one that up until then, you hadn't let me even wash without screaming. But when you see people hurting, my little baby, you would give them everything you had if only to make them feel better. And I was not going to take everything I had from my precious daughter. I was not going to let your first memories of the world be tainted with violence and pain. I planned on leaving. But then, your father did the only good thing he ever did." She sucked in another strangled breath. "He left, after beating me enough to require your sister, at eight years old, to somehow get me and you to the hospital."

Her voice cracked.

"And that's where your dad found us. Your real dad. The one who took you to softball, who plaited your hair, who cared for you when you were sick. Because of your father, I found your real dad. But it was at the expense of Lucy's innocence. I waited too long with Lucy and that's my sin I will carry with me. It's why she's different than you. Because I left her in that place too long."

"No, Mom. Lucy is different because she's different," I said firmly. "Because that's how beautiful the world is, to give us that. You did not stop her from being who she was meant to be by being human. By having hope."

"And the world has somehow not stopped you from being who you are, despite everything," Mom murmured, cupping my face. "I'm so sorry I kept it from you," she said.

"I understand," I said, crying freely now. "I didn't tell you and Dad what happened because I wanted to protect you from any and all kind of pain. That's what you do when you love someone. You want to be true to them to show them you respect them, but sometimes the truth hurts, and you can't hurt someone that precious to you without losing respect for yourself." I squeezed Mom's hand. "I respect you, Mom. I love you. And I'm proud of you for being strong enough to live through that. To find Dad. To give us a beautiful life without any inkling of that ugliness you carried around inside."

Mom was sobbing now. We were notoriously the emotional

half of the family. "My baby," she croaked. "It takes no effort to create a beautiful life when you've got beauty around you. When you've got family. You need to remember that. What's inside of us can alter the outsides, I know my little yogi is an expert on this." She smiled at me. "But it's the people on the outside, like your Heath, who can help repair the inside. I know that because your dad did that with me."

I was sobbing too.

Because she was right.

Weren't moms always?

Heath

The drive was silent at first.

Heath didn't mind that.

Didn't feel the awkwardness most people felt in silences. He preferred them. That—and many, *many* other things—had enchanted him about Polly. This bright, seemingly loud girl, was happy in silences. Didn't rush to fill them. Just bathed in them.

He suspected she might've gotten that from her father.

Though he knew the man was not bathing in silence right now. He was stewing in it. In blame.

Because he was a good man. A good father. Heath recognized that because he knew what a bad one looked like. He spent the first sixteen years of his life looking at a bad one. Being beaten up by one.

So it became easy for him to spot a good one.

It was solidified when Pete finally spoke.

"Was it bad?" he asked.

His words were choked, forced out of him. Because Heath knew the man did not want to know. Wanted to stay in ignorance to the truest horrors his daughter encountered. It would've been easier for him to bear. But he was a good man and a good father, so he didn't want easier. He didn't want to be ignorant when his daughter had to live with horror.

Heath's grip tightened on his steering wheel. "Yeah," he bit out. "It was bad."

He supposed he could've lied. Might've been kinder.

But Heath wasn't about being kind. Only when it came to Polly. And he knew this man wouldn't respect him if he lied. For whatever reason, this man's respect was important to him. Beyond the fact she was Polly's father and she adored him. It was because he wasn't Polly's real father.

He knew this.

He knew Polly didn't know this.

Only reason he knew was because he'd looked into everything about Polly when he got back. Because he was half fucking insane with not having her. Not being able to control the situation.

So he'd treated it as a mission.

Gain intel.

And what he'd gained had hit him.

Hard.

Her mom getting brought into the ER by an eight-year-old Lucy carrying a two-year-old Polly. Her mom beaten to hell.

By the father that was never seen again.

Pete was the attending nurse.

They were married a handful of months later.

Polly wasn't old enough to remember the violence, thank fuck. Lucy was. But no one told Polly. Because that family, every one around her, made it their mission to protect Polly from the little ugly truths of the world.

But they couldn't protect her from everything.

"You love her?" Pete asked, clenching his fists.

"More than anything in this world," he said.

Pete nodded.

"The man that hurt her?"

"Dead," Heath said.

Again, he should've lied.

Pete didn't seem shocked. Or disgusted. His shoulders sagged in relief.

"Thank you," he murmured.

"Didn't do it for you."

"And that's why I'm thanking you," Pete said.

Silence lasted a little longer.

"Gonna marry her," Heath said, breaking it for once. "Whenever she's ready. So it could be tomorrow or two years from now. Doesn't matter to me when. Just matters it's happening." He glanced to Pete. "But it matters to me that I'll have your blessing. Because I know that shit matters to Polly. And Polly is everything to me."

Pete smiled. "Son, she's everything to me too. Been hoping to pass her onto a man that says what you just said. Did it against my better judgment the first time around, and that's somethin' I'll carry with me. But I'm thinking you'll make sure I don't have to carry anything else."

"No fucking way," Heath promised.

"Then you've got my blessing."

Polly

Heath and Dad arrived home once Mom and I had finished crying and then broken into a bottle of wine.

My dad's face was weary the second he met my eyes like he was expecting something. A hurricane.

He and Mom had obviously planned this.

And he was scared.

Terrified.

I saw that in the man I loved and respected above all others, the younger, bearded man beside him coming in at a close second.

My wine glass hit the coffee table with enough force to spill liquid everywhere. I ignored this, Mom was already getting up to clean up after me.

I was in my dad's arms in the next moment. He went back on his heels, but he caught me. Of course he did. He always caught me.

We were silent for a long time before he let me go.

There was a fear in his eyes, even if he didn't say anything.

So I knew I had to.

"You're my dad," I said firmly. "That's not changing. That's *never* changing. You are the man who taught me how to fish. Who wiped my tears away. Who walked me down the aisle. Who didn't judge me when I signed that paper dissolving that marriage." I paused. "You never judged me. You never told me I was making mistakes, even though it was glaringly obvious."

He smiled and squeezed my hands. "Honey, mistakes are different for everyone. One person's mistake is another's miracle. It was a mistake in the DNA of the man who fathered you that brought you to me. My biggest miracle."

His eyes moved to where my mom was standing, most likely crying.

Then he went back to me. "My biggest accomplishment is being a father to two beautiful, and wildly different girls. And the biggest mistake I could make as a father would be to try and steer your life for you. To tell you not to do something just because it's not how I would do it. How I would *want* you to do it. I want you to be happy. And to be happy, unfortunately, you've gotta make mistakes. Ones that hurt you, ones that kill me watching your pain. But we cannot have happiness without pain. Without mistakes."

He paused, bringing my hands up so he could kiss them and then let them go. "So, no, sweetie. I'll never judge you. Never doubt your spirit, your mind. You make decisions that you think serve you best at the time. That protect your peace. Even if they end up ruining it. No one person can ever tell another they're making a mistake. Because that would mean there is one way to live life. A script. And even if there was, one of the proudest moments in my life is watching my daughters go off script. Scary as hell."

His eyes went dark and I knew exactly what he was seeing. The future we'd almost had.

"Scarier still when it looked like I was gonna lose Lucy's light because of her spirit," he choked out. "But that's a burden we all carry. And I'll protect you as much as I can." He glanced to Heath. "You've got a man that'll do the same. Though I wish it could be as easy as finding someone who loves you the way you deserve to be loved in order to protect you from the world. That just ain't the case. Person who's gonna protect you the most is always you. And I've always known you'd do that, even if it didn't look like it to the people on the outside. Especially because it didn't look like that to the people on the outside. You're one of the rarest things in this world, my little bug. And don't you forget it."

I was full on sobbing now.

As was Mom if the sounds behind me were anything to go by.

Dad looked to Heath.

"You got her?" he nodded to me.

I was in Heath's arms in a heartbeat.

"I always got her."

CHAPTER TWENTY-TWO

Two Weeks Later

"HEY, please don't call me to tell me you haven't thrown up again, I'm so very happy for you, but I'm late," I answered Lucy's call as I was rummaging through my purse for my keys.

Some things never changed.

"You're always late," Lucy replied.

I poked my tongue out at her even though she couldn't see me.

"Don't poke your tongue out at me," she demanded.

I froze. Straightened. Looked around to see if Lucy was hiding in her car.

She was not.

"Are you psychic?" I asked seriously.

"Dude, if I was psychic, I would be using my powers for evil, not to spy on you," she replied. "I just know you're Polly."

And she was right.

I was Polly.

Not exactly the same. I was scarred now. But every day, I was getting more like me. I watched the sunrise, every morning. Sometimes alone while Heath slept. Most of the time with Heath beside me. Or inside me.

I taught my classes, five times a week, multiple times a day. And I derived so much joy from it.

I still volunteered. I was helping Jay with expansion.

I still helped my friends out with whatever crazy plan one of them had.

But I also had Heath.

Really had him.

Every single day.

And he was planning for the days ahead.

Since he'd purposefully left the iPad screen onto a house listing.

I'd obviously picked it up because I was nosy.

And also because the house was beautiful.

It was by the ocean.

Old.

Beautifully restored.

It had character.

"Do you like it?" Heath murmured from behind me, arms circling me.

"No, I hate the beautiful yet quaint cottage by the sea," I deadpanned.

He chuckled, and the sound vibrated all the way to my bones.

"Why are you teasing me with it?" I asked. I definitely couldn't afford it, since I had little of Craig's money left and I was planning on something else with the small amount I did have. The small amount that wouldn't even make a dent in the deposit needed for such a house. It might've been quaint, but it was seaside. In L.A.

"Not teasing if you like it," he said.

"What do you mean?"

"I mean, we can set up an appointment. View it. If you hate it as much as you say, we'll keep looking. If you don't, we'll buy it."

I froze.

Heath noted this, as he noted all changes, big and small so he let me go and I turned to face him.

"Buy it?" I repeated.

He nodded.

"To live in...together?" I clarified.

He grinned. "We live here together." He gestured around the apartment. "What's the difference if I buy you a house to build a home with you?"

"It's different," I snapped. "It's grown up and real."

"Newsflash, we are grown up and real," he said.

"You would do that?" I whispered. "Buy a house for me?"

"For us," he corrected. "And yeah, I'd do anything for us. For you."

I chewed my lip. "This is a lot."

"Babe, it's our future we're plannin' not a military coo," he said, voice amused.

I chewed my lip. "I know that," I snapped.

He pulled me into his arms and all the stiffness that had emerged with his words melted with his touch and I relaxed into him immediately. Well, my body did. My mind was still running.

"Baby," he murmured, cupping my face. "Talk to me."

That was it. Talk to me. He was so direct. He saw something was bothering me, he noticed it. And that in itself was something. Because in my experience with men—and I had a lot—they didn't notice much or distinguish the subtleties in a woman's demeanor. Or even the fricking obvious mood changes.

And even when they did, it was rarer still for them to address it.

Men didn't like conflict, as a rule. Of course most would like to portray different, about their lack of fear directly correlating to their abundance of 'manhood.' But they were terrified of fights with women. Or even heated discussions. Anything that would make them uncomfortable, they avoided like the plague.

A huge generalization, but I'd done the legwork, so to speak.

It rang true.

For every man I'd dated except Heath.

He noticed the subtleties.

And then he cared about getting to the bottom of them.

He wasn't afraid of conflict.

Of any kind.

Shit, I loved him.

"Well, I've lived my life spontaneous," I said. "I've never planned. And it's been quite common for me to decide to do a cross-country road trip when I've got a full tank of gas and nothing on that day. Or especially if I've got something on that day. I'm used to that. The unknown doesn't scare me like it does other people. But this? Plans? Future? It's terrifying."

He kissed me. "That's a good thing, baby. Bein' scared means you're livin', really living."

We looked at the house the next day.

And I loved it.

"We'll take it," Heath said immediately the second my eyes lit up with the view of the ocean.

Heath hadn't even blinked at the fact he had to provide the capital. "You've given me a home, least I can do is buy you one."

"You're not concerned I'm only with you for your money?" I teased.

And he had money. Not that you could tell. But considering we were buying a beachside cottage in Malibu, albeit rustic and not at all like the flashier ones around it—it was the shabbiest on the street, which was why I'd instantly fallen in love with it—it was still Malibu. And he was buying it all with cash.

"Well, I'm only with you for your looks, so it works," he teased.

I was yet to tell everyone about the house, but I reasoned that I could tell Lucy now.

"Lucy—"

"Oh, fuck!" she hissed.

I froze, because of the utter pain in her voice.

"Lucy, are you okay, is it the baby?" I demanded, fear choking me.

"Yes it is," she hissed. "And I was right, this baby is an asshole."

"Lucy, I need more information."

"That's why I was calling," she bit out. "To give you the information that I'm in labor. But then you had to start talking about physics and my child had to contract my womb with the power of its father's stubbornness," she ground out.

"Lucy, I told you, five fuckin' minutes on the phone," Keltan's tight voice entered from the background.

"And I told you, when you push a baby out of your vagina, you get to make the rules. Until that point, you shut up and drive me to the place where they give me the drugs."

"And where they'll deliver our child," Keltan added.

"Whatever," she muttered.

She sounded calm.

Much too calm.

I was, however, freaking the fuck out.

"Lucy, you're having your baby," I chanted.

"I'm aware," she replied. "We'll meet you at the hospital. And

I expect you to have a martini ready for me the *second* this baby comes out."

Then she hung up.

I WAS PACING.

Pacing in a hospital, waiting for news on Lucy.

Heath was watching me.

It was like before.

Except instead of waiting for news that would shatter our world, we were waiting for news that would brighten it.

"How does it take this long? It's crazy," I muttered.

"I know," Rosie put in from where she was trying to balance her soda on her belly. "Mine is going to be quick, in and out. Like a hair appointment. Two weeks from today."

Luke caught the soda can as it toppled, resting his hand on her large bump.

"The birth of our child is nothing like a hair appointment," he clipped.

She smiled. "Of course not."

He frowned and glanced at his phone.

"It totally is," she mouthed over his head.

I giggled.

Then Keltan burst into the room.

I held my breath. Because even though this was a joyous occasion, my mind was taunting me with all the things that could go wrong. Now I knew that the worst could happen, I kept bracing.

But Keltan was beaming, his eyes red. "We've got a daughter," he said, voice somehow a yell and a whisper at the same time.

And then I let the joy chase away the dread.

"SUNSHINE." Heath snatched me into his arms as I left the room, my arms were still heavy from the weight of my niece in them.

My heart still full from the sight of her and Lucy and Heath.

I leaned until Heath's arms and he kissed my head, searched my eyes. "You okay?" he asked gently.

I knew why he was asking.

Because he was worried about what this was doing to my barren and empty womb. Seeing all the beautiful things that my sister had that I wouldn't have. And though I did feel a pang of pain in the spot where I'd lost my child, it wasn't as much as I'd expected.

Because I'd lost something precious and irreplaceable. But I hadn't lost everything. I had my sister. My family.

Heath.

And just because I couldn't grow a child inside me didn't mean I couldn't be a mother.

My father taught me that.

That there were plenty of children out there that needed love. And it didn't matter whether that love was born in blood or not. I did have to discuss the idea of adoption with Heath first since being a part of a couple meant talking about things like adopting babies before you actually did one.

I had something more important to say first.

"I think we should get married," I said in answer to his question.

He jerked.

He was silent for the longest time, long enough to think I might have to repeat myself.

I wasn't scared he'd disagree. The man had just brought a house for me, for goodness sake. He'd stuck with me through everything. Loved me since I was eighteen.

But before I spoke, he moved. Out of my arms and down onto one knee.

And he retrieved a small box.

I gasped when he opened it.

"Are you psychic too?" I whispered, looking at the white gold, antique, oval cut diamond ring.

It was the ring. The exact ring. My ring. It was simple and beautiful. It was bursting with personality. With a story.

And there was no way Heath could've known I'd say what I just said. So the only reasonable possibility was that he was psychic.

It would explain a lot of things.

He grinned. "No, Sunshine, sorry to disappoint, but I'm not psychic. I've been carrying this around for months. Waiting. For you." He grabbed my hand. "'Cause I knew you'd decide you'd be ready. And you'd declare it at an unexpected moment, because you're you. And I wanted to be prepared."

A tear trailed down my cheek. "How long were you going to carry that around for?" I asked.

"Forever if need be."

Another tear trickled out.

"But thanks for not making me wait forever," he murmured. "My beautiful Polly, will you marry me?"

It was simple. No poetry. But he didn't need it.

"Yes," I choked out.

It was only then that he slipped the ring on my finger.

ROSIE WENT in to have her baby as scheduled two weeks later.

And she was sure there wouldn't be drama.

But she was Rosie.

So there was drama.

Drama that nearly broke Luke.

That nearly broke the entire club, who were sitting in the waiting room.

Luke had first emerged, in full scrubs, telling everyone about his son, grinning from ear to ear. There was a low roar from the men in leather who had taken over the entire waiting room. But then a doctor rushed to Luke, pulled him aside and murmured something.

Then Luke froze.

Then all color, all joy drained from Luke's face.

I wasn't the only one who saw it.

Cade, Rosie's brother, had all but tackled the doctor.

And then the joy drained from his face.

We waited in that room for three more hours. There were no more smiles, no more roars. Nothing but ugly and painful silence.

Something had happened.

Complications.

Rosie had to be rushed into surgery.

"This can't be happening," I whispered, Heath's arms tight around me. "She's had enough. We've had enough. It's time for peace. She deserves it."

Heath kissed my head. "I know, baby."

He didn't placate me then either.

Because it was bad.

Really bad.

But she was Rosie.

And she pulled through.

And there was a fragile, chaotic peace once more.

Eight Months Later

We didn't rush into the wedding like everyone thought we might.

I didn't want to rush.

I wanted to enjoy it.

Plan it.

Just live for a little.

And we did.

We moved into our house.

Into our *home.*

I opened my yoga studio 'The Problem With Peace' where I helped people find peace, but I also encouraged them to find it in chaos.

I babysat when my sister was going out of her mind. Treasured and spoiled my niece and nephew.

I healed. Slowly. But surely.

And now I was getting married.

In a church.

Heath hadn't even blinked when I told him I wanted to, despite the fact I knew he wasn't religious. Not one word was said about it as we did weekly meetings with the priest, who was kind and easy to talk to.

He hadn't had one single opinion on a dress, the flowers, the location.

"I'm marrying you for you," he murmured when I'd asked him if it bothered him, all of the plans that he wasn't in control of. "Don't care about the wedding. As long as it involves you in a dress, promising forever and then me taking off that dress and fucking you all night."

Then we hadn't talked about the wedding. We were intent on recreating the wedding night.

I smoothed my dress.

Though it didn't work since the dress wasn't exactly smooth. It was white, hand-beaded silk.

Sheer organza covered my collarbone and turned into long flowing sleeves. Tiny lace flowers were scattered atop the organza, heavy at my shoulders and then fading down my arms. The organza was draped across a tight, strapless, beaded bodice, with more flowers stitched atop.

It flowed down from my waist, long and whimsical, with a long train behind me.

It was the dress.

My dress.

"Holy fuck."

I turned around.

"Sunshine," Heath ground out, eyes feasting on me. "Never in my life have I seen a more beautiful woman."

I didn't speak, didn't spout crap about the bad luck of seeing me in my dress. He'd already seen me in one wedding dress. We'd had the bad luck.

So instead of all that, I ran to him, into his arms.

He caught me.

Of course.

I didn't hesitate to press my lips to his.

He didn't hesitate to kiss me back.

"I just wanted to see what it was like to kiss you," I murmured against his mouth.

"And now you'll never have to know what it feels like to stop," he growled.

And then he kissed me again.

I was late for my own wedding.

But I was Polly.

So they expected it.

Two Months Later

We were sitting on the sofa, me with a glass of wine, Heath with a beer. He was reading, and I was doing some research for new versions of meditation at the studio.

It was a normal night.

Whatever passed for normal for us at least.

"What do you think about Luna?" I said, snapping my head up.

Heath glanced up. "For a girl or a boy?"

I scowled at him. "For a girl, of course."

"You suggested Malin for a boy yesterday," he shot back.

"It's a unisex name!" I protested.

"Any unisex name is a girl's name," he muttered.

"That's such an alpha male thing to say," I snapped.

He grinned, yanking me in for a kiss without spilling our drinks. "I remember you seem to like all of the alpha things I do to you."

I blinked once he was done kissing me.

"What were we talking about again?" I whispered.

"The name for our daughter," he reminded gently.

"Right," I breathed.

We had been talking about names since I'd broached the subject a month ago. I'd expected him to be tense, tentative, to mention it being too soon.

Instead, he'd made slow, beautiful love to me, then he'd made an appointment at an adoption agency. We'd gotten on a list quickly and without hassle, which was strange considering it was notoriously hard to get on such lists.

But Heath was Heath, so we got on.

Judy, our caseworker, warned us it could be a long wait.

"It's okay, we've got time," Heath had murmured, yanking me to his side.

And he was right. We did have time.

The ringing of my phone jerked me out of the past. And then of course I had to dig around in the sofa to find it.

"Hello," I answered on the last ring, about to sip my wine.

"Polly? We've got a baby for you."

I froze, the glass halfway to my mouth.

Heath was instantly alert.

"I'm going to warn you," Judy continued. "She is currently suffering from Fetal Alcohol Syndrome. She's in an incubator since she's premature and will be for the next three weeks at least. She will be hard," Judy said, her voice hard as if she were trying to prepare me. "And not in terms of her health, but that will be a struggle too. But because we've seen various behavioral and mental health issues. This is a big commitment. This is harder and uglier than the reality of a normal baby. There will be no judgment if you say no."

I had put the phone on speaker the second she spoke her first sentence, so Heath had heard everything too.

"We'll take her," Heath said immediately, snatching the words from my mouth, and my heart.

If there was ever a moment when I thought my love for him might kill me, might literally explode my heart, it was then. It was his lack of hesitation, the look on his face, the love he had for a child that we hadn't seen, that was full of all the ugly realities of the world and that would be the most beautiful thing we'd ever seen.

Our child.

"I WILL NEVER GET RIGHT with the fact that I lost my baby for a reason," I said, looking at the little baby in the incubator. She was so small. So small but somehow she took up all the space in the room. "But I think if there ever was one, it's lying right there."

I nodded at the tiny, helpless, damaged human being.

Heath's arms tightened around me.

"It's because the universe knew that there were little beautiful people like this that needed us. And that we'd need them," he murmured the profound words with enough force to bowl me over, if he wasn't holding me, that was.

We continued to watch the little being in the incubator.

Our daughter.

EPILOGUE

WE FOUND our son only three months after we brought our daughter, Skye, home. Everyone said it was too soon. Especially with the extra care Skye needed. A lot of people thought it was because we were sleep deprived and delirious.

"I bought kitten heels in the first three months of Amelia's life," Lucy said. "It's like when Mercury's in retrograde, no big decisions. And the kitten heels, thankfully I could return when I was lucid...ish. But a child, you cannot—well, not without people judging you, at least. Not me. There have been times where I would've returned Amelia for a houseplant or something that didn't cry for six hours straight if I could. Of course, I love her more than life, but they don't tell you about how fucking insane lack of sleep can make you."

Lucy was right, we were sleep deprived. But I operated off little to no sleep as it was, and Skye seemed to like being awake in the night, just like her mom, so it worked out.

And I was her *mom.*

It didn't matter that she wasn't mine biologically.

"Blood doesn't determine who your parents are," Dad said, cradling the peaceful baby in his arms—Skye was always peaceful when she was given love and tenderness. "Love does."

And Heath and I loved our little girl with all the pieces of ourselves.

She was ours. In more than blood.

But she was a lot. She did have problems. But we seemed uniquely qualified to handle them.

She cried a lot. Screamed, in fact. But her father was cool, calm under pressure, and he cradled her restless and fragile little body, laid it upon his bare chest, and somehow, it soothed her.

Like it had soothed me when I was broken.

I walked with her strapped to my chest, up and down the beach at three in the morning. She liked the witching hour.

Now I knew that everything happened for a reason. Everything ugly, horrible and unthinkable Heath and I had been through in our lives gave us the tools to give our daughter beautiful peace.

But she was still a newborn baby.

And they didn't like sleep.

So we were tired when we pushed the stroller into the shelter. It was now one of three in the city, with Jay expanding. I helped manage when I could, but I was also building my second yoga studio inside the next shelter he was converting.

It was safe to say that the people of L.A. liked my particular brand of peace.

And people liked Greenstone dealing with their chaos, so Heath was busy. Not busy enough to miss feedings. To give me time to do things like shower, brush my hair and remember to put on deodorant.

He was a hands-on dad.

Skye was his princess.

So we were busier than ever, yet we made sure to volunteer once a week. Heath came every single time, not just for security. But to contribute. Because he wanted to be involved. Because of his past. Because he found that a lot of people had parents like his, and those people didn't react the same way as him. Didn't have the opportunity to react in the same way as him and they ended up on the streets.

He worked with them to find jobs.

And that's how we found our son.

He was too skinny for a start.

He was jumpy.

Didn't talk to anyone.

Didn't let anyone touch him.

But he touched my heart the second I saw him. I had a reaction, one I couldn't explain then, and I wouldn't be able to explain at his high school graduation or his wedding.

Because I believed in love at first sight.

That people belonged to each other.

And he belonged to me.

I didn't tell Heath immediately and he didn't have the same reaction as me. Not until Skye started having an episode. One that was common with babies like her. It was something more than a crying jag. It was horrible, heartbreaking to watch. Because nothing could calm her down. She had to cry it out.

People at the shelter knew this, knew us, and they understood Skye.

And they knew that it was made worse when people tried to comfort her. She barely quietened when Heath gently rocked her —and she had a special bond with her dad already.

Heath froze as the skinny, bruised boy came up. He was on high alert when his daughter was involved. But something gave him pause.

Skye's screams silenced the second he put his hand on her tiny chest.

Utter *silence.*

Heath gaped at the boy.

And he was a *boy.* Upon closer inspection even younger than I'd thought.

Ten, at the most.

And he was at a homeless shelter, wearing dirty and torn clothes, sporting a bruise and a sadness in his eyes that broke my soul. And he gave my daughter peace in the midst of chaos even Heath and I couldn't calm.

He was ours since then.

It wasn't easy getting him to trust us.

To realize we weren't going to hurt him, leave him, scar him more.

It wasn't easy getting the adoption to go through.

But it was worth it.

ACKNOWLEDGMENTS

This series is different than all of my other books. I seem to write each book when I need to write a real story. A painful story. Full of flawed characters and the uglier side of love. I need to write it because then it shows me (and more importantly, you) that it's okay to be flawed. To make bad decisions. To learn from them. That the pain will seem unbearable sometimes, and love won't be like books and movies promise, but it'll all work out in the end.

I am so thankful for the people who helped me through all my struggles, to get me here, to the end of this book. I'll forever treasure the wonderful people I have in my life.

Mum. You're always going to be here. Right at the top of this list. Because without you, I wouldn't be here. I wouldn't have turned my love of reading into writing if you hadn't told me I could be anything I wanted to be. You're the one I can call at one in the morning, in hysterical tears and you tell me it's all gonna be okay. You're also the one that makes sure there's a basket of cheese and wine at my front door the next day. Thank you for your faith in me. Thank you for always being my best friend.

Dad. Another person that's forever going to be at the top of this list. A list you're never going to read, but I know you're around, somewhere. You taught me to be a bad ass little girl before the world stole you away. I carried those lessons with me and now I'm a bad ass woman. Because of you. I miss you every single day.

My girls, Polly, Harriet, and Emma. The truest of friendships take no notice of postcodes, of time spent without speaking, and that's what I've got with the three of you. I am so very lucky to have girlfriends who are always there for me as a shoulder to cry on, a partner in crime, or someone to drink wine with.

My #sisterqueen, Jessica Gadziala. What would I do without you? No, seriously, what in the heck would I do? You are always there with support, wisdom and a kick up the ass when I need it. I can't wait to take over the world together.

Amo Jones. I'm so lucky to call you a friend, a sister, a soulmate. You've been with me since the beginning and I'll be with you till the end. Ride or die.

Michelle, Annette, and Caro. You ladies are something special. I cannot tell you how much your support has meant to me this past year. I love you all, to the moon.

Ginny and Sarah. Thank you for putting so much work into this book, for helping me turn it into what it is now. You ladies are everything to me.

Ellie. Thank you for taking me on and for staying true to my voice while editing this book. Thank you for being awesome. I love you. Strong independent women for life!

And you, the reader. Thank you for reading this book. You have made my dream come true just by taking a chance on me. I will be forever grateful.

ABOUT THE AUTHOR

ANNE MALCOM has been an avid reader since before she can remember, her mother responsible for her love of reading. It started with magical journeys into the world of Hogwarts and Middle Earth, then as she grew up her reading tastes grew with her. Her love of reading doesn't discriminate, she reads across many genres, although classics like Little Women and Gone with the Wind will hold special places in her heart. She also can't get enough romance, especially when some possessive alpha males throw their weight around.

One day, in a reading slump, Cade and Gwen's story came to her and started taking up space in her head until she put their story into words. Now that she has started, it doesn't look like she's going to stop anytime soon, with many more characters demanding their story be told as well.

Raised in small town New Zealand, Anne had a truly special childhood, growing up in one of the most beautiful countries in the world. She has backpacked across Europe, ridden camels in the Sahara and eaten her way through Italy, loving every moment. She's currently living London, loving life and traveling as much as humanly possible.

Want to get in touch with Anne? She loves to hear from her readers.

You can email her: annemalcomauthor@hotmail.com

Or join her reader group on Facebook.

ALSO BY ANNE MALCOM

The Sons of Templar Series

Making the Cut

Firestorm

Outside the Lines

Out of the Ashes

Beyond the Horizon

Dauntless

Battles of the Broken

The Unquiet Mind Series

Echoes of Silence

Skeletons of Us

Broken Shelves

Greenstone Security

Still Waters

Shield

The Vein Chronicles

Fatal Harmony

Deathless

Faults in Fate

Eternity's Awakening

A Dark Standalone

Birds of Paradise

Made in the USA
Coppell, TX
05 August 2022